D0396661

WHEN
IN
ROME

ALSO BY LIAM CALLANAN

The Cloud Atlas

All Saints

Listen and Other Stories

Paris by the Book

Callanan, Liam, author.
When in Rome : a novel

2023
33305254002755
ca   03/14/23

WHEN IN ROME

a novel

LIAM CALLANAN

DUTTON

DUTTON

An imprint of Penguin Random House LLC
penguinrandomhouse.com

Copyright © 2023 by Liam Callanan

Penguin Random House supports copyright. Copyright fuels creativity, encourages diverse voices, promotes free speech, and creates a vibrant culture. Thank you for buying an authorized edition of this book and for complying with copyright laws by not reproducing, scanning, or distributing any part of it in any form without permission. You are supporting writers and allowing Penguin Random House to continue to publish books for every reader.

DUTTON and the D colophon are registered trademarks of Penguin Random House LLC.

LIBRARY OF CONGRESS CATALOGING-IN-PUBLICATION DATA
has been applied for.

ISBN 9780593184073 (hardcover)

ISBN 9780593184097 (ebook)

Printed in the United States of America
1st Printing

BOOK DESIGN BY LORIE PAGNOZZI

This is a work of fiction. Names, characters, places, and incidents either are the product of the author's imagination or are used fictitiously, and any resemblance to actual persons, living or dead, businesses, companies, events, or locales is entirely coincidental.

TO MOM AND DAD

You walk close to your dreams.

—ELEANOR CLARK, *ROME AND A VILLA* (1950)

PROLOGO

September 2019

TODAY IS DIFFERENT FOR SO many reasons, but chiefly this: the city has decided, as she has, that Rome is precisely where she is supposed to be.

Claire will try to communicate this to Monica. Best of friends for thirty-four years, business partners for thirty; they're telepathic, or should be, but these past weeks since Claire left the States for the second time, it's been messy, and it's taken Claire a while to sort things out.

But now they are. They weren't last month. Not even last week. But today, Claire's changed. Inside. Outside. Thanks to Rome. She has its key in her pocket. After this past summer, it's her city now.

Except this one part—this one corner bar, the counter where you stand to sip the espresso you painstakingly ordered (not knowing that simply asking for a caffè would get you the same thing), at *this* bar, the narrow counter feels like the province of men. She's never seen a woman standing there, not dressed as she is. But today, Claire stands, orders, waits, and studies the wall behind, where shelves bear not syrups but spirits.

Paolo, the barista, starts to smile at her as he always does, like they were lovers once but parted on good terms. Today, though, he catches himself.

"Signorina," he says. "You look different!" She smiles. "You look good!" He smiles.

They have tried, and try, different things. *Signora*, which feels too old. *Suora*, which isn't quite right but still causes her to swoon slightly, because the word, short as it is, has sweep, and whenever he said it, she felt like he'd just dipped her to the floor.

So, *Signorina*—but it's too jangly and bright and diminutive. And also too young; it's impossible for him to say it to her without a smile. Some weeks ago, she'd finally offered him her name, which he accepted and then never used. Too intimate, apparently. But for her to use his felt totally natural.

"Paolo," she says. She would like Monica to meet Paolo. She would like Monica to meet everyone she's met in Rome. Maybe then Monica would understand. Claire tries explaining this to Paolo, but it's no use, and she retreats, condenses. *I would like you to meet an old friend of mine*, she wants to say, but, like always, her limited fluency truncates this into something more emphatic. "Meet my old friend."

Paolo peers around her, as though the friend is there.

No, no: she waves her hands to erase what she's said. Too late.

"How many grandchildren does your friend have?" Paolo replies, and smiles again.

The smile discounts the jab, but still, she's surprised: Google told her earlier that *vecchia amica* means—

"Very old friend, yes," Paolo says in English.

"No, like 'good friend.' Not old. Fifty-two."

Paolo says the next part with his eyes—*Fifty-two is plenty old*—

and then shrugs, says he would like to meet her. Now his real work begins. He taps the coffee scoop clean. Back in the States, the signature sound of the coffee bar is not the hiss of the espresso machine but the hammering of the scoop to clear it of old grounds. *Thunk, thunk, thunk.* Hammering, hammering, as though the baristas were building a house or recycling steel.

When it was the other way around, when it was Claire correcting Paolo's English and not him her Italian, the word in question was *fluffy*. That's how he'd described another customer's voice once.

"Her voice, this is very fluffy."

"No, Paolo, *fluffy* means 'soft' and 'light.' Airy. Gentle."

"So I am right?" Paolo had said or meant. In English, what he'd said was, *So I am precise?* And Claire had laughed because absolutely nothing in her life then, least of all Rome, was precise. Everything, from the final cab fare to the number of tomatoes or cherries—or, really, precisely *what* would finally wind up in her market bag—to her confidence that, at age fifty-two, she'd finally, fully decided how to spend every day of the rest of her life, was approximate.

Paolo's smile is active now, lit from within. He has told her his age—forty-five—and she does not believe him. He looks to be her daughter's age. Dorothy is twenty-nine. Paolo is maybe thirty. Thirty-five. But when he smiles like this, he is no longer thirty-five, nor even forty-five. He is the right age.

"What do you call your grandmother?" he jokes. "When does she arrive?" He slides the saucer and tiny cup to her, and after that, a small, elegant caddy of sugar packets, which is the only time the two older men at the other end of the short counter look up. Claire returns the caddy unused, and they look away, satisfied. Italians everywhere cascade sugar into their coffee, but Paolo takes pride in his product—impossible to improve what God has already sweetened, is the gist of it—and so sugar is not the custom here. That said, sugar was always provided to her without complaint during early visits. Indeed, without a single word. Then after she'd tipped yet another sugar packet into yet another espresso, Paolo held up a finger, made her a second cup, and asked her to try that one without sugar: *no amaro*, he said, giving each syllable more than its due, and she'd blushed, having confused the word *bitter* for *love*.

If only Monica really was coming. Claire has outpaced her Italian skills, made musing fact. Claire's been daydreaming, pretending, and now Paolo seems to think Monica is actually en route.

Claire will believe this, too, then. She has found that Rome can favor imagination over reality, and that acquiescence to this can serve her.

Paolo has been staring at her for some time, which is unusual, or would be until Claire realizes that she's not answered his question.

"My grandmother?" Claire says.

"Your friend," Paolo says. "Her name is what?"

"Monica," Claire says.

"Ah, Monica," Paolo says. "The mother of Saint Augustine."

Claire did not realize that life in Rome would involve such constant reference to theology, history, art history, philosophy, the lives of the saints. It's strange she didn't anticipate this, of course, because these things *are* such constant companions here. It would drive her churchless daughter, Dorothy, batty. Back in the United States, if the Starbucks barista spoke to Claire at all, it wouldn't be about a fourth-century Doctor of the Church, even if that barista was busily scribbling *Augusteen* on a cup. In Rome, on the other hand, grand references blossom every day. Not just during conversations with Paolo, but on the sidewalk, at the market. Buying turnips earlier occasioned a brief discussion of Nero.

Another sip, two. The foamy crema on top is so sweet she worries she's forgotten herself and put the sugar in anyway.

Monica would say, *Add a cup of sugar, what the hell*, or Monica would tell her not to, *What are you thinking?* But what Claire's been thinking lately is that Monica's been telling her what to do for thirty years in matters large and small. It helps, and does not, that Monica is usually right.

Claire lifts the cup, but it's only the dregs now. She's seen people— men, women, Italian, not—spoon up the final drops, but she worries it will betray too great a need, and besides, it doesn't make the moment last longer. That's the problem. She's not found a way to make the tiny espressos endure. It's her only sadness about these moments with Paolo or at any other counter in the city. Too brief. But that's what it's all about. People think—she thought—Italy was all about the lack of speed, but plenty happens fast here. Speech. Scooters. A tazzina of espresso.

Changing your life.

"Oh!" Paolo says, misinterpreting Claire's silence as reticence. "Your friend, she is bringing a man with her?" He switches back to his sad smile. "I am understanding now."

"No," Claire says, and it is a moment before she herself understands. The thought of untangling this is exhausting, and so she doesn't, but it gives her an idea. She tells Paolo ciao, he gives her outfit one more look, up and down, and then she's out the door.

She walks, imagines finding Monica's face in the crowd. Monica would take one look at Claire, the smile on her face, and tell her, *Yes, this is perfectly right!*

No, knowing Monica, she wouldn't.

But if Monica did, then everything—what Claire's done, will do here in Rome—will feel right.

It doesn't, not yet.

All along the way, people look at her, and some men even nod, duck their heads.

A discovery, an omen: gifts have been left for someone (for her?) all along Via Cavour. Books. She sees the first, an Italian paperback, *Il Manoscritto Incompiuto*, its cover a woman reading. The paperback is on the sidewalk outside a shoe store. Her initial thought is that someone has dropped it, but it's been too carefully placed; it's resting against the building just so. She picks it up, crosses the street, sees a tiny door left ajar—an ancient access panel for water or electricity?—and in here are shelved three more books. She's alert to them now; someone has seeded the entire walk with books. They are in planters, in windows, idling beneath menu boards. It's like a secret passage through the city.

She follows the trail to Piazza dei Cinquecento, waits for the green walk signal, doesn't panic when it changes to yellow after just a few seconds, and finally reaches the other side. She smiles. It is impossible to cross a Roman street successfully and not feel favored by fortune.

Before her, Rome's main train station, Termini. She joins the flow of people flooding in. There's a glass-walled bookstore, bright and busy, just to her left, and she catches a glimpse of her reflection.

She can't help but pause, and so misses seeing everyone, but most especially Monica, who is, impossibly, here.

In Italy. In Rome. At Termini.

Claire misses seeing Monica approach, seeing Monica see her, seeing Monica's face fall.

By the time Claire looks up, Monica wears something like a smile.

Claire's shock is total—Monica is *here*, really here—and Claire does the only thing she can think to do, which is throw open her arms for a hug.

People turn.

Monica shakes her head but leans in for the embrace, and when she speaks, still deep in the hug, it's muffled, because her words must work their way through so much fabric. Claire can't see everyone else yet, but she can hear Monica's question clearly.

"Why the fuck," Monica says, "are you dressed as a nun?"

PART I

....

Four Months Earlier

I. OLD CAMPUS

Rome waited for her Monday, but tonight was Saturday, and Claire was in New Haven, Connecticut, at her thirtieth college reunion. One night, one person she wanted to see, ten lies told before she did.

One. "You haven't changed. You look wonderful."

Not a difficult lie; many classmates did look wonderful. But she couldn't help noticing that those who looked most wonderful were the ones who *did* look different. The women who'd gone gray, the men who'd gone bald, everyone who'd settled into their skin and was doing no more for their skin than grinning into the showerhead each morning.

Claire wasn't alone in the lie; many people had told her that she looked radiant, or happy, or exactly as she'd looked when they'd last seen her, thirty years ago. None of this could be true. She wasn't radiant, or happy, and she hoped she didn't look the way she had the last time most of her Yale classmates had seen her, which was red-faced and crying, running from a stage the night before graduation.

Two. "Marcus? Sardeson? I've not thought about him in years."

False. Marcus was—

Is—

Oh, just read the Class Book.

Three. "I've never read the Class Book."

The Class Book came out before each reunion, updating everyone on their classmates' lives. Claire read it avidly, even though everyone always seemed to be winning something or had prizewinning kids.

Claire often skipped reunions and always skipped sending in an updated bio, but this year was different. She'd been working on a draft.

> *For thirty years, I've sold commercial real estate at a*
> *boutique firm my college roommate, Monica, took over from*
> *her dad. I've specialized in decommissioned religious*
> *properties—old churches, seminaries, convents. I was*
> *and am a single mom of a single daughter and (I think)*
> *we're both single now. I tried to run some marathons but*
> *never finished. As many of you know, I tried to become a nun*
> *during my Yale years but failed. I recently turned fifty-two*
> *and feel like I'm failing that, too.*

Her classmate Marcus had never contributed to the book, either—she'd always checked—and she'd often wondered what he would say, if he would mention Claire. No, that was vanity. Marcus had plenty to talk about besides her. He had, for example, been nominated for a Best Supporting Actor Oscar within a year of graduating. And though he'd never summited those heights since, he worked steadily enough. Sometimes acting, sometimes directing, sometimes writing, often doing small, specific jobs—rewriting a scene, coaching a young actor—for more famous friends.

They *were* friends, Claire and Marcus, that was true, but what kind? She would have loved to have read about that: *I occasionally see classmate Claire Murphy,* Marcus might write, *my old college crush...*

No, he wouldn't say that; among other things, it wasn't news: everyone had learned in quite dramatic fashion what Claire and Marcus were to each other just before graduation.

But no one would read anything Claire or Marcus had or hadn't written; the organizers had decided against continuing the tradition. The book consumed too many resources, was too focused on the past.

And so, at this reunion, a new project with a new prompt, less question, Claire thought, than curse:

What next?

So much that question assumed: that one had the freedom to choose what came next, that one had a clue what to choose if one did, that someone would tell the truth when they answered.

Four. "I love my job."

Claire had not set out to have the career she did. Just months after graduating, she was pregnant, single, and unemployed, and Monica had swooped in. She'd found Claire a place to live and a home at her family's Manhattan-based firm, which stumbled into what would become Claire's specialty when an order of nuns called. The sisters had been told their convent's expansive, empty parking lot was worth money, and it was—much more than they'd been offered. Monica put Claire on the case and a career was launched.

Claire went on to sell a variety of properties over the years, in New York, nationwide. Some sites had been beautiful. A seminary and retreat house on the California coast. An island in Michigan. A mountaintop lodge. Other sales had been less idyllic. Old rectories and convents ridden with mold. Parochial schools closed by building inspectors decades before. A church in the round with wall-to-wall carpet in maroon plaid. The buyer leveled it the day after purchase and put up prefab trailers, which he rented out for self-storage. The old parishioners had gathered around the rented chain-link fence and wept. Or so Claire had been told.

It could be tricky to persuade sellers to sell, but Claire had a gift for seeing things both as they had been and as they might be, perhaps because that's often how she saw herself. She was no longer surprised that not all her clients shared this mindset. Old buildings becoming something new—a church becoming a restaurant—could scare them, especially the men, as if they sensed they, too, were overdue for overhaul or demolition. The women, Claire found, scared less, were more given to panorama, always looking forward and back, never losing sight of the now.

Claire tried to show her clients that life would be better when they moved. The roof wouldn't leak; the boiler wouldn't blow; the cat would stay peacefully curled in the chair instead of constantly prowling for mice. Claire helped her clients find futures. Or so her pitch went.

Couldn't someone now do the same for her? For the longest time, her goal had simply been survival: her mother died when Claire was twelve, her father just two years ago. Claire had needed to stay alive for her own daughter, and had. But Dorothy was twenty-nine now, had a house, a job, a life. Claire had—a job. She hadn't realized, until she had, that you could lose your life without dying.

Many of her clients had vast debts. They had to pay settlements, pensions, mortgages. They had to pay to mow the lawns of cemeteries that had filled long ago and whose "perpetual care" fees were long-ago spent. They had to pay for the upkeep of buildings they shouldn't have built in the first place.

It was difficult to traffic so much in endings, especially recently. She was aging into the demographic she usually dealt with, elderly priests and nuns, and had a newfound appreciation for their befuddlement: once upon a time, they'd taken vows. And thirty, fifty years on, all that meant...what? A padlock, a fence, a backhoe beeping its warning.

Claire, too, had made a life-altering decision once. Or so she'd thought. It turned out she'd had to keep making the decision again and again.

Where was Marcus? She texted him; he didn't answer.

Five. "I no longer bargain with God."

Monica caught Claire ducking out of the cocktail hour, headed to the back gate, which they both knew led to Yale's Catholic chapel. Monica raised an eyebrow and Claire lied her fifth lie.

Blame real estate, a tin soul, or losing a mother young, but Claire had long ago developed a transactional prayer life to address matters large and small. *God, may the dentist not find cavities, and I will give up chocolate for a month*, she'd pray, and emerge from the office smiling. Sometimes, especially in adulthood, her initial bid was too low: *Land the plane safely, God, and I will swear off wine for a week*. The plane had then shuddered so violently that the oxygen masks dropped; she upped it to no wine until year's end, and they were safely on the ground thirty minutes later.

She understood that all this was nonsense, that brushing prevented cavities, that pilots landed planes, but she found the practice, like her belief, hard to shake. This for that, that for this: it was no way to live or think or pray, and so she was trying to stop. She really was.

But what about Saint Joseph?

Monica had once caught Claire burying a small plastic statue of Saint Joseph in the front lawn of an old sailors' chapel down in Rockaway. Of course Claire had done this; doing so would ensure the property sold. Many Catholics knew of this practice; every broker did. Religious supply stores religiously stocked Saint Joseph in multiple sizes, instructions included free. Harmless. But Monica had been alarmed, and so Claire had brought the matter to Marcus, as she did most of life's curiosities.

You do what? Marcus said. And then he took the question somewhere she didn't expect, something he often did, something she loved about him, but not this time. *Did you do anything like that in college?* he asked, and she lied and said no and he pressed and so she lied better, invented a story of a midnight courtyard years ago in New Haven, parting daffodil bulbs, a small Saint Joseph planted just so to benefit Claire and Monica when students drew lots to pick their senior-year room.

Claire had done nothing of the sort. She had made a deal regarding Marcus, though, at the very end of their time in college.

He'd never known about that deal. But soon he would, because she was going to tell him.

Here, at reunion.

As soon as he showed.

To collect herself first, she'd thought she would find an empty pew and sit.

"The chapel?" Monica said. "What's up?"

"I don't bargain with God anymore," Claire said. Was it a lie if you wanted it to be true? Deals, after all, were entanglements, and she wanted now to disentangle from everything—from everyone—to stand clear for a while in order to see better what came next. What, not who, because, repeatedly, *who* hadn't worked out.

"You might miss something, or someone," Monica said. "Can't it wait?"

It couldn't.

Thirty years on, this once-studying-to-be-a-nun not only still had the chapel key, she'd brought it to reunion. Claire liked keys. Each represented a history, a possibility. She collected them, kept them long after she remembered which went to what. But this key she knew. Not that it would work. She balanced her drink on the chapel steps.

The key slid in easily.

Inside, the nave was narrow, tall, white, the windows clear glass. There was very little decoration. It felt a world away from Yale, which had made it even more of a refuge during her undergrad days.

Sometimes Marcus would come in with her. Once, he'd persuaded the chaplain (or rather, he'd persuaded her to persuade the chaplain) to let him mount a play here, and that had led to Claire and Marcus scrambling through the crawl space above the ceiling to adjust the lights.

The truth she owed Marcus, or part of it, was this. Just before graduation, just after giving up her plans to take vows, Claire had made a deal to never get involved romantically with him. She'd had her reasons—it was for Marcus's benefit—but she'd never known how to explain that to him and so had never tried; over the years, she'd had a hard time explaining the deal to herself.

Of all midlife's surprises, the most curious to Claire was that she'd

begun going to church again. Monica said it was about Claire losing her dad. Or losing Dorothy's dependence. Or turning fifty. It was
something, Monica seemed to think, and once Monica found a cause,
she'd find a cure.

But there was no cure. Losing her dad to cancer had been long on
the horizon—he smoked—but the ending had been so sudden Claire
hadn't had time to make a deal, which would have infuriated her
father anyway.

Two years on, his death still hurt, though differently, manageably.
What had gotten worse was her feeling of untetheredness. Her mother
had died when Claire was twelve. Her father when she was fifty. And
Dorothy—Dorothy, please God, was absolutely fine, healthy (and tall)
as a tree, but Dorothy was about to turn thirty. Monica was right:
Dorothy didn't need Claire as she once had.

Claire had been so worried about the years piling up behind her
that she was startled to discover her life increasingly felt like a count-
down, well underway. But to what?

She eased into a pew. Her breathing slowed; her mind began to
clear. Her heart still bumped along anxiously.

A minute or two passed. Not working.

She kneeled, winced, then sat again. Too much running too late
in life, her doctor said. But what did he know? He'd also blamed the
buzzing she sometimes felt in her limbs, her inability to sleep well,
on caffeine. Monica agreed. But Claire felt like *she* was buzzing, all
of her, like a power line swinging before a summer storm.

She got up to go. She needed to talk to God, yes, but she needed to
talk to Marcus more. Because for roughly an hour's worth of her last
marathon she had thought Marcus was dead—long story—and all
she could think of during that hour were all the things she hadn't

told him, starting with the stupid deal, and all the questions she'd never asked him, and everything he'd never asked her.

With one last look up at the lights, she turned, walked out of the chapel, and locked the door behind her.

Six. "Locksmith."

Everyone had a badge hanging around their neck with two blanks: *Name* and *What next?* Many left the latter blank; others scribbled *life* or *another drink.* Monica's read, *Overlord.* She was the reunion chair, but Claire suspected Monica would have written *Overlord* regardless. Monica was Claire's greatest champion—she loved her—but it could be exhausting being Monica's subject.

A brave few, meanwhile, had taken the question seriously: *painter/ poet*; *foster parent*; *grandparent*; *better person!*

How would Marcus answer? And: Why wasn't he here yet? Was he even coming? He'd said he was. He'd come to Claire's father's funeral, been so kind since, checking in, calling, writing. Just enough, never too much. He'd always been that way, but especially so of late. She'd been looking forward to seeing him, telling him—

I want to be a locksmith!

No, but that's how Claire had facetiously filled in the *What's next?* blank on her own name badge. She'd encountered many locks in her career and had once opened one with a paper clip.

Peering at her badge now was someone Claire didn't know, a woman who'd been in pharmaceutical sales and had then become an Episcopal priest. She'd already had her *What's next?* moment and aced it. Her badge read, *Rev. Susan Clark* and *hope.*

"Locksmith?" Rev. Clark said. "I like the metaphor. A lot."

But it wasn't a metaphor, and not true, either. Claire wanted to *be,* to feel—what's the right word, Reverend?—enmeshed, enfolded, enclosed. Her career had one big hole where the meaning was supposed to go. Let's talk about *that*. What should Claire do next?

"I could use someone who knows real estate," the reverend said.

Sigh. Claire listened patiently while the reverend explained: she was in a dispute with her local airport about an interfaith chapel's forced relocation to a parking garage.

Claire breathed deep, nodded, and then took out her phone and dialed her favorite fixer. If Claire couldn't arrange her own future, at least she could secure someone else's.

Ultimately, it would take two months, some money from Claire, some instructions from the fixer about whom the reverend should call when.

"To my favorite locksmith," read the card on the bouquet Rev. Clark would send to Claire's office, where the flowers would sit on a windowsill, bleaching, browning, unaware that Claire had been gone for weeks by then and would never return.

Seven. "Marathons? Oh, I've run four and counting."

If Claire was counting truthfully, the tally stood at three, none of which she'd finished. Though she fully planned on finishing the fourth this October: Milwaukee's Lakefront Marathon, which was basically flat except when it was downhill. Hills had gotten her in San Francisco, weather in Chicago.

In New York, her father, still alive then, had run the hard miles with her, sixteen through twenty, leaving her the last 10K to suffer, savor, solo, so as to be a victory all her own. Despite a perpetually untied shoe, he'd kept a good pace, told long, mile-consuming stories about how he'd wished he'd been a professor not of English but geography all these years. Did she know that Europe and America were moving away from each other two and a half centimeters a year, that Nebraska had a mock Stonehenge made of upended autos? She did not.

Did he know cigarettes were bad for you? He did, and yet she knew he had some in his fanny pack for when he peeled away. Advil, too, and she still has the travel-size sleeve he gave her that day before parting.

Her phone rang a mile after her father left her side: Monica. She'd seen a news item that Marcus was hurt, possibly badly, fatally, filming accident, helicopter, a fall.

Claire had just seen Marcus a few weeks before. He was passing through town on his way to that very shoot. They'd eaten at a vegan place, Ladybird, his choice, a good one for once, and then wandered the Lower East Side. Over the years, he'd become the world's slowest walker, easily distractable, never let a plaque go unread. Depending on weather and mood, it made her either go *insane*—or relax, like she was on vacation. They took a selfie at the river with his phone, and then a car whisked him away. Dine and depart: the pattern of decades; one or the other always left too soon.

It would later be reported, first by the *Hollywood Reporter* and later by Marcus himself, that it was a stunt double, not Marcus, who'd been hurt, not killed. But there in the Bronx, Claire was already on the ground, her dad nowhere near.

She felt then that what she'd long feared would come for her father was happening to her: the heart skipping one beat and then another, and then you're on the ground, cheek hot against the asphalt, looking at your life sideways.

She had shut her eyes tight and concentrated.

God, a proposal—not a deal—*what if I*—

She imagined her father simmering and she stopped. He still believed in God, he often told Claire, but wasn't going to talk to God again until after he died, and then God was going to get an earful.

While Claire's mother, a devout Catholic, was alive, he'd gone with her to Mass every Sunday. Maybe faith wasn't a choice but encoded in your cells, Claire sometimes thought; maybe you didn't just get from your parents your eyes and hair and height, but the stubbornness to believe that something answerable was listening always, and when the time was right—mile ten or twenty or age fifty-two—that something would answer, by sign or deed or wonder.

She rose and staggered off the course, race finished.

Eight. "I don't remember graduation."

Claire remembered every second, and, as a cruel bonus, every second after: driving home to Milwaukee with her dad asking questions all the while, which was miserable; exit interviewing with the order of nuns she'd thought she'd join upon graduation—which, given everything, made sense, but was still miserable; ignoring Marcus's calls and cards, miserable; fleeing to Monica's first apartment in New York, going to bars and clubs and parties with her, a "one-woman Roman Catholic rumspringa," a phrase Monica said she'd trademark and franchise, as it was working so well—which was, interestingly, not entirely wrong.

During this stretch, Monica urged Claire to have sex with someone, anyone, the less meaningful, the better. Given Claire's new path, virginity was no longer a virtue but a burden: she should lighten her load.

Foolishly, it *had* been a weight, one Claire had spent college worrying would fall. No more. So, the boy in the corner at the party, talking to no one, gripping a beer, studying the spines of books on the block-and-plank shelves, all titles from one syllabus or another: "Someone majored in history!" she shouted over the music, the B-52s, inescapable that summer.

"Where'd you go to school?" he shouted. She told him. Sweat or beer had plastered his shirt to his chest. He wasn't as tall as Marcus, but just as lean. "Jail?" he shouted back, and she nodded.

Months later, the overnight clerk at Duane Reade, an older woman, told Claire to put the off-brand pregnancy test aside, get the expensive one. "If it's worth coming here at 2 a.m. to find out, it's worth knowing for sure." But Claire already did.

Claire had been in absolutely no place to have a baby but, with a clarity that had accompanied little else in her life until then, decided she was. She couldn't explain it, so Monica stopped asking.

Monica did keep pressing her on getting in touch with the father, whom Claire had never seen again, by choice, after that night. His name was Len, and when Claire finally received his reply—*Here's $100*, he wrote, *don't contact me again*—she saw she'd chosen right.

Monica insisted on writing back, though, so Claire let her.

Here's $200, Monica wrote, *hire a lawyer.*

Then, unbeknownst to Claire, Monica wrote Marcus.

Nine. "I have no idea what I'm going to do in Rome."

Maybe go dancing, which Claire loved. So few men did, especially as they aged: another reason she dated less and less. Take Byron, her latest ex. He'd been gallant, reserved, a former monk. She'd met him at a church-basement mixer that followed late Saturday afternoon Mass. Saturday, because he observed "silent Sundays," no talk from dawn to dusk, the opposite schedule of his life in the monastery, and the silence had been annoying to her, then gratifying, the more she discovered how little they had in common. Claire briefly thought they might figure things out, but he was also firm in his hatred of dancing—*Monks don't dance*, he'd said, like the title of a documentary Claire would never watch—and that was that.

Tonight, though, as the dance floor filled, she spun with delight. She smiled at classmates who danced with her; she smiled at the ones who tried to talk (*I heard you're going to Italy?*).

Some weren't just watching, but filming.

The idea had been to allow classmates who couldn't attend in person to sign up for slots to appear on a tablet under the tent. Anyone physically present who wanted to talk to a virtual attendee could sidle up to a long table, where the tablets had glowed brightly all night. It was a wonderful idea and a terrible one: some tablets, unvisited, featured a forlorn face; others broadcast the empty chair of someone who'd abandoned the exercise; no one seemed to be able to hear anything.

But now they were dancing. People picked up the tablets still broadcasting a face and held them aloft. Monica caught Claire's eye and sent her a tight smile. Since they were due to be donated to Code Haven, a Yale-student-led effort to teach middle schoolers programming, she wanted at least a few intact at the end of the night.

Not Claire's problem. The music was great, the night air cool, the dancing transcendent. She'd arrived at reunion wobbly; now she didn't have a worry in the world.

And then a tablet fell.

Its bearer had come streaming into the middle of the dance floor from the tablet table, yelling something that no fifty-year-old pair of ears could separate from the din. Then someone had tripped and the tablet dove from her hands to the floor, facedown. Monica went to retrieve it, but Claire was there first, thinking she'd spare Monica the pain of seeing a cracked screen.

But it wasn't cracked. It was bright and clear and bore the startled face of Marcus Sardeson.

There you are, Claire thought, the same thought Claire had thought a thousand times over the years: Marcus at her dad's funeral; at Dorothy's graduations; arriving at the occasional catch-up coffee or dinner or happenstance layover overlap; meeting decades ago, outside a secret society's darkened "tomb" at Yale.

But she wasn't going to tell him what she had to tell him via tablet. He'd told her he'd "see" her at reunion; that wasn't this.

Why aren't you here? she thought, though she wouldn't be much longer herself. Italy called.

Rome was a challenge, a bribe, a dare. Her destination was a massive, crumbling seventeenth-century villa turned convent occupied by a dwindling number of American nuns from the Order of Saint Gertrude. Their specialty was teaching, particularly at the college level, and for a while, the order had run a small college in Rome, then a study-abroad program. But the students and staff were long gone and the remaining women were debating whether to sell. They'd need an Italian firm's help eventually, but someone had recommended they consult with Claire first. That could be done by phone or video, of course, but Monica had told her to fly over, the firm would pay.

The nuns there need a friend, Monica had said. *They need you.*

They likely didn't. Claire knew well that there was no more capable class of people worldwide than religious sisters. They ran hospitals and schools and nonprofits. They prayed; they marched; they labored;

they served. They braved poverty, misogyny, and a church that could and often did go out of its way to make their lives hard. And their lives were already hard. Many of their institutions, buildings, and bodies were aging. They needed cash. They didn't need Claire.

Over thirty years, Claire had dealt with the despair (her own, her clients') of disposing of old properties in different ways. She'd sent flowers; she'd had photos and historic documents framed; she'd visited aging nuns in the retirement homes she'd helped them find. She'd sat with them, prayed with them. Lately, she'd done even more. She'd cut her percentage on deals. She'd started competing less eagerly for new business. Letting the phone ring through to voicemail on old business. Not answering Monica's emails subject-lined "Re: WTF, part 8?!"

Claire didn't answer because she didn't really know. She'd fetched up at fifty-two with nothing more than some money in the bank that accrued interest as steadily as it did guilt, a bungalow she rented out in Milwaukee, and a condo in New York so bland it looked like she'd bought the demo unit (she had; still inside the door to the empty cabinet above the fridge was a sticker that read, BONUS SPACE!), *and* a daughter who had somehow skipped from age nine to age twenty-nine and was now too old to put her head in Claire's lap and have Claire lightly run her fingers through her hair.

Claire had all this and, now, a ticket to Rome via Alitalia the Monday after reunion. Twenty days in Italy. A little work, a lot of vacation. A reset, Monica called it. Apartment in Trastevere, near the convent and the best park for running in Rome. Monica would fly over to join her at the end.

The end: no, Claire knew exactly what she was going to do in Rome. Not reset, but quit. Quit, while she was four thousand miles from

Monica and the howls that would ensue, four thousand miles closer to a new life as an apprentice pasta maker, or tour guide, English teacher, off-the-books barmaid, visa overstayer, all the things her classmates had done after graduation that she had not, because she'd been busy working, caring for infant Dorothy, experiencing what life was like when you only slept for an hour every other day. Now, she could volunteer in a vineyard. A kitchen. A girls' running club. She could sleep. Claire was fifty-two. *Only* fifty-two. She could do anything, just not this job, not anymore.

Ten. "Great."

Reunion, party, dancing, life: all great. Yep. Really. Thanks for asking! Why the tablet? Are you sick? No? Good! I worry. Talk later?

And with that, she handed Marcus off to the next pair of hands. She had to. Even virtually, seeing—holding—Marcus could send the world tilting. Still, giving him up so fast felt like a mistake.

And it had been a mistake to lie even one lie tonight, a mistake to agree to go to Rome, to join Monica's firm all those years ago. *A little piece of me goes into every transaction*, Monica once chirped to a client, like this was a good thing, when it was actually much worse; it was a true thing, and the more little pieces that got sold, the less of you there was. Claire could reassure herself that it was good work she was doing, helping congregations convert unused property into money that could pay bills and—possibly—do good. But it felt like blood money all the same. Or not blood, but that other liquid that came with hurt: tears. Her money felt soaked.

Claire wasn't the type to cry in the middle of the dance floor. Crying was for bathrooms and cabs and dropping off your one and only child at college freshman year. Claire darted from the tent and across the courtyard. She found her way to the back gate, let herself out, and a moment later she was back atop the chapel steps, where she retrieved the drink she'd left there earlier.

Everything *was* great. She took a sip. It was always pleasant to drink outside, even on chapel steps.

Marcus didn't drink. Never had. It had been a marvel at first, then irritating.

How're things, Claire?

That's what he'd asked via the tablet before she'd passed him off. With that face. That face, that honest, patient smile.

Who'd chickened out? Claire, for not telling him about that long-ago deal that had kept them apart? Or Marcus, who'd not shown up in person?

She'd come to the reunion because Monica had made her, because Claire had told Monica that Claire was soul-sick, that it wasn't just about being alone (it was, partly) or entering a kind of second adolescence (complete with acne) or having become the kind of person who dreaded Friday night as much as she did Monday morning. Reunion, Claire had known, would be terrible.

You might be surprised, Monica had said, always one to oversell.

Claire had thought, briefly, about not getting up from that pavement in the Bronx, about letting the marathon run over her and then traffic, too, when the course reopened. She *had* gotten up—of course she had, she had a daughter—but Claire thought now about that moment before she had, before she'd known if she'd be all right. In those brief seconds, she'd assessed things, all that she'd done and failed to do, and thought, *Not great*. And then she'd gotten up.

She rolled her glass between her palms. And now she was down again, sitting outside a chapel, while Monica and all her classmates were still inside a reunion tent.

All her living classmates. Monica had grimly pointed out how many had died before their time. At least, Monica said, Claire was *alive*.

And yet, Claire thought.

She closed her eyes, but all she saw was the crumbling convent that awaited her.

Inside, Monica was talking to Marcus.

"A thousand dollars says she's on the steps of the chapel," Monica said.

"The chapel's not going to work," Marcus said.

"Agreed," said Monica. "Best to hold off, anyway. She's in a strange mood tonight."

"I should have gotten right to it," Marcus said, "skipped the tablet part."

"You'll have other chances."

"We're getting older," Marcus said.

Monica pursed her lips and nodded. "Then act it?" she said.

Marcus wordlessly handed Monica the tablet and walked to the car waiting outside the front gate.

II. IL CONVENTO DI SANTA GERTRUDIS

EMBEDDED IN THE CONVENT'S BROAD brick façade was a massive metal slab, scabbed with rust. The door? But the doorbell did not seem to work, and there was no alternative: no intercom, no knocker, no clue as to how to let them know Claire was here, short of dragging an outdoor table from the café across the way and hurling it wallward.

A waiter, T-shirt, apron, too young for her or maybe not, came out of the café and smiled. She smiled back. Her phone buzzed; a text from Monica: *Update?* Claire couldn't even flirt without being monitored. She put the phone away, nodded to the man, turned back to the convent door, smacked it with a fist, and stumbled slightly as it swung open. The waiter was now looking at her with the same question they'd asked at the reunion: *What next?*

This, Claire said to herself and stepped inside the convent. She looked for who had answered the door, but all she could see was a small, empty, wood-paneled vestibule and another door, ajar, leading farther in.

The first part, the worst part. Meeting the clients. Claire preferred to sell properties empty. Empty of furnishings but also, ideally, empty of people, of stakeholders, torchbearers, people who cared. Give her the attorneys of the Congregation of Saint so-and-so every time. All business, conferral via phone and FedEx, nobody cries.

And yet, here she was, in Rome, in person, real live people reportedly somewhere inside. It was why she'd taken a day—just one, she told herself, and then it was two—to settle in, explore the city. She deserved some time to herself before the work began.

Friends had promised her a Sahara, seared by a wincingly bright sun; perhaps that lay ahead, but for now, late May, the skies were a cool blue and the air soft. She had passed a sunglasses store named for Elvis, bought a pair, and their tint made the city even brighter than it had been before—walls, cars, clothes, vibrated with color, fountain water glittering like cracked crystal as it sputtered from lions' lips.

She had bought postcards, coffee pods, shoes. She almost asked where to buy cigarettes when she walked through a cloud of sidewalk smoke that smelled like her father's brand. She bought a phone-charging block shaped like a miniature popemobile and a large leather shoulder bag, reversible, black and red. She tried to buy a bottle of wine, but the man would only take cash and she only had five euros. He took the bill, spent a moment looking at her and then the wall of wine behind him. She walked out with a screw-top special, but that was fine; she didn't have a corkscrew.

At one point, she'd stopped on the palace-lined Via Giulia for a quick lunch. After ten minutes, she realized there'd be nothing quick about it; after another ten, she realized that was the point. She studied the passing crowd, their clothes. The men wore suits, closely tailored, vibrant blue, almost too blue, she thought, until she realized it was cousin to the national football team's uniform. No polos, no golf shirts with corporate logos, no khakis, no effort.

The women looked even smarter. Especially the ones her age. They wore dresses here, which stupidly felt like a revelation, but it was. Cap sleeves or sleeveless, modest, never strappy. Classic, never frumpy. Above the knee, below: it varied, but what didn't was that each woman, every woman, in the entire city, so far as she could tell, had found her own flattering length. It wasn't that every pattern or color was beautiful; it was very much that everything fit beautifully.

And the entire city, Romans and shorts-and-sneakers-wearing tourists alike, seemed paired up or gathered into groups. Walking along, she'd wondered if she was the only solo traveler in all of Rome, and had decided later that night, last night, looking out her window, glass of unscrewed five-euro red in her hand that tasted like fifty euros, that she probably was. Thirty years of dates, and some men had lasted just the night (some, less), some a year or two; many had been clumsy; some had been kind. But none of them had *fit*. And so here she was, in a city of four million, alone. Which was fine, wasn't it? She was here to work. On this last job, on whatever lay ahead.

So back to work, back at the convent entrance.

She called out *hello* and then *ciao*, and finally, *It's Claire, Claire Murphy.*

Nothing.

It would not be beyond Monica to have created this gig as a ruse, a way to lure Claire into, say, a surprise party. Claire hated surprise parties as much as Monica loved throwing them: there had been one at the zoo, where Monica had booked them an overnight stay on the grounds in a tent. The lions had roared a lullaby. *We have a contingency plan for everything*, the ranger reassured them before bidding good night, and Claire could only think, *But you've not accounted for my friend here.*

Still, Rome, Italy, a convent? Claire leaned back out, looked up and down the street. No sign of Monica. And yet, she was always there, inside her head.

Claire shut the convent's exterior door behind her. The vestibule was dark, dank, a smell she'd smelled a thousand times. Though different here, yes, deeper, older. Danker.

She went to the next door, opened it, and entered. Might as well get this over with.

Surprise, no one shouted. And still, Claire gasped.

Claire's father liked to say that Claire had grown up an only child with one hundred sisters. He refined the joke over the years, revised the number down: twenty or thirty sisters. Fifteen. Claire herself wasn't sure. At the Milwaukee convent where Claire had worked from age twelve on, sisters came and went—more the latter than the former—all the time.

The convent was attached to the parochial school Claire attended. The sisters had founded the school a century before and for many years staffed it, but most had long since retired, died.

Schoolkids visited the remaining sisters regularly, gave piano concerts, sang carols at Christmas. In return, the nuns read picture books to the younger grades, offered homework help in math, science, theology, and art to the higher grades, or, in a few cases, worked strenuously to avoid interacting with the children altogether. But those women were rare, and even the coldest hearts warmed to the task set before them in Claire's seventh-grade year, which was comforting Claire when her mother died.

Claire should have remembered everything about that time. But she didn't. Forty years on, she mostly remembered previously preserved memories, not the events themselves. She had a memory of a hospital bed in their living room, but not her mom in it. She remembered her dad buying a new fridge, a wild extravagance, because it dispensed ice chips. She remembered never using that feature again, not once, after her mom died. What photos Claire had looked older now—worn, creased—but her mother in them looked younger every year. In one photo, Claire was little, wrapped in a postbath towel head to toe, arms trapped but her mouth wide open, screaming with delight. This cozy wrapping, her mother's specialty. Claire remembered that.

Her father did not wrap as well. She remembered that, too, and that he'd told her she would *come out of this stronger*, which, fine, she had, but it hadn't been what she had wanted to hear or what she had wanted to have happen. She'd wanted to hear what the nuns told her: *This is absolutely terrible* and *You poor thing*, and *Cry, by all means, cry*. And when the nuns quietly asked if Claire might serve as their receptionist in the afternoons, answering a phone that rarely rang and a doorbell that rang less, Claire honestly thought she was helping *them*.

The tea Claire made for the sisters was tepid and weak. She tracked mud in from the garden and, in spring, weeded out what would have become lilies. She sometimes lost the mail, including bills, between the front door and the reception desk.

The sisters said nothing. They helped her study for math, complimented the cookies she made, even the batch when she'd run out of all-purpose flour and used decade-old semolina instead. They didn't tell her, as some of her teachers had, that crying over her mother was no longer called for. They didn't cluck when, a year on, Claire mentioned that her father seemed to have a standing date on Fridays with a particular woman; they didn't cluck when Claire later said those dates seemed to have ceased. They simply hugged her and listened to her and reminded her that there was a saint for almost every need. Saint Anthony to find something lost, Saint Cecilia for the choir audition, Grace Hopper—not a saint, true, a younger nun said, but *one might keep her in mind when wrestling with mathematics.* With some ceremony, they entrusted her with a great ring of keys that Claire, miraculously, managed not to lose.

Oh, and one other thing, Claire—

Yes?

Would you pray for us?

What a strange thing for them to ask! These women, who had everything, who were holy and good and complete in a way that Claire never would be, why did they need anyone's help, least of all a young girl like Claire's? It was astounding, really. Only later did she realize they'd been teaching her a lesson in a subject she was still trying to learn, humility.

But she did pray for them, for years, through high school and college and into adulthood, until the signatures on the Christmas cards the nuns sent grew shakier, shrank in number; and then one July came news that the last, a sister improbably named Ernest, had died.

"She and the others all loved you so," Sister Ernest's caregiver wrote Claire, and Claire immediately went to a church.

Why? Nostalgia? Her mother's influence? The nuns'? Her bereft and angry father's? All that, but also curiosity. She'd always believed, but wasn't always sure where that belief went or led. "Spirituality..." a friend might airily begin, and Claire would think, ask, *Yes, yes, but* where *is that located, and why, and how,* and the friend would shut up.

"What do I do now?" Claire prayed. Not to God that time, though God was welcome to eavesdrop while she prayed to the nuns. To Sister Honora, who'd taught her to knit; blind Sister Saint John, who asked for Lytton Strachey's *Elizabeth and Essex* be read to her again and again; Sister Ernest, who taught Claire that eggs cooked best low and slow and whole chickens high and fast. Sister Mary Grace, who hailed from a long line of plumbers, who taught Claire how to repack a faucet, the pros and cons of copper, and how to tell the gas line from the water line in a basement's latticework of pipes. Sister Jane, who told her to not even bother with boys who didn't make her laugh. All the sisters, who'd taught her how to pray, that not only was it just like breathing, steady and constant, but that done right, it was breathing itself.

And Claire wasn't breathing, not just yet, having stepped through the interior door of a convent in Rome only to find herself outdoors again, in a setting so beautiful it rivaled any property Claire had seen or sold.

She had a spec sheet; she had satellite photographs; she had a calculator. The convent occupied two hectares in the hilly northern reaches of Trastevere, an ancient neighborhood of tangled streets and tangled vines just south of the Vatican, just across the river from the heart of Rome. Two hectares was five acres. The U-shaped main building averaged about six thousand square feet per floor, and there were five floors. At thirty thousand square feet total, it would still fit easily inside Saint Peter's Basilica, but it was far larger than the nondescript brick convent where Claire had worked as a teen.

She found a small stone bench and sat. Around her unfurled a vast rose-filled cloister, or courtyard, equal parts garden and hallucination. This, the spec sheet said, was called the roseto.

The building rose all around her, each story fronting the roseto with outdoor corridors dimly visible behind a forest of arches. The arches themselves grew smaller on each successive level, which made the uppermost floors seem even more lofty. The masonry was painted a red that mutated with altitude, becoming paler and pinker as each floor neared the sky. Thickly populated murals crowded the fascia on the very highest level: angels, saints, animals, mountains, stars, clouds, battles, nuns. Claire was too far away to see the work clearly. The exuberant excess of spending money so lavishly on work legible to so few made her shiver.

The most vivid color came from the bougainvillea, a flowering vine in magenta so bright it hummed. The vine surged up two floors from the roseto before petering out. Its outsize presence suggested an answer to two questions. Why hadn't the building fallen down by now? (Vines were holding it up.) And why was it so difficult to peer into the building's shadows? (The bougainvillea was consuming all the sunlight.)

Across the roseto and opposite the front entrance rose a cream-colored chapel, seemingly constructed of meringue. Curlicues of masonry cascaded down its sides; the cross above the roof's peak looked to be losing a battle to stay above the froth. Two faded red doors stood sentry atop a series of grand steps that descended into the roseto, which Claire now saw was split into four quadrants. A bright blue sky rippled overhead. She would have sworn the one outside had been gray.

Claire closed her eyes. She smelled not just roses, but lavender and honeysuckle and lemon—and, faintly, wood rot. From the satellite photos, she knew that most of the parcel consisted of a walled, parklike enclosure behind the chapel, but none of the photos had prepared her for all this. Her own teenage life in the Milwaukee convent—a sooty, cream-brick building with a 1950s asbestos-clad addition—had not prepared her. Her decades in and out of countless church properties had not prepared her. The Convento di Santa Gertrudis was no convent, but a fragrant universe.

Well. It'd sell quick.

She opened her eyes, looked back at the door to the vestibule. Whoever had thrown up the drab façade out front had known exactly what they were doing. Slow the intruder down: first a wall, then this reveal. It would be the rare person who didn't do as Claire did, which was stop and sit, stare, and listen.

She'd never heard such silence before. She'd known quiet, of course. That weekend when Monica had lost her phone. Or late nights with a feverish daughter who'd finally fallen asleep. Early-morning runs. Evenings when she was the last one out of the office. A canyon overlook in the Dakota Badlands. At an old church she'd just sold, giving it a final all-is-well check before handing the buyer the key.

But not silence, not like this. This silence had texture and shape; it felt attached to each molecule of air. Everything inside her was falling silent, too. She breathed in the roses. She closed her eyes. The bougainvillea's image burned through. She held her face up to the sun. *Thank you, Monica, for this idea, this trip.* Claire almost felt bad that she was going to quit. But the guilt could wait. For now, she relaxed. One deep breath after another: she felt her jaw release, her shoulders, her spine.

She'd never been to Rome before, but she'd been here before.

When Claire started at Yale, she was—or was preparing to be; the rumors weren't clear—a nun. This had not come up in the letters the roommates had exchanged over the summer. Claire wrote them that she lived in Milwaukee, had gone to an all-girls Catholic school, had lost her mother. Upon learning this brief bio, Monica's own mother had said, *Be extra nice to her*, which Monica had thought unnecessary. Claire seemed interesting and different and smart. She not only had been the first to write Monica back but had also used fewer exclamation points in her letter than their other future suitemates had. What's more, Claire had suggested they go in together on a subscription to *The New York Times*, the paper to be delivered to their door daily. And Claire was from Milwaukee. Monica was fuzzy on exactly where that was—Michigan or Manitoba or somewhere west of Manhattan, where Monica had lived her whole life—but what she did know about Milwaukee was that beer came from there.

And now here she was. Claire did not look unusual in any respect, unless exceptionally plain apparel was unusual—pastel orange T-shirt, khaki shorts, sandals. The necklace with the cross was a statement, but not a loud one. What struck Monica most, what someone later said out loud, was this: *She glows.*

Claire introduced her father, who looked so much like a college professor that Monica almost cut him off while he explained in his burred smoker's voice that that's what he was. He wore his own set of sandals, and though his hair was gray, he wore it, like Claire, in a ponytail.

It was the woman with them who gave it away.

This woman, parent-old but somehow not parent-like, did not glow. But she didn't have to. She was over six feet tall and as solid as the sofa they were struggling to move into the room. Monica had heard both Claire's dad and Claire call this woman *sister*—which was a bit fussy and odd, but maybe that was how they did things in Milwaukee—and so Monica finally worked up the courage to call the woman Mrs. Murphy, because this had to be Claire's stepmother.

This made the woman laugh. She shoved the sofa once more with a hip and then spoke. "Oh—oh! No, it's not like that at all." She stuck a thumb in her chest, jangling her own, larger cross necklace, and repeated Monica's line to Claire: "Mrs. Murphy!" She shook her head, looked at Monica. "Sister Anastasia," the woman said.

Monica blinked. Milwaukee was stranger than she'd thought.

"A nun," Claire's father said. "She's a nun. In fact—"

"Dad, I told you," Claire said.

Sister Anastasia waved a hand and spoke. "I serve as the leader of a community of religious sisters, the Society of Saint Clement, the Clementines. *Nun* isn't quite the right term, but it'll do. So will 'Anastasia.' Or 'Ana,' whenever I am around, which, because you still look worried, I'll reassure you won't be much."

"Oh God, Claire, you didn't tell her?" Claire's dad said.

"Tell me what?" said Monica.

"That your roommate is preparing to join our community," Sister Anastasia said. Monica stared.

"I wanted to join *before* I started college"—Claire glanced nervously at Sister Anastasia—"and then start classes as, more or less, a novice."

"In the religious formation sense," Sister Anastasia said.

Be nice to her. Monica's own mother's admonition meant Monica couldn't say what she now thought, which was, *This is nutty.* College, the first great adventure of Monica's short, privileged life, and *this* is who she gets as a roommate?

"Do a lot of people do it this way?" Monica asked.

Everyone looked at Claire to hear the answer, but Claire, her smile suddenly gone blank, had nothing to say. Sister Anastasia opened her mouth, but nothing came out. Monica was too embarrassed and confused to say a word more. So it was left to Claire's dad to speak.

"She's not done anything yet," he said to Monica.

Claire's glow should have dimmed as one week wore into the next. But it did not. In the dining hall, crossing Old Campus, crossing the street. She glowed in class, where even professors who'd long ago put aside being impressed or intimidated by any of their reportedly brilliant undergraduates found themselves intimidated by her. She was fearlessly smart. "But *I* think," Claire might say, and a mildly panicked nod of acknowledgment from the professor would follow. She was someone straight out of Hollywood, the Middle Ages, the convent: a nun in training.

Claire had expected to hate Yale—the school too fancy and too proud of that—but found, sheepishly, that she loved (most of) it. She walked through campus like someone who had fallen through the thin curtain that separates one universe from another and stands up, blinking, marveling at all she's just discovered. College! Professors and students and meals that went on for hours because you couldn't stop talking. She loved the post office, where letters from her dad and the Clementine sisters back home awaited. She loved the Catholic chapel, simple and spare, which looked like the one back at the Clementines' convent but was also pleasingly different. Dorm complexes that looked three times as old as they were, protected by dry moats. And there was a carillon with bells and expanses of grass called quads and she couldn't believe how blessed she was. God had seen to it that she should experience all this. She wrote sparkling letters to her dad, rapturous letters to Sister Anastasia and the other sisters. She rattled on about all she was doing, the people she'd met, the friends she'd made. Yes, some on campus rolled their eyes at her, maybe even snickered, but: give them time to get to know her.

And, just across the hall, this boy. Marcus! He was sweet and smart and a little lost. (And skinny! Too skinny? Was he okay?) And so *curious* about her, her life, her life in the convent. He couldn't stop asking questions, said it was from his training as an actor. Claire couldn't wait to see him onstage. Marcus! She mentioned him every week in every letter until the week she didn't, and then she never mentioned him in her letters again.

Back in Rome, footsteps. Claire opened her eyes. Before her, stepping out of the vestibule, appeared a woman: bright orange running shoes, shorts, and a tech-fabric tank. A nosy tourist? She must have followed Claire through the front door. Claire would help the nuns (when she found them) with their property sale, sure, but first, the would-be locksmith would help them buy a lock.

The woman hadn't met Claire's gaze yet, as she was too busy struggling to free her hair, a shoulder-length mess of going-gray curls, from a balky ponytail. "So, what do you think?" she said. "Can you help?"

Claire looked around, cautiously stood. The woman sounded, and acted, American—helpless—and Claire tentatively approached, arms half-raised. The woman looked up; her face flashed first with panic, then laughter.

"No, love, the convent." She looked up and around as Claire had. Claire could suddenly hear everything in the world. "I'm in charge here," the woman said, abandoning her hair to shake hands. "Sister Felicity."

"And I'm mortified," Claire said, gesturing to the door Claire had let herself through, the hair Claire hadn't fixed.

"As are we," said a new voice.

Claire turned to find two other women. The taller of the two stuck out a hand. Gray hair cut short, button-up yellow blouse, tan polyester pants, black orthopedic shoes. Midsixties, Claire guessed. In this life, in her prime.

"You must be Claire Murphy," the woman said. "Our brave leader here warned us you were coming, and promptly took off for a run." She looked Sister Felicity up and down. "I'm Sister Georgia," she said, turning to Claire. "And this is Sister Thérèse."

Sister Thérèse was shorter and younger by far, even younger than Claire's daughter, Dorothy. She was also the only one of them wearing a habit—just a veil, black, a faded blue T-shirt, denim skirt, a wooden cross on a string. She had a spray of freckles across her nose and, unless Claire was mistaken, a tiny hole in her left nostril, which must have once (still?) allowed a nose ring. She was holding a dingy yellow hard hat.

"Claire," Sister Thérèse said, and then swept Claire up in a hug as unexpectedly tight as it was brief. "It's so good you're here," she said, and then, looking around, added, "I wish you weren't." She held out the hard hat: "Guests are supposed to wear these."

Sister Georgia sniffed.

"We all are," said Sister Felicity. "But I am the leader here and I'm waiving the rule for lunch, as we're eating outside. She gestured toward a corner of the roseto where a table had been set beneath a small lemon tree. "*I* am very glad you're here," said Sister Felicity.

"As am I," said Sister Georgia.

"Oh, and so am I, of course," said Sister Thérèse, "*Welcome*. But God wants us to help ourselves."

"We are," said Sister Georgia. "Hence Ms. Claire Murphy, whom we've summoned from across the great wide ocean."

"Mother Saint Luke didn't want—" Sister Thérèse began.

"May she rest in peace," Sister Felicity said, and then explained. "Mother Saint Luke passed two months ago. The oldest sister in our order worldwide."

"She loved it here," said Sister Thérèse.

"We all do," said Sister Georgia. "That's not the point."

"She'd been here for ages. Had done everything," said Sister Felicity. "Taught, gardened, worked as a photographer, film-set chaplain, maybe an actress herself—"

Sister Thérèse tried to correct Sister Felicity about something, but Sister Georgia talked over her. "A very good 'actress,'" said Sister Georgia. "Which leaves me in doubt that all she claimed was true—"

"She left us a key," interrupted Sister Thérèse.

"Not just any key," said Sister Georgia.

"Nothing more than a keepsake," said Sister Felicity.

"The note with the key said, 'In case of *emergency*,'" said Sister Thérèse.

Claire exhaled. She loved keys, but how were they already on to this? A key, a chalice, a cloth, a statue, a box: it could be anything. One time a sale was held up because the clients couldn't find a saint's reliquary—a right ear, she recalled. And so here, a key. *Was* it missing? Not clear. Sister Georgia looked away.

Sister Felicity smiled again. "I think the most pressing emergency is that Ms. Murphy will faint if we do not feed her immediately."

Sister Thérèse frowned. *You old women*, her eyes said. Claire read that clearly, just as clearly as she understood the label was meant to apply to Claire, too. Claire watched herself through Sister Thérèse's eyes as they walked to the table. Claire moved more stiffly than all of them. It had been a long flight.

"Let's join hands," Sister Felicity said, and extended hers, closed her eyes, and bowed her head. They all did, Claire last. The quiet returned, and with it, a wave of vertigo, memory.

"Amen," the sisters said, and sat.

One earthenware bowl held cut-up tomatoes and basil dressed with olive oil and coarse salt, another radicchio, wet from washing. Nearby, a basket of pizza bianca, cut into rough squares. Mismatched plates and glasses and silverware. A pitcher of water "fresh from Mother Saint Luke's favorite fountain," Sister Thérèse said. Sister Georgia shook her head at this. Sister Felicity asked if she wanted more tomatoes. Claire looked at her plate and then the serving platter. She'd somehow eaten them all.

Sister Georgia and Sister Thérèse went through the property's history while Sister Felicity fetched more food. The oldest parts of the convent had been built four hundred years ago. The property had begun life as a merchant's villa, spent periods as a linen factory and later a stable, and around two hundred years ago, nuns took over. First one order, then another. The Order of Saint Gertrude had arrived at the start of the twentieth century. "Perfect timing," said Sister Felicity as she returned with a new plate of tomatoes. "The world fell apart, then the building."

The Gertrudans, founded in Germany in the nineteenth century but now with a solely American membership, used the Convento di Santa Gertrudis—a name they'd bestowed—as a Roman outpost. But as their teaching opportunities dried up, their ranks winnowed. Twenty years ago, there had been one hundred Gertrudan sisters worldwide. Ten years ago, fifty. Now there were twenty. Fifteen were spread across three nursing homes in Delaware. Two shared an apartment in Cambridge and taught at Harvard. Four lived in Rome, or had until Mother Saint Luke died. Now there were three.

To hear them describe Mother Saint Luke made it sound like they'd lost forty. The three only knew Mother Saint Luke in her last years; she was, they reported, "complicated," "demanding," and "charming," this last word not exactly a compliment. Sister Felicity said Mother Saint Luke enjoyed a good party, and for years was a fixture around town at cultural events, the livelier the better, and rooftop parties the best. "Sister La Dolce Vita" was one of her nicknames in the ex-pat community, which Mother Saint Luke reportedly disliked, but, in the eyes of her fellow sisters, did not dislike enough. Her connections had their uses, though. If ecclesiastical or municipal bureaucracy needed navigating, Mother Saint Luke led the way. If there were simply no more Italian artichokes left in Rome in June, if the market insisted on selling you altogether inferior French artichokes instead, give Mother Saint Luke an hour and bus fare, and she'd come home with a sackful of locally grown carciofi, dirt still on the stems. Mother Saint Luke had a solution for every problem, which is why they missed her most keenly now.

Her death had sent the Order of Saint Gertrude's membership worldwide below twenty-one, triggering a clause in the order's constitution that required the remaining members to decide whether to continue as an independent order, seek a merger, or "reach completion" and dissolve. Each route would require lengthy discussion and discernment, but in the meantime, the order's superior general was "empowered to make emergency decisions to safeguard remaining finances."

Sister Felicity was interim head only of the Convento di Santa Gertrudis, a role she'd assumed upon Mother Saint Luke's death. The order's superior general, Sister Rose, sat in Massachusetts. Sister Rose had long wanted to dispose of the costly Roman outpost, and as soon as Mother Saint Luke had died, she'd invoked her emergency powers to do so. Barring other developments or offers, the convent was set to sell September 4 to a group of American investors.

What's more, Sister Rose, who, unlike these three in Rome, favored the order merging or dissolving, had scheduled a straw poll regarding the order's future for the same day as the convent's sale. This was not coincidence, Sister Felicity explained: closure would be in the air. The three outnumbered sisters in Rome would lose the vote and the convent the same day.

Which, as of this lunch, was one hundred days away.

Claire nodded soberly. An utterly familiar story. Albeit one that, for once, didn't seem to involve her. She could quit her job even sooner than planned. The convent was already sold, or almost.

"That's terrible," Claire began, "but honestly, given the market, given conditions"—she nodded to the row of helmets—"you're lucky this Sister Rose found a ready buyer. You won't need me, in any case." She dusted off her lap. How to leave? Be gracious. The lunch alone had been worth the flight.

"She's priced it at two million."

Claire began to feel queasy. She hadn't fully researched the market but knew the convent was worth many times that. You could sell the curb out front for two million dollars or euros. Melt the front door down for scrap, another million. Take a scrub brush to it first, discover solid gold underneath, and you could buy half the hill.

"Her brother is the buyer."

"Can we not discuss money?" Sister Thérèse asked.

"Well," Claire began. They were getting robbed, basically.

"Find us a better buyer," said Sister Felicity.

"I—" Claire had meant what she'd said about lucky. Robbery or no, Americans or no, few would take on a headache like this. What if you wanted to rezone? Was the centuries-old title clean? *Was* there a title? Did the sisters even know where any paperwork was?

"A buyer who'll let us stay," Sister Georgia said.

What entity did evictions in Italy?

"That's not normally how—" Claire began.

"Just buy us some time."

Claire nodded again, tried to smile. One last job. Buy them some time. At the expense of her own.

It was a beautiful night for opera. The stage was south of the Colosseum, outdoors, set amid the multistory ruins of the Terme di Caracalla, ancient baths where voices had echoed for millennia. Bleached-brick walls towered all around her, made pale pink canyons of the walkways. The sky was an electric blue. She was glad she'd come. She couldn't have spent another evening alone in the temporary-stay apartment Monica had found for her—flimsy IKEA furniture, Marimekko knockoff linens, giant canvas print above the bed of poor Audrey Hepburn rendered in neon pink—and while the sisters seemed happy for her to linger, to the point of Sister Felicity offering up some of Mother Saint Luke's whiskey, even a candlelight tour of the convent, Claire needed sleep.

But then a passing tram had had an advertisement for the opera, and she'd thought of the stories about Mother Saint Luke, and it wasn't hard to imagine the old nun insisting, *Tonight, the opera, you must, we'll save the convent tomorrow.*

And so here she was. Outside, under the stars, at the opera. *Thank you, Mother Saint Luke.*

An empty seat sat next to hers, and she couldn't help but think of her latest ex, Byron. Antidancing, yes, but a serious opera fan. Too serious, and about everything, but Claire had liked this about him, and any opera: the moment when the concertmaster tuned the orchestra. The sound swelled, silenced, and Byron would lean just the slightest bit forward.

He was gone, though, and she was alone with an empty chair.

May I join you? Mother Saint Luke would have said, and Claire would have—

A brief vision passed through Claire: two nuns at the opera, one of them old, one of them Claire.

She shook her head. Opened her program. Her mind had done this to her before; certain cities, certain jobs, certain women religious, led her to daydream, conflate her past and future.

Prickly Sister Georgia had stopped Claire as she left tonight. Claire had briefly gone speechless, worried the old sister would try to recruit her that very moment, worried that part of Claire wanted to be found so worthy.

But no: Sister Georgia had taken Claire's hand in hers and pressed a small key into it. For the door? No. Mother Saint Luke's emergency key. Claire had meekly protested; Sister Georgia had shaken her head, clasped Claire's hands around it. *Help us find what it opens.* Claire had said she would, and the woman had held on, stared at Claire.

The moment then felt like the moment now, as the orchestra fell silent.

The feeling of Mother Saint Luke sitting next to her became so vivid she almost turned to look.

But Claire didn't. She didn't give in. Never had, not since.

The conductor raised her hands and Claire clasped her own, remembered the sharp teeth of the key, Sister Georgia's stare.

Everything was about to start.

III. FONTANA DELL'ACQUA PAOLA

Six a.m., the city quiet but for the tweet and caw of birds. The apartment's countertop machine and its pods had already delivered Claire her cup of coffee; she'd finished it, cleaned the cup, dried it, put it away. The bed was made, too, and she sat on the edge of it, trying to ignore neon Audrey's garish gaze while Claire attempted to pray.

No deals on offer; just presence, gratitude. Or so she was trying. This was her second attempt of the morning. Her first had been at the open window—clearer signal there, right?—but while trying to figure out what to say, she had gotten distracted by the massive, deep green tide of ivy cascading down a wall across the narrow street. A bike was parked below, a scooter, too; a DO NOT ENTER sign had been adulterated with graffiti she couldn't decipher.

At some point she began crying. She didn't know why; it wasn't uncommon of late, and it no longer scared her, or even much interested her. Her father had wanted to take her to Europe on a Fulbright fellowship one year, but he'd failed the physical. Maybe she'd been thinking about that. Or Dorothy, who couldn't have gotten off work on such short notice but would have still liked to have been invited on this trip. Or Audrey Hepburn, who'd died too soon and wasn't much company anyway in this empty apartment.

Lord, Claire would not pray, *let the sisters sell their convent to a better buyer.*

No, she'd given up, or was trying to give up, praying about property.

Also, this particular matter didn't need prayers; a solution was easily at hand. Bert Ligouri, an old client of hers in Chicago, exceedingly decent guy, medium-size portfolio, loved all things Italy and Italian. She'd call him, would have a verbal offer before she hung up, written offer in a week. Likely for less than it was worth, but Claire would make sure it beat the offer from Sister Rose's brother, and she'd get Bert to rent it back to the sisters for cheap, at least until he figured out whether to apply for a "golden visa," citizenship by investment. She'd do everything short of slapping a bow on it before giving the offer to Sister Felicity, and she'd add the bow, too, if she could find one. *Sisters, here is your future.*

She looked at her phone.

They'd be all set.

Celebrate with a meal out she'd pay for, good wine, table outside in a garden, cacio e pepe—on every tourist's checklist, yes, and every other restaurant's chalkboard, but perfect all the same, pasta stirred up right inside, and served from, a hollowed-out thirty-kilo wheel of Pecorino Romano—and then they'd all go home. The nuns to the Convento di Santa Gertrudis. Claire to . . . here, this anonymous apartment. Or home to New York and her own anonymous apartment. Bonus space.

Her phone buzzed. A text. Dorothy? Monica? She had let them know earlier that she'd landed safely, sent a picture of the apartment and another of the convent's ugly façade, but she hadn't called, still hadn't mastered the time-zone math, spent her waking hours half-awake.

The phone buzzed again. She checked it. Marcus. *Hey! I'm . . .* read the preview snippet and she thought, *Hey, yourself, I'm busy praying.* But she wasn't. She was sitting in an apartment that was its own giant wheel of cheese; where she needed to be was outside.

She had a moment's panic that something was wrong with him—he'd had a big scare in college, brief, but it had scrambled everything then, and in some ways, everything since.

Why give in to paranoia, though? Besides, she was still peeved he hadn't answered her texts from New Haven; she would read his text later. Maybe steel her nerve and tell him what she'd planned to tell him at reunion. That old deal, the truth. For now, though, she'd take a snap from her window to send him later.

She studied the scene: below, a series of shops anonymous behind steel shutters; above, a distant horizon of pigeon-colored domes and spires; immediately across from her, a low roof with a rusted white metal café table, linens on a line, a red, yellow, and blue playset in rugged plastic. Not scenic. But better than the inside of her apartment. She leaned out to take the photo.

"Claire!" sang a voice from the street.

Startled, Claire dropped the phone.

And though throughout the coming summer she would visit many churches, kneel many times, falteringly pray in anger, sadness, confusion, gratitude, and, occasionally, joy, if anyone asked in later years what her most religious experience in Rome was, she'd say there, then, that moment, her phone plummeting two stories, a startled Sister Thérèse trying and failing to catch it, Claire rushing down the stairs to hear Sister Thérèse say, "I have an idea," as a brief but critical unplugged period of Claire's life began.

Claire had spent her first hours in Rome in a mediated cocoon, wireless earbuds jammed in, lush podcasts guiding her about. *Here is the Castel Sant'Angelo, second-century tomb of Hadrian, sixteenth-century siege refuge of popes . . . Sit and sip Fanta on the ramparts where archers once emptied their quivers through arrow slits… Closing time varies by season.*

Another podcast urged her on to Saint Peter's, the Vatican, its museums, but Claire had thought she'd tackle that another day; she skipped ahead an episode to learn more about the angels lining the Ponte Sant'Angelo, *look for the one with dice, see Matthew 27:35, where the soldiers "cast lots" for Jesus's garments.* Here, the podcast producers had added ambient noise of an angry crucifixion crowd, which Claire had trouble hearing over the noise of the actual crowd around her.

So she fled to the Domus Aurea, Nero's underground palace, where she was issued virtual goggles but wanted a parka, it was so cold in the wet, sunless passageways. Her goggles glitched; she exited, toured the park above, which was pretty but had none of the intricately tiled ruins her podcast had described: Where was Poseidon, his trident, chariot, *timeless horses at full gallop*?

Nineteen miles west, it turned out: she'd accidentally fast-forwarded to the episode on the Ostia Antica archaeological site, which she never would get around to visiting, though it sounded lovely and quiet and well-tiled. Confused and defeated, Claire had suspended her touring and retreated to her apartment.

Monica fretted over her, she knew, said without saying that Claire had lost a step, should see a doctor. But Claire was fine. She could run the nineteen miles to Ostia and swim with Poseidon the nineteen back. What was wrong was that she'd lost her father to lung cancer and her daughter to late-onset adulthood. Turning fifty had exposed a fuse in Claire, and two years later, reunion, crowded with memories and wants and things unsaid, had lit it. To what end, she didn't know yet, but its burning kept her on edge while she figured out what to do next.

Sister Thérèse knew exactly what came next: maritozzo. A breakfast treat, Sister Thérèse explained. After which she'd take Claire to her favorite phone fix-it shop. By the time Sister Thérèse finished talking, she'd already tucked Claire's shattered phone in her pocket.

Claire started to protest—she'd already had her pod coffee—but Sister Thérèse sniffed and said that wasn't breakfast. Or coffee. She also shook her head when Claire suggested she run back upstairs and get her purse.

"This morning, we eat for free!" Sister Thérèse said.

As they walked, she explained that Monica had called the convent looking for Claire; she'd not heard from her? She'd asked if they could check in on her.

Claire wondered if Monica somehow knew it was happening again, that Monica's mind's eye had spotted her at the opera, thinking about vowed life. *Don't worry, Monica. It's just the overwhelmingness that is Rome. The awfulness of that apartment. Complete exhaustion.* "I've long been Monica's 'project,'" said Claire.

"Fun!" said Sister Thérèse. "Anyway, I volunteered for the duty because I needed to talk bribes with you today."

Or Claire thought she said *bribes*; maybe Sister Thérèse wanted to talk *brides*. Either way, she seemed content to not have Claire clarify. Not that Claire could have gotten a word in edgewise; Sister Thérèse talked nonstop as they moved through Trastevere. *Here* was the best gelato; not there. Try the seadas—an amalgam of Sardinian cheese, chestnut honey, orange peel. *This*, meanwhile, was the best place for supplì—deep-fried rice balls—but they run out. Don't bother calling ahead, even though the sign says SUPPLÌ AL TELEFONO: that refers to the cheese-filled ones that stretch a telephone-line-like string of mozzarella from mouth to hand as you eat. And here was where, on Sundays, you'd find the massive Porta Portese flea market; don't enter from the north unless you want to wade through blocks and blocks of cheap knockoffs before getting to the good stuff. Sister Felicity had once suggested they sell Mother Saint Luke's key to an antiques dealer there. Sister Thérèse rolled her eyes and then smiled.

Sister Thérèse seemed so comfortable with Rome's rhythms; Claire wondered if she had any regrets when she disappeared inside the convent's door each night.

But she wouldn't ask that question that way. Instead Claire said, "Sister Thérèse, how did you decide to be a nun?"

Sister Thérèse threw back her head and smiled. "I shall be quite glad to tell you," she said. "But first, another miracle: maritozzi!" She swung open the door of a small corner shop and shouted a greeting to a tall, bearded man presiding over a rapidly emptying glass case.

The shop was crowded. It was difficult to tell where the line started or ended, or if there was a line. Everyone was shouting at the man, but somehow he heard Sister Thérèse's high, musical voice above the din.

"¡Hola, Sor Teresa!" he called.

"Where's the menu to order?" Claire asked.

"There's only one thing worth ordering," Sister Thérèse said to Claire. "Due maritozzi," she called back to the man.

He feigned shock. "Due maritozzi? Ma c'è solo uno di me."

"Dices eso en español," Sister Thérèse said.

"Solo uno—" He waved a hand in surrender and then handed over two huge ovoid buns, split like hot dog rolls and overstuffed with whipped cream.

"He's dating a woman from Seville online; I'm teaching him Spanish," Sister Thérèse said. "I'm also trying to teach him not to make the same joke every time about becoming my husband—these are called maritozzi; 'husband' is marito."

"Ciao, Sorella!" the man said.

"Gracias," said Sister Thérèse, and they left.

There was no way to eat the roll delicately, but it was extraordinary, like falling face forward into a cream-thick cloud—and the taste improbably transported Claire back to the Wisconsin State Fair, held every summer near her old home in Milwaukee, famous for its massive, softball-sized cream puffs. Rome's version was lighter, less sweet, and apparently available daily, as opposed to once a year during state fair season.

"These are amazing."

Sister Thérèse wiped her face. "Impossible to eat, but yes."

"How did you find this place?" Claire looked back at the way they'd come. "All those places?"

"During the semester," Sister Thérèse said, "I take a different way home from school every day. I'm in Rome! And life is short."

"School?"

Sister Thérèse laughed. "Claire, how long did you think you'd be here? Did you do *any* homework on us?"

Claire burned red beneath all the whipped cream while Sister Thérèse explained. This summer, they were busy preparing the convent for the possible sale. But during the school year, Sister Felicity taught economics and Sister Georgia theology in an American university's study-abroad program. Sister Thérèse taught Spanish two mornings a week at a Canadian seminary and English three afternoons at a shelter for the few refugees who'd been allowed to travel north from Lampedusa.

Their order's superior general, Sister Rose, meanwhile, had just won tenure at Harvard, where she taught eschatology in the divinity school.

"Impressive," said Claire.

Sister Thérèse rolled her eyes. "*Her* future is set, so she doesn't care about ours."

"I don't know Sister Rose," Claire said, "but I agree with you that the way she's arranged things—"

"Rigged."

"Makes it difficult. But there might be a way"—Claire wished she'd at least left a voicemail for Bert Ligouri before dropping her phone from two stories up—"to get some money, buy a little time before—"

Sister Thérèse stopped and stared. "That's exactly what I want! *All* I want. A little time. A month, two—enough time for Anna to make up her mind and get back over here! How much will that cost?"

Anna?

A promising prospect, it turned out, one who, if she joined the convent, would nose their numbers back above the magic threshold. Who was she? Where was she?

But Sister Thérèse wouldn't say any more.

Sister Thérèse also hadn't answered Claire's question about becoming a nun, but maybe she hadn't had to. All Claire wanted was to be Sister Thérèse. Not really. But it had been so long since she'd worked with a sister so young, so full of faith that everything would work out, given just a little more time. Anna, whoever she was, was a fool to have left Rome. Sun, maritozzi, tomatoes, Sister Thérèse, and the Convento di Santa Gertrudis. And time. Sister Thérèse thought she had so little of it. But Sister Thérèse was in her twenties, in a convent, in Rome. She'd already accomplished so much Claire hadn't.

"Anna is a lovely young woman whom we will never see again," said Sister Georgia. It was three hours later and she and Claire were sitting in the roseto, having tea. Claire had been left in Sister Georgia's care while Sister Thérèse went to get Claire's phone repaired. To distract herself from the thought that her phone was unfixable, Claire had brought up Anna as soon as Sister Thérèse left.

"Lovely woman," Sister Georgia kept saying, though each time she repeated the word *lovely*, Claire suspected she meant the opposite. Sister Georgia was quite clear on another point, though: Sister Thérèse's expectations for Anna were too hopeful by far.

Anna was a friend of Sister Thérèse's from the Peace Corps, a job Sister Thérèse had had before taking vows. Anna had gone on to Fordham Law but was "restless," as Sister Thérèse would put it, and she'd invited Anna to spend a work sabbatical with them in Rome, see what she thought of the life. Anna had spent much of the winter at the Convento di Santa Gertrudis, and it had gone well. The sisters had thought maybe, yes, they might invite Anna to discern, a first step on the path to becoming a sister.

But then Mother Saint Luke died and Anna left.

"She was upset?" Claire asked.

"Mother Saint Luke's passing upset all of us, but no. Anna was upset because Sister Thérèse suddenly became convinced if Anna joined us, we'd be back at twenty-one sisters, and thus out from under Sister Rose's 'emergency powers.'"

The Order of Saint Gertrude would survive; the convent wouldn't close.

But there were so many things wrong with this plan: the sale was already in motion; just because someone indicated an interest in becoming a sister didn't mean they'd take vows immediately. It could be months, if not years.

"I can't read minds," Sister Georgia said, "but I can read faces, and I agree with everything yours is saying."

"Poor Sister Thérèse," Claire said, embarrassed she'd betrayed her incredulity so plainly.

"Ha," Sister Georgia said. "Sister Thérèse is in her glory. She loves a cause; she has one."

"But if Anna has said no—"

"There's the rub. She hasn't. Anna keeps saying she needs more time. So Sister Thérèse is frantic to find that time for her. But I know. Sister Felicity knows. *You* know."

"You and Sister Felicity could just say no, then. It's not solely Anna's decision."

"Sister Thérèse is going to have her heart broken; I'd like someone else to break it."

"Anna should just say no and be done with it."

"She should," said Sister Georgia. "She can't, I suppose, not yet."

"Why?" said Claire.

"It's a powerful thing," Sister Georgia said, "to be wanted so much."

They sat and talked. And talked and talked. Neither Sister Felicity nor Sister Thérèse returned, and Claire wondered if she'd been summoned to Rome to spell the two younger sisters from listening duty. Next to Mother Saint Luke, Sister Georgia had been in the convent the longest, seen the most.

Every so often, Claire would answer a question, but she did so in fewer and fewer words.

"I know a yawn starting when I see one," Sister Georgia finally said.

"No, Sister," Claire said, but the power of suggestion was too strong. She yawned.

"Exactly," said Sister Georgia. "Now, here's what we'll do."

And by that, she meant what Claire would do: Sister Georgia said the best antidote to jet lag was exercise, and she mapped out a little walk around Trastevere. Be back by seven for a simple dinner. Sister Georgia would go with her but for her knees. Claire protested, mentioned her own knees, said she'd find her own dinner. Sister Georgia shook her head. "Mother Saint Luke would be horrified if we let you go yet another night without company."

Once upon a time, Claire would have held her ground. But the thought of going back to neon Audrey, all that blond wood and soulless melamine, daunted her. She didn't want to be alone tonight. Or tomorrow night, either, or the next. She'd call Monica, tell her to move up her flight. Send a ticket to Dorothy.

Or Claire would have another meal with these three fine, fierce women and their departed force of a friend, Mother Saint Luke. When Sister Georgia asked Claire a question, she'd occasionally pose it as Mother Saint Luke. *If Mother Saint Luke were here, she'd ask you, Claire, about your family . . .*

Walking to the first of three fountains Sister Georgia had instructed her to visit—the second was Mother Saint Luke's favorite—Claire went through the conversation again. Claire had talked about Dorothy, about Monica. And, briefly, Dorothy's father, Len.

Maybe it was poor Sister Georgia who'd been assigned listening duty.

Coming up on the first fountain, a huge stone bath perpetually filled by a looming lion, Claire remembered she'd even recounted an anecdote about Dorothy's first swim lesson. (She'd run right off the diving board when no one was looking; Claire had leapt in to save her, fully clothed.)

How clever of Sister Georgia to make Claire think she, Claire, was being imposed upon, and not Sister Georgia, who likely just wanted a nap herself, but instead had kept asking Claire questions, mostly about Dorothy: Is she independent? (*Yes, she's twenty-nine.*) Good job? Home? (*Yes, yes.*) A special someone? (*Usually.*) She's named for? (*Blessed Dorothy Day.*) Treats her grandparents well? (*My mom died when I was little, Dad not too long ago; Dorothy took it better than me.*) In the end, they'd covered everything but Dorothy's favorite color (bright, loud, University of Wisconsin red).

Claire almost felt like she was being vetted, assessed as not a real estate broker but a convent candidate. *Oh, you've no idea, Sister*, Claire thought. It had happened on jobs before, Claire sensing a convent's desire to have her join them. Usually unspoken, though sometimes directly expressed by someone like Sister Georgia, a sister who didn't have a lot of time. Nothing ever came of such moments, but it was flattering.

Claire cupped a hand beneath the lion's mouth, sipped what water she could. Sister Georgia, again, quoting Mother Saint Luke, said every Roman fountain had its own flavor; it depended on which ancient aqueduct fed it. This one came from Lake Bracciano, which reportedly swirled with eels. Claire cupped another hand. If this same water fed the Convento di Santa Gertrudis, maybe she could slow the sale that way: the toilets might be a protected habitat.

She walked on. The water had tasted fine. Cold, nothing of eel. Not surprising. To hear Sister Georgia tell it, Mother Saint Luke was prone to drama.

For good reason, and not just because Mother Saint Luke had left behind a key marked "in case of emergency." Sister Georgia had explained that, though Mother Saint Luke had *not* been an actress for director William Wyler during the shooting of *Roman Holiday*, she had been an au pair for his family, at least until she'd missed escorting one of his daughters home from school. Walking alone, the daughter had been scooped up by a stranger on a bike. Returned safely after a few hours, no harm done, and no one blamed the au pair, but she blamed herself. Asked the sisters of Convento di Santa Gertrudis to take her in for a spell to recover and repent; she stayed sixty-seven years.

Initially, she'd stayed inside the convent's walls, never venturing out. But eventually, she emerged to teach literature and film at universities around town. She loved fountains. Visiting them, sketching them, drinking from them. She loved Rome's water. Wine. She was perhaps the only person who loved Italian whiskey. She loved visitors, particularly artists.

Mother Saint Luke loved giving tours of the convent—the frescoes, the floors, the roseto, the chapel, the overgrown garden, or il parco, behind it, where she'd established a hermitage she'd use from time to time. The Gertrudans had wanted Mother Saint Luke stateside for her final years; again and again, she foiled their plans. *Come stay*, she would write to her American superiors, *come stay and see why I can't leave.* In her final weeks, she dictated countless letters to Sister Thérèse that were never sent: the recipients were all dead. *Cher Audrey, come stay with us in Rome. Mr. Wilder, bring your family. Come stay, come stay, come stay.* If Mother Saint Luke couldn't move about in the world anymore, she wanted it to come in.

Of course Mother Saint Luke hadn't wanted to go back to the States. The convent was resplendent, even in decay. And outside its walls, eternal Rome. Not just the statues and stairs, but the white-socked cat sitting on a sill, the two young men animatedly arguing with two old men, all four smiling. The waiter snapping a white cloth over a tiny table, the aproned woman Claire's age bending to chalk

Strozzapreti on a chalkboard. The young boy looking down at Claire from a balcony. She waved; he retreated.

No matter: these flowers, that tree, the late-day sun summoning new details on every block. She wanted to take pictures of all of it and was delighted that, phoneless, she couldn't. Everything was brighter, better, without her phone. She'd ask Sister Thérèse to never bring it back. Claire would start a business that specialized in electronics-free tours. They'd take pictures with eyes alone. That green scooter, that black bike, this—

This ugly, ugly fountain.

Which, if Claire had followed Sister Georgia's directions correctly, was Mother Saint Luke's favorite.

Above a small, shallow pool almost flush with the ground rose a recessed space bracketed by Doric pilasters and capped by a ruffled seashell. An exhausted lion—or boar?—dribbled water over a misshapen—boulder? It looked half-melted, and whatever it was, or had served as the pedestal for—a statue of a prisoner?—was gone. Muffled music thumped nearby; Claire turned to see a vape shop.

The fountain was not crowded. Claire would give it that. Debris floated in the shallow pool.

Sister Georgia said Sister Thérèse had a theory about why the fountain was so important to Mother Saint Luke. This was the Fontana del Prigione, the prison fountain. After all these years, Mother Saint Luke must have still felt guilty about the kidnapping. Had they ever caught the kidnapper? The prisoner-less fountain reminded her of that, and that she herself should have gone to jail for dereliction of duty.

"I don't necessarily agree," Sister Georgia had told Claire piously. "But it's good to be reminded of our failings. She was a holy woman, but like all of us, a sinner."

But—

But Wyler had gotten his kid back. And it didn't sound like it was entirely Mother Saint Luke's fault. And it didn't sound like Mother Saint Luke. Not that Claire knew her beyond these stories, but she'd known plenty of women religious her age. Each of them entirely unique, but not a one would ever presume to imagine herself on a pedestal, much less in a Roman fountain, even one as dilapidated as this.

Claire looked around again at the empty street, the vape shop, the dirty fountain, the vines encroaching from the hillside beyond, the molten marble lump where Sister Georgia insisted a penitent Mother Saint Luke pictured herself a prisoner: no, not at all. But why *had* Mother Saint Luke dragged the sisters here? For that matter, why had Sister Georgia dispatched Claire?

Claire looked at the fountain for another long minute, and a shiver ran through her. She looked around. Something was wrong—was off. She reached for her phone, remembered she didn't have it, and decided to skip the third fountain Sister Georgia had specified. She walked back to her apartment, but when she got there, she walked straight past it. It suddenly felt unsafe, neon Audrey no longer funny but menacing. A Vespa swooped past. She knew this, too, without her phone: the scooter's name meant *wasp*.

Years ago, the man had just "scooped" up Wyler's daughter, Sister Georgia had said. "Scooped," like gelato, making it sound okay. It was not. Claire was not.

Claire hurried up the street now, not fully sure what she was feeling or why, only that she needed, right now, to be inside. She wished she'd brought Mother Saint Luke's key along.

Take me in, Claire had said to the Milwaukee nuns when she was all of seventeen. She had loved those women, and they had loved her back with a warmth that was nothing like the love her mother had once had for her, but somehow had made for a sturdy substitute. College, the world, adulthood, looked messy and chaotic and full of men. The adult world had taken her adult mother. The church looked safe, had a two-thousand-year footprint on the planet versus Claire's seventeen. *Take me*, Claire had said, *I'm ready.* Saint Clare of Assisi had turned down marriage and money and entered a monastery at eighteen. Claire was no saint, but she'd read other stories (in books given to her by the nuns themselves) of women who'd joined convents at twelve, thirteen, even nine. Some of the older sisters in that very convent had joined in their teens. Few as young as Claire, but still. And while Claire hadn't necessarily heard God calling out to her, wasn't *thinking* all the time about becoming a nun some sign of God saying something? Wasn't wanting it enough? Sometimes you got on the train just as it was leaving; sometimes you got to the station early and waited for it to arrive. Wasn't all that mattered that you were on the right track?

Oh, Claire, Sister Anastasia had said long ago, *what a gift having you with us would be.* But apparently it wasn't a gift the Clementine sisters in Milwaukee could accept, not with Claire just seventeen. *Go to college, a good one*, the nuns said. *Study hard, but live simply, devoutly. Prepare. Spend summers with us learning, studying, praying. When you graduate, we'll be here, and so will your vocation if it's truly a gift from God.* Claire didn't understand, but she came and showed them her acceptance letter from Yale. Yale!

What did Claire care? She'd applied on a lark; if she got rejected by enough places, the nuns would *have* to take her in.

Her father had been thrilled, and even more so with the financial aid, but Claire told the nuns: *I'll tear up this letter if you take me in now.* Sister Anastasia shook her head. *Go,* she said. *Go to Yale and live the life of a young woman preparing to take vows, to become a sister of the Society of Saint Clementine. If you can do it out there, then maybe you'll be able to live it in here.*

And Claire had gone to college and she'd lived the life, and it had almost, almost worked, until it hadn't.

Claire had shown up in the emergency room last year with what turned out to be a panic attack. Even though she'd been in the midst of three disastrous deals and had just learned she'd been lied to by a kindly old monsignor, she'd disbelieved the diagnosis. She hadn't *panicked* since college, since that night before graduation, onstage.

The diagnosis had been delivered by a busy triage nurse who'd told her to sit down, put her head between her knees, breathe deep, and sit in the waiting room until she heard her name called. *But I'm dying,* Claire said, and even if there had been enough oxygen in the world—there wasn't—her lungs refused to take it in. Her heart and ears ringing, vision darkening, vertigo surging.

Now, as she was ushered back inside the convent by Sister Georgia, Claire felt similarly. Different light today made everything new: the archways crowded with yet more frescoes; floors inlaid with a universe of stones; ceilings coffered or vaulted or so soaringly high you had to squint to make out what floated there. Animals. Birds. Angels. All of them static, but a small price for, say, the painted bird to pay to float in full plumage forever. The convent's base color was persimmon, but today it had ripened into red. Everything was wavering, even the birds' wings.

Sister Georgia fretted over her.

"I should never have sent you on that walk. *Sleep* is the best cure for jet lag. Or crossing by ship! How Mother Saint Luke came in 1951. Italian Line, the *Giulio Cesare*, I believe."

Sister Felicity appeared now, or had been there all the time. "Are you okay?" she asked.

"I'm fine," Claire said, a lie, which the sisters' faces registered as such.

"The sisters disagree with me," Sister Georgia said, "but I'm certain that Rome trembles with dozens of tiny earthquakes each day. I'm forever stumbling."

Claire smiled. She did feel a bit wobbly, but now that she was sitting, not nauseous. Not ready for dinner, either.

"Where's Sister Thérèse?" Sister Felicity said. "She can walk Claire back to her apartment."

"Do you want to just lie down?" Sister Georgia said.

"I'm right here," Sister Thérèse said, walking in from the vestibule, holding up Claire's phone. "Ta-da! Just needed a new screen, praise be to God."

Even from a distance, Claire could see that the screen was crowded with messages.

"How much do I owe you?" Claire said.

"Lie down here. For an hour or the night," Sister Georgia said, turning serious. "We have a guest suite. It's terribly uncomfortable, but we could keep an eye on you."

"Oh, that's a wonderful idea!" said Sister Thérèse.

Sister Georgia looked at Sister Felicity. Then Sister Thérèse did, too. And finally, Claire.

Sister Felicity had had on a guarded look of concern, but now her eyes softened. "Please forgive us, Ms. Murphy. The very first thing we should have done is offer you a roof, a bed."

* * *

And it was in that bed later that Claire, luggage retrieved, dinner skipped, towels issued, finally texted Dorothy.

Can't talk. Can text. In convent.

The room was small, painted sky blue, had a twin bed, desk, and chair. On the desk, a bud vase with a single rose, orange flecked with red, like the heart of a peach. A leaded window labeled DO NOT OPEN!! was cranked wide open.

Dorothy's reply arrived: *U do realize I post screenshots of yr texts.*

Ha, Claire replied.

The next text from Dorothy took longer; but it was indeed a screenshot of Claire's original text, the words circled in red, annotation added: *MY MOM IS COOLER THAN YRS*. Hearts of different sizes and colors were scattered everywhere.

Wait, what—

Claire's phone rang. Dorothy.

On the one hand, Dorothy was precisely whom Claire wanted to talk to. It was rare that more than two days passed without a call between them, and though Claire had warned her she might be slightly more out of touch in Italy—and this was even before she knew she'd be dropping her phone from on high—she felt badly that she hadn't spoken to Dorothy since landing. In fact, not since New Haven, some days before.

Though Dorothy and her mother were born twenty-two years apart, people sometimes mistook them for sisters. This haunted Dorothy, Claire understood. Turning twenty-nine, for example, was stressful enough without someone assuming you were the kid sister of someone who'd just turned fifty-two.

"At least they always think you're the younger sister," said Claire, who had experimented with going gray. (It had looked lovely, but "for business reasons," Monica had urged Claire back to her buttery highlights.)

Of late, however, Claire had come to feel less like Dorothy's mother or sister than like Dorothy's daughter, given the way Dorothy kept tabs on Claire. Which may have been why, love Dorothy as she did, Claire didn't want to talk with Dorothy just yet. It wasn't that the nuns had said she couldn't use her phone—their own quarters were distant; she wouldn't be disturbing them.

But she might disturb Dorothy, especially if Claire said anything kind about the convent or its occupants or its deep, beautiful quiet. Dorothy was at best wary of religion and, what's more, had little patience with Claire talking shop.

Before encountering Sister Thérèse that morning, Claire had had no plans for this evening and had looked forward to that emptiness. This morning, her plan had been to walk, eventually find food, let the city unwind around her and she with it. But then she'd dropped her phone, eaten a maritozzo, drunk from a fountain, decoded another. Then she'd felt—something.

No, she was being coy with herself; she felt this: What if she stayed, not just for an hour, not just a night or two—

But what a strange, strange thing to think: Claire, at fifty-two, in a convent. She hadn't been able to hack it as a teenager; what would make it possible now?

Maybe being fifty-two.

She listened. Absolutely nothing.

Dorothy!

Can we not? Claire started to text. *It's just so quiet here.*

She deleted that. Maybe what Claire could do was find a landline.

She could stay in touch with Dorothy even if she dropped her fixed phone from a higher height. Which she wanted to do.

In the meantime, a new text arrived from Dorothy. *Sorry, realized it's 9 there. Way past your bedtime. I shouldn't be texting and driving anyway. Talk tmrw!*

Claire had half a thought to call Marcus and see if anything was up. When Dorothy was younger, her escapades and milestones had been good fodder for conversation; concerts, championships, graduations, good excuses for the unofficial godfather to visit. Claire was sad all those milestones had passed. And she missed Marcus's visits. They could talk endlessly about anything.

Claire rose from her bed and went to the window. Below, a hillside overgrown with what looked like honeysuckle ran down toward the Tiber. Above, stars. Somewhere, a citrus tree—something had to account for the sharp, sweet citrus smell. She closed her eyes, opened them, felt her breathing slow and steady.

A sea of roofs rippled toward distant mountains. People loved Rome. The sisters seemed to. Claire did, more and more. Claire had liked the opera; she'd liked that the café waiter had smiled at her; she'd liked that, to judge from the looks on the sidewalk here, she was at least visible (though not to drivers); she liked that you were never more than two or three wrong turns away from a quiet, narrow street, inevitably aglow with flowers or lights or laundry.

And then there was where she was, this broken paradise, the Convento di Santa Gertrudis.

Claire left the window, lay in bed, browsed on her phone. Dorothy was, as Claire had told Sister Georgia, just fine. Then she looked up the third and last fountain Sister Georgia had told her to visit, which Claire had never gotten to, the Acqua Paola. Even on her phone, it looked to be absurdly large: more waterfall than fountain, pouring into a vast pool. Or maybe it was a church. The marble façade was capped with a large cross; five arches made up the base, and the middle one looked very much like the front door of a cathedral, but for the water pouring out of it. Mother Saint Luke's devotion to the bedraggled missing prisoner fountain began to make more sense. Acqua Paola, so much closer to the Convento di Santa Gertrudis and so much lovelier, was nevertheless *too* lovely, too showy for a woman who'd vowed poverty.

She'd tell Dorothy all about that when they finally did talk.

Dorothy, who was just fine.

Claire turned off the light and put the phone on the floor. Thought of Dorothy when she was little, depending on Claire for everything, including bedtime stories. *Good night, room* . . . Claire always fell asleep before Dorothy, could feel even now her breath hot in her ear, whispering, *Wake up, Mommy . . .*

What if Sister Georgia *had* been surreptitiously assessing her, seeing whether she was free of obligations, familial and otherwise?

Right. Fun to imagine. No: vain to imagine.

Claire rolled over. The sheets smelled faintly of lavender.

But what *if*?

What if Claire were a restless, seeking soul in Rome and came through the convent's door and stayed the night, a month, a year?

She imagined telling Dorothy, Monica. *I've decided to . . .*

She imagined telling the alumni magazine, *Ciao from Rome, where I . . .*

She imagined telling Marcus, right in the roseto below.

She did not imagine that he had just landed in Rome.

IV. PIAZZA CAVOUR

LET US MEET MARCUS. LET *someone* meet Marcus, went his own steady plea during his first weeks at Yale in 1985. He'd been assigned a double and his roommate hadn't shown.

There was a quad across the hall from him; this was where Claire and her roommates lived. An odd arrangement, but they were in an odd spot—atop a tower on Old Campus, the large, patchily lawned quadrangle where Yale kept its first-year students. The floor had once served as a penthouse suite, a place where a professor and his family could live and rule over all the students below. But no professor had deigned to do so for years, and so the floor had been carved up into space for six students—the legendary Sanford Hall sextet. Jokers from lower floors loved doubling down on the double entendre. Marcus did not. In fact, he mostly kept to himself until the night he met the entire first-year class all at once.

He was eating dinner in Commons, the massive, baronial dining hall where freshmen ate. Eating alone, even though he could see his floormates at a table across the way. He was too embarrassed to join them. Claire had walked in on Marcus the first day in the bathroom, not knowing it was co-ed. She'd heard someone singing in the shower and thought it was Monica—the voice was high but husky. But then he'd grabbed a towel and emerged, wet and smiling and nervous. He was skinny, hairless, all joints, like one of the little wooden mannequins they'd used in high school art class. He apologized, she said not to, and instead of leaving, she stood and stared at him for five seconds. Felt like five hours.

Time slowed again now as a group of guys sauntered over to where Claire and Monica and their roommates sat. Someone said something and the women exchanged looks. Marcus saw Claire try to smile. Then one of the boys began to sing the title anthem from *The Sound of Music*.

Marcus nodded. He'd been in the show in high school. Ninth grade. He'd tried out for the part of Georg von Trapp—Christopher Plummer's role—but they'd given him young Rolf. He made the best of it, understudied all the male parts.

Yale had a dozen or so a cappella groups, choirs, a glee club. Someone was always singing somewhere. It really was an amazing concentration of talent. Or annoyance, depending on your point of view. These three were annoying, even more so because they were so bad. The more Marcus listened, the worse they sounded.

And the more embarrassed Claire looked. The boys sang on; people quieted and stared. Monica began whispering to Claire, who shook her head but began fingering the key ring on the table between them.

The Sound of Music. The nuns.

He'd have figured it out faster if he hadn't been replaying memories.

They were mocking her.

Other tables began to join in. Laughter rose. Monica looked murderous.

Marcus watched, thought, took a deep breath.

"*Ohhhhhhhhhhhhhhhh . . .*" Marcus began, his voice drawing him up, out of his chair, then atop it, then onto the table. The acoustics were terrible, but he had a great pair of lungs—which is why he'd won the lead in *Oklahoma!* senior year—and was using them to the full now: "...*klahoma.*"

Twenty feet away, the boys sang on. They'd switched to "Maria."

Marcus started again, louder, drew out the *O* longer. A couple of tables away, another boy rose and picked up the refrain. Then another. Another. Suddenly every a cappella kid wanted in. Others climbed on tables, but Marcus could feel it, all eyes were on him. He'd never played a room this large: twelve hundred seats. Halfway through the song, he had half the room. By the end, whistling, shouting, calls of "Encore!" rang throughout the great hall, and then everyone sang the chorus a final time. Even—he looked—Monica and Claire.

Marcus finished, accepted congratulations and audition invites, and made his way to Claire's table, where he saw the three boys talking to her.

"It's fine," Claire was saying to her dinner plate.

"Hey, Marcus," Monica said, hand gripping a spoon. "Give us a sec. These guys were just apologizing."

"For what?" one of them said.

"Listen," Marcus said, his voice still pitched as though he were addressing the whole room. And though there was now a background roar of conversations, the nearby tables fell silent. "If you *ever* mock her again, you will never sing again, because I will rip your throats out." Claire blanched. Monica looked on in wonder. The boys looked startled but not chastened until Marcus added, "I was *in The Sound of Music.* I played the boyfriend who betrays them all."

"Hot, but vaguely psychopathic," said Monica.

"That one," said Marcus, not breaking his stare.

Then it all went quickly. Monica chuffed—she may have been

stifling a laugh, but the boys seemed appropriately abashed. Apologies were mumbled, the boys fled, and the women did, too. The onlooking tables inched away.

In less than a minute, Marcus was all alone once again.

Until the next day, when Claire appeared in his doorway.

"Can I come in?" she said.

"Sure?" he said.

So far, this conversation was going better than the first he'd had with her, when he'd been still wet from the shower and stammered through a monologue asking whether it was okay that she lived on a co-ed floor. No! If it was okay that *he* lived on the floor. Not because— or that—anyway, if—he didn't mean to suggest that—

Claire had shaken her head, said it was fine: *I walk with Jesus.*

That's cool, Marcus had said, terrified he would say the wrong thing, or that he just had.

But now, here in his room, it looked as though he'd been cleaning for a week awaiting her arrival. The bed was made with hospital corners; the desk surface was bare but for a single piece of paper with a pencil lying across it. A narrow bookshelf held a full set of orange-spined Pelican Shakespeares, a red-and-blue Merriam-Webster, and a maroon *Bartlett's Familiar Quotations*. Tacked to the wall was a reproduction of Laurence Olivier's 1948 *Hamlet* poster and another, in Italian, of Olivier starring in William Wyler's *Carrie*. The floor had a small oval rag rug, ugly and immaculate.

"Wow," Claire said.

"What?" Marcus said, and then, assuming she was talking about his posters, started in on his love of Olivier—an ar*cha*ic kind of fandom, sure, but—

"No, this room," Claire said. "Monica and I—if you ever saw—well, our room, it's not like this, tidy, and it won't ever be."

"Oh," said Marcus. There was only the one chair. If he sat in it, she'd have to sit on the bed, which seemed wrong. If he sat on the bed, though, that seemed wrong in a whole other way. So they stood. She didn't seem to care. She had a ring of keys with her, more than he had—did she have a car? Access to special rooms? What did nuns do, or need? She put the keys on his desk and went to the window, where he had three plants: a fern, a spider plant, and a schefflera. He'd tried that as a conversational gambit with a girl from another dorm the first week—*I love plants!*—and she'd looked at him with such sorrow that he'd turned away. He was nerdy and shy, would have been no one's pick to become the class's sole Academy Award nominee (Best Supporting, 1992) and the subject of not one but two *People* magazine lists ("Most Eligible Bachelors," 1996; "Whatever Happened to…?" 2016).

Onstage or atop a table in Commons, he could say anything. Offstage—well, so far, he'd hardly said more than, "Oh."

She didn't seem to mind. She studied his posters and slowly read the title of the Italian one, "*Gli Occhi Che Non Sorrisero*." He'd been waiting for someone to ask about this and began rehearsing his little speech, about how *The Eyes That Didn't Smile* was a strange title for what had been, in English, simply *Carrie*, after the Theodore Dreiser novel *Sister Carrie*—but then Marcus found his heart was shouting at his head to shut up.

Claire read it again, faster and with more confidence this time, and then turned to ask Marcus something—what, he'd never know, because she stopped short, having clearly changed her mind as soon as she saw his face.

"Marcus, are you all right?" she asked.

And then she laughed.

He was not all right. He was ruined. It wasn't that she was smart (she was). It wasn't that she was beautiful (she was). It wasn't that she was kind and thoughtful and—what's the word?—good (she was, she was, she was). It wasn't that her Italian was perfect (it wasn't). It was her laugh, easy and ready and joyful.

She told her story. No, she wasn't a nun yet, but was trying to live the life as best she could. Example: Yale had offered to house her in a special single-occupancy suite up at the divinity school, but if she became a sister, she'd take a vow of poverty and already felt an aversion to anything that smacked of luxury or privilege or singled-outedness—and so much here did. Besides, the divinity school was atop a hill at the edge of campus. Good sledding, she'd heard, but otherwise distant from everywhere she needed to be.

"So I'm here," she said, and smiled. "And I'm *here*..." Was she an actor, too? She knew how to ride a pause. "... to say thanks."

"Oh. Those guys were jerks."

"They were having fun," Claire said.

"At your expense."

"Until you came along," she said. "And anyway, they had a point."

"They—sorry—which was what?"

"Are *you* spending summers studying to be a nun?" Claire said. "Are they? Is anyone here but me? I belong at Yale as much as Julie Andrews belonged in a convent." She straightened. He wondered if she would have preferred that he'd broken a chair or two over the boys' backs. "Did you really play Rolf?" she asked.

Marcus nodded. "I'm afraid so. *He* was a jerk. Sorry if I come off that way, too."

"You don't, but enough acting. Who are you?"

A deep breath, a mask dropped, and out it came. Finally, someone to listen. *He* was the one who didn't belong. He'd been by the Dramat, the undergraduate stage—it dwarfed his high school's. He'd found out one of his Yale classmates already had a manager and another had had a one-act produced off-Broadway. He'd been by the bursar's office to sign his loan papers; Yale was helping him some, and so was a local scholarship from the Rotary Club, but it looked like—he didn't understand, exactly?—he was on the hook for a lot. What was he even thinking about, acting? He'd already looked up the late registration deadline for the state college back home. The bus would take two days, but he had enough for the fare. He hadn't decided yet but thought he would probably leave.

They talked deep into the afternoon; the light faded, and with it, his voice. So, *this* was college, Claire thought. Conversation without end with interesting souls. She loved the sound of his voice, round, deep; he could talk about anything and she'd listen.

After he transferred, he'd major in accounting, he said.

There was no accounting major at Yale, Claire knew, because she'd looked it up when her father asked about one. He wanted her to have a fallback if the "nun thing" didn't work out. Until that moment, she'd not imagined it not working out. She was going to major in geology, maybe chemistry; Sister Anastasia said their high schools needed women who could teach science. Claire had been by the Yale bookstore annex, where the books were stacked in columns. The science textbooks looked as big as pizza boxes and twice as thick. English majors' books—individually bound plays like the ones Marcus had on his shelf—looked frail by comparison.

He wanted to transfer?

"Don't leave," Claire said finally, and he didn't.

Thirty-four years later in Rome, he debated whether he should. He still had time to make a clean getaway; Claire wasn't due for another five minutes. The sun was yellow, the sky was blue, but the atmosphere felt wrong. The café he'd picked—or that a blog had chosen for him—was closed and so he'd switched to this one, right around the corner, realizing, too late, that it was named for Claire's first fiancé, Café Henry, complete with English spelling.

Calm down. Henry had never proposed. Marcus thought he had this memory correct. Henry was a jeweler, had showed up at dinner one night—she clearly loved telling this story—spilled a small manila envelope of rings onto a napkin: *Pick.*

Is this a proposal? Claire said she'd asked, and he'd said, *Depends on which one you pick.* She'd left.

Still, she'd been with Henry a year by that point; Marcus had once asked why she'd stuck around. He remembers this conversation, but not where they were; was it the time they'd walked the Brooklyn Bridge, or the time they'd met at that bookstore, or maybe at Joanie's wedding?

Henry did *all* the chores without asking, apparently, *and, Marcus, he had the most beautiful hands.* Awkwardly, Claire had broken up with him before Monica collected some jewelry she'd left at his store for cleaning. When Monica finally did go, she insisted on the friends-and-family discount earlier promised. He said no. *Still*, Claire said, *you can't blame her for trying.*

You couldn't, and Monica tried a lot. For example, when Dorothy was three months old, Monica had tried to get Marcus to marry Claire.

It had started with a letter, which led to a call and, finally, a visit with Monica.

Maybe Marcus would tell Claire this story in sunny Rome today.

About Monica meeting him that night at a bar in Midtown, Cassidy's, about Monica's crazy idea: Marcus should, at that moment, marry Claire.

Because *that* would have made sense. Because he was twenty-two. Because he was starting a film career that had him living out of a suitcase. Because he was heartbroken. Claire had had a baby with another fucking guy she'd just fucking met in the city at some random party.

But mostly it didn't make sense because Monica was asking him this, not Claire.

Because it's my idea, Monica had said, *my, to borrow a word, fucking brilliant idea.*

Monica had put one and one together and gotten three, marriage. A year out of college, a stuffed bulldog on the table between them, a baby gift. Monica had given it to Marcus to give to Dorothy.

Monica swore she never told Claire about this conversation. He certainly hadn't.

What she really needs is help, Monica had told Marcus.

She's got you, he'd said.

He can believe how angry he was—he was a baby then himself—but not how stupid.

She needs family, Monica had said.

She's got her dad.

He's furious.

He'll come around, Marcus had said.

Will you? Monica had asked.

He would eventually, because he loved Claire, even though she'd run from him that night before graduation—why?—and though it in fact made no sense, Marcus might indeed have asked Claire to marry him that very night, had Monica, who knew everything, not admitted, *I don't know*, when Marcus had asked, *Will Claire say yes?*

"Really?" Claire said. She stared at him. She was in Rome, with Marcus, at a café outside in the sun. She'd awoken that morning in a seventeenth-century convent on a thin metal cot that had somehow borne her through the best sleep of her life. She'd had a reverse princess-and-the-pea moment, had gotten down on her hands and knees to study the cot, see what made it so comfortable. Nothing. It just was. And now Marcus was here. They hugged lightly and sat, he on the edge of his chair. This was the Piazza Cavour, he explained; the palace presiding over the piazza was the Italian Supreme Court.

"I thought it'd be handy," he said, nodding to the court, "if we needed to settle anything."

He looked anxious. So was she, but the sun was helping.

She'd texted Dorothy earlier, mentioned that she was unexpectedly meeting Marcus this afternoon, and Dorothy's reply had been downright giddy, complete with a string of hearts. Then another string of hearts, glasses clinking. Dorothy truly loved Marcus. He loved her back, had long been her godfather in every way but officially, remembered her birthdays, invited (and paid for) her to visit him on location when the location was cool. Claire half wondered if he had Dorothy hidden somewhere nearby now—it would explain his uncharacteristic anxiety—but hoped he didn't, or if he *had* somehow brought Dorothy to Rome, that she and Marcus would have a few hours together before they met her. Because Claire wanted to talk to Marcus about Dorothy, about how she might react to Claire quitting, doing something new, especially as that "something new" was evolving in a way she hadn't fully anticipated.

She'd welcome Marcus's wisdom. As much as he was Dorothy's unofficial godfather, he'd also served at times over the years as Claire's unofficial god-spouse, someone other than Monica whom Claire could consult about various quandaries.

Claire knew—she assumed Marcus knew, too—that Dorothy had long wanted them to be actual spouses. Not because, Dorothy would always emphasize, Claire needed the parenting help. Thank you, Dorothy. Claire hadn't and didn't. She had raised Dorothy on her own, through the many years when Dorothy's father, Len, sent only child support and through the many more years when, having "quit banking for Jesus," he sent only Bibles—children's Bibles, teen Bibles, big ones, purse-size ones.

Claire had more than proved that she could fend for herself and her daughter just fine. Dorothy did well for herself, too. Dorothy and Len now met at least once a year, usually near the megachurch in Dallas where he played bass in the praise band. The meetings were Dorothy's initiative, God bless her. Part of being an adult was acting like one, or so Dorothy claimed she'd told Len. Claire watched it all carefully, didn't interfere, didn't question where the impetus to reunite had come from, though she suspected it had something to do with the illness and death of her own father, Dorothy's grandfather. Family grew more important as you grew older. Anyway, it sounded like Len was mellowing. Dorothy reported he'd even begun to say *How's your mom?* without frowning.

Mom was fine, thanks. She looked at Marcus. The old pull, like waves tugging at your feet along the shore. But Claire knew better than to wade in deeper. There had been occasions over the years when Claire idly wondered whether she and Marcus would wind up together. But the timing was never right—he'd be in a relationship or she was or they both were.

And of course there was that other reason, that deal only Claire and God knew about.

Maybe she'd talk to the sisters about that. Someday. Today, Marcus was here.

What *was* Marcus doing here? One option: he'd arrived out of the blue to ask her why she'd run from the stage that night before graduation.

Or so went a recurring anxious fantasy of hers, that he would finally press the point. He'd never outright asked why she'd run but sometimes nervously joked about it. She'd grin weakly in reply or stammer something about having been embarrassed, which wasn't entirely untrue. But it was incomplete, and sometimes he'd let the silence build as he waited for more.

Today, though, she was the one leveraging the silence. They'd met, sat; he'd ordered. She smiled, waited. His brief explanation on the phone had sounded like one long lie, but she was going to give him another chance here under the restaurant awning.

She studied the Supreme Court building. Marcus said he'd heard locals called it the Palazzaccio. Claire said that sounded pretty. Marcus said it meant the opposite. But it wasn't ugly, not to Claire. Much of the piazza before it was given over to a deep green lawn and, even more unexpectedly, palm trees lolling this way and that, which gave Claire the dizzy feeling that she was somewhere farther south, on some seaside vacation.

But something else was making her dizzy now, a notion Sister

Georgia had inadvertently or slyly seeded the night before, which, over the course of the day, eating, praying, being with the sisters, exploring the beautiful, crumbling convent, had deepened into desire, and even as she sat here, was surfacing as an actual, if farfetched, idea: Living in that convent or another, forever. Taking vows. Becoming a nun.

Could a woman with a child do this? Yes, she could, if that child was old enough, independent, possessed of all the things Sister Georgia had asked about. Claire had met such sisters over the years, ones with adult children. Such sisters were memorable. Capable. Powerful. They'd figured it out. Claire could, too.

But that she felt this strongly after a mere twenty-four hours, after one night's perfect sleep—was that evidence of her having lost her mind? Or the opposite? In good ways and bad, she felt younger than she had in years.

Thank God Marcus was here to talk about this. He was the one person she could always go deep with, deeper than—she would never tell her this—Monica. Monica only ever wanted to fix things, got frustrated or laughed when Claire brought up things she couldn't fix, like existential loneliness.

Sometimes Monica was right to laugh. But sometimes, as now, Claire wanted someone—Marcus—to say, *I'm listening.*

"Cheers," he said.

One word, one smile, was almost enough to erase any thought of vowed life, past or future. She always forgot that about him, that keeping up with him by email and phone was as different from seeing him in person as Milwaukee from Milan. She felt less lonely around him, though being around him reminded her how lonely she was. What was it? Tuesday? Thursday? At home, it wouldn't matter: she'd leave work, go to the gym, grab a salad. Or mix it up and get the salad first. She never got to day-drink in front of a supreme court.

She wondered if his days ever felt as empty, if he ever blamed her for that, as she did herself. They could have been together, but for her divine dealmaking regarding him. Though it was silly to blame that. Maybe the simpler truth was that they didn't belong together, never had. That was why he'd never asked her why. He knew.

And maybe the sisters intuited something about Claire, too?

"Salute," she said and took an emboldening sip. "So. I have something to ask you. Something big."

He squirmed. "What a coincidence," he said carefully. "I have something big to ask *you*."

She hardly heard him; should she just come out and ask, *What do you think I should do with the rest of my life?*

But Marcus didn't look ready, not to ask his question or answer hers.

"Let's start with lower stakes," Claire said. "What are you doing here, besides stalking me?"

He smiled, and when he did, she thought, *He looks older*, or rather, willed herself to think this, especially before he thought the same of her. But the problem was, he didn't look older. Rail thin, which, as ever, meant that he could wear anything, even jeans and a blank black T-shirt, clothes for a man half his age.

"Do you know ——?"

He mentioned a woman's name, an actress Claire didn't know. Claire always asked after Marcus's love life, precisely because she thought doing so signaled she didn't care. Evidence: he never asked after hers, though she sometimes shared regardless.

"How old is she?" Claire said.

"We're not seeing each other, to answer your question," he said. "She's fifty-four."

"Good for her," Claire said, and maybe it was. Being fifty-plus had to be good for someone.

"Good for me!" Marcus said. "She called and said, 'Marco, you want to rerecord that dialogue, I have an hour free in Roma on this Tuesday in June—'"

"You flew here for an hour's work?" Claire said.

"She's an amazing actress. And this is an amazing city," Marcus said. "And, most amazing of all—"

She took a big swig of the wine, white, late sun made liquid. Marcus didn't drink, never had. He'd lost a beloved high school drama teacher to alcoholism. Their first year at Yale, he and Claire had spent long nights in Sterling Memorial Library, especially on weekends, to avoid parties that might involve an excess of alcohol or nun-taunting clowns. Back then, Marcus and Claire sticking together had meant staying out of trouble. It had also meant long minutes of staring at him when he was bent over a book, unaware. Sometimes it might even mean her foot would accidentally brush his as she stretched. She didn't realize she was starting to stretch her own leg now until it abruptly met the table's metal post.

"Claire?"

She'd always wanted to be a better listener. Her clients uniformly were. She'd never met a religious sister who didn't have a good ear, one tuned not only to the audible spectrum but to the thoughts and prayers that lay beyond it as well. Right now, looking at Marcus, Claire thought she heard something he wasn't saying. What? She waved her glass. Let him talk.

"I'm not going to use a minute of what we got, I don't think,"

Marcus plowed on. "She's the one who wanted the rerecord, and of course I said yes, but the truth is, I think that scene is already gone. The studio gave us notes, and—"

"Marcus," Claire said. He seemed to want her to interrupt, and because she'd just figured it out, she was happy to oblige: this film Marcus had made, an early one, he'd proposed to the female lead, over drinks, at a tiny table at— Claire had forgotten this, though it had seared her at the time, their college days then so proximate. But of course: they'd filmed it *here*. She remembered the light, the piazza. She remembered wondering if the wine in their glasses was fake. "You shot a film here," Claire said. He went ashen for a moment but then looked around, shook his head. "Tiny table," Claire said. "Wine. A proposal. No ring, I remember that: cheapskate." Marcus twisted around, shook his head again. "Pretty girl," Claire went on. "Looked a bit like Monica. Too thin."

"Oh!" Marcus said. "Santa Barbara. We shot that in Santa Barbara. I'd forgotten all about it. God, even the title. *Sun*-something." He looked at the palm trees, the lawn, reconsidering. "I can see what you saw," he said. He took a sip of water.

They fell silent. He stared at his glass, she at him. There was something he wasn't telling her. Fair enough, there was something she wasn't telling him. They sat, unable to speak, unable to part.

Was it a failure of God's creation that a human mind, a body, a soul, cells, could hold on to a connection like this, thirty years past its expiry? Normal creatures moved on. The palm trees in the square across the way; their fronds browned and fell and new green fronds grew in their place. What no other woman had told her about turning fifty was that there were moments when you felt fifteen again. Or maybe that was just Claire's own peculiar set of cells. Maybe this was the genius of creation. Or Rome. What would it be like to get engaged here? You could not go two blocks in central Rome without seeing someone kiss, not one block without seeing a cross or saint or church, not one step without seeing a color, a detail, something you didn't expect. Your old friend, Marcus. Your old love. Your old life.

Traffic and church bells aside, Rome was suddenly quiet for a city where every knob was dialed to ten.

Yes, there was a time when she had wanted to be married to him, to be with him, to have him nearby. There had been a time, early on, when she had *needed* him at her side. And he hadn't been. It was three years after graduation before she saw him again. *I missed you,* he said at the door to her apartment, which was grand to hear, but what she really wanted him to say, what she expected the first words out of his mouth to be, were, *I'm sorry, you needed me, I wasn't there, I'm sorry.* Instead he said, *I missed you* and *I brought this for Dorothy* and handed over a small stuffed dog. Three years, and all he'd brought was a stuffed dog for a girl who hated dogs, a fact he would have known had he been around those three years. Claire had swallowed hard. Because maybe she owed him an apology, too. Because she had missed him, too. Because she'd run from that stage and never explained why to him. Because he still did have some kind of magic, which magically extended to toddler Dorothy, who emerged shyly from behind Claire's legs and accepted the dog. The girl who hated dogs went on to make this one her pillow companion for the rest of her childhood. So credit to Dorothy or the dog or Marcus for subsequently working so hard at being a godfather, but Claire had forgiven him and he her. Probably.

I have something big to ask you: what if, in Rome, she said, *Where were you?* But she wouldn't, because he was here now. And she sensed that, as she navigated this strange flowering inside her, this sudden, renewed curiosity regarding vowed life, she would need his support like never before. Just the task of explaining all this to Dorothy, Claire would need help with that. *This is important for your mother*, Marcus could say. *Yes, it's okay that she's moving an ocean away from you.*

But was it? He might have to convince Claire, too.

"Marcus," she said, extending a hand, not sure what she was going to say or ask. His hand edged toward hers but didn't quite take it. "Ask your question."

"Can I ask another one first?" he said.

Like that, the tension eased, and she felt confident enough to joke, "I think you just did."

"Dinner? Tonight?" he said.

Claire retracted her hand, relieved at the reprieve. "Can't," she said. "I told some nuns I would join them for evening prayer." He looked defeated. "I'm free tomorrow night," she said, "unless you're 'recording' your Italian star."

"I think she'll give me the night off," said Marcus, "for an old friend."

Claire smiled. "Not that old."

She looked at the palace, then back at Marcus.

"You look great," Marcus said.

"So do you," Claire said.

Then he asked, "So, do you want to ask your question?"

Claire's smile widened into a grin. "Would you like to tour a convent?"

The night before, Claire had gone on an informal convent tour of her own. Though she would eventually sleep very well on her magically comfortable cot, her first minutes alone in her room felt electric; she was more awake then than she'd been since arriving in Rome. She looked for a book to doze off to, but as she did, she heard someone walking by outside. The sisters, come to check on her? Sister Georgia, most likely.

Outside the door, there was no one.

Claire had dealt with supposedly haunted properties before. An old Saint Vincent de Paul store in Sheboygan, Wisconsin, that had become a restaurant reported doors opening and closing on their own. They'd hired a psychic, who told them to do what Claire had told them to do in the first place. Don't entirely erase the past; preserve some architectural detail or artifact from what the building once was. At the town library, they'd found a grainy photo of a priest blessing the store in the previous century; they framed and hung a copy. The doors stayed closed.

Claire dressed, grabbed Mother Saint Luke's key, which Sister Georgia had pressed upon her before the opera, and made her way down the corridor in the direction the footsteps had gone. At the base of some stairs, she stopped and listened again. Nothing, and then, fainter, more footsteps. Upstairs, one flight, two, and then, on the uppermost floor, perfect silence. None of the sisters lived up here. It was dark and the moon was hiding someplace she couldn't see, so she had to navigate by starlight down the open-air corridor. The roseto was lost to darkness far below. A faint floral smell came and went with the breeze.

A row of doors stood shut. She tried the first; locked. The second, too. The sisters said they'd tried every lock in the convent with the old key of Mother Saint Luke's, but had they? Claire took it out. It was a snaggle-toothed skeleton key, but smallish, as though for winding a clock. She tried it in each of the doors without success. Then a door marked ARCHIV. swung open as she inserted the key in the lock.

The light worked. A bigger surprise was that the room was small and held not dozens of books on shelves but just one in the center, a large ledger, which lay open on a table. Though it was in English, it took several minutes for Claire to decipher the handwriting—many different hands, pens, over different years—and realize what she was looking at. An inventory of belongings. Claire had seen similar ledgers at monasteries; aspirants had their effects cataloged and stored so that they could be returned in the event the visitor didn't ultimately take vows. If they stayed, the items were repurposed or discarded after some predetermined amount of time. At a Trappist monastery in Kentucky, she'd seen a decades-ago entry for a Ford Model T, which the abbot had thoughtfully put up on blocks to preserve the tires in case the would-be monk wanted to drive away.

Julia, 23 yrs., Glendale, California, USA, clothes, books, hairbrush, hand mirror. Bin 6.

The room was lined with wooden cubbies, each with a perforated door. Claire went to number six. The key didn't fit, but inside it looked empty. She went back to the ledger and saw the note, in a different hand, in the last column. *Returned, May 20, 1938.*

Elizabeth had deposited a gold necklace. Ruth, opera glasses and an umbrella. Amalia, *nine hats*, and so many other things that she had been assigned several bins. Though the notation said that Amalia, too, had left in 1949, the unknown scribe noted she'd left her possessions behind. What was Mother Saint Luke's name before religious life? Harriet, Sister Georgia had said. And she'd come during the shooting of *Roman Holiday*. Early 1950s? Claire flipped back through the ledger. More clothes, hats, steamer trunks, valises, lockets, curios, a Hermes Rocket typewriter, Baedeker guides, keys to scooters, and one Bugatti race car from the late 1920s, *blue with green stripe.*

And then, there she was, Harriet. Clothes, books, sketchbooks, *a Kodak Tourist II camera with leather case, personal letters,* and money—*4,000 lire.* Bin 26.

In case of emergency. Maybe Mother Saint Luke hadn't meant for the key to function as an actual key but rather a mnemonic device. *Remember what's been tucked safely away.*

The sisters would have been through all this already, surely. But the layers of dust in the room suggested not. Claire went to Bin 26. The key didn't fit. Again, though: maybe it didn't have to. She pulled on the knob, and it opened. No clothes, no books. No scooters or cars or typewriters. Instead, an empty box marked PERSONAL LETTERS and an empty Kodak Tourist II bourbon-brown leather camera case. In the back of the bin, something not marked in the ledger: a small metal flashlight with a cracked lens.

Claire heard nothing as she made her way back downstairs. No footsteps, not even, strangely, the sound of the city outside. She kept her own light off as she climbed into bed and tucked Mother Saint Luke's key under her pillow for safekeeping. She'd found nothing, or so it would appear to anyone who hadn't spent years in and out of old convents. But Claire had, and so Claire knew: she'd found the start of a trail.

V. VILLA PAMPHILI

DOROTHY WAS A NIGHT OWL; Claire was not. This discrepancy had never suited them, but in Rome it worked well. Midnight in Madison was 7 a.m. in Rome. The morning after meeting Marcus, Claire went outside, put in her earbuds, and finally called. Dorothy picked up on the first ring.

"So?"

"The big news is, I'm getting good sleep," Claire said. She'd already raved about this to the sisters, who'd looked at her oddly. But it was true, so true that she'd asked the sisters if she could relocate to the convent for the remainder of her stay in Rome. Claire had assured them she'd pay. Sister Georgia had tut-tutted; Sister Thérèse had suggested a rate of a million a night—they'd be able to counter-offer Sister Rose's brother in a week!

Sister Felicity, cautious, said if Claire really wanted to stay with them, she was of course welcome, and as their guest. Claire said she'd insist on paying. Sister Felicity said she'd insist on Claire joining her for a run in her favorite park.

"And, um, you met an old friend?" Dorothy asked.

Despite Marcus having just used that term the afternoon before, Claire's first thought was of the sisters. Another sign, surely. "Well, they already feel like three old friends."

"What?"

"Oh, you mean Marcus!" Claire said.

"What are you *taking* for sleep?"

"That's just it," Claire said. "I'm sleeping—"

"Wait—just stop. I don't care about your sleep. Talk about Marcus. You, and Marcus, in Rome, by the Supreme Court."

"How'd you know where we met?"

A pause.

"He actually calls," Dorothy said, "unlike my mother, who prefers to string her daughter along via cryptic texts. He called, said he was in Rome; I said you were in Rome."

Claire felt guilty for not being in better touch with Dorothy, worried now that it wasn't just jet lag but a deeper disorientation. She needed to be calling Dorothy, but she also needed Dorothy to not worry about her. Claire needed to not worry about herself. Or about what Marcus was doing in Rome. "He mentioned this starlet," Claire said. "Do you think he's seeing someone over here?"

"He saw *you*," Dorothy said.

"You know what I mean," Claire said.

"I really don't," Dorothy mumbled, sounding sleepy. "Not what either of you mean."

Dorothy was drifting off, so Claire took the reins of the conversation, discussed the day ahead: she was collecting Marcus this afternoon for a visit to the Convento di Santa Gertrudis; in the morning—the early morning, as in, Claire was walking to meet her right now—Claire was going for a run with one Sister Felicity.

"Now you're just lying," Dorothy said through a yawn.

"She's a runner," Claire said. "It's not like she runs in a habit." Claire hadn't even seen her in a habit yet but knew the women wore a simple one—skirt, blouse, veil—to daily Mass, for prayer and ministry. Sister Thérèse seemed to wear hers more frequently.

"I love you, Mom," Dorothy said. "You are deeply crazy, and I'm sure the nuns know that, too. But I love you." It sounded like she was talking into her pillow. "Tell Marcus," she began, but didn't finish.

The walk had gotten steep, and Claire had to syncopate her speaking with her breathing. "I love you, too, dear girl."

The line fell so quiet that Claire was sure Dorothy had fallen asleep.

But no, Dorothy was still awake: "I miss you, Mom," she said, and Claire wondered, *Which Mom?* The one wandering Rome or the one from childhood, who hadn't time to worry about anything other than Dorothy, every minute of every day.

Claire softly wished her good night and received only quiet breaths in reply.

Love was Dorothy's superpower; she had a boundless, constantly replenishing supply. Claire wasn't sure where her daughter got it from; possibly it had cascaded down the gene tree from Claire's own mother. It certainly hadn't come from Dorothy's dad.

Monica said having Dorothy was Claire's way of guaranteeing that she'd never join a convent. The Milwaukee nuns, the Clementines, were open-minded and open-hearted, but a woman with a baby? They'd find her food and shelter, but not a vocation.

Claire hadn't been thinking that a baby would keep her from vowed life. In those early days post-Marcus, post-Yale, she'd been thinking minute to minute, breath to breath, or forgetting to breathe as her life changed all around her.

Dorothy was a gift, to Claire, to the planet, and if the serpentine route Claire had taken over this earth was the only way she got to give the world Dorothy, she'd gladly wind that way again and again.

Claire decided she would visit an Italian church at some point and say just that—*Thank you, God, for Dorothy*—but then Rome decided that some point was now: the Basilica di Santa Maria in Trastevere had its doors thrown wide open to the early morning. She checked her watch. Did she have time? She imagined telling Sister Felicity she was late because she'd felt a call to stop and pray. Claire liked the sound of that; in she went.

Hollywood could spend millions on special effects but never build a time machine as efficient, or profoundly disorienting, as the ones scattered about Rome. As here: the sky that arced outside was inarguably 2019's; inside, every step put her centuries further back: 1900; 1500; 1100. And somewhere beneath her feet, if the brochure was to be believed, a foundation from the year 220. Gold, everywhere. Mosaics pixeled with stone. Marble columns stout as oaks. She sank into a pew, looked briefly for the wall said to weep holy oil—Hollywood could learn from that, too—and began to pray.

The same old silence.

She offered thanks for Dorothy, for Rome, for the run she was about to have.

Nothing.

It wasn't that she needed a movie director to handle this, too, have an angel descend or a column crack or even her phone to ring. It wasn't that Claire thought there was nothing beyond this world. She just occasionally wanted some sign of it. She sat in the silence along with another woman four pews ahead. Maybe she was waiting, too.

They'd find it, wouldn't they, what they were looking for? If the woman already had, could she please tell Claire how? What you said, where you sat, what you asked?

How did you choose?

On her way out, Claire went closer to the altar to better see the strange mosaic floating above in the apse. Twelve spritely lambs, Saint Peter in a toga, six popes, all looking a little confused, perhaps because Jesus, in the center, wasn't paying them the least attention. Instead, he had his arm slung around a woman, his mom. Seven hundred twenty-eight years old, the artwork, and it looked like it could have been made yesterday. Mary appeared tired; Jesus, protective, devoted, awkward. Claire had never seen anything like it. "Hang in there," Claire said, and headed out.

Claire paced the small gravel parking lot at the edge of Villa Pamphili, the massive park and gardens that Sister Felicity had designated as their running spot. It was less than a kilometer west of the Convento di Santa Gertrudis, and once there, the women would have plenty of running room—approximately five hundred acres, Sister Felicity had promised, and almost all tourist-free; though the gardens were hardly two miles from the Colosseum, they were a little too far southwest of Rome's main sights to fit on most tourist maps.

She'd wondered why Sister Felicity had asked to meet her here at the park entrance instead of back at the convent but was now grateful. She'd gotten to see the basilica, that surreal and beautiful mosaic. And though she'd had to run the rest of the way to not be late, she was happy to have the extra distance; her marathon training would have to begin in earnest in a few weeks. October, Milwaukee's marathon, was not so far away.

"Claire!" Sister Felicity called from across the street.

Claire waved. Sister Felicity looked different. Not outwardly, just to Claire, who'd finally googled her and immediately wished she had earlier.

From *The Wall Street Journal*:

THE ULTIMATE TRADE

High-Flying Star of the Street Swaps Corner Office
for Convent Cell

Here Work Habits Come with a Wimple

Felicity had had her own boutique firm, capital for women-led businesses, had grown it, diversified it, cashed out after a cancer scare. She'd taken a lap of the world, met some religious sisters, met some more, made her decision at age forty-five.

But *how*? Claire didn't marvel so much at why—the mystery was why more women didn't become nuns, given all that you got to give up, all that you gained—but the how. Sister Felicity seemed settled, strong. Claire had felt that way once. She envied Sister Felicity the fact that she still did.

"Good morning, Sister," Claire said. Sister Felicity reached for Claire's hands. Claire extended them, uncertain.

"Dear Lord, I ask that you run with us today," Sister Felicity said. "That we breathe in your grace and run with your heart. May every step we take glorify every step your Son took on this good green earth. Amen."

"Amen!" Claire replied, and they were off.

The gardens were vast, varied, an outdoor museum of the world. A weed-choked, stumbling ascent to a salmon-colored triple arch did nothing to prepare Claire for what came after: sweeping savanna presided over by towering umbrella pines, their canopies like dark green cirrus clouds. Then formal gardens, the completely overshadowed villa itself, fountains (some spouting grass instead of water), followed by thick forest, pomegranate trees and palms, locust, cedar, spruce, elm. Dense corridors of oleander, white and pink, the fragrance so thick it almost choked her. And hills.

Back home, Claire cruised along at a gentle, respectable nine-minute-mile pace. Or even slower ten-minute miles on days with hills, or days after she'd been out late, or days when her knees were hurting, or days when she'd had a fight with Dorothy—most days, in other words. Today, it felt like Sister Felicity was taking them out at a seven- or eight-minute-per-mile pace, and what's more, Claire could feel that she was holding Sister Felicity back. How long had Sister Felicity said they'd run for? She hadn't. Every time they appeared to be reaching the park's limits—some sign of a boundary road, a passing car flickering through distant trees—the path would fork, and another landscape would unfurl.

Claire was not holding Sister Felicity back. Rather, Sister Felicity was dragging Claire, shouting a one-sided conversation all the while. Sister Felicity felt sorry, was the theme: she felt ashamed that Claire had flown all the way over to help them with a problem that was only a problem because Sister Felicity and the other two sisters were making it so. Then they'd made things worse by inadvertently encouraging her to move into their toppling edifice. Claire should move back out. They *all* should move out, really, and just be done with the business.

"Stop," Claire wheezed.

"No," said Sister Felicity, taking the pace up another notch, "I'm serious. I'm the leader here; it's time I led."

"I need to, I need to, stop," Claire said, and stopped.

Sister Felicity ran on several more paces before she realized Claire had dropped away. "Oh, Sister," Sister Felicity said, "is everything all right?"

Even bent forward, hands on knees, Claire heard the slip. Maybe Sister Felicity usually ran with one of the other sisters. Sister Thérèse? Not Sister Georgia. Maybe another nun from nearby.

Claire felt her vision irising in but fought it off. Deep breath, one, two. *What if...* she'd thought the other night, falling asleep. It made no sense. Women her age, her situation, didn't join convents. Did women of any age anymore?

But Sister Felicity had joined. So, too, Sister Georgia. Young Sister Thérèse! And before them all, Mother Saint Luke. And countless women before and hundreds of thousands of women now living worldwide, many of whom were *not* getting good sleep because they were wondering where their next vocations would come from.

It made no sense, no more than having this realization now, on the brink of collapse. If Claire fell to her knees in the park this morning—this amazing park—and said, *Bless me, Sister, take me in*, Sister Felicity would shake her head and say, *This makes no sense.*

But flying to Rome to sell the beautiful source of so much community, grace—and sleep!—did?

Maybe the only conditions under which such realizations arose were ones like these, when all life's distractions were pared away and only fundamental needs remained. Oxygen, water. Belief?

"Bless me, Sister," Claire said, still bowed.

There was a pause and Claire wondered if Sister Felicity hadn't heard her or was confused by what she'd just heard. Claire herself was confused that she'd said it. But then she felt Sister Felicity's hands hover over her head, heard the woman say words not quite audible. When Sister Felicity was finished, Claire rose.

"I'm not quite sure why I—"

"You honored me by asking," said Sister Felicity. "And pardon my blindness. I called on you for help, never looked to see if you needed ours."

"You have enough to worry about," said Claire.

"When your firm said you were flying over," Sister Felicity said, "I thought—forgive me—*Oh no, one of* those *types.* Vacation disguised as work, flying on the company dime. We needed someone serious, and you—and then you needed us. You weren't feeling well. We hadn't been needed in a while. We're rusty. I'm rustiest. Speaking of"—she looked at Claire panting—"let's walk a bit."

As they walked Claire thought, *This is where I want to be right now, whom I want to be with, a community I want to be part of.*

Monica would be asking her, *What the fuck is wrong?* Dorothy would be asking her, *How is Marcus??????* Marcus would be asking her about Mother Saint Luke, and then her key, or dinner or drinks or coffee or Audrey Hepburn or *Do you remember?* And *What's the meaning of it all?* And *Do you really want to know, Claire, why I'm in Rome?*

Claire did. But she also wanted to know a better, broader purpose for being in Rome herself, and she sensed Sister Felicity could help her find out.

She looked at the path ahead of them, a broad, straight allée lined with hulking nettle trees three and four stories tall. Sister Felicity squinted as though measuring the distance, then looked at her watch.

"If you need to get back," Claire said, and then wished she hadn't; she was giving her opportunity away.

"It's like a puzzle," Sister Felicity said after a pause. "Some mornings, I wake up and find the pieces scattered all over the floor; other mornings I wake, go to prayer, and then return to find God has helped everything fall into place, that with that help, I'm *this* close to solving it, all of it, but for one more piece."

She looked at Claire.

Caught unawares, Claire said the most inane thing possible. "I love puzzles."

"I bet you do," said Sister Felicity. "You'd have to in your line of work. I'm sure it's one puzzle after another, always looking for that missing piece—"

Claire, unprepared for the conversation she'd just imagined having, tried a diversion: "Or key!"

Sister Felicity paused a moment, then smiled. "The key, of course. Mother Saint Luke's key. I understand Sister Georgia gave it to you." Claire nodded and Sister Felicity sighed. "I don't believe in talismans, but it was Mother Saint Luke's; it's hard not to think some grace attaches to it."

"Or that it unlocks a closet full of all the cash you need," Claire said.

"You're right to tease me," said Sister Felicity. "On the subject of money, Sister Thérèse always does. She knows my Wall Street past, holds it against me."

"That's not fair," Claire said.

Sister Felicity stopped and turned to face Claire, hands on hips. "What's not fair is—what's not fair to *you*, is that when you showed up in our rose garden, I thought—I shouldn't admit this—I thought, the missing piece!"

What if, Claire had wondered while falling asleep last night, she had come to Rome for a conversation about a vocation. And now she saw that it would sound, look, not unlike this. People said—Claire knew—vocations started with a pull, a tug, a call, and for thirty-odd years, ever since leaving the path to the Clementines in Milwaukee, Claire had wondered when or if she'd ever be called back. She hadn't thought she would. Now she wondered if she just had been called. If, say, the pull to train for a marathon had actually been to train for this run with Sister Felicity.

"It's so damn—sorry—hard, Claire. So much harder than my old job. So much better, but so, so much harder. I don't need—I don't want to need buyers. I need bodies, good souls, women like you, who ask me for a blessing and bless me by doing so."

A young family was passing, girl in a stroller, soccer ball in her lap. "Guests are the last thing you need," Claire said. "I can move right back out. I will."

Beg me to stay, not just for a week or two, but forever.

Sister Felicity, eyes glassy with tears, turned to Claire. Claire's eyes welled, too.

"Sister—" Claire said.

Sister Felicity tried to laugh, wiped away a tear. "Now we're both crying."

"Scusi?" said an older man in a green track suit. He offered Sister Felicity a handkerchief, which, to Claire's surprise, she took, used, and returned. A minute on, a woman who looked to be roughly Claire's age patted Claire's wrist as she passed.

Sister Felicity steered them to a bench to avoid further consolation. And out it came, what Sister Felicity had discovered, the missing piece. Sister Felicity *had* thought it was Claire, not just her people-first reputation but also her promise of money, of a miraculous financial solution that would allow them to stay, save the Convento di Santa Gertrudis, save the Order of Saint Gertrude. But that was far too great a burden to place on money—let alone Claire—and thus couldn't be what God wanted. Sister Felicity had figured that out this morning, when she'd caught herself asking God for a buyer who'd pay in euros instead of dollars, which would make transferring the balance back to the US just one step more difficult, slower, thus delaying their departure, however infinitesimally. Ridiculous, evil, wrong.

The solution they needed, what God wanted, Sister Felicity explained, could only ever be human.

A small match rasped into flame inside Claire.

"We need to get Anna back," Sister Felicity said.

"Anna?" Claire asked, though she knew. She let the match burn.

"Anna, Sister Thérèse's friend, the prospect who spent time with us, who wanted—I pray still wants—to join us, get our numbers growing again, get us back on a path to twenty-one sisters active in the order."

What if, me? Claire thought. *What if I'm being called to join you, now? What if God's been calling me for decades and I haven't heard because I've had my fingers in my ears, or Dorothy has, or Monica?*

"I can help," Claire said.

"I know you can," said Sister Felicity. "I'm glad you're here."

Sister Felicity thought Claire was still talking about the convent's sale. Claire had to be more clear.

"Sister Georgia," Claire said, and paused, belatedly wondering if she was betraying a confidence, "doesn't... think Anna's return is all that likely?"

"Ask Sister Georgia if the sun will rise tomorrow and she'll only give you fifty-fifty odds."

"But even if Anna did return, it's not like she'd take vows fast enough to forestall the vote. That's already been triggered."

And neither would, say, Claire's vows happen fast enough. But she'd be faster than Anna: Claire had had experience with vowed life as a teenager.

Although the abrupt abbreviation of that experience might count against Claire.

"I see you *have* been talking to Sister Georgia!" Sister Felicity said. "Beware. She's crafty. And also, in this case, correct. The vote is coming, Anna or no. But if I am able to boast of an aspirant actively discerning"—Sister Felicity put a hand on Claire's knee and an electric jolt went through her—"and *you've* been able to work some all-but-impossible deal improving our finances, well."

"You really think you'd win the vote?"

"I believe, Claire. I believe in God the Father Almighty, and I believe in God's will, whatever it may be. But I most especially believe, if Anna comes, with your help, resources will come." She smiled. "More *women* will come." She rose. "Let's go." They began to run again.

What to say? Nothing, at least while Claire was pounding through a park, burning up miles faster than she'd ever done in her life. The pause, the cry, the plotting, all seemed to have rejuvenated Sister Felicity, who was now gliding along smoothly, swiftly, resuming her monologue. Claire spoke when she could, which wasn't often.

"The truth is, I'm fine with selling," Sister Felicity began.

"You are?" Claire asked, confused. "You just said—?"

"I'm trying to ease the pressure on you," Sister Felicity said. "If the best you can get us is a traditional buyer, closing in thirty days, three sisters and their suitcases out on the sidewalk after, that's—well, it's not fine, but it won't be Sister Rose's brother." She coughed, recovered. "Because, some days—most days—I think it's crazy to stay, but then Sister Thérèse invokes Mother Saint Luke's memory and I think it's betrayal to leave." She looked around. "And then there's Rome—and this Eden for running. I don't know."

Claire looked at Sister Felicity as the woman loped along, breathing easily, eyes worried. "I made a mistake with Anna," Sister Felicity said. "Sister Thérèse made a mistake, too, telling the poor woman our future rested solely on her, but I'd made a mistake earlier. Sister Thérèse had sent Anna to meet with me to announce her interest in us, and Anna told me she'd come to Rome to find herself."

"How old is she?" said Claire. An innocent question, though Sister Felicity didn't take it that way.

Sister Felicity snorted. "Exactly. Anyway, I laughed, and it probably sounded like a mean laugh. It's just that every month or so there's a backpacker at the door who's lost something—a lover, a passport, some or all of their sanity—and they're all, to a woman, looking for themselves. I want the ones looking for God."

"And you told Anna that?"

"Not in so many words." Sister Felicity ran on and, after a minute, started speaking again. "The problem is—no, I shouldn't flatter myself—*a* problem is that I *did* find myself when I took vows; I found this new self that didn't need or want money, that, other than running, was ready to slow down, be still, be quiet, love God." She paused. "Back in the day, I had a mouthguard—"

Claire nodded. Claire ground her teeth at night so much she wore out a guard per year.

"My dentist had me wearing one day *and* night—I was grinding my teeth at my desk," Sister Felicity said. "While running. Sleeping. All the time." She shook her head. "And now this convent—our predicament—it's all dragging me back. Contracts and deeds and dollars and euros. I can feel it in my jaw. I just want to be, to serve, love, work, pray."

"Sister, you can—you will! I'm here to help—this is exactly what I do."

And it was, though Claire saw she'd do better by doing the opposite of what she usually did: instead of facilitating rezoning, obstruct it. Instead of hoping for a clean title, find ways for it to be infringed.

Yes, she could do all that. But she also felt like she was on the verge of doing something else, here, now. Earlier, the silence in the millennias-old Trastevere church had left her longing, but running had revealed a path—or something? Claire felt like she was making it up as she went along, but she liked going along beside Sister Felicity.

Sister Felicity half laughed. "Al fresco psychotherapy? I don't think so."

Maybe not, but Claire kept up her questions, eventually finding out, among other things, the name of the firm Sister Rose's brother worked for. Sadly, Claire knew them: a national firm with tentacles everywhere. In Milwaukee, Claire had watched them offer hard-up churches reverse mortgages—a good bet, most thought. It's hard to foreclose on a church. But they did, and then leveled them, built apartments they didn't maintain, flipped the buildings, and then started again. The best Claire had ever done against them was fight them to a draw; otherwise, like Sister Felicity, she fought to avoid them.

"You'd think your superior would never seek such a partner."

"You'd think," said Sister Felicity. "But she says her brother has a vision."

"There should be rules," Claire said.

"Against visions?"

"Brothers," Claire said.

"Find me a better buyer," Sister Felicity said.

"Or a better Anna," Claire said.

Just say it: *I'm right here, Sister! Forget about your prospect Anna—I'm the one who could get you back to twenty-one members! I'm the one who could forestall the vote!* But Claire couldn't. She heard herself with Monica's ears, anyone's ears, heard the nonsensicalness of it. Religion was a delusion; God, vapor; vows, nothing more than messages sealed in bottles cast into a shoreless ocean.

Except Claire didn't believe that. After this run, Claire believed in Sister Felicity and Sister Felicity didn't believe that.

"I truly believe God sent Anna to us," Sister Felicity said. "And I somehow managed to send her away. But if—when—she comes back, I will beg her forgiveness. And God's."

Where was Sister Felicity when Claire was seventeen, not yet at Yale? Instead of perching on the Clementines' convent stoop in Milwaukee, why couldn't have Claire knocked on the Gertrudans' door in Rome? Sister Felicity would have snatched her inside and locked the door behind.

Claire adopted Sister Felicity's horizon gaze and studied what she saw there, the possible past, thirty-some years of living as a nun in Rome, waking to bells every morning, never yawning from lack of sleep. God everywhere, every day, in the sun, the frescoes, the roses, the meals. Women visible through the archways above, moving this way and that, silent smiles passing from one to the other. Claire overseeing it all—she'd be the abbess, or second-in-command to Sister Felicity—and the convent, like their lives, would be full. Except—

"How old is your daughter again?" Sister Felicity asked.

Except Dorothy would not exist. Claire would get the best sleep of her life every night of her life, and the atoms that made up Dorothy would make up something else. This park. A glass of wine. A stuffed dog. Impossible.

"Twenty-nine," Claire said. "But I don't think Dorothy could get you to twenty-one. Twelve years of Catholic school—I tried—and she'd had her fill."

Sister Felicity laughed. "Good to know," she said. "I was more thinking that you must miss her, and whether that changes with age. God didn't call me to be a mother, but that doesn't mean I'm not fascinated by the women who are strong enough to be mothers."

"The fascination's mutual," Claire said, and who knew whether that nudged a door more open or not? Claire was exhausted, and not just from running. She was glad to see they were again approaching the triple arch that had marked the start. They fell back into a walk.

The run had been good; they always were. And hard ones like this cleared the fog: Claire saw that reality held in Rome just as it did in other parts of the world, except maybe in her brain, which had briefly considered itself on a path leading straight back into vowed life. This, of course, made no sense. Because Dorothy. Because Claire had a job, a job right here in Rome. Some doors stood ajar not to invite entrance but because they awaited a responsible person to pull them shut, keep safe what was already inside.

If Sister Felicity was aware of what Claire was thinking, she didn't show it.

"I wish I'd met Mother Saint Luke," Claire said as they walked.

"I wish you could have, too," Sister Felicity said. "She was a force. Take the date of the proposed sale. Another debt we owe her. They'd wanted to do this deal months ago. But not long before she died, she got them to agree to September fourth. Which is—was—her birthday. Also the date of the fall of the western Roman Empire. She famously enjoyed that, said it was evidence that God never takes away something without replacing it with something better."

"She bought you time," Claire said.

"Ha!" said Sister Felicity. "It's what I heard about you—you're good at the endgame."

"I don't like to think of it as an endgame. Besides, you've got one hundred days until September fourth."

"If only," Sister Felicity said, and looked at her watch. "Ninety-eight now, and in an hour, New York time, ninety-seven."

"Do you have the deed, the title—a history, anything? We might find out a duke actually owns the building. Or his heirs. They could contest the sale."

"Wouldn't that put us out on the street regardless?"

"But it might take more time."

"I'll put Sister Georgia on it. She loves a good paper chase."

They exited the park and kept walking back to the convent. Sister Felicity stopped at a spigot—a nasone, or big nose—that stuck out from a wall and endlessly emptied into a trough. Locals were lined up, filling containers. When it was their turn, Claire cupped her hands and drank.

Sister Felicity, by contrast, bent to the spigot and stoppered it with a palm, which sent a stream of water vertically through a previously hidden hole in the spout. She drank deeply, while Claire looked on in fascination: to be as comfortable in Rome, in vowed life, as Sister Felicity.

"Did they walk you through the house rules?" Sister Felicity said as they walked back. "I'm a terrible host. You've already been with us two nights."

"You're excellent hosts."

"Keep a flashlight handy. First one up makes coffee. Always wake up before Sister Thérèse." They'd reached the convent door, and Sister Felicity bent to pick up an empty bottle. "Never go inside without picking up at least one piece of litter outside." Claire nodded. Sister Felicity would make a fine first—or second or third, depending on which histories you believed—female pope. "We usually go down the hill to Mass at seven. You're welcome to come." She checked her watch. "But I'll have to aim for a noon Mass today. Join me?"

"Actually, I'm meeting a friend for coffee—and then we were going to visit the convent after—"

"Right, right," said Sister Felicity. "Sister Thérèse said something about this." Sister Felicity shoved the door once, twice, and finally got it shut with her hip. Then she looked up and smiled.

"And we never lock the door," Sister Felicity added. "Your friend, she's welcome at Mass, too."

"He," Claire said quietly, as she followed Sister Felicity inside.

Claire would get the sisters what they wanted.

And if they wanted her?

Dorothy lay awake in bed, face glowing gray from her phone. She felt old, older than every other twenty-nine-year-old in the world.

There was the name: too many assumed Dorothy was named out of a love for *The Wizard of Oz*, a book more than a century old. But it was more than that, like a gray thread had been woven through her DNA (and already through Dorothy's hair, alarmingly). In middle school, she'd briefly switched her name to *Dorty*, then decided she wasn't cool enough for it; she was a Dorothy, every inch, and saw the world, and particularly her mother, through older eyes.

Her mother needed the help, needed someone who set boundaries

(Claire couldn't date men Dorothy's age or younger; her days of dating coastguardsmen were *done*), explained mysteries (Wi-Fi, routers, and you), and made sure Claire got home at night, thanks to an app they'd jointly installed ten years before.

Claire, however, either had lost track of the app or had become wise enough to not alert Dorothy that she was still attempting to track her. If she was, good luck; Dorothy had adjusted her own setting to "invisible." But Claire had not, and Dorothy had to bite her tongue every time she saw Claire doing something that surprised her daughter. Even before Rome, Dorothy was sometimes left wondering what her mother was up to—eating vegan on the Lower East Side at 11 p.m.? But such outings were rare. Claire's regular pattern—work, gym, salad bar—was so established that Dorothy felt the route had burned an afterglow into her screen.

Dorothy tried not to pry, though. She let mysteries go unmentioned because she felt oddly closer to her mom this way. She felt protective of her. They were all they had. Dorothy commiserated when dates went bad (and suggested giving Marcus a call) and she hummed when they'd been promising (and suggested, even so, giving Marcus a call). And there'd been other men over the years—had to be—but Dorothy let Claire have her secrets. And if Claire ever got in trouble, Dorothy could find her on the app, her mother a reassuring blue beacon.

But Claire wasn't in the US anymore. She was in Italy. Dorothy had been curious to see if the tracking would still work, and it seemed to, though the results were spottier. Her mother might flash from one part of Rome to another in seconds, then spend endless minutes caroming around a park.

Dorothy studied the phone another moment. What was her mother *doing*? Did her mother ever have nights like this, wondering where

Dorothy was? During her teen years, they had had a rule: no curfew, but Dorothy must always come to Claire's room, no matter how late, and say goodnight.

Dorothy always did, even though Claire was always asleep. Dorothy always wondered if she heard her; the next morning, Claire always said she did.

"Good night," Dorothy whispered, and tried, once more, to sleep.

VI. THE RARE BOOK
AND MANUSCRIPT LIBRARY

COFFEE. COFFEE COFFEE *COFFEE*. IT wasn't that Claire was addicted. Her early years with Dorothy, yes. (Sorry, Dorothy.) But in Rome she couldn't stop drinking it; it was everywhere. At first, she had let guidebooks lead her to shiny places with jacketed waiters—older men, those waiters, pursuing their life's calling, and she marveled at how well such a calling had treated them—but what came to fascinate her more were the closet-size neighborhood places, where the same care and crockery came from a counter that also sold alcohol. Maybe biglietti for the bus. Cigarettes. Pastries oozing something sticky. The sole decoration a wall calendar sponsored by AS Roma, Vodafone, or Jesus, sorrowfully exposing his sacred heart. The only constant was that there were strict rules, inevitably broken. You paid first, or after. You ordered inside, or sat outside. You paid the cashier or the waiter or the barista, or, like Claire, you went to a place where one man was all three.

Claire had only been in Rome a couple of days but had already become a regular at a coffee bar close by the convent, befriending in the process Paolo, a barista who seemed to be on duty no matter the time of day. Monica had given Claire a complicated anti–jet lag vitamin regimen, but Paolo's coffee was cheaper and tastier and came with complimentary Italian lessons.

Or, Claire thought she had befriended Paolo, but when she arrived with Marcus, the reception was chilly.

Claire felt the other patrons at the small coffee bar staring at them, too, or maybe just Marcus. Were they trying to figure out where they'd seen his face before, or whether he'd be successful in convincing Paolo to serve their coffees in takeaway cups? (Paolo said no.)

They left; there was so much to see. Policemen throttling by on twin, inexplicably sea-blue motorcycles. Tour groups trailing behind a guide's limp umbrella. Windows high above shutting themselves against the heat of the day, already rising.

Claire was stiff as stone after her run, but somehow unhurt, and she couldn't stop smiling. She'd not run a marathon, but she'd possibly covered a greater distance. Sister Felicity had made it clear that she officially wanted her—to help, to stay. Claire wanted to help, to stay, too. But Claire also wanted to discuss her "what if"—what if she became a nun—and why no amount of reasoning with herself, even when those reasons involved Dorothy, would make the question go away.

And Claire also wanted to know why Sister Georgia had so intently handed over Mother Saint Luke's "emergency" key. Claire had decided not to mention her visit to the archives, the empty bins, what she'd found, and not found, in Mother Saint Luke's. She didn't want the sisters to know she'd been prowling about at night, especially as they'd told her they'd tried the key everywhere inside the convent. Maybe they'd think she was showing them up.

But they hadn't mentioned trying the key anywhere outside the convent. That left her the rest of Rome to check.

"The key to what?" Marcus asked. They were outside the door of the Convento di Santa Gertrudis, and Claire was wondering if she was about to make a mistake, bringing Marcus inside. But she'd invited him, Sister Thérèse had said it was okay, and here they were.

And who knew? Maybe Marcus could connect them with a production that needed a rentable ruin. Marcus had sent location scouts her way before.

And maybe inside, where she felt so at home, she'd finally tell him the truth about what had happened between them all those years ago.

"That's just it," said Claire, "they don't know."

"Ring the bell again," Marcus said.

They needn't have waited, the door, as Sister Felicity had said, was left unlocked, but Claire felt uncomfortable letting herself in with Marcus in tow. She barely felt comfortable letting herself in alone. But Marcus, having him here, that made her feel completely comfortable. So far. If he asked her to ring the bell one more time, though, she'd stuff him in a cab to the airport. The bell didn't work, never had.

"We're trying to make a good impression," said Claire. She wished the nuns were, too.

"Try the key," said Marcus. He smiled. The joke made clear he didn't believe the key unlocked anything. This annoyed Claire, and so, to annoy him, she fitted the key to the lock.

The key slid in—and then stopped.

"Oh my God," Marcus said, feigning surprise. "It works."

She jiggled it. Nope. She shook her head, quietly relieved—she liked her quests more arduous than that—and removed the key. "We'll wait another minute, then we'll call."

"You have enough Italian to do that?"

"They're American," said Claire.

Sister Georgia abruptly opened the door. She looked Marcus up and down before turning to Claire.

What had ebbed since her arrival in Rome: Claire feeling she had the upper hand. Excepting her first few years at the firm, Claire had long felt her clients' equal, if not their superior, no matter how lofty their title nor lengthy their legacy. She knew her business; she was ever in control.

In Rome, though, things were different: not just the country, but the property, somehow the clients?

"We missed you at Mass," said Sister Georgia.

And Claire herself felt different here, subject, it seemed, to daily humbling.

"It's Monday?" Marcus asked Claire. What Marcus knew about Catholicism he knew through Claire, and he presumed he knew everything. He did not. Example: though Claire abstained from meat on Fridays in Lent, Lent fell in spring, not October, which is when he'd once, feeling gallant, snatched a burger from her mouth in a Yale dining hall: *Did you forget, Claire? It's Friday!*

"They go every morning," Claire said, "not just Sundays. And apologies, Sister Georgia. I was running with Sister Felicity. And then I had to collect... my friend, Marcus Sardeson. Sister Thérèse said it would be okay."

Sister Georgia looked at Marcus.

"Buona giornata," said Marcus emphatically.

Sister Georgia shook her head. "Incorrect, as is Sister Thérèse thinking she could approve such a visit." She opened the door further. "But come in, come in, both of you. Welcome the weary traveler and all that. Sister Felicity and Sister Thérèse are out, and I've things to do, so you'll have to tour on your own."

Sister Georgia pointed to the rack where the helmets hung. "Wear a helmet unless your head is as thick as mine," Sister Georgia said. "I'll be in and out of the office. I understand I have an assignment, Claire? I'm to look for paperwork, a title, impedimenta? And then the roses. Though it's already so hot." She looked at Marcus. "Do you know anything about roses?"

Claire did not, and was worried Sister Georgia seemed to think Marcus did. His ignorance would count against Claire. Maybe if he offered to roll up his sleeves and weed, or—

"Roses?" Marcus said merrily and shook his head. "Only 'That which we call a rose / By any other name...'"

"He's an actor," Claire said, apparently to herself, because neither was listening.

Sister Georgia fixed Marcus with a stare, then finished the line, "... would smell as sweet."

Marcus continued, "I take thee at thy word—"

Sister Georgia cut him off. "Too soon! I have five more lines."

And so it began, back and forth, with ever-greater smiles. For a strange minute, Claire found herself wanting both to be Juliet to his Romeo and to be Sister Georgia as Juliet.

"You're terrific," Marcus finally said to Sister Georgia.

Sister Georgia put a hand on Claire's arm. "This is why the rule about male visitors is so strict." She waited a beat, smiled. "*Normally.*" She clasped Marcus's hand in two of hers. "Such a pleasure," she said.

"Thanks so much," said Claire, but Sister Georgia was already walking away.

"I like her," said Marcus. "Maybe I could get her cast as an extra sometime."

"Maybe she'd cast *you* as an extra," Claire said. "She's a star."

They wandered the roseto. The Clementines in Milwaukee had had a little rose garden, but Milwaukee was no place for roses.

"You're quiet," said Marcus.

"I'm thinking of Yale," she said, and she now was. Every spring, the campus shone with daffodils; it was hard to find a place where you couldn't spot a cluster of them rippling in the breeze. A memorial, she'd heard, given by a family to honor their late son.

Marcus looked out, nodded. "This is exactly what it would look like if they didn't hit us up for money each year. A once-grand edifice, now bent under a hard-hat edict." He gestured toward the row of helmets as though to fetch two, but she shook her head.

"I never give Yale money," said Claire, and they climbed an outdoor staircase to the second floor's arcaded corridor overlooking the roseto. As undergrads, she and Marcus had bonded over their unease with Yale's opulence. Marcus was the first in his family to go to college; Claire, of course, had plans to become a nun and take a vow of poverty. And yet, there they were at Yale, where at least one of the dining halls featured a massive Tiffany chandelier, and on occasion, glittering just outside, chef-carved ice sculptures. The library and gym looked like churches, though each was taller, larger, grander, than any cathedral she'd ever been in. Every other building seemed to have a concert piano sitting idle, waiting for someone to play it. The Beinecke Rare Book and Manuscript Library was sheathed in 250 translucent marble panels and housed one of just twenty-one complete copies of the Gutenberg Bible that still existed. Harkness Tower, meanwhile, had a fifty-four-bell carillon. Woolsey Hall, an organ with almost thirteen thousand pipes.

The Clementines' convent in Milwaukee had had countless Bibles, all of them dogeared paperbacks, and a cassette deck with a mono-speaker.

"I always give," Marcus said. "I underpaid at the time for what I got."

"Which was what?"

"Well, I met you," Marcus said.

She walked on.

The part of the convent that surrounded the roseto consisted primarily of individual cells, though there were some larger, specialized rooms—a library, a meeting room (long and narrow, with benches on the sides), a workroom with broad, high tables whose purpose Claire couldn't identify but which Marcus said looked suitable for fabric cutters in a costume shop. A strong, chemical lemon scent pervaded all.

"Yale's in better shape, but nowhere in southeastern Connecticut will you find this kind of view," Marcus said, moving from the corridor into a bedroom whose door, and window beyond, were wide open.

Once upon a time, the sisters had rented this room out to the (female) public; this room resembled the suite they'd assigned Claire but was simpler, dustier. A small stack of towels still sat on the foot of a twin bed with a pat of soap on top. There was a tiny desk with two cards taped to it: "A Prayer for Travelers" and "Hail Mary." The latter included a version in Latin. There was also a laminated, handmade card of "Handy Italian Phrases."

> My name is: *Mi chiamo*
> Where is: *Dov'è*
> I want: *Voglio*
> Get away from me: *Stammi lontano*
> I will pray for you: *Pregherò per te*

"'Get away from me'?" Marcus asked.

"If you insist," said Claire, and went to the window.

"I was just reading my line!"

"Actors," Claire said, and scooted to one side. "Come here, dummy. There's room." She patted the sill.

From this vantage point, Rome looked like a village—low terracotta roofs, the occasional spire or dome. No office towers. The Vittoriano, or Victor Emmanuel II Monument—glistening white at a youthful 166 years old—sat squarely in the middle of it all, stubbornly organizing the city around it. Here and there teetered more umbrella pines, whose tousled, top-heavy, cotton-candy silhouettes reminded Claire of picture books she'd once read to Dorothy. They'd loved reading; Dorothy still had copies of all her old favorites and Claire secretly bought still more. For grandkids, she told herself, but she didn't wish children on Dorothy yet. What Claire really wanted was what she couldn't have, which was for her twenty-nine-year-old daughter to put her head on her shoulder once more and say, *Read it again.*

She looked at Marcus. He would have been a good dad. He'd always said he'd never wanted kids, but she didn't believe that. Not the way he'd been with Dorothy, even during her teen years, when she'd been able to tolerate no other male of any age.

"'I want,'" Claire said.

Marcus leaned through the window beside her to look and then withdrew into the room.

"Look how this window frames the city," Marcus said. He leaned out again, as if looking for someone. "Do you know that funny little spot over on the Aventine Hill? Have you had time to go around? The Priory of the Order of Malta?"

Claire shook her head. She was listening and not. Thinking about Yale had gotten her to thinking about that younger self, the one who'd fallen in love with Marcus, the one who'd been in love with Jesus, or thought she'd been. She'd definitely been in love with vowed life. The community, the quiet, the simplicity. A room like this. She'd been like this, and she missed that younger self who didn't worry so much, not at what was in the mirror, not at what the mirror couldn't see.

Marcus was still talking. "It's a group like—I don't know what they're like," he said. "I think, a millennium or two ago, they were knights in shining armor. Anyway, my last time here—when was this?—you go up to their front door, which is always closed—"

"Marcus." She was going to ask him. Just ask him. *Dov'è the woman I was, and what if I became her again?*

"Claire?" he said.

She looked at Marcus, who was looking at her, waiting.

Life was linear, not a loop, she told herself. That was the good news and the bad news. It meant that no matter how much it felt like you were reliving the past—again and again, in her case—you weren't.

It also meant—"Knights, right," she said—you were always running out of time.

"So," he said, cautiously resuming, "they've got this keyhole—we could try your key!"

Claire's cue to laugh, or at least nod, but she did neither. She suddenly felt protective of the key, and herself. Neither was his to toy with.

"Well," Marcus said, "fine, no key. It's not the point anyway. You're supposed to look through the keyhole. It turns out you're actually looking into their garden, or *through* it, because your eye is led down a gravel path to a distant but perfectly framed view of Saint Peter's."

"Why are you here, Marcus?" Claire said.

"You . . . invited me along?"

"I mean here in Rome."

Marcus turned to face her full on and Claire almost flinched; he was using his public face, his screen face. Not an unkind face, but a professional one that came with the full force of a thirty-year career around cameras.

"I'm finishing one project," Marcus said slowly. "And maybe starting another."

"Maybe?"

"I need buy-in from a critical partner."

"What's his holdup?"

"Hers."

"I think Sister Georgia's all in."

Claire had seen some of Marcus's self-funded documentaries over the years. They were often about faith. Passion projects. They played festivals, and later online, if you could find them. She blamed herself, happily, for his obsession, though the results had been uneven. The first, years ago, was about the Dalai Lama visiting Cedar Falls, Iowa. She'd loved it. Others in the series, less so. A recent one had featured a Russian Orthodox monastery in Siberia. In winter. Claire had gotten a headache after watching it; so much of the film had been so dark that she'd squinted the entire time. But even that one, all of them, were distinguished by a slowness. It could get too slow, but the slowness somehow conveyed—she'd always wanted to tell him this—not just fascination, but openness, respect.

Claire felt like she was the only person who understood Marcus's career. This was a source of pride and dismay. She'd winced at critics who'd faulted Marcus early on for leaping from the indie scene into more lucrative roles. She'd winced again when they faulted his various attempts to return to his indie roots—or do Shakespeare, though he was now too old for Romeo (no matter what Sister Georgia thought), and too young for Lear. These days, he was mostly behind the camera, consulting here and there. He had a good eye, good pen—and good friends, who'd invite him on set for a day or a week to pick his brain. Dorothy said she'd even spotted him in a car commercial. Claire hadn't asked about that, though there was no shame in it—was there? Marcus's career goal was to stay working.

"Tell me how it starts," she said.

"What?"

"The movie. Any movie. I always wondered. Do you start at the start? 'We open in Rome...'"

"For me?" He left the window. "Research first," he said, bored now. "Then you try to visualize..."

What she wanted to do was go downstairs, quietly exit, find a table, and talk about, sure, framing. But frame this: two people, two continents, two different times of life. Wide shot, close.

She kept looking at him. If she looked, waited, long enough, he would get it. He was her life once. And she his. They'd been twenty, and they hadn't needed to stand a half floor above each other to see what was going on. If he had a film of that, she'd watch it, study it for some clue of what she was supposed to do now.

He reached for her, and for a split second Claire thought not only that he, finally, recognized what she recognized, but also that he was going to kiss her, which would be the first time in exactly thirty years and—give her a calendar and she could count—seven days.

She closed her eyes.

She felt two fingers alight on her left temple and two more on her right. She stopped breathing and waited, and then felt Marcus gently turn her face away from his and toward the roseto below. Listening to him breathe reminded her that she should, too. She opened her eyes.

"What do you see?" he said.

She looked at him.

"Okay, I'll go," Marcus said. He pointed to the rose, speckled with yellow leaves. "That's my acting career. I've not had a good role in years, and my last outing—"

"Won a Golden Globe?"

"The film did, not me, and the studio basically bought that. That was an awful role. All those motorcycle films have been awful. And dangerous. Though at least I know how to ride them now."

"Oh, *that's* why you took those roles. To learn to ride. I always wondered."

"It paid for things."

She looked down. "And the rest of the roseto? Empty?"

Marcus looked. "Some days. Depends on where you look. You go."

There was suddenly too much to see, to say. She didn't want the Gertrudans to leave their convent. She didn't want to leave Rome. Maybe Marcus had been right, the way the city framed things for you, and it had framed this for her, drawn a border around her, and said, *You, here.*

She had to tell him that, but she had to tell him something else first.

She felt like the railing was giving way. She saw the Convento di Santa Gertrudis, but also the Clementines' convent in Milwaukee. She saw Monica's apartment and hers down the block and the side-by-side Carolina beach condos Monica had been pestering her to buy. She could see all the convents she'd ever sold and all the padlocked churches and seminaries that she'd helped turn into apartments and restaurants and parking lots. She could see the three marathons she'd failed to finish. She could see Dorothy at her graduation from college and from high school and the annual, all-evening mother-daughter spa appointments they'd always booked during her teenage years to obliterate the nights of the father-daughter dance.

And all the men Claire had dated, she could see them, some good and kind, but none who'd ever given her vertigo.

"It's farther down than you think," she said.

A short history of kissing Marcus, told in numbers. Two: how many times she'd kissed Marcus freshman year, at least according to what she'd told in confession to the priest, who'd jovially laughed and said, *Three and you're out!* Zero: the number of times she brought up the topic with Sister Anastasia. Three: the *true* number of times Claire had kissed Marcus, according to Monica, who counted the kiss they'd performed while acting out a scene in Professor Biggs's Restoration Drama class. One: how many times Monica had kissed Marcus during an ill-conceived plan to serve as Claire's "rodeo clown," jumping into the ring to draw off the bull. Four: days Claire didn't speak to Monica. Three: weeks she didn't speak to Marcus.

It would be senior year before they kissed again, and then it happened twice.

The first time was in February, a dark, raw season. Yale, it turned out, had been hard. Studying to be a nun, even harder. Reconciling the two, hardest of all. But she had figured out a way to continue to be close friends with Marcus without getting too close. The roller coaster of freshman year, of kissing and then scolding herself for kissing Marcus had ended ignominiously, with Monica walking in on Claire and Marcus late one night in the room she and Claire shared. *Have I got a story for you*, Monica said, stumbling in from a disastrous party two entryways over. Then Monica snapped on the light and saw them on the bottom bunk. "Get off her!" Monica shouted, though he was under her. Given that Monica was ambivalent at best about Claire's vocation, Claire didn't understand the fury in Monica's voice.

But years later, in Rome, Claire better understood jealousy and friendship and secrets—she better understood Monica—and was less surprised by Monica's surprise than by the fact that Claire had been there in bed with Marcus. Fully clothed. *Nothing happened*, Claire said after he slunk away, and nothing had—stupid buttons and maybe mutual fear—and when Monica opened her mouth to speak, Claire, for once, spoke first: *And nothing will.*

And nothing did for the rest of freshman year, sophomore year, junior year. It helped that Claire began to feel a greater kinship with the Clementine sisters back home as her summers with them grew more intensive; it helped that Monica embarked on a series of her own romantic distractions; it helped, and did not, that Marcus started dating around.

Now it was senior year, their last semester, he wasn't dating anyone, and she couldn't help feeling that they were running out of time, though to do what, she couldn't say. She'd told him they could be friends, nothing more, and the fact that he'd shrugged and stuck around made her love him all the more, inspired her to do things she shouldn't have, like this very occasion: Marcus had somehow gotten himself assigned a seminar paper on the "rooftops of Yale" and, more improbably, had gotten himself access to the roof of the Beinecke Library, whose director was a theater fan. The library housed the university's collection of rare books and manuscripts; its unusual 1960s architecture made the building its own strange treasure.

Claire hated heights but hated even more the thought that Marcus might invite someone other than her along, and so here she was, terrified. And confused. Because she'd thought they'd be outside, on a rooftop, gazing up at the stars. But instead, they were inside—the library building was actually a box inside a box. The outer box of translucent marble cloaked, nested-doll style, an inner, smaller, multistory box of glass. The roof of the interior glass box stopped a meter or so short of the exterior marble box, which meant that, if the Marcus-charmed library director instructed an incredulous security guard to enable this, you could climb up through the stacks, out a hatch onto this inner "roof," and then wriggle your way to the lip of the glass box. Then you could lie on your stomach and peer down at the atrium floor, seventy feet below, where some of the library's most valuable items were on display.

"There's the Gutenberg Bible," Marcus whispered. "First book in the world printed with movable type."

"You already pointed that out," Claire said, her eyes shut. The guard had accompanied them and then somehow managed to get them locked out. He was back at the hatch, radioing for help. Marcus was killing time.

"This is amazing," Marcus said, resting chin on hands. The surface beneath them was slick, powdered with dust. Though it was flat, there was absolutely nothing—no railing, no ridge—to keep you from falling if, like Marcus, you kept inching your way forward.

"I want to go back down," Claire said.

"I had a TA who was obsessed with this place. Do you know they have a First Folio?"

Claire couldn't hear much of anything; she was scared to discover that she was scared, deeply, physically. The ground floor was so far away. She had been nervous in her early days at Yale but, deep down, thought herself fearless; she trusted in the Lord; she'd had her missteps freshman year but, since then, had held her own on a secular campus preparing for future life as a nun. She was invincible.

And now she was holding his hand. Had he taken hers or she his? She wasn't sure, only that she was glad for it and gladder still when he suggested they roll over on their backs.

They looked up at the ceiling, just a few feet away. This was the underside of the outer roof, and it was traced by a network of pipes and wires not used to being seen.

"Think of everything beneath us," said Marcus.

"I'm trying not to," Claire said.

"They have Lewis and Clark's maps," Marcus rattled on. "The pen Lincoln used to sign the Emancipation Proclamation. Ezra Pound's *teeth*."

"No."

"Actually, you're right. My TA said they're in his file, but it's unclear whose teeth they are."

Finally, she laughed. She turned her head to look at him and he looked back. There wasn't a lot of light to see by, but there was enough to see him smile. He looked a little pale, she thought—unwell? But she surely looked paler. She smiled back, bared her own teeth.

The security guard's radio crackled back by the hatch.

The silence of the library rose all around them and they looked at each other for a while. She stopped smiling, but her mouth remained slightly open, like his. He was going to try to kiss her, but look: he couldn't. She'd worked so hard to enclose herself in this bubble, and it was working. She was exemplary. Marcus understood that. The Clementines did. God did.

Claire had asked one of the younger nuns in Milwaukee what the most difficult vow was. There were three most every Catholic priest and sister took: poverty, chastity, obedience. The woman told Claire that the challenge was different for everyone, and moreover, *difficulty* probably wasn't the most productive way to think about vows, but that chastity, celibacy, wasn't as hard as many thought, "provided you thought about it in the right way."

What if you thought about it in terms of love? Because there, in that impossible space, that's what she felt.

Thirty years on, in Rome, Claire left her roseto overlook and walked toward Marcus, who had his back to her. Though she remembered that line so well, *provided you thought about it in the right way*, she did not remember what the right way was, or is. She remembered the library's hush, though, everything still but her; she remembered the smell of his hair; she remembered thinking that if no one saw them, this one time, this last time, it wouldn't count. She remembered the medieval Bible beneath them, how the whispers between them, softer and softer, closer and closer, became the brushing of lips, a kiss.

The second kiss that semester came months later.

The night before graduation, Claire rose from her front-row center seat at the end of his senior year show and climbed onstage. He looked surprised, his costar even more so.

It was this kiss that Marcus thought of while looking out from a high floor at the Convento di Santa Gertrudis, not the one atop the

Beinecke tower, but there, then, onstage, Claire's hands on his chest, his shoulders, the back of his neck, her kissing him deeply, passionately, irrevocably, the feeling so much like falling he felt a jolt even now.

"Ready?" Claire said.

VII. VIA MARGUTTA

HE WAS, FINALLY: ROME, RESTAURANT, ring, tonight. This made so much more sense. Over drinks at Piazza Cavour would have been too sunny, too soon.

And earlier still? Under the reunion tent at Yale would have been fine. The scene precast with all the extras you'd ever need. Proposing in New Haven would have brought everything tidily full circle. But he'd overthought it—first appear on the tablet, then magically appear in real life—and he'd overrelied on Monica's and Dorothy's encouragement: *Now, now!* Good thing they'd promised to keep all this a secret. Though how long did promises last?

Now, now. There was, admittedly, a different way to do all this. Forget proposing. Slow down. Invite Claire out to LA or find a way to visit New York more often. See each other for occasions beyond funerals. "See each other," period. Hang out. Date. Reacquaint himself with all that he'd always loved about Claire, the way she'd swerve a conversation, how she didn't tolerate glibness, how she not only wanted to know what you really thought but wanted you to really think.

Do all this for months, a year or two. Wake up some future Sunday together, prop yourself up on an elbow, say, *Hey, I've been wondering…*

But Marcus *had* been wondering, about how he'd waited thirty years since she'd kissed him onstage, or thirty-four if you counted back to him emerging from the shower, about how he knew Claire better than anyone else in his life, including (should have been a sign) the two women he'd been married to. He'd rushed into those marriages, true, but he'd always had the sense that he was short on time.

Maybe it was because the last time he and Claire had kissed, really kissed, she'd run away. So many times over the years he had wanted to ask why. So many times, including now, he told himself not to ask, for fear of an answer he wouldn't want to hear. Claire and her keys! Was that an obsession of her adult years, or something that had started at Yale? No matter. Sometimes what was wanted was a door that stayed shut.

Especially if it meant another might be opened.

Tonight, then. Why was it so much easier to climb atop a table and sing than sit at one and speak? Because he was who he was. And Claire was like no one else.

When they'd parted at the front door of the Convento di Santa Gertrudis, he'd given her a light hug, an even lighter goodbye—*I'll text you the address for dinner*—and then he was down the hill, gone.

She'd watched him, felt a faint worry—he seemed preoccupied—but it was quickly obscured by the larger worry before her and, once inside the convent, all around her.

Ninety-seven days the sisters had left at the Convento di Santa Gertrudis unless someone could figure something out. Someone: Sister Felicity. Sister Thérèse. Long-delayed Anna.

Sister Georgia had done the most so far, and she'd come up short: though the file marked DEED was promisingly empty—what if there *was* no deed?—it turned out Sister Rose had it in Boston, and a digital record existed here in Rome. An old map of the property, meanwhile, drawn on silk, showed a narrow road, apparently unbuilt, running straight through the back garden—had the city wanted to build such a street? Claire loved a good eminent domain fight!—but the map was also illustrated with fire-breathing dragons. Suitable for framing and selling, but not for a court of law.

So it would fall to Claire. She then took a deep breath and called her old client, Bert Ligouri. He was thrilled to hear she was in Rome, made her take down the names of four restaurants she had to try. Would have *loved* to put in an offer on the convent, but hadn't she heard? He'd gotten out, liquidated everything, set up a foundation. The sisters sounded like nice gals, though: He'd write a check right now, a thousand dollars, where to?

No, she thought later, as a cab delivered her deep into Rome for dinner, ninety-seven days would not be nearly enough time.

And yet it was measurable, guaranteed. Short of an errant meteor or actual dragon, the convent had that much time left on this planet, ninety-seven days, no question. In fact, it was hard not to imagine that the convent, its corridors and windowsills, its chapel, its cots and crucifixes, its brick and stone, and even its roses, would last much longer than that, longer than her, than anyone now alive.

She'd ask Marcus about that tonight—she had *so* much to ask him, couldn't believe he couldn't stick around forever, the two of them regularly meeting up at Paolo's coffee bar, to talk about Rome, this last half, third—fourth? fifth?—of their lives. How long did they have? Not being morbid, just efficient. Everyone had their own personal meteor coming anyway. *What are you going to do?*

Marcus?

What should I *do?*

She'd figure out a way to ask him. Not straight off; she'd learned a thing or two from him about timing over the years. Until then, they'd talk about other things. Dorothy. Him! She stopped in front of a tiny church. Or they could talk about the old reliable, real estate.

A sign on its door cried, VENDESI! A cement escutcheon above the entrance bore a stout cross. Maybe it wasn't a church. She tried the door. Nothing. It was silly, but there was no one around; the lock looked ancient; maybe Mother Saint Luke's key was an old type of master key. She slipped it out of her bag. God, she *would* miss this, the first time you opened the door. She didn't like that first meeting with the clients, but she loved that first encounter with the space: *What were you? What's next for you?*

Claire leaned close to look through a window slit in the door. She wouldn't try the key yet.

Yes, it was a church.

She was in the Centro Storico, Via Margutta, right where he'd said he'd meet her. It turned out to be a quiet side street, just off swanky Via del Babuino, and was lined with small, spare galleries and boutiques. Most were closed for the night; a few had left on a single light to illuminate a vase, a scarf, a logo. She'd walked slowly, studying the beautiful windows. Could she be this person? Not a nun, but a retiree in Rome, the American tourist or expat, single, successful, someone who shopped, acquired, filled closets.

Never. She'd all but worn a uniform over thirty years in real estate. She was known, even teased, for dressing plainly, forgoing makeup. She'd never acquired a Tiffany chandelier. She checked her phone; she had five minutes yet to meet Marcus.

Walking over here tonight, she'd tried an experiment, tried seeing the city through the eyes of a sister. Did Claire know enough to do that? Not really, so not much of an experiment, but she'd noticed how some things had looked slightly different. The small vitrine set in the wall above the intersection of two pedestrian streets, the one containing a painted wooden Virgin Mary statue, hand up in blessing, unconcerned that the flowers about her were plastic or that someone had wedged a tiny toy station wagon beneath her feet—this looked less like kooky shadowbox art and more like God had left a light on.

She peered in the window again. This church was deconsecrated, no pews, no art, and the altar was in pieces, but bring the right buyer—thirty-foot ceiling meant you could easily build a sleeping loft. A sacristy meant water was back there, possibly a bathroom. You'd have to do the kitchen from scratch, of course; on the few occasions when she'd done this sort of project, church to single-family residential, the architect usually put the kitchen in the chancel— where the altar once stood—or the apse, the curved part at the back. Or, for particular clients, not the kitchen but a king-sized bed took the place of the altar. Claire preferred that area left bare. Residential clients who bought churches usually filled them with too much stuff. But on this street, you'd want to do retail anyway, not residential, and this church was so tiny that—wait, was that water damage? She pressed her face closer.

Different eyes: not a sister, not a Realtor, but someone looking for a pied-à-terre to share with an old friend. *Marcus, you get spring, I get fall.* She closed her eyes. Or: *We both get summers.* What would Christmas be like? *Claire,* he might say, *I got you something…*

She had a strange, sudden urge to hide. She put the key to the lock. It didn't really fit; she forced it, and then it was stuck.

That was her. He knew from a block away, but he'd have known from ten blocks, thirty years.

Precious few people got more beautiful with age. And smarter. Funnier. He was not among them. Claire was.

Ask her now.

But the ring was at the restaurant.

Just ask her.

But it was so dark, and she seemed too deeply distracted by—of course—a church.

"Hi." Marcus surprised her, quiet and warm, and now put his face to the glass, too. "Can you get in?"

She smiled quickly at him, hiding the lock, the stuck key, behind her. "Hi."

"Let me guess," he said. "The magic key doesn't work?"

"Don't have it."

"Impossible."

The night was hot, smelled everywhere of jasmine. She'd forgotten; she was no better at lying to him than he was to her.

"It's stuck," she said, and stepped away, exposing the lock.

"And here I wanted to spend more time in a mildewing old convent."

"I like it there," Claire said softly. Then she turned. "And anyway, *this* is a church. Was. Help me get the key out."

"Do you have any WD-40?"

"Funny, I usually toss a can in my purse before a date, but I didn't tonight."

She'd meant it to be funny, anyway, but the word *date* landed oddly.

Marcus looked serious as he reached around her, jiggled the key, and removed it. He handed it back to Claire. "Does it depress you, all these endings?"

How had he done that? "Can we save the hard questions for later?" she asked. She smiled again, but he was studying his watch.

"You know, I was worried," he said. "The restaurant is technically not on this street, but up a steep flight of stairs. I wasn't sure you'd have the right shoes."

"I always have the right shoes," she said. And she did: not the platform sneakers she'd initially laced up, but the strappy, chunky heels she'd bought, inspired by their near-universal use among Italian women. And they'd been for sale right there on the sidewalk earlier that afternoon, lined up on a tarp.

It was possible they were not authentically the brand whose mark they bore.

"The strap's come undone," he said.

"It's for good luck," she said, a line of her father's about his own perennially untied shoes. At her dad's funeral, Marcus had done the exact same deed, fixed a loose strap on her shoe, though he'd done it wordlessly, as he was helping her from the car. And afterward, he'd kept her supplied with water and bites of food during the endless—so many students, current and past!—condolences line. When a neighbor, drunk (but her father's instructions had insisted on an open bar), thought it would be funny to rehash with Claire an old dispute about a fence, Marcus had drawn him off. Later, out of the corner of her eye, Claire saw them at the coffee urn, Marcus serving the neighbor and then the next person and the next, people assuming he was some sort of coffee attendant. And why not? He was playing the role with flair. Marcus always said he didn't know what he'd do if he didn't do movies. Claire said he'd make a good nurse. He always took good care. He didn't rattle. Claire wished he'd been there for her father's final hours. She smiled for the first time that day and cried for the not-first time, but in gratitude, admiration. Dorothy would call it love.

Maybe Claire would, too. And tell Marcus that, which she never had. Tell him tonight. You could tell a friend that, right? You *should* tell a friend that you loved him. Could you tell a friend that after entering a convent? Why not? But she looked at such a conversation through her earlier eyes and suddenly wished for the Virgin Mary's toy station wagon to arrive and speed her away.

Marcus looked at her, started to kneel. There was the crown of his head again, the whorl of hair there she saw so rarely, not since their Saturday nights in the library at school, him reading, her watching. Then they'd switch.

She had a sudden thought, as fanciful as it was painful—*a marriage proposal would look like this*—and so crouched down herself to scuttle the scene. "It's tricky," she said, beating him to the strap.

"Apparently," he said, remaining on one knee, studying Claire's foot carefully as if to learn the art. She stood, extended a hand, helped him up.

"Whose job is that on set?" she asked. "Is that what a 'key grip' does?"

"No," said Marcus. "And though it doesn't sound as cool as 'I do my own stunts,' I do tie my own shoes."

She went to his side, took his arm, leaned in, almost said the words, *I just love you*, before she caught herself. A seismic thought she'd had before but never voiced.

And wouldn't now. He'd think she was joking. But look at that face—you could—*she* could—tell it, ask it anything.

So she would.

"Marcus," she said. "A question."

She drew a deep breath and he did, too.

"I'm listening," he said.

"I'm considering—starting again. Starting over. Or finishing what I started."

"I don't understand."

"Neither do I, really, and that's what makes it kind of exciting! All this time, for the call to still be there, and—"

"What call?"

"To become a sister. To take vows. Enter a convent. Join the Order of Saint Gertrude." She looked at him. "Your mouth is open. It's been open. Say something."

She was thinking about becoming a *nun*? Here, in Rome, in that crumbling villa?

For the rest of her life?

And—she wanted to know what he *thought*?

"All right, *I'll* say something: it's a shock," Claire said. "I know."

"I'm not saying that."

He hadn't had to; she could see it. Also: she knew him. "I'm shocked, too," she said. "Again, I didn't come over here thinking this would happen. Which, weirdly, makes me trust this feeling all the more." She let go of his arm. "But it also—I don't know. I'm confused. I'm sure *they* are going to be confused when I tell them. Which is why you showing up here is perfect timing."

She might wind up telling him about that long-ago deal now, too—though did it even matter anymore? Her wanting to tell him at reunion was to have been a step toward a disentangled future, one free of deals and debts and disappointments. But it would have been only a step, with so many more to follow. Here in Rome, a bypass had emerged. She could spare them both the awkward truths—her telling him why she'd run, him telling her why he'd not followed—by slipping into a life she'd long thought was locked against her. Once inside the convent? The deal didn't matter, but even if it did, they were covered.

He looked up the stairs, then down the street. "Do you want to go somewhere and... talk?"

"Yes." Claire poked him in the chest. "I want to go to dinner." She put a hand on the railing and started up.

After a moment, he followed.

The stone staircase climbed between two buildings into a maze of yet more buildings beyond. A tangle of Christmas lights fringed the summit. Marcus checked his phone and then rang an apartment bell at a nearby door. After a long minute, a man appeared in a white apron, smiling from ear to ear.

They went down a scuffed hallway, muffled music behind this door, that door, and entered a studio apartment that had been converted into a small restaurant. Two tables of diners looked up at them, grinning at the now-shared secret. *A restaurant, here!* The chef returned to the kitchenette and a young woman took over, escorting them through French doors to a large patio, where six couples sat at separate tables. Candles glittered in jars, and all Rome glittered beyond. Magnolia trees and, as ever, bougainvillea, foaming in magenta clouds, vivid even in the dark, provided privacy from the street below. Umbrellas shielded them from the apartments above.

Heaven. The chef could bring whatever he wanted, even an empty plate; the sommelier could pour her a glass of air. She wondered—

She wondered what the sisters were doing. If they should have invited the sisters along tonight.

It was a sign—of something—that what would have sounded silly yesterday sounded less so today.

There was no menu; the food just came. Artichokes, roasted and split. A bowl of tomatoes and olives and corn cut from the cob. Then pasta al sugo di coda, thick with tomato, celery, and golden raisins, the sauce redolent of the oxtail that had simmered in it and which starred in the subsequent, and for them, final, course.

No additional diners arrived, not a single couple left. Claire wondered what she and Marcus looked like to the other tables, but whenever she sneaked a glance, she saw that no one else was looking at anyone other than the person directly across from them.

Claire relaxed. Marcus relaxed. They talked about everything except what Claire had just said down on the street. They talked about Yale and they talked about Hollywood. They talked about turning fifty and turning twenty-nine. They talked about Dorothy, Monica, bad movies, good ones, what to do on a Saturday night when they found themselves alone—nothing, they agreed—and where their favorite spots on earth were—right here, right now, they agreed, though Claire thought he was just being polite.

"Do you think it's just because I'm in Rome that I'm feeling the way I do?"

"What *are* you feeling?" said Marcus, newly intent.

She shifted in her chair.

"About why I might want to take vows? Like I said, I'm feeling a... call," she said cautiously. She didn't want to scare him, or herself. She *was* feeling, more and more, called to be in Rome, in that convent. She was just worried that—she didn't know what was calling her. Something beyond her, yes, bigger, yes. But she'd looked in the mirror and not seen the look—yet?—that she'd seen in the sisters' eyes.

In her teens, she'd worried similarly to a spiritual director, who'd reassured her: *Sometimes God gets there ahead of you.* Thirty-some years later, she worried to herself the opposite was true, that she'd gone too far ahead, and down the wrong route.

Saying *call*, then, was also like calling out, hoping to be heard.

"Okay," he said, too quickly. If she was saying this to the sisters— and she'd have to practice if she did—she knew this would prompt a thoughtful pause. *Called.* For Marcus, it seemed like it was just an item on a checklist. "And?" he said.

"That's kind of a big one," she said.

"All right, how do you feel 'called'?"

"'How'?"

"Or 'why,' or whatever," he said. "You're holding back."

She looked at him. He'd picked at his food tonight, but he'd been insatiable at Yale, food or talk. Back then, he'd ask questions all night. Monica had found it annoying, would wander off to bed, but Claire would stay up with him until all hours, tending the perennial topic, why *were* things the way they were? Which, even though that never-ending discussion regularly ran rampant across everything from astronomy to zoology, Claire later understood was about some-thing simple, the two of them.

Tonight was a little taste of that. Different: the absence of the feel-ing they'd had at eighteen, nineteen, twenty, that if they just stayed up late enough, talked long enough, they would figure everything out.

"I feel lonely," she finally said. "And when I'm with those women, when I'm in that drafty, moldy, helmets-required convent, I don't."

Marcus nodded slowly, and relief washed over Claire, having fi-nally said this aloud. She could kiss him for being so understanding. So many other evenings, other men, none had felt like this.

They fell into silence. They were that comfortable, Claire thought, no more need be said. Which was good; she didn't know what she would say. She'd just said she wanted to take religious vows, and yet this felt like the most romantic night of her life. Marcus looked beautiful, hands, hair, lips, eyes.

"Why," Marcus said then, "didn't I ask you to marry me when I had the chance?"

It took Claire only a second to answer this question, but it was a long second, long enough to go to college, collect the truth that waited there, and return.

Graduation week, senior year. They had five days until the ceremony itself, but the campus was already transforming: the quad where they'd spent their first year had sprouted a stage, signs, thousands of white folding chairs the night had stained a faint blue. New Order poured from one dorm's windows, Madonna from another. (She liked "Like a Prayer" just fine; she just hated everyone nudge-nudging her about it.) They'd commandeered two chairs to talk.

"Do you remember—" he began, and then coughed. The sentence could have led to anything: freshman year, when they'd lived in the sextet, the building easily visible just across the way. Sophomore and junior years, when they'd kept things strictly platonic and become, they agreed (didn't they?), better friends as a result; then senior year, January, the Beinecke, which no one saw—save God, apparently, because she was being punished: Marcus had gotten the lead in the spring show, which involved him kissing his costar every night. Claire knew the girl, Eva, and had hated her long before her time onstage with Marcus. Eva sat in the front pew of Saint Thomas More Chapel every Sunday, pointedly asked after Claire's welfare whenever Claire failed to show. Monica said it sounded like Eva was competing with Claire to be the better sister in training, but Eva didn't have designs on being a nun. Eva definitely had designs on Marcus.

Claire had been to every performance of the show so far. Marcus had had girlfriends before, nothing serious, but this was different. Every performance, their closing kiss got longer, Eva's hands sank lower. Claire wasn't sure how much farther they could go, but she had a front-row seat—between her father and Sister Anastasia—to the last performance, a pregraduation show for families.

"Remember what?" Claire asked.

Marcus waved a hand. He looked tired. "Nothing," he said.

"I can't believe you're missing graduation," Claire said, switching from one irritation to another, the cascade of good fortune Marcus was riding: the visiting professor who'd been dazzled by him; the young star who'd backed out of a movie that was already shooting in Toronto; the audition to replace him that Marcus had done *over the phone*; the director, the agent, the press, the A-list cast, the fact that they needed him this week; after his last bow with Eva, a plane was coming to pick him up at tiny Tweed Airport, fifteen minutes from campus. He'd miss graduation. Still, a tremendous break, and maybe something had broken over his skull, because Marcus had been walking around campus looking mildly concussed. She'd even made him go to the health clinic and was glad she had. They'd found a fever, maybe some asthma, given him something. He was better now; the cough was fading.

Everything was. Poking Marcus about leaving was a way of not talking about something else. Not about holier-than-thou Eva. Something that Claire didn't yet know how to say. Not to Marcus, not to herself, not, most importantly, to the nuns back at the convent in

Milwaukee, whom she was planning to tell: *I don't think I want to take vows anymore.*

The Clementines, after their initial hesitation, had become increasingly eager for her to finish college and join their ranks. They were counting on her, her smarts, her energy—her youth—she knew. Claire had been counting on the sisters. They'd welcomed her back each summer, each summer a chance for the sisters to say, *Yes, it looks like this is going to work.*

But Claire had fallen in love.

She hadn't told Marcus. Something inside her, raw, medieval, specious, wanted to punish her for falling in love with Marcus when she'd been preparing to promise herself to God alone. And something else, just as insidious, suggested that the reason she'd not left the convent path earlier—like five days into freshman year—was because she'd been scared to. Not scared of what God would think—God didn't "think"—but because it was scary to stand outside the door of the life you thought you would lead.

Here she was, days from graduation, months, if that, from formally entering the Clementines. And just hours from what felt like a pending explosion.

What a mess. She should talk to the sisters back home, to the chaplains here at Yale, to God. The message they might deliver: *Men come and go, Claire—*

And they did, and would, but that was the point. She'd fallen this hard now; she would again. It was better this way, to quit before she started. It was more honest this way. As for a future with Marcus? She'd see! They'd see. One step at a time. First, this conversation.

"I may... not be leaving," Marcus said. He put a fist to his mouth like he was going to cough again, but no cough came.

He'd be at graduation after all? Claire had to force herself not to be excited; if he wasn't leaving, something must be wrong.

And something was: he'd just come from a physical.

"A what? Why?" said Claire.

"A physical," he said. "Have to have one, for the underwriters. For them to insure the film, they have to know how big a bet they're making, even on a newcomer like me."

For years, she'd remember that word, *bet*. She'd blame that word.

"How big a bet *are* they making?" said Claire. This was an irritating way of telling her how big a part this was.

"Well, the bet just got bigger," he said.

Do it now, Claire thought, tell him now. Tell him that you're quitting the convent before he tells you all about the coming money and fame, so that he knows that you love him for who he is, the kid that he is, with the tidy room, the big smile, the bigger voice that sings to the rescue when the jackals (jackasses) circle. That you love the quiet within him, which strangely, and somehow perfectly, reminds you of what you love about convent life.

Tell him that you love him, not the star being born.

"A second opinion is what we're after," he said.

Had they only had a stenographer with them that night. A transcript would have been helpful in the years that would follow. She could have reviewed it from time to time to clarify what had been said. She remembers words, *hemogram* and *lung* and *cancer*. She remembers—this is important—that there was no reason why he should have developed lung cancer; he'd never smoked, neither had his parents. So an X-ray was coming, another type of blood test, "it's probably nothing."

"It *is* nothing," Claire said, and then set about making that true.

Later that night, Claire let herself into Saint Thomas More Chapel with her key, knelt, and prayed. Prayer wasn't always quiet, someone had once told her, and it wasn't that night, as she knelt in the dark, angry at Eva, angry at Marcus's doctors, angry at herself, angry at God, and finally said, "Save his life."

There *is* a transcript of this conversation. A divine one, tattooed inside her chest, the way divine conversations are.

And why should I listen to you? God said (that is, she was imagining what God would say to her; they'd been closer not so long ago). *You've gone astray.*

"I know," Claire said. "I'm already planning on giving up the convent, community, vowed life." And it was true: she had nothing to offer, she was about to give up everything. And yet she had to help Marcus.

So she made her promise. She'd give up Marcus.

God said nothing in reply—because she hadn't been talking to God, of course, just her imagination, and her imagination was flabbergasted by how readily she'd offered this deal.

And she would later be flabbergasted by how quickly God delivered. The test, the lung? The next day, the second opinion said balderdash. A third opinion did, too, suggested that the hemogram should have been run differently anyway; in any case, no matter, no blast cells.

"No what?" Claire said weakly.

Marcus was so excited he couldn't hear Claire sniffling on the other end. He was calling from Canada. "You said it was nothing," he said. "*Believed* it was nothing, and it *was*!"

She'd promised, she believed, and the miracles kept coming: the film production figured out a way to get him back to campus not only for graduation but for the final performance of the show as well. Claire sat, eyes shining, between her dad and, from the Milwaukee Clementines, Sister Anastasia, front-row center.

At intermission, her father and Sister Anastasia agreed that it was a good show. Claire nodded and said nothing. She thought if she opened her mouth she might throw up. She was grateful when the lights dimmed, hiding her face.

After the final song, Marcus and Eva began to cross toward each other for their *final* final kiss. Claire rose from her seat. She couldn't not. She needed to explain everything to everyone but didn't have the words; this gesture would have to do. Her father looked up, confused. Sister Anastasia didn't notice Claire had left her seat until she saw Claire climbing a small set of stairs to the stage.

Then everyone saw, and Claire saw them see. Not a triumph, which her heart had sent her pounding up the stairs in search of, to claim her beloved from the arms of a woman who scarcely mattered, but an emptying.

Claire, who'd promised herself to the Clementines and God, who'd told everyone from Yale to Yakima that she was becoming a nun, who'd endured taunts and temptations, who'd stubbornly, if wrongly, believed that she was better than most people, including Marcus, because she trod the harder road, was abandoning that road.

"Claire?" Marcus said onstage, just before, as she had promised, she kissed him goodbye.

"Claire?" he asked again, twenty-five years later.

Why hadn't he ever asked her to marry him? "Because," she said, and paused to convince herself that she was hurting him less now than she had then, "I would have had to say no."

* * *

Any priest or sister, anyone at all, really, so long as they had a heart, could have told Claire her promise was not a promise, that God wasn't a slot machine, yank the handle, see what you get. But Claire had promised, she had yanked, she had won; Marcus was alive and well and in Rome.

What a deal: promise that she'd never intertwine with Marcus romantically—much less marry him—and Marcus would recover from whatever illness plagued him. And Marcus would never be burdened, as she was, with knowing what she'd done.

He still wouldn't if she said nothing further. But if she didn't speak, she'd be entangled with that old self and all its debts forever. She'd thought Rome, the convent, would usher her neatly past all this, but apparently not.

So tell him. It would hurt, but at least he'd know it hadn't been about him, her running away.

It had always been about him.

She could run again now, run forever.

She looked down at her feet. They didn't move.

He got up and had a brief discussion with their server, the chef. She didn't see him collect the ring.

"Everything all right?" she asked when he returned. He looked ill.

A walk home. A dark street. A pause outside the convent door. He waited. An ocean away, Dorothy waited. Monica waited. The women waited on the other side of the convent wall. Somewhere in Rome a lock waited for its key.

She remembered kissing Marcus center stage, yes. Everyone there that night did. But she didn't remember climbing the steps to the stage, what that had sounded like, or what it sounded like when the shouts began. She remembered the endless, glowing silence between those two points, before and after, which sounded like Trastevere did now. She remembered the look on his face when he saw her cross the stage to him, or maybe it was when he first saw her at his door in Sanford Hall.

What are you doing here?

She'd held on to her belief—or rather, vice versa—and all that had delivered her to Rome, halfway up a hill on a quiet street, beside a boy she'd loved, and somewhere shared between them, a memory of the young woman she'd been. Claire loved her, too, still.

This older Claire, she hadn't run. Give her that. She waited with him outside the door of the convent now.

"Good night, Claire," he finally said, and she watched until she lost sight of him walking down the hill into Trastevere.

The next morning he sent a message saying he'd been called back to California unexpectedly.

He'd return, he promised.

PART II

I. IN FLIGHT

DOROTHY HAD BEEN BORN IN New York City but raised in Milwaukee; Claire had moved them to Wisconsin after she and Monica determined that it gave the firm more credibility with heartland clients. Plus childcare was so much cheaper, and Claire had had a hunch that, eventually, it would be easier to get Dorothy into Yale if she didn't hail from the crowded East Coast applicant pool.

Dorothy didn't apply anywhere other than the University of Wisconsin–Madison, which Monica thought no less strange than attending school on Pluto. Forty-five thousand students. Football! Cows! Badgers! Dorothy loved it. Claire stayed in Wisconsin for four more years to claim in-state tuition rates and then decamped back to Manhattan; Dorothy, who now did HR for a health-tech company, had vowed to stay in Madison for the rest of her life.

And whenever Claire visited her, especially in the summer, especially today, she could see why. Though Dorothy was years out of school, she still frequented a favorite campus spot, out behind the student union. Called the Terrace, it was one of the loveliest pieces of collegiate real estate in America, a vast, multilevel patio that descended into a sparkling lake. Nothing at Yale came close. Outdoor stands sold plastic cups and pitchers of beer so cheap that, to a New Yorker, it felt like drinking for free. Above, cottony white clouds buffeted along. Students sunned on the dock, skimmed by in boats and canoes. A band was setting up. In February, as Claire knew from her own Wisconsin days, it would be a frozen hellscape, but in June, it was sublime.

Claire lifted her cup and took a sip, coming away with a thin mustache of foam.

"Do you like it?" Dorothy asked. "I can get you something else."

Claire wanted what sunny, smiling Dorothy had. Contentment, stability, confidence that she was living the life she was supposed to. *How did you know you were supposed to be in HR?* Claire once asked her. *I didn't!* Dorothy gleefully replied and started talking about an upcoming vacation. Claire's gift to Dorothy was that she'd enabled her to graduate debt-free. Now Claire wanted the favor returned somehow, but Claire's debts and entanglements weren't financial.

Still, look at Dorothy grinning. How did she do it? Alcohol, maybe. "I love it," Claire said.

"You don't," Dorothy said, and took a large gulp from her own cup.

Claire felt herself being studied, which was fair: on the flight home from Italy, Claire had locked herself in the tiny bathroom and studied the mirror. She saw a woman who'd changed her flight home three times, who'd overstayed her initially planned twenty-day visit by an extra ten days, and who'd come to begin each day in the convent chapel, finished it quietly reading spiritual texts, and spent the intervening hours trying to save the convent.

Sister Georgia remained dauntless in her research, even in the face of dragons; she'd begun walking the neighborhood to see if she could find other signs of the perhaps-proposed road, and when that failed, started scoping out places where *she* would propose a road to the city. How about bulldozing "AD," a new, neighboring business whose initials stood for not *anno domini* but *American Donut*? The lack of Latin was bad enough, but the adulterated English?

Claire's efforts, meanwhile, to find a rent-back buyer had stalled—no one wanted to beat the offer on the table—and so she'd started contacting foundations. Bert Ligouri's foundation was too small; she needed someone with cash, an international mindset, spiritual outlook. Mostly cash. So far, of the ones that had gotten back to her, the gist was: we invest in people, not places. *You're investing in me*, an exasperated Claire told a wealthy couple from Indiana. Good luck, they told her kindly. The same thing, coincidentally, that Sister Felicity had told Claire before she left for the States. For her part, Claire hadn't told the sisters anything about vocations, vows, permanent plans, but she sensed they sensed something in her.

Someone would have to say something soon. As of this beer with Dorothy, there were sixty-eight days left before the dissolution vote and sale.

Peter, whose name had started appearing in emails and texts, was due to arrive in minutes, as soon as he got done with his job in the city's planning and zoning department. *You'll have plenty to talk about*, said Dorothy. And maybe they would: Claire had been waiting for an appointment with Rome's Soprintendenza delle Belle Arti, whose role in Italian officialdom apparently could include determining whether the Convento di Santa Gertrudis was an encumbered, unchangeable monumento nazionale d'arte—or just old. Claire could ask Peter for his take.

And also for advice on how to break the news to Dorothy that Claire was returning to Rome and, God and the sisters of Saint Gertrude willing, beginning the path to taking vows. Maybe she would explain it to Dorothy in terms of looking for a sign.

"Mom?" Dorothy said. "You don't have to lie about the beer."

It wasn't a sign she'd find on this sunny summer terrace, that much Claire knew.

"I'm not," said Claire. "Yum." She drank. It tasted like someone had been washing oranges in a stoppered sink and then ladled the dishwater into cups, bubbles and all.

"It's a good summer drink," Dorothy said.

"It's a good summer place," Claire said. It really was. She realized Dorothy had fleeced her all those times she'd gotten Claire to pay for summer school in Madison: no one could possibly get anything done here in summer. It would be just one long, beautiful haze.

"You could get a place here," Dorothy said.

A cue.

"Listen," Claire said. "Before Peter gets here—"

Dorothy abruptly put down her cup and put her hand lightly to her chest, a burp or a pause. A toddler memory flashed before Claire: that amazing day care Monica had found for Dorothy that taught the kids sign language before they could speak. A hand smeared across the chest meant—Claire couldn't remember—*more* or *please* or *Mom*. Dorothy's face now contorted into bottomless, toddler-like concern as well. "What do you mean, 'before Peter gets here'? What's—oh my God, are you all right? I *knew* there was a reason for the text blackout."

There was, of course. Over the past weeks, Claire had been working nonstop. Thinking nonstop. Spending hours in and around the shedlike hermitage in the parco, the convent's back garden, which had once belonged to Mother Saint Luke, to whom, as the days passed, Claire had felt more and more comfortable speaking about everything. Marcus. Dorothy. Herself, about whether or not to finally, after all these years, take vows. Mother Saint Luke had said go for it.

Maybe Mother Saint Luke knew how profoundly lonely Claire had been back in the States. Lonely, despite colleagues, friends, Dorothy, Monica, New York, a city of nine million. Maybe Mother Saint Luke knew Claire talked to herself there, too. If she did, then she knew that Claire wished for what she had in Rome. Alone time without loneliness. Community without claustrophobia. Belief without boundaries.

"I'm fine," Claire said, and turned to look Dorothy straight in the eye. It wasn't just about Claire. It was about the sisters needing help; it was about Rome, 5K runs past palazzos. Coffee as she'd never had it. Wine as she'd never had it. Tomatoes—*tomatoes*, fresh, olive oil, salt, or just eat them like apples, maybe lick the salt from your hands, then take another bite, more salt.

And God. God? God would come along soon enough. She was—would be—in Rome. God would find her. She just had to be in the right spot.

"You're drunk," Dorothy said, "or stalling."

"Stalling," Claire said, as both would soon be true.

Seeing Marcus, too. That had helped. Her, anyway. It wasn't closure—she hadn't told him all she needed to—but she felt like she'd made progress. She'd make more.

Peter arrived. He kissed Dorothy on top of her head and plopped down a small plastic pitcher with yet more beer.

"My mother doesn't like the beer," Dorothy said. Claire had never heard Dorothy call her "mother" before and now worried that it was something her daughter did all the time. *Mother*, like Claire was eighty-nine, an elderly nun who kept a hermitage in a walled convent garden and a key for paranoid emergencies.

"That's not true," Claire said.

"My mother also doesn't like getting to the point," Dorothy said. "She was about to make an announcement when you walked up."

Two young men nearby took off their sunglasses, their hats, and then their shirts.

Claire *could* just get a place here. A condo across the lake, on the water. She could see Dorothy for picnics in the summer. Come baby-sit for the beautiful grandchildren Dorothy would have with Peter. Rome was too far.

Claire had fretted to one therapist or another during Dorothy's day-care years that her daughter might have abandonment issues; her mother at work all day, her father nothing more than a signature on the occasional check or *Keep Christ in Christmas!* card. But the therapist had turned it around on Claire, asked her if Claire had felt abandoned when her own mother died; Claire had cried all the way home.

Claire loved Dorothy like breathing. Dorothy could visit Claire anytime she wanted, in Rome.

"I'm going back—thinking of entering—going back *in*," Claire said quietly. Dorothy stared at her. Peter cocked his head and then twisted around.

"Bathroom's on the ground floor," he said, "not too hard to find, but you've got to work your way through the rathskeller first. Then a quick jog right. Sorry! I'm making it sound more complicated than it is."

Claire was, too.

"In *where*?" Dorothy said. Her interest in Claire's prior flirtation with vowed life had peaked around sixth grade, when Dorothy declared she wanted to become a nun—as in, enter a convent at that very moment, to hell with seventh grade—and then ended abruptly with her first crush in eighth grade. Claire had accompanied Dorothy to Mass at the Newman Center her first weekend in Madison, her first year. Since then, Dorothy had wandered away from church.

"A convent. Vowed life," Claire said. Dorothy looked at her, pursed her lips, then rocked back. The two young men behind Dorothy were laughing about something on a phone. "I was all set to enter a convent once before," Claire said to Peter. "I don't know if this has come up. I doubt it. Fascinating as I am, I'm probably not the subject of Dorothy's every conversation."

"Close to," Peter said. "She's very proud of you." Claire smiled at Dorothy. Dorothy was agape in shock. "But no, we've not gotten to this part," he said.

"Well, it was a long time ago," Claire said. "I was very young."

Peter nodded, took a sip. He looked a little lost. Claire should turn the conversation back to zoning. "A nun?" he said.

"Yes," Claire said, watching Dorothy out of the corner of her eye. This was not the right way or time to tell her. Dorothy liked being consulted, not surprised.

"What—the—fuck, Mom?" Dorothy said quietly.

"This is the first you're hearing it?" Peter asked Dorothy.

"No—I mean, yes," Dorothy said. "I sensed something was up. Three weeks in Rome became six. And yes, I knew she'd planned on becoming a nun when she was a teenager, and that was crazy, but people do stupid shit in their teens. You have a Tasmanian Devil tattoo on your ass." Peter smiled at Claire by way of reply. "But she's talking about going into a *convent* now," Dorothy went on. "At age fifty-two."

"You don't look a day over forty—" Peter started to say. He was clearly about to add another digit but stopped.

"Thanks, Peter," Claire said.

Awkward pause.

"How big is the tattoo?" Claire asked.

"Smaller than Dorothy's," he said amiably, whereby Claire learned Dorothy had one.

"What would you do with—with—everything?" Dorothy said, half rising from the bench. "Your job at the firm? Your apartment? Your bank account? Your keys?" She turned to Peter. "My mom loves keys."

Peter nodded.

"Or is it like, just a day job, you report in the morning to the chapel and then go home at night?" Dorothy asked. "Is it in Manhattan? It couldn't be Rome; you don't speak enough Italian."

"It is in Rome, Dorothy, and it's—"

"Rome!" Dorothy shouted. The two shirtless guys behind her looked up from their drinks and unembarrassedly scanned her, head to toe. Claire did, too. Dorothy was tall, six feet, most of it legs. It had made her look ungainly as a child but not as an adult, not in summer in Madison, not by the water, wearing shorts, with her new date, with her mom telling her that she was leaving the secular world behind, returning to Rome.

"That sounds so cool," Peter said. "I didn't know they still did that. I thought it was all—you know, so many churches are just museums or hotels now in Europe, in Rome. But I suppose some aren't. You'll live in one?"

"What the hell are you *talking* about?" Dorothy said.

"I don't know why you're upset," Claire said. "You're an adult now, and I'm still an adult."

"Because I'll never see you again," Dorothy said.

"That's not true," Claire said. "It's not that kind of convent."

"That's good," said Peter, putting on what he must have thought was a thoughtful face.

"It won't happen right away," Claire said. "There are stages, even before you take simple vows. And even then, it's seven years before you take solemn, or final vows."

Peter nodded. "They say it can take ten thousand hours to master a skill."

Peter, Claire thought, was a few hours short when it came to charming a girlfriend's mother.

"It may not happen at all," Claire said. "I need to spend some time thinking; the sisters do, too—in the end, it's up to them to invite me—"

"What about me?" Dorothy said. "Do I not get a vote?"

"Dorothy."

"This is why you flew out here, then?" Dorothy said. "To tell me this?"

Claire was not drunk, not on beer, anyway, but on Rome, the Gertrudans, her imagined future, so much so that she only now realized that she'd flown here in pursuit of an impossibility: Dorothy telling her that all this was a good idea, that Dorothy thought her mom was doing something brave and beautiful, that Claire would still see Dorothy several times a year because Dorothy would just fly over for the weekend, the week. (With what money?)

Impossible.

Here was Peter, eyes glinting from the beer, a port in the storm. Claire turned to him. "You take vows," Claire mumbled. An hour ago, he'd thought he was meeting his girlfriend's mom for a welcome-to-Wisconsin drink. "Poverty, chastity, obedience," Claire went on, and her fervor began to return. She *could* do this. She would. "There can be other, specialized ones, but those are the main ones, or the ones I'll take."

"Wait," Dorothy said. "Marcus! Because—does he know?" She turned to Peter. "Marcus is—"

"We're throwing a lot at Peter," Claire interrupted.

"At *Peter*?" Dorothy said.

Peter took this as a cue to examine his pitcher, which was all but empty. The plan had been to go to a restaurant for dinner, but Claire now felt too woozy to stand.

* * *

"Just don't become a nun, like, tomorrow," Dorothy said the next day at the airport. They'd struck an overnight, talk-about-anything-else truce, which Dorothy was breaking now. "Give me time."

This was easy to agree to. September 4 was sixty-six tomorrows away. Also, as Claire had said, the process wasn't quick, the outcome not guaranteed.

"And promise me you'll *talk to Marcus*," said Dorothy, who apparently would carry a torch for the man forever.

Claire nodded. She had a more urgent concern: "What should I tell Monica?"

"That I love her and I have someone I want her to meet," Dorothy said.

"Peter?" He'd seemed nice enough, but—

But would Claire miss all this in Rome? Courtship, babies, marriage.

What would Claire have missed had she become a nun at seventeen? Yale, Marcus, Monica. Middle-age dating. Selling old churches. Sitting alone in front of the TV weeknights with a jam jar of wine.

Her precious, precious Dorothy.

"I'd like her to meet the lunatic impersonating my mother," Dorothy said.

"I love you, sweet girl," Claire said, and Dorothy hugged her hard. Claire rubbed her hand in a circle on Dorothy's back: *More*.

Claire and Marcus had once unexpectedly met at Chicago's O'Hare airport. Marcus had just sent her a long, newsy email, as he did roughly once a year, and she'd been pecking out a reply on her phone while waiting for a flight to New York. Fifteen typos in, she'd given up and called him to say hi. It sounded like he was in an airport; she was, too—

She got herself put on a later flight and he'd done the same for LA. They sat at his gate because it was quieter, and they talked. Unlike with other friends—even Monica; heck, even Dorothy—there were never moments when the conversation lagged. They talked about what they'd seen and read, mutual friends and enemies and futures. They told each other everything. Almost. He'd have made a good interviewer, she thought, or therapist, or professor, or copilot. He made a good friend. *She* made a good friend. The conversations were, if anything, better than they'd been in college, more informed, less parochial. She trusted his advice; he eagerly sought hers. That months, even a year, might pass without contact never seemed to affect them; when they finally did meet, or write or call or text, all the prep work—decades of it—had been done. They could pick up where they'd left off.

When the gate agent called his flight to Los Angeles, Marcus told Claire to wait, said he was going to see if there was another yet later. She shook her head—common sense said there wouldn't be—and shook her head again when he came back smiling with the news that he'd rerouted himself to California via New York.

He fell asleep over Ohio, didn't stir when Claire laid a blanket over him. A flight attendant came by with a basket of snacks. "Does he want anything?" the man whispered. "Do you?"

Claire looked at Marcus, then the flight attendant. She mouthed, *No.* The man moved on. She looked at her watch. She should have routed herself west. Flying east, you always lost time.

Claire took a cab from the airport straight to her meeting with Monica. They'd briefly disputed the location. Claire's favorite bars in New

York were near NYU, Goldie's and Flavio's, across the street from each other. Or, on game days, Kettle of Fish, the Wisconsin bar.

But Monica claimed the Yale Club of New York City, a skinny citadel in midtown, had the best bartenders in the city. Claire had never been won over by the bar or the club, especially in their younger days, when white-haired men would get waved in at the door and Monica would be stopped and asked for her member number. A confrontation would ensue, even, or especially, if Monica and Claire had some unsuspecting non-Yale dates in tow. Monica relished the encounters, loved the moment when she finally presented the member card that the doormen and dates had by then convinced themselves did not exist.

Nowadays Monica herself was not only waved in but regally welcomed, which Claire could tell Monica liked almost, though not quite, as much as being turned away. But it was still fun to sit in the Main Lounge, which stretched the length of the façade overlooking Grand Central Terminal, and drink and snack and people watch. Fewer white-haired white men, but still too many. Then again, it was three thirty in the afternoon. Claire wondered who else had time to while away such hours.

Of course: the two of them did. For that matter, the room was probably full of commercial real estate brokers and aspirant nuns. You just had to look closely.

A waiter arrived; Monica dispatched him for two martinis. Claire had initially turned the offer down but then thought the drink might serve her well.

"I'm giving you space, if that's not clear," Monica said. "I want to hear what you have to tell me, and I hope it starts with an explanation of what that weeks-long stretch of radio silence was all about and is followed by an explanation of why you haven't figured out that convent sale yet *and* what on earth is going on with Marcus. But I'll wait."

In their twenties, this lounge had been the unlikely place to dish about dates gone wrong or, more rarely, right. Their customary spot was a pair of chairs beneath a portrait of Gerald Ford, LLB, 1941. "Let's go see the president" was their code, and whenever they deployed it, they'd felt not only impossibly clever but invincible, united, the city at their feet, Ford at their back.

Now Claire felt panicked, and not just because a new, piercing portrait of Sonia Sotomayor, JD, 1979, was looking on from an adjoining room.

Monica waited and then said, "Do you remember?" and the litany began. Flings and flops, love won and lost. Early on, they'd discovered the Yale Club—indeed, all of Midtown—was no happy hunting ground; Monica had gone uptown and Claire all the way to Staten Island. The coast guard had a base there. The guys were courteous, tan, fit, and efficient. They had no trouble understanding what one called "operational windows": that is, how much time Claire had until Dorothy's babysitter had to go home.

Most important, after a year or two, the guardsmen always moved away. Claire still got a Christmas card or two from Maine, San Diego, Kodiak. She would smile at the name and sigh—in relief that they'd found someone else.

The two women sat in silence. Monica wanted to know about Marcus. So had Dorothy. Fine. In a minute, Claire could give the report. Marcus was great. Looked great, smelled great. Listened great. He had been in Rome to record something, Claire wasn't sure why it couldn't have been done remotely, but then you could have said the same about Claire's trip. But they weren't going to talk about that.

Conversations that included the word *God* made Monica uncomfortable, which made Claire uncomfortable.

But how to talk about Rome otherwise? The waiter arrived with their drinks. Monica sipped at hers and stared at Claire. Claire looked the waiter in the eye and said thank you. "My pleasure," he said to Claire. He was slim and silver-haired and smiled quickly as he left.

"Could you leave at least *one* man for the rest of us?" Monica said. She looked at the Ford portrait.

Claire looked at the martini. She loved the drink but not the glass. Byron, her too-serious ex, once said it made him feel like a squirrel at a birdbath and the image had stuck with her. Another thing to hold against him. She suddenly wanted an Aperol spritz; in June, in Rome, early evening, the drinks were their own source of light. Outdoor tables across the city glowed orange with them. She looked around the room. An Aperol spritz would look out of place here.

Claire lifted the martini carefully, drank, and put it down. "The nuns in Rome, they invited me to stay with them, and I did."

"I know, that's sweet."

"I think—they seem—it's *possible* they might want me to join them."

"Poor dears," Monica said.

"I think I—" Claire said. So this wasn't going to get easier. It had been easy when Claire was seventeen, when she knew what she wanted out of life and life out of her.

But that had been before she'd lived a life.

"I think I want to try," Claire said.

Monica leaned back and stared at Claire as she sipped again at her glass.

Monica had initially sought to major in physics—what she called the "invisibilities" of life fascinated her—but the weekly problem sets did her in, and she dropped the subject. She would often point out, however, that she'd kept up with her second-hardest major, the life and times of Claire. For a long time, Claire had stumped her. How did all these pieces that were Claire—roommate, Yalie, Marcus studymate, inner-tube water-polo captain—add up to nun in training? But after graduation, Dorothy, when it got harder for Claire, the math got easier for Monica. Childcare cost this much, housing this much; how about your salary equaling this much?

Later math, trickier: How much was enough to retire on? Age math, trickiest: somehow the more years you added, the fewer you had left.

Right now, though, the math was basic: one drink, and Claire felt like she was going to pitch forward onto the floor. She'd somehow already swallowed half her birdbath. "I need to go to the bathroom," she said.

"Liar."

"Monica," Claire said, almost a wail.

"I'd say, 'start at the beginning,' but I *was* there at the beginning, or almost, so you don't need to go back that far. And I've been closely watching you, of course, for the better part of a year now. A little weekend away here, then one there, talk of this retreat and that. Mass on Sundays. You said you were plotting your next chapter. Dorothy thought we had more than a year, but I knew. I tried to convince myself I didn't, but I did. There'd been less talk of dates."

The same was true of Monica, though, so far as Claire knew. For most of her twenties, Monica had been too busy helping Claire and Dorothy to see anyone seriously. In her thirties, she'd taken over the reins of the firm, began sending regrets—and gifts—instead of attending all the classmate weddings she was invited to. Finally, in her forties, Monica had dated a guy, Clay, who was separated from his wife in every way, including geographically (she worked for an NGO in Latvia). He was going to marry Monica, have kids, as soon as they divorced. Everyone but Monica had known how this would end, and they'd been right. Afterward, Monica had not left her apartment for a month. Now, Monica would often joke, she was too busy running Claire's life to pay much attention to her own.

"I don't want to date anymore," Claire said. "I want to discern—to become a nun again."

The old man just beyond Monica's shoulder, who'd been seated in a large red leather armchair reading the paper, quite convincingly paying no heed whatsoever, now paused and turned his head fully around.

Monica noticed him. "I know," she said to him. "I couldn't believe it, either."

He smiled. "My residential college was Davenport. Nineteen sixty-six."

Claire raised her glass. "I was in Davenport, too. So was this one." She gestured at Monica.

"We're not meeting new people tonight," Monica said to him and turned back to Claire. He frowned, looked hurt, and went back to his paper.

"There's no need to be rude," said Claire.

"Look at you," Monica said. "So scolding."

"Monica, I need your help," Claire said and looked away. "Dorothy thinks I'm out of my mind."

"You are," Monica said. She reached out a hand. "You're also incredible. I have thought that since the day I met you. I *do* think you're crazy; I think this is officially what the kids call a midlife crisis. You are overreacting to a strange season of life when we all go haywire and want the comfort of institutions. Look! I'm sitting on the second floor of the Yale Club at age fifty-two. We like to be part of things bigger than us, that tell us who we are."

Claire looked around the grand room. "I'm not this." She looked up. She wasn't this place. Add some black mold, broken windows, and a cross or two, and this was the type of place she sold.

"You are Sister Whatever, then?" Monica said. "A nun."

"I really feel—" Claire paused and then said what she felt, which was "something." She said the word to her glass. The olive stared back. How many women drank martinis before they took vows? She took a sip. Even more after, probably. Was she doing this for the right reasons, or had she, too, succumbed to the tyranny of math? One more sister in the convent, and the Order of Saint Gertrude survives. Except it wasn't that simple. Nothing was, ever.

"Spit it out," Monica said. "Not the drink. This 'something,' a word that makes me feel like you're treating me like a two-year-old. God: tell me about *God*. Does he look like Ford—"

"Monica," Claire said. Claire was beating herself up just fine. She didn't need Monica's help.

Monica waited. "Okay," Claire said, "to start, not really a 'he'—"

"Then Justice Sotomayor? I hope so, for the universe's sake."

"Stop teasing."

"I'm testing," Monica said. "I think you're saying 'something' because you actually don't know if it's God or the wind in the trees."

"God *is* the wind in the trees."

"Pretty," Monica said, popping her martini's olive into her mouth. "So okay, I'll stipulate that you believe. Billions do. I'm not so lucky. And though I don't know shit, I'll bet to take vows you have to *really* believe. You have to tremble with it, tremble so much it frightens you."

Claire couldn't look at Monica. Or Ford or Sotomayor. Or Bushes, father and son, Clinton, Taft, their portraits all looking on.

"I am scared, Monica," Claire said quietly. "Really scared."

Claire had thought she'd have this moment with one of the sisters, or even the ghost of Mother Saint Luke. And maybe she still would. But it was happening here first, with her best friend and martini-fueled atheist, a calling to account. Not the easy question, *Do you believe?*, which actually wasn't easy at all, but the *Are you ready to give your life over to this belief?* question. Are you ready to be worked *through*, be borne along like a leaf in the wind in the trees?

Claire didn't know. That was the scary part. She said she was being pulled by "something" because she wasn't sure. But that something was probably inside the Convento di Santa Gertrudis. It definitely wasn't here in the Yale Club, or on the Terrace beer patio in Madison, or at her desk at their firm.

Whatever it was, was in Rome.

"Don't cry," said Monica softly, who looked ready to. Claire wasn't. "You're going to do this, aren't you?" Monica asked. "Quit the firm, move to Rome?" Claire nodded. It sounded like Monica was about to say *Are you really going to leave me?* and Claire waited to see what that kind of vulnerability looked like. But instead Monica said, "Not right away, though?"

"Nothing in the Catholic Church happens right away," Claire said, but what she was saying was, *Look, it's still me, same old Claire, just a little more sorted.*

"That convent's closing real soon," Monica said.

"I'm working on it."

Monica took a deep breath. "Well, don't be scared," she said. "I'm on the case."

And then she ordered another round.

* * *

Monday night, Monica insisted on not only booking a town car for Claire but riding to JFK with her. Claire had avoided the whole weekend talking further about Rome. Instead Claire and Monica had walked and slept and ate and talked and laughed. They weren't acting, just avoiding. But now, riding to the airport, Claire wanted the weekend back. She had to talk this all out. Traffic was slow; the car was quiet. They could talk now. But Monica was twisted away from Claire, looking out the window. Claire looked at her. She knew this hair, this head, this woman, this friend. She knew the color of her eyes, that Monica heard better with her left ear than her right, that grapefruit made her sneeze.

A hand tentatively slid across the seat toward Claire, as if of its own accord; Monica was still staring away from her, outside.

Monica had held Claire's hand when Dorothy was born, had been the first to hold Dorothy after Claire. Claire had held Monica's hand when Monica had heard the news that she couldn't conceive. They'd both held each other's hands when the other was finally deciding that this guy, too, was not the one.

Claire took Monica's hand, squeezed it, held on. She was glad Monica was "on the case," whatever that meant. Monica turned briefly, smiled, turned back to the window. Claire studied her. Monica had so much to give and she gave almost all of it to Claire. Occasionally, it was too much. Often it was too much, especially lately. Still. Claire knew she was lucky. She tried not to complain.

Maybe she could do better than not complain. Maybe—and who knows where this new thought came from, Rome?—Claire should tell Monica thanks.

She turned to look out her own window.

Cars, trucks, trains, planes, flashed by. People honked. Lights flashed. Sirens moaned. The city roared. Claire squeezed Monica's hand tighter. Claire wasn't afraid of the city, the world, but if you had a choice, why wouldn't you choose stillness, peace, light, God? Why wouldn't you find a way to live that allowed you to open wide in safety? Few understood because few saw. Few, save three women in Rome, and a few hundred thousand other women worldwide.

If by signaling serious interest—by declaring she wanted to join— if that meant Claire would get them to twenty-one and thus prevent the dissolution vote from taking place, great. Better than great. But ultimately, this wasn't about a deal; this was about ending a lifetime of deals, bets, barters. Entering vowed life wouldn't mean sacrificing friendship, motherhood. She wouldn't be able to hop on a plane whenever she wanted to, but they could visit her.

And when they did, they'd discover something beautiful—the Claire who once was, who would be again. Happy and content and relieved and fulfilled. Who wouldn't want that for a friend, for a mother? Claire looked down at their hands, still clasped.

They weren't losing her. They were getting Claire back.

The return ride to Manhattan was absurdly long, three hours, roughly how long it had once taken supersonic jets to cross the Atlantic. But Monica didn't care. It gave her time to plot, to make some calls and make some more.

By the time she reached her door, the plan was already in motion.

II. LA FONTANA DELLE TARTARUGHE

When Claire took off from New York, the convent had sixty-two days left. When she landed in Italy, sixty-one. Otherwise, she was delighted to discover that everything was even better than she remembered—the convent, the sisters, Rome, even her bed. True, to walk the city at midday in July was to saunter the surface of the sun, but that's why they went back and forth to Mass in the early dawn.

A week passed. Fifty-four days. Claire did runs and chores in the morning, worked the phones in the afternoon when her American prospects began waking up.

Fifty-two days left. She was fifty-two years old. This would augur well for that day's calls. It did not.

When the calendar showed fifty days remaining, the sisters decided to honor, or obliviate, the milestone by detouring for maritozzi on the walk back from Mass. Afterward, egged on by sugar, the sun, the calendar, Claire decided to just tell them.

I'd like to become a sister of the Order of Saint Gertrude.

Or, she decided she *would* tell them, because she found herself unable to say the words during the walk. By the time they'd reached the convent's front door, she was pale and sweating. The café waiter looked on. Sister Thérèse thought Claire might be ill. Sister Felicity agreed, said not to worry about the sale—today—Claire had been working so hard.

Sister Georgia studied Claire and then went wordlessly inside.

They fetched water, took her to her room. But Claire was fine now. She didn't lie down. She looked out the window, mouthed the sentence again and again. She just needed more time. She had fifty days. To practice. To pray. To find someone, possibly herself, who could save everything.

In the meantime, they worked on saving the convent. When Claire wasn't minding the door fending off tourists, she was in the convent office with Sister Georgia, searching through papers for a way to stave off the inevitable. Evidence of a forgotten bank account, or a scrap of historical significance that might helpfully stall a sale. Claire's meeting with the Belle Arti bureaucrats had gone surprisingly smoothly. Too smoothly. The Convento di Santa Gertrudis would make for a fine hotel or other commercial establishment, the officials said, particularly if that interior rose garden was converted into parking.

Ah, but Claire had been down this road—or parking lot—before. What if, she asked, during construction, culturally significant artifacts were found?

No, no! Mio Dio! Everything would have to stop.

"Artifacts? Did you show them Mother Saint Luke's key?" Sister Thérèse said. Claire shook her head and sent the young nun to dig deep around a rose or two.

Sister Georgia expanded her efforts to the convent's library, searching for treasures buried or bound. Sister Felicity was doing everything else: cleaning, cooking, double-checking facts provided in the prospectus that Claire was working from. (Did the basement really have fifteen hundred square meters of usable space? Was the cantina, or cellar, mentioned in some documents actually a second basement, and if so, where was it?)

Claire loved the convent, she really did, but there were days when all she could see were cracks in the masonry, beetles contentedly waddling across the kitchen floor. Cleaning layers of concretized guano from a high room whose broken window had allowed pigeons to roost for months was one thing; discovering there was no water to wash up with after—no hot, no cold, not even a half-drunk bottle of Pellegrino—was another thing altogether. A plumber came and went, but they needed a dozen plumbers, painters, sacks of gold. There was no need to clean or fix anything—it would be sold as is—but Sister Felicity said it was a matter of pride. Which was hard to feel when you fell asleep smelling of bird shit. Days like that went slowly.

Or they did until you looked up at the calendar. Forty-five days. Forty. No maritozzo, no word from a magic benefactor—even Bert Ligouri's promised thousand dollars had yet to arrive—and the only word from long-delayed Anna was that she was further delayed, "for family reasons."

"Pray for her," Sister Thérèse said.

Sister Felicity said she did some of her best praying when she ran, so out Claire went. She still planned to run Milwaukee's marathon in mid-October—or at least to train like she was—and in late July her training regimen called for twenty-four miles cumulatively by week's end.

Again, to avoid the twin onslaught of heat and tourists, she went early in the morning, when the city was hers to share with hardly two dozen others. The night nurse in teal scrubs on a teal scooter, buzzing home. The monsignor in a tatty beige cardigan (in July!) out with his dog. Wary, stylish soldiers lounging by jeeps outside myste-riously important palazzos. The pair of nuns in gray, striding to early Mass. Street sweepers with long, skinny brooms and pigeons with steel-gray beaks, all cleaning with equal languor, neither group quite able to pick from between the cobblestones the last of the confetti children threw during Carnevale, or the rice from the recent wedding. No other runners—they were all in the parks—but one or two walkers, women, nodding their conspiracy to Claire: *At this hour, the city is ours.*

Claire avoided the Villa Pamphili to give Sister Felicity space, and so ran everywhere else. The Circus Maximus, which looked like a high school's quarter-mile track until you descended into the grassy bowl and began running—and were still running, almost a mile later, having yet to complete a circuit. The Spanish Steps, meanwhile, numbered well over a hundred—she always lost count, but made sure to run up at least thirty before slowing her climb. By her fourth visit, she was able to run halfway up without stopping. On her next visit, she ran the whole way up and then turned, gazed, breathed. The sun looked as though it had been stirred into the paint every building used, all of it now rosy peach.

She surreptitiously tried Mother Saint Luke's key everywhere old; newer locks obviously wouldn't accommodate its profile. To keep it from getting stuck again, she'd grease it with lip balm, locally available and less messy than industrial spray lubricant. She'd had some success at what she thought was the Teatro dell'Opera's stage door— the key slid home easily; *of course* Mother Saint Luke would have had a backdoor key to the opera—but it wouldn't turn. The door opened anyway, and an irritated man appeared. "Piano, piano," he whispered, and Claire thought he was referring to the distant music inside, but later learned it meant *quiet, quiet.*

No matter. Soon enough, the sun would hang overhead like an anvil, no place to hide. But she couldn't be happier. Claire was no better at Italian than she'd been the day she'd first arrived; she might have been worse. Locals more often replied to her in English now. But something *had* clicked, and it felt like a click, the kind the optometrist's Phoropter makes swapping in and out lenses—this one? or *this* one?—to find a new prescription for the patient in the chair. *This one*, Claire wanted to say.

This one, because everything made sense. The buildings were red and yellow because the sunsets were red and yellow, and so were aperitivi and tomatoes and flowers, and the city was green, too, greener than she'd ever realized. Trastevere teemed with trees, vines, flowers. London plane trees, umbrella pines, blue plumbago, wisteria, bougainvillea. She'd once thought of Rome's spectrum ranging from bleached-bone white to sooty gray, the color of the Colosseum, the Forum, the façade of Saint Peter's, the Capitoline Hill. But none of that was Rome, or it was not Rome entirely: everywhere she'd previously seen no color at all, she now saw shades she hadn't seen before. The Trevi Fountain was faintly purple at certain times of day, tourmaline at others. Cauliflower, for that matter, was purple some days at the market, but sometimes green, or a creamy white. All the vegetables shone as if dressed for the opera.

Many Romans, meanwhile, looked dressed as if they were *in* an opera. So went the cliché, but so went Rome: caped policemen, tuxedoed waiters, military academy students in dress uniform with plumed kepis, double-breasted fronts, and, hanging from their hips, little gold—piccolos? no, daggers; wait, specifically, actually, stilettos. Which, but for a daring few, most women did not wear here because the cobblestones would maim them. And while Claire still loved copying the chunky heels local women preferred, she'd noticed, of course, that none of the nuns she saw wore heels of any height.

And she did see nuns. Everywhere, every day she ran Rome. They contributed to the theatrical atmosphere, but more thrilling by far was that they were real. They wore habits of gray or black. Navy blue or sky blue. Dazzling white with a black belt. Or a rope cinch. Or they wore layers, green, blue, brown, white. They traveled in pairs. They wore sandals except when they wore running shoes. To see even a single nun on the streets of New York—or Milwaukee—was hardly unheard of, but rare enough that you might mention it back in the office. In Rome, seeing a nun meant you'd see two more within the hour or within the next block.

Where were the men, the priests? She saw one or two. More near the Vatican. But they didn't fascinate her the way the sisters did. She wanted to stop the women, ask them: *Why, when, how, did you choose this life?*

And why, at times I can never predict, does the question become, Should I choose Marcus?

If she could just keep running Rome forever, she felt like she might find the answers, but she, and the Convento di Santa Gertrudis, didn't have forever.

They had weeks, which passed. Claire worked. More calls to America, more visits to offices around Rome, fewer results.

July 29. August suddenly loomed, and hard on the other side, September, the end.

Thirty-seven days left.

She'd come to decide she'd let her actions speak for her; she'd pray, work, live their life, tackle any task put before her and some she'd put before herself. She'd run and run and show them she could not be stopped.

Claire still awoke each morning: *Today's the day I'll say the words;*

I'll tell them I want to join. And each evening, she'd say, *Tomorrow.* And each day she would think that the words were burning so brightly inside her that she didn't have to *say* anything, that they would just know, or see. Everyone would! Even people halfway around the world.

"Back to one!"

Top of the scene, bottom of his career, another sunny day in Southern California, hot as hell. *Back to one* meant everyone had to go back to their starting positions and he might as well be going back to 1990. What was Marcus doing, shooting a bit part in Burbank? He would be better off if he did go back to the beginning of his career, given that his career had begun with a lauded film, a Best Supporting nomination, red carpets.

Someone had come up to him at the lunch break, paper and pen in hand—*Would you sign?*—and he'd worked hard not to smile. It had been ages.

"Whom to?" he'd asked, and the person had looked confused. It was a birthday card for one of the camerawomen. Everyone was signing.

Work was work: he'd heard it a million times; he'd said it a million more. He wasn't shooting a feature, but worse was when the phone didn't ring, and it hadn't recently, not until Monica called.

He'd been wrong to loop Monica in before reunion. He'd only wanted to work out the logistics of a champagne toast postproposal, but then Monica had interrogated him like she was the father of the bride: *What are your intentions?* (Happily ever after.) *Why the rush?* (It's been thirty years.) *Can't you just go steady first?* (Monica, can we not do this?) But they had, and some of Monica's suggestions had made sense, including asking Dorothy for—not really her "permission," but her take.

Dorothy had been thrilled, of course, and Monica had said, *See?*

And Marcus had *not* said that the only reason he hadn't asked Dorothy in the first place was because he wanted to spare Dorothy her heart getting broken, like his, if her mom said no.

Did it make sense that he loved Claire even more because, in Rome, she had turned him down? True, she'd not officially said no—because he'd not had enough courage to officially ask. But she'd told him what she was up to, what she was planning to do with the rest of her life, become a nun, which better deserved the adjective *death-defying* than any stunt he'd ever done. He loved her for this. She was doing—*something.*

He was doing a life insurance commercial.

The grips wheeled the Vespa back around. Because the fates had been increasingly cruel to him, the supposed location of this commercial was not some random sunny spot but, specifically, Rome. He'd winced when he read that in the script; thought, *Nope, can't do this*; told his manager, *Of course, can't wait.* Both were true.

The gig was easy enough, one shot in what would be a montage of life events. An outdoor wedding in a quiet square in "Rome" beside the famous Fontana delle Tartarughe. Marcus actually knew the fountain well. Built in the 1580s. Copies worldwide, including one on Nob Hill in San Francisco—and another in New Haven few knew about. Not that he'd tell anyone that story. Not that they'd care. They were all in Burbank, gathered by this prop fountain, famous, if it was, for being in the backgrounds of Three Stooges movies and, later, a '90s sitcom. Instead of the original fountain's four boys poised atop four dolphins helping, in turn, a series of turtles *just* nose over an upper basin, the Warner Bros. fountain featured just the four dolphins. Heavy sigh.

"Ready?"

"I'm ready," he said. Let the ignominy begin.

The makeup assistant, before she'd dashed away, had purred, "I don't know why they mistook you for the father of the bride," to which the woman playing the bride joked, "Maybe it's because she didn't touch up your gray?"

The bride, a singer, was the buzziest person on the set but wore it lightly; she'd been nothing but a pro throughout. Demanding, yes, but he'd worked with all types and had grown to like the de-manders best, so long as they knew what they wanted. She did.

He settled in to look at his bride. She had a nice smile. He smiled back. He thought of Claire. Then someone shouted and everything broke. Some tour group escapees had wandered into the background.

Marcus had shot parts of three films himself in various corners of the lot early in his career, back when he'd thought he'd be a leading man forever, and he remembered all the secrets, which fake store-fronts you could cut through, where Clint Eastwood parked, where Marcus was standing when Monica called him (an hour ago) and said, *I have a plan.*

Had Marcus still been in his leading-man days, he'd have had a plan, too.

Not necessarily a good one. The leading men he'd played always seemed to be leading lives that led nowhere. "Inaction heroes," said a zeitgeist essay way back when in *The Guardian*, which wasn't wrong. It got difficult when he realized he wasn't so much playing such parts anymore as becoming them.

And here? The director was frowning. The bride went to talk to him. Marcus looked at the fountain, the flowers. The priest-officiant was a chatty guy who talked to Marcus like they were old friends, had worked together many times, and Marcus had been nodding along, though he had no idea who the man was. Marcus had given a PA his phone—a self-imposed rule and ostentatious sacrifice; everyone else's came out at every *Cut!*—so there was no way to google who the priest was.

"Everyone back to one!" the assistant director called again.

The bride, her face barely hiding a secret, hustled back.

As Hollywood secrets went, Marcus's own wasn't much, but here it was: he didn't like it, not in front of the camera, not behind. Hadn't liked it since 1991 or '92, hadn't liked it since he'd discovered it wasn't like high school or college theater, that it *was* a job, his job, and a job that he'd have to win again and again, day after day, year after year. He was trapped.

Yes, in such a lovely prison—sunny hills rising just beyond the freeway, sometimes snow on the farther, tree-lined peaks. Maybe he could do that, be a forester. Yale had a forestry school! Or a firefighter. Or a cowboy or cook.

Things he would never, ever, say out loud to anyone, except to his therapist and then only once because the man had told him to make a film about *that*, an actor who doesn't want to be one. The therapist might or might not have heard the irony; instead, the therapist turned to *I don't mean to dust off an old line like, "Do you realize how lucky you are to have the career you do, the life you do…"* The words *were* dusty, but that was fine because Marcus was dusty, too, and so was the next line in the script, which the therapist didn't even have to say: *Then just quit.*

What next? The question they'd urgently asked at reunion like it was a bulletin from the future, when in fact it was the tired old tide from his past, coming in, going out. He hadn't quit acting because he hadn't known what he would do with the rest of his life, other than imagine what it would be like to live it alongside Claire.

The clapper came out, the scene was announced, the director yelled, "Action," and everything lurched back into life.

"Do you take this woman to be your lawfully wedded wife..."

Maybe the problem with the scene really was about him, he thought, and decided to put more feeling into it. The commercial apparently was about decisions, about how you could make many bad decisions in life so long as you made one good one, life insurance. Not that anyone would notice or care—he did—but Marcus had decided his character's motivation was that he would be the best of the wrong choices.

He leaned down to collect his kiss. Marcus was glad they'd agreed on the rule that you never kiss in rehearsal, only when the cameras are rolling. He thought to mention this to Monica, whose ever-evolving, under-planned, now capital-*P* Plan was that she, Dorothy, and Marcus would go to Rome and confront Claire, put her on the spot.

Here came the bride, a funny look on her face.

He puckered up.

"Da-*ad*!" she said, giggling as she put two hands on his chest. "I'm *not* going to marry him!"

Marcus's jaw dropped. They'd turned him into the father of the bride after all.

The director yelled, "Cut!"

So, that old ploy. Wyler had pretended to be furious at Audrey Hepburn on the set of *Roman Holiday*, her first big role, to get her to cry. It worked. Worked here, too, though it needn't have. Wyler yelled at Hepburn because she wouldn't, couldn't, cry. Marcus could have cried if he'd been asked, or looked shocked, or winced, or done a double take, or wooed a nun playing Juliet, or delivered all fifty lines of the king's Saint Crispin's Day speech from *Henry V.*

Because he was—

The bride grinned and gave him a little hug. The crew applauded, for either his acquiescence or his performance or both. Marcus smiled. Automatically. He liked applause. He glanced at the fountain. The dolphins appeared to be rolling their eyes.

As he turned to leave, he caught sight of the officiant, whose look of pity was the only genuine thing Marcus had seen all day.

Claire had always worried about money. Of course she had. Dorothy's father, Len, was no help, and even if he wanted to be, when he became a praise-band bassist, he had no money to spare. It was all on Claire. Monica had long been her safety net, but to be caught by a net was to be caught in a net. Oh, to have carefree cash like Marcus had! Claire actually had no idea what he had, but: Hollywood. She always marveled at the property transaction reports out of Southern California. Seven-, eight-digit sales by and to actors whom no one had heard of in ages.

Claire's phone rang as she neared the Tiber. Another day, another run. More praying. She checked the phone. Monica. Earlier in the week, she'd had a discussion with Monica that had gone sour. *If I really do this,* Claire had asked, *one thing I have to do is get rid of all my money. Vow of poverty and all. So: How? Humor me. A thought experiment.*

Call me back when you're not drunk, Monica had said. Claire hadn't been and hadn't called.

The phone rang again. Claire slowed to a walk.

Claire was frustrated with herself. She'd not been able to say the words she wanted to say to the sisters, and her idea to let her actions reveal her intention wasn't working.

She'd thus decided she needed a way to show the sisters she was serious at least about changing her life. More than faithful attendance at daily Mass and diligent work around the convent, around Rome. She needed incontrovertible evidence. Something that would convince them all—the sisters, Dorothy, Marcus. Monica. Herself. Something that, even if Claire finally did say the words, she couldn't go back on.

Like her money. What if she gave it all away?

The phone rang a third time. Monica. "My love," Claire answered. An old endearment between them, old enough and sincere enough that Monica paused for a moment on the other end.

"She lives!" Monica finally said.

"Like never before," Claire said. It was early morning for Monica, afternoon for Claire. Claire had slept late this morning, too late for a run, and Sister Felicity had urged her out the door at the end of the day. *It's good for you*, she said, but in a way that made Claire wonder if her absence would be good for the sisters. Claire had been asking a lot of questions.

"So," Monica said, "have you talked to Dorothy?"

Claire stopped walking. She was near the Garibaldi Bridge, beside one of her favorite pieces of sculpture in Rome—favorite because in a city where most statues wore togas or nothing at all, this figure looked Dickensian, top hat, great coat. He was leaning against a sepulchre he seemed to have just exited.

"What happened?" Claire began scanning her messages, her email. Nothing. What time was it in Madison? Drunk drivers were endemic in Wisconsin, but their peak hours came after midnight. Still, Dorothy insisted on making her way across Madison in all kinds of weather, at all hours of the day, on scooter or bike. A dusty tram thundered behind Claire and over the Tiber.

"She's fine," Monica said. "Sorry. Totally fine. Physically, anyway. I just think she's making some bad decisions."

Claire relaxed, but only slightly. Monica frequently critiqued various Dorothy choices, but never to Dorothy directly. Monica saw her role as not quite coparent, but someone with more say than an aunt. From day care on, she'd always taken an active interest in Dorothy's upbringing, and, for the most part, Claire hadn't minded. Dinners out, girls' weekends, and, when Dorothy was little, Disney World. And though not every adventure succeeded—Monica spent most of the Disney trip drinking at Epcot—Claire didn't protest. Monica had wanted a family; it hadn't worked out. It had worked out for Claire and Dorothy, thanks to Monica. If the price was being second-guessed by Monica on decisions large (Claire) and small (Dorothy?), so be it.

"Peter's not a bad decision," Claire said.

"Bikes," Monica said. "She just spent six thousand dollars on one. It has a motor. She lives in a city that's icebound half the year. She handed the bike place the whole amount and they're not delivering it for twelve months."

"She told you all this?"

"Her mother's in Rome."

Claire took the phone from her ear and looked at it. A woman passing by looked at her. She could just hang up.

"Sorry, sorry," Monica said, her voice tinny until Claire put the phone back to her ear. "I think she thought you wouldn't understand.

I was actually kind of proud. I thought she was calling for a loan, but she'd saved up."

"She knows you're still mad about graduation."

Monica had given Dorothy a thousand dollars cash for graduation, which had startled Claire. Not just because it was four or five times the value of Claire's gift—a simple, sumptuous gold chain, something that would look fantastic on Dorothy, and which Dorothy would never buy for herself—but because, a thousand dollars. Claire had money in the bank, a share in Monica's firm, but she'd never cease to be the kid who grew up in and around a threadbare convent with a single parent, later becoming a single parent herself. She never worried about destitution—not because she had Monica as a backstop but because she was Claire Murphy. She knew how to hustle, save, pray. She knew better than to drop a thousand dollars on a kid.

"I'd forgotten all about that," Monica said, unconvincingly, because who could forget? It hadn't been just a thousand dollars, but a thousand-dollar-bill: *Grover Cleveland, get to know him*, and before Monica could explain none had been printed since 1945 and that it was worth triple its face value to collectors like the one she'd bought it from, Dorothy had handed it to her soon-to-be ex-boyfriend and said, "I *told* you I'd make up the rent." He kissed her and ran off. Dorothy threw her arms around Monica and said, "I just love you," and while Monica's face didn't quite read the same in reply, only Claire could see that and only Claire—and every other mom who'd ever lived—knew that Monica had paid a bargain price for such an embrace.

"And you'll forget all about this bike," Claire said.

"I blame this Peter person," Monica said. "He *races* bikes, apparently. I don't mean, like, on foot—"

"Monica, what's really up?" Claire asked. She was on Via Arenula, still tracking the tram line. The buildings on this side of the Tiber were no taller than they'd been in Trastevere, but they were several centuries younger, looked freshly painted or power washed. Above her, balconies jutted out from buildings, their copper railings oxidized green. More than once Claire had thought to tell a nun or pastor: *That copper spire, those green copper gutters on your old building? You could sell them for scrap for almost as much as your entire property is worth.*

"Say you did double down on your madness," Monica said, "say I'm not able to get a judge to appoint me your conservator—"

"Don't joke."

"This part is no joke, and you know it: Dorothy's not ready for your money," Monica said. "And she won't be ready for it tomorrow, either, or next year, or when the next boyfriend appears. She'll buy another bike. She'll buy artisanal tricycles for aging cats. She'll paint her house University of Wisconsin red. She'll dye her hair to match."

"And that's fine, Monica. It's ridiculous but it's also fine. It is—will be—her money."

Monica drew a long breath. Claire did, too. The hill was getting steep. She'd meant to make her way up to the Villa Borghese through the narrower, back streets of Ludovisi, but in her anger had blindly followed a road that led to the broad Via Veneto. The American embassy, many embassies, were in this neighborhood. The crowds had thinned, so much so that Claire wondered how the expensive boutiques here did business. Twenty minutes ago, Claire had been passing Largo di Torre Argentina, a large sunken ruin that hosted a feral cat colony. On the sidewalk overlooking the site, a man had been setting up card tables of souvenirs. PAPA FRANCESCO, sometimes just the words, sometimes the smiling face of the pope himself, appeared on plastic tumblers and demitasse cups and magnets and towels. Two for five euros.

But up here, it was thousand-euro shoes, three-thousand-euro coats: all so exquisite someone would probably argue the pieces were underpriced. But wasn't it gross, too? Claire felt drawn to the Convento di Santa Gertrudis because she felt it might still her mind, calm her soul, but now she saw how much else it might clarify: money, responsibility, friendship.

"Her money?" Monica said.

Just two words, but the question actually being asked was more complex: Did Monica want to spend the money necessary to buy Claire out of the firm when she quit, money that would, yes, go to Dorothy?

No, it turned out: Monica did not.

Claire's face flushed. She wasn't Monica's equal in negotiating, but this wasn't negotiable. It *was* Claire's money. The partnership papers documented that. The buy-sell agreement mandated that. And it would become Dorothy's, and her daughter could do whatever she wanted with it: buy beer straight through to Armageddon or fill a kayak with cash, push it out into Lake Mendota, and set it ablaze—

Or buy a convent in Trastevere?

But Dorothy would never do that. In part because Monica wouldn't give Claire the money to give to Dorothy. It was like that, then?

Claire stopped walking.

"You don't have to buy me out," Claire said quietly. She took a deep breath. It was that easy. Giving up, giving everything. "Keep my share. Just make sure Dorothy's okay. She's not great with cash."

"Claire!" Monica said. She sounded wounded. "I would never—"

"Monica," Claire said, still quiet. She wished the sisters were listening in. "Giving up everything will be the best deal I ever make." Wise to just hang up now, but that would be rude.

But Monica already had.

Months ago, that would have stung. Now it was just more clarity, suited the Claire who'd started showing up in the mirror, the one who did nothing more with her face than cleansing and moisturizing, hadn't used a hair dryer in weeks, could probably give up the mirror soon, too, having come to trust that she looked like she felt, which was great.

She didn't regret the trip home; she'd needed to go, for Dorothy and Monica, but she saw now that she'd also needed to go for herself. To see this new life from a distance, clearly, see what a fresh start really looked like.

It looked amazing. And even better up close. She continued on to the top of the hill, expensive cafés and boutiques disappearing behind her as she walked into the Villa Borghese, a large park far across town from the Convento di Santa Gertrudis. This part of the gardens was protected by a section of the ten-meter-tall Aurelian Walls, which had encircled much of Rome since the third century. And here was a tunnel through; nothing could stop her now. Rome itself was showing the way.

On the other side of the wall, the Borghese gardens looked sunny and bright, speckled with just enough shade. Families meandered down broad paths. It was a beautiful day for a run. But the call with Monica had scraped her raw. She went down a gravel path until she found a bench that was not only empty but out of sight of any statuary—she didn't want any company, human or stone—and looked at her phone. Her screen was clear; no postcall texts from Monica. Or Dorothy.

Or Marcus.

In her earliest New York days, Claire had lived in Turtle Bay, on the same block as E.B. White's tree, the little "battered" willow he'd written about in his essay "Here Is New York," arguing that it exemplified life's ability to persist in a hostile environment. Or so Claire had been told. She'd never seen the tree, which was, or had been, behind a small apartment building across from hers on East Forty-Eighth. What she remembered better was the first line, about what a man moving to New York needed—he needed luck—and how Monica had given her a bound copy with the male pronoun replaced with an exuberantly blue-penned *SHE*.

But Claire had never felt more fortunate in a city than she had in Rome, and, conversely, never less indebted to luck. She was in the midst of finding a new life, here. Her forties, early fifties, had felt like one steady decline, a Milwaukee lakefront marathon without the cheering. Now, here in Rome, not least because she'd just climbed an actual hill, things were trending up.

Monica had once gotten a call from Claire at 3 a.m. Dorothy was sixteen months old. Fever of five thousand degrees or thereabouts. Pediatrician's answering service not answering. Monica got them to Mount Sinai Beth Israel and then somehow got herself kicked out for making too many demands, simple ones like *Save this baby*. Claire had blubbered that they would be fine: *Go pray*.

And so Monica had found herself in Stuyvesant Square Park, out behind the hospital, in front of New York's piddliest fountain, a thin stream of water jetting up out of a slender copper pipe. Pray? She threw in a quarter, took a deep breath, went back upstairs to do battle.

And look at Dorothy now. Beautiful and alive.

And look at Claire, six time zones away. Life at the firm was, to be honest, easier without her.

Life itself? Harder.

Monica had been back to Stuyvesant Square over the years. More tears, more coins. Today, after hanging up with Claire, she'd walked there without knowing she was. She leaned on the fence, looked at the fountain, then her phone. The Plan was stalling. Claire hadn't texted or called back to ask if Monica was okay, or to explain or apologize. Monica looked in her purse, but she already knew she didn't have a coin. She could toss in her phone. She stared at the hospital, the water, the fountain, the fence around it. Her parents, her father in particular, had raised her to believe in one thing only: herself. The universe above was empty, inky distances cluttered with the occasional rock or fire cloud. To stare up into all that and see nothing took courage.

And maybe more than she had, at least today. Panic is what Monica felt. Was she really standing here alone? If only Claire believed in her the way Monica did Claire. If only Monica understood how, exactly, Claire believed.

III. PIGNETO

EARLY MORNINGS IN THE CONVENTO di Santa Gertrudis could be cool, even cold, even in summer. It took the sun until almost midday to find the center of the roseto; until then the stone walls and corridors stubbornly preserved the night's chill.

A week after her call with Monica, thirty-two days until the convent's possible close, Claire found Sister Thérèse pruning roses. They were looking well. The hopeful archaeological dig had turned up nothing, but turning the soil seemed to have helped the plants.

The readings at Mass that morning had included the parable of the man who goes away and leaves his money with servants for safekeeping. Two invested and grew their shares on his behalf and were rewarded upon the man's return; the third buried his share and was punished.

"Looking for money?" Claire said. "Find any artifacts?"

"Sister Georgia told me to look for a road," Sister Thérèse said. "And why?"

Claire tried to explain the dragon map, the one drawn on silk, perhaps showing the planned road. She told Sister Thérèse that finding the road wasn't really the point, more that someone might regularly presume to cross through the property without consent. Like assuming you could park in your neighbor's driveway in perpetuity. "Adverse possession."

"Like Satan?" Sister Thérèse said, very gravely.

"I don't know your neighbors that well," said Claire with a smile. "I also haven't seen them regularly walking around in here. This angle may be a lost cause."

Sister Thérèse toed the dirt. "How's it going with Mother Saint Luke's key?"

"No luck yet," Claire said.

"Here, neither," Sister Thérèse said, standing, hands on hips, studying her work.

Claire had received an email overnight from a tech investor she'd asked for ten million dollars; she'd read a story that he was trying to give away all his money and "go broke" by year's end. Turned out he didn't want to go *that* broke. Still, he'd googled her, he said; she was cute; coming to California anytime soon? Dinner? He'd buy.

"If you had ten million dollars, Sister Thérèse, what would you do with it?" Claire asked.

"Burn it," said Sister Thérèse, without pausing. She was younger than all of them and never looked more so than when she was frowning.

"No, really," said Claire. "What if *I* gave you one, two million dollars?" How much *did* Monica owe her?

"Please don't," Sister Thérèse said, still looking at the roses.

"Is everything okay?" Claire asked after a pause.

"No," Sister Thérèse said. "And that reminds me. Sister Georgia has an errand for you."

"Can I help?" Claire said. She'd gone looking for Sister Georgia but had found Sister Felicity first, on an upper level of the convent, knee-deep in a dusty task, flattening a cache of empty moving boxes. It was extraordinarily hot, but Claire would happily work alongside

Sister Felicity for a while, especially if it meant they could talk about Claire's vocation, her "call," the source of the *something* whose pull she still felt, and whose haziness still confounded her.

And something new, which was old: Marcus. The longer he was gone from Rome, the more Claire thought about him. Walking with him, talking with him, eating with him. She kept replaying the memories of when he was here, as if they might end differently, with her in Los Angeles or him here or anywhere, really, with the two of them together.

Push-pull; it was tiring, and she worried she was tiring the sisters. Her plan to show instead of tell them was faltering. Was it because of things she'd already told? They seemed ever-more wary.

Was the reason Dorothy?

Marcus? But he'd won over Sister Georgia.

Or was it that Claire hadn't come out and said it, *I'm ready, take me in.* She felt ready, or close to. Just not ready to say it yet. Just one more phone call home, with Dorothy, with Monica. With Marcus, if he'd answer. She could take another trip back to the States, but why? She'd prepared them. All she had to do now was prepare herself.

Show she was serious.

What better way, in light of the Gospel of Saint Matthew today, than to announce that she was taking steps to give away her money, all of it. What better way for her to show she truly understood what a vow of poverty was?

But she realized she didn't.

"What was it like, Sister," Claire asked, "vowing poverty?" Given her background on Wall Street, Sister Felicity must have had to divest herself of a substantial sum.

Sister Felicity looked at her pointedly for a moment, and Claire thought she might just tell the sister—ask her—*Will you have me?* But Claire didn't.

"It was like this," said Sister Felicity, nodding to the pile of boxes. The room was floor-to-ceiling full, and as they had worked their way from the door to the room's far corners, Claire was sure she heard rustling.

It took Claire a moment, and then she saw, everything, always a test, in every room, a parable. Sister Felicity had owned many things—many boxes—but it hadn't been until she was preparing to take vows that she'd realized her life's "boxes" were all fundamentally empty.

Not bad, Claire thought; she was more advanced, theologically speaking, than she'd thought. She humbly shared her clever exegesis with Sister Felicity.

The sister laughed. "No, I mean it was a pain in the ass." She apologized. There was decluttering, she explained, and then there was getting rid of *everything*, winnowing down to a toothbrush, underwear. Running shoes.

And then there was the money. If Claire, for example—and only for example—were joining the Order of Saint Gertrude, she'd be required to take a vow of poverty, but there was a lot of small print. In any case, Sister Felicity would prefer that the convent not directly benefit from—say—Claire's assets, either. The donor of a large gift who then joined the community might have too much influence, even if that wasn't her intent. When Sister Felicity had joined, she'd given her money to...

"I love it here," Claire blurted out.

"We've noticed," Sister Felicity said after a pause.

Claire wasn't surprised at what Sister Felicity said, but she was somehow surprised that either of them were saying these things aloud. Claire had imagined so many conversations, but to have an actual one turned out to be heart-thumpingly different.

"I want to stay," Claire said.

"We've noticed that, too," Sister Felicity said, her face very serious now.

Claire waited. Here it was, the moment. The call she'd heard? It *was* real. Her future *was* here. In Rome, with these women, this convent, these boxes. She'd move even larger mountains to find the money they needed—she'd beg them to take some of her own—she'd get them back to twenty-one women worldwide. No, her journey to vows would not be complete by September 4, but hadn't Sister Felicity said evidence of someone actively showing interest might turn the vote in their favor?

Sister Felicity had remained silent while Claire's thoughts raced.

"And?" Claire finally prodded.

Sister Felicity smiled. "And we've been waiting for you to decide."

"I—"

And where were the words? Claire knew where her feet were, where her money was, where her daughter lived and Monica, too. She did not know where Marcus was and she wanted to, because he knew how to deliver a line.

Sister Felicity watched Claire and waited. Claire stared back, unable to speak.

"And we'll keep waiting," Sister Felicity finally said with a smile.

"Sister Felicity," Claire began. She wanted the woman to embrace her but she showed no sign she would, so Claire said the first thing that now came to her. "Is it supposed to be this hard?"

Now Sister Felicity grinned. "Yes," she said.

* * *

What to do? Break down boxes and pretend nothing had happened? Break down, period? No. Even if she couldn't yet say the words, Claire could still show she was a good candidate. Off to find Sister Georgia, then, and find out what errand needed doing. Claire hoped it was far away. She needed to get clear of the convent to think.

"Are you okay?" Sister Georgia asked when Claire found her, and didn't seem to care when Claire, annoyed, replied, "Spiffy," perhaps because the errand was urgent.

Sister Georgia explained that things had previously progressed so far with Sister Thérèse's prospect, Anna, that they'd scheduled a psychological assessment, a now-standard part of the vocation journey. This would be conducted by a sister with a degree in organizational psychology and offices in Prati, but Sister Georgia had booked Anna a "practice run" with an old friend of hers, a psychologist and former priest named Frédéric. He now had to be told the appointment was postponed.

But Frédéric didn't answer his phone or his mail. When Claire asked why they didn't email him, Sister Georgia laughed. No, the thing to do was to have someone visit him in person.

"Bring the key," said Sister Georgia.

Mother Saint Luke's key. Claire had thought it part of the convent's charm. Now it felt like just another chore.

"Sure," said Claire. "Fred can help?"

"Frédéric, and I doubt it," Sister Georgia said. "But to get to his place, you'll have to change buses at Termini, and *that* is where the key might come in handy."

And thus unfolded Sister Georgia's theory about where the key would work: in a storage locker at Termini, Rome's main train station.

Sister Georgia had been with Mother Saint Luke in her final days—they all had, but Sister Georgia had spelled Sister Thérèse for the night shifts, and "that's when you hear the stories." Not just of Rome, but of 1950s Hollywood, of 1950s Rome, of parties at the Italian president's summer palace down the coast at Ostia.

During those last long nights, Mother Saint Luke sometimes asked Sister Georgia to summon a cab to the train station. Mother Saint Luke insisted she had a ticket, she had to pack, she had to claim her luggage at Termini. "'In case of emergency,'" Sister Georgia said. "My theory is that it was her own insurance plan. If she woke up one morning fed up with the Convento di Santa Gertrudis—and we sisters all have such mornings, everywhere in the world—she could steal down to the station and slip out of town."

"But she loved the Gertrudans." As did Claire, so why—

"She did," said Sister Georgia. "We all do. And as you've experienced, we all have those mornings."

Claire missed the bus, switched to the tram, which bypassed Termini. She doubled back only to discover that they hadn't had lockers for years. She'd shown some soldiers on patrol the key; they ignored her and said to keep an eye on her purse.

On to Pigneto, Frédéric's neighborhood, which *was* distant, far across the city from Trastevere. It took Claire two more trams to get there, and the second, a narrow, rattling green streetcar from the 1940s, looked as though it had rumbled right out of a museum. When she got off, she felt she'd been transported to a different Rome, one that looked not unlike the Rome she'd just left—here, too, buildings in tomato and orange, ochre and caramel—but younger, diverse, and, despite the almost total absence of tourists, with busier side-walks. It was as if here, far from the Tiber and the Colosseum and Saint Peter's, people in Rome could go about the business of being people, not playing extras in an endless history drama.

Graffiti was sprayed on everything, some of it arrestingly beauti-ful. Exiting the metro, Claire was greeted by a three-story mural of a moody sea-green she-wolf as the founders of Rome—Romulus, Remus—and a pope suckled at her teats. Other façades featured con-temporary faces, massive photorealistic eyes. If the rest of Rome made her feel like she was walking through the ruins of a patchily remembered past, Pigneto made her feel like she was sifting shards of a forgotten future.

Street level was given over to the present: there was hardly a stretch of stucco that wasn't tagged somehow. *Sono qui* seemed to have a good run of it lately, and Claire tried to translate the phrase on her own. Hear me? Hear where? But then she finally gave in and went to her translation app: *I am here!*

"The nuns sent me?" Claire said. It had taken her pressing the buzzer almost through the wall to get anyone to answer, but she wasn't go-ing to fail this test. Because it was a test, right? No mere "errand," this. "Sister Georgia? Convento di Santa Gertrudis?"

The man who'd opened the door was hardly five feet tall, with the bald head and trim white beard she had expected, and a small gold earring in his left ear that she had not. He looked her up and down silently and then said *come in* in a language she didn't recognize.

"Oh—no," she said. "I was sent to tell you Anna isn't coming." She made a phone of her hand. "We tried to call."

"Anna," he said, nodding, not understanding. "Convento di Santa Gertrudis."

"Yes," she said. "Anna: not coming."

"Anna," he said. "Coming." He opened the door wider and then stepped out of the way so that she could enter. She looked back at the stairway. "Anna," he said.

If it was to have been just practice for Anna, why couldn't Claire practice, too? She went in. Sister Georgia had wanted them to meet, after all.

The apartment, like him, was tiny and old. There was a little sitting room with dusty-rose-pink walls. Beyond was a dining alcove with a small table, two chairs. An aluminum window looked out into the prematurely yellowing leaves of a plane tree.

"Italiano?" he said. Claire shook her head. "Français? Deutsch?" No, no. She was doing badly already. She smiled in case this was part of the test: *Reads facial cues, check.* She felt particularly bad about her Italian. If only she'd not spent so much of her time in Rome talking to American bankers. Money, as Sister Felicity had said, was distracting.

"Flemish," he repeated, slowly, this time in English.

Ah, so Sister Georgia, the linguist, was setting her up. Or tying her up; maybe the sisters were cranky today because they needed a break from Claire.

Claire belatedly decided to extricate herself, but he was already miming his offerings: coffee (no), tea (no), biscuits (okay, fine). There was much clattering, and a long wait, while he worked in a compact galley kitchen. Then a great crash, cursing, but before she got to the kitchen to help him, or announce her departure, he appeared in the doorway, hand raised.

"Stay."

A moment later he emerged with a sleeve of cookies, two glasses, and a bottle of wine.

"Oh, I don't—" she started to say.

"Is good," he said.

Well. The glasses were small.

He filled them to the brim. He sipped at his, snapped his fingers, rose again, and got a pad of paper.

"I am your guide," he said. "Understanding?"

Claire nodded, but it wasn't enough for him.

"To understand?"

Claire said yes aloud. This was a good time to explain who she really was, but he shook his head and got out a phone, said something into it, and then stared at the screen. Whatever he saw seemed to suffice, and he showed it to her. A translation app of some sort, not the one she used, but still: his language on one side of the screen, hers on the other.

I LIKE A TINY ANGEL, the English side read.

"Who doesn't?" Claire said, straightening up, thinking of Dorothy, a tall angel. He did not reply. "I do, too," she said, and still nothing. "I agree," she said, and finally he nodded.

"We are starting," he said. Above his head, on the wall, hung a small wooden cross, and beside it, a black-and-white oval photograph of a woman. "We are having ten—ten thousand questions you to answer."

"That seems like a lot," she said, expecting him to laugh. He frowned. "Yes," she said. He frowned. "I agree," she said, and he nodded and continued.

"How much have you to steal?" he asked.

A dicey one, right off the bat. Had she ever stolen from clients? No, absolutely not. Had she ever profited handsomely off a deal? Yes. Did that sound like stealing in Flemish?

Or did he mean that literally, like, how much money did she have on her? The nuns would want to know if she was the kind of woman who went strutting about with wads of cash.

Or the key! She should show him that.

He scribbled something down. Shit. Her nonanswer had just become an answer.

"Love," he said. He waited; Claire waited.

But in the word's wake, all she could think of was Marcus.

"Yes?" she said, and Frédéric waited again. The clock in the kitchen ticked. A cat appeared, large and orange, and he reached down to pet it.

"Go," he said. The cat didn't move. "Go," he said again. Claire watched the cat watch her. When she looked up, she saw that Frédéric was pointing at Claire. Leave? Because she'd thought of Marcus when he said *love*? How had he known? She hadn't even known she'd think of Marcus until she had, and now she could think of nothing, no one else.

She'd thought it would be easy. Not this interview, but entering a convent, taking vows. That the dire circumstances of the Gertrudans, combined with her perfect résumé—years working around religious people and places, an earlier encounter with vowed life— would make this process all but automatic.

"No go," she said, like that made any sense. She should leave. She'd delivered the message, she'd drunk his wine, met his cat—

She stood up rapidly, startling the cat and knocking over the wine. She apologized but started moving to the door.

"No go!" he said. "Love," he said, nodding. "Go," he added softly. The cat flicked a tongue at the wine and then looked at Claire.

"I love your cat," Claire said quietly. "I love Rome. I love the Convento di Santa Gertrudis. I love those women, even Mother Saint Luke. I love her weed-choked garden, her stories, her key. I love Dorothy. I love Monica. I love that they are always looking out for me. I love the stillness of the convent. I love praying with the women at Mass, how sometimes I almost feel like I am being picked up by my arms and moved. I love—religious life, which sounds strange to me because it's strange to say that out loud in my world and even stranger to an ex-priest psychologist who doesn't speak English."

"Go," he said quietly.

"I love the thought of living in the convent forever, teaching, working, whatever the Gertrudans will have me do. If they want me to move back to the States, I wouldn't love that, but I guess, the point is—the vows are—poverty, chastity, obedience—but the point is—the point is, I don't know what's happening. When I left Rome, I had a feeling; when I came back, I thought I had a plan. But now I don't know."

He nodded.

"I miss my dad," she said. She wasn't teary; the opposite, if there was such a word, and maybe there was in Flemish. She saw this clearly. "I lost my mom so young, and, well, time. That loss is a scar, maybe tender to the touch, but healed over. But my dad, that's going to feel like just yesterday for a lot of tomorrows. My therapist said, just talk to him like he was still here, but it's like here in Italy, in this room, it's a language I don't speak very well."

Frédéric didn't move.

"It's lonely is what it is. And I thought, after I got here, I finally had it beat. The Convento di Santa Gertrudis—"

"Yes," said Frédéric.

"There we go—yes, the convent, those walls, it was like a fortress against loneliness. And now, somehow, it's stalking me there, too. Maybe I should have found a convent where the walls were in better shape." She studied her hands. "Maybe I should have found a door I could lock instead of open." She looked up. "I have this key."

He said nothing. He'd understood nothing, or he was making her point for her.

"I should leave," Claire said quietly. He shook his head. What else could she say? Love. She had loved her parents. She loved Paolo's espresso, Roman mint in the market, the way the knobby cobblestones felt under her feet, especially when wearing those great heels. She loved sitting in the roseto, by herself or with the other women, the murals and frescoes swirling about them like whispered prayers, fading, but ever-present. She loved that after fifty-two years, she was on the verge of making a choice as profound as any she'd made before. He stared at her, waiting, his lips parted as if to say something, but she surprised them both by speaking first.

"I love Marcus," she said. She looked around: the walls were still intact, the floor beneath her still held. And yet.

"Who?" he said.

The interview couldn't have gone twenty minutes. But the pedestrian street had been transformed while she was inside. Before, it had been a thoroughfare. Now it was a party. Everywhere, clusters of little tables, lights zigzagging above. People were drinking, walking, talking, and someone was playing a snare drum, just the one drum, the one drummer, a drumstick, and a brush. Maybe he was waiting for the others to get there. Maybe he was the main event. Maybe he, too, knew what he loved. Claire found a table nearby. She had planned on leaving as soon as a waiter found her, but when the waiter came, she decided to stay. He said something to her in Italian and because she didn't want to break the spell, she said, "Sono qui!" And he smiled and brought her a glass of red wine and she sat and listened to the night rise around her. Upstairs in an apartment sat a man with his earring and a cat. Down here sat a woman with her wine. A curly-haired trumpeter arrived, and a woman with an electric bass. They warmed up and slowly found their way into a melody, which soon fell apart. Then the trumpeter tried something, the drummer followed, and then the bass. And then they flew. It shouldn't have worked, what she was hearing, and every few minutes, it didn't work, but for the most part, fragile as it was, it flew.

When she got home, Sister Georgia was sitting on a stone bench in the roseto looking up at the night sky.

"Good evening, Sister," said Claire.

"That took a while," Sister Georgia said. Claire started to say something about the jazz, the night, Pigneto, Anna, Marcus, but Sister Georgia waved a hand. "No need to explain."

"Thank you," said Claire.

Sister Georgia patted the seat beside her on the bench.

"I was kidding," said Sister Georgia. "Of course you need to explain. Tell me everything."

The trip home had settled Claire, but not so much that she'd tell Sister Georgia "everything."

"Do you—do you speak Flemish?" Claire asked.

"He's an interesting guy, isn't he? Before he was a psychologist, he was a missionary priest, to the Congo, and then he got kicked out of the country for helping to organize against the Belgians and then out of the priesthood for—well. We're supposed to be talking about you."

"He thought I was Anna," Claire said.

"Oh dear," said Sister Georgia, looking more pleased than concerned.

"I tried to explain but—"

"He's losing his languages, one by one, with age. Did he try any Latin on you?"

"Sister, I—"

"Did the key come up? He and Mother Saint Luke were fast friends for a stretch. He's also a poet."

"The lockers at Termini are gone."

"Just as well," said Sister Georgia.

Claire shook her head. "I—I'm not Anna. But for a while there, I was. I don't know Anna at all. Not why she came, why she left, if she's coming back. But I think I—I think I made a mess of things. I mean, not just literally—I spilled his wine—"

"You had *wine?*"

"But we got to talking—or I did—and somehow I—" Claire felt like she was speaking Italian or Flemish or some other language she no longer knew. She thought she'd made her decision to join the order, but it was somehow unmaking her. "There are days when I know what I want, when I'm *sure* I know what God wants for me, and there are days when I find myself looking for empty boxes, long-gone luggage lockers, and other reasons not to stay. This morning I was ready to tell Sister Felicity, 'Take me!' The other morning, I missed Dorothy so badly my heart hurt. I wanted to call my friend Monica, but it was too early—or late. I wanted my friend Marcus to call me."

"Tell me about Marcus," Sister Georgia said.

Claire shook her head.

Sister Georgia waited a moment. "Did you talk about all this with Frédéric?"

"We talked about love."

Sister Georgia sat back and looked at Claire for a while, both hands on the bench. Then she looked away. A minute passed before she spoke. "I entered the Gertrudans with a class of eight. Eight! Those were different days. Still, two of the women chose to leave after a week, two more after a month. They said they had thought it would be more 'fun.' The remaining four of us felt quite proud of ourselves. We'd chosen to stay. And we lasted almost forever, or earth's closest approximation of that, seven years, which is when you profess what are called final vows. But six months before that ceremony, the woman from that class I was closest to, Helen, came up and told me she was leaving, too. And she did."

Claire had been content to listen, but Sister Georgia stopped, as though awaiting an interruption.

Claire said, "Is she still—"

"Oh yes, she's still alive. The other two died relatively young, may they, too, rest in peace. But Helen sends me cards every year—kids, grandkids. Dogs. A horse. I used to throw the cards away without opening them, but I've softened." She smiled.

"Does Helen visit?"

"She did, once, during a European grand tour. And she told me in person what she'd always written, which is that I was so much 'stronger' than her, 'better' than her, 'braver' than her, for living this life." Sister Georgia shook her head.

"It is the harder path," Claire said. She was grateful to Sister Georgia for this story—for any story, to get Claire out of her head, to put her in a position where Claire might soothe Sister Georgia rather than vice versa.

"Then join me on it!" Sister Georgia said sharply. "For years, people have clucked about the burdens I bear and apologized for not helping to shoulder the load. Enough!" Claire put out a hand. Sister Georgia glanced at it and turned away. "I'm just getting started." Fragments of music came over the walls: an electronic dance beat bumping by in a car; a sighing accordion somewhere; a distant guitar. Sister Georgia breathed deep. "And that's the thing, isn't it? I'm *not* just getting started. I'm sixty-eight. Forty-four years a sister. Good times and bad, but I've never been alone. God has been with me. My community has been with me, even as it shrinks." She looked at Claire. "We need help. The people of God need help. The church is broken, broken, in so many places, so many ways. The Convento di Santa Gertrudis—the order itself—could collapse tomorrow—dear God, may it not—but we still need you, you and your heart that hurts." She stood. "I talked with Sister Felicity. She thinks it's too soon, but I don't."

Sister Georgia stared hard at Claire.

"Too soon for what?" Claire said, almost too scared to ask.

"For you to start your journey with us," Sister Georgia said.

This morning, the words would have thrilled Claire. This morning, she'd had everything figured out, until the floor fell from beneath her. Now the words settled in her chest, alongside those other words, *I love Marcus*, like a stone.

"I've failed at finding a better buyer or a way to stay. I failed by thinking this was all about money," Claire said, staring down at the ground. "I most definitely failed my interview with Frédéric." She took a deep breath. "And I've failed to tell you what I want."

Now was the time to say it, but Sister Georgia stared the words back into her.

"Because?" Sister Georgia said.

And Claire finally said the one thing she could confidently say: "I don't know."

"Failure is part of the process," said Sister Georgia, and waited until Claire met her gaze. "So is making up your mind."

Claire wanted to disappear, or start over, or shake her by the shoulders and say: *Help me.* But none of that happened. Instead, Sister Georgia spoke.

"I'm sorry," Sister Georgia said. "That was rude. And unhelpful. Discernment isn't simple, nor is it short."

Claire took a deep breath, found a smile. "I get that," she said. "A while back, I decided to train for a marathon."

Sister Georgia shook her head. "Isn't it funny? The worst choices we make are the hardest to talk us out of."

Claire never ran at night back home. The schedule never worked— business dinners and just being too tired after the day, but now that, after taking leave of Sister Georgia, she was running, she wondered why she'd never run Rome at night before. The air was cool, the streets were deserted, but she wasn't afraid. She was going to run a marathon this fall? She needed to get thirty-six training miles in this very week. She continued putting one foot in front of the other, following the road that ran along the Tiber. Eventually she'd dart through the massive Porta Santo Spirito on her way to Vatican City—

A horn tore past; lights blinded her. She thought she'd been running on a sidewalk, but apparently not. Or the driver thought he'd been on the road or didn't care. Neither did Claire: God was looking out for her, but she was also looking out for herself.

Rather than continue on the Lungotevere, an unofficial multilane raceway that hugged the twisting Tiber, she swerved cityside, descended below grade to the old road, a narrow canyon now, fifteen-foot brick wall to the right, the darkened hulk of Queen of Heaven to the left. Regina Coeli: Sister Thérèse had once explained why Romans had named their ancient, still-operating city jail for Jesus's mother, but all Claire remembered was the stray detail that at certain times of day, family members would perch on nearby hills and rooftops to shout messages to the incarcerated. She ran a little faster.

She cheated death again at an intersection that must have been two hundred feet across. Horns, lights, sirens, shouts; a scooter passed so close she felt its slipstream. Faster, faster. She felt like she was being chased. Maybe she was.

She loped down Via dei Penitenzieri, passed through the Vatican's old walls via a massive arch, and instantly everything fell silent. Fewer cars to kill her, but somehow it felt more dangerous, more unsettling, than when she'd been by the jail. She wasn't officially on Vatican territory, but she was close.

There were more than nine hundred churches in Rome, but Claire had only wanted to see one. Not Saint Peter's, which she was closing in on now, but the Basilica of Saint Clement, beloved of the Clementine sisters in Milwaukee. Would that there were still some Clementines to send a postcard to. But Saint Clement was clear across town from the Convento di Santa Gertrudis and the lines at Saint Peter's were always too long, so she had gone into the churches without lines. Not just the one with Jesus awkwardly hugging his mom, but so many others. The Church of San Luigi Dei Francesi just off the Piazza Navona, with not one but three Caravaggios, none entirely visible because the other pilgrims were too cheap to toss a one-euro coin in the light box. Claire had. *The Calling of Saint Matthew* came to life. One woman teetered, the correct response. Or the Jesuit mother church with its trompe l'oeil ceiling and, the afternoon when Claire had visited, an organist noodling through the *Star Wars* theme. The tiny nun-operated elevator at Saint Cecilia in Trastevere. The Madonna dell'Archetto, Rome's smallest church, dome hardly bigger than a golf umbrella, yet designed by the same guy who'd done the US Capitol.

Tonight, though, Saint Peter's. The outside, anyway. She emerged onto Via della Conciliazione. More lights here. This was the broad boulevard Mussolini had embarrassingly, and threateningly, laid like a red carpet leading from the Tiber to the Vatican's front door. She needed a drink, but Mussolini had put in precious few of the drinking fountains that ran ceaselessly throughout the rest of Rome. She finally found one halfway up the block. Not a proper nasone spigot but a small dragon, outsize wings arrested midflap. Unlike a normal nasone, there was no way to stopper it and send the water jetting upward to drink, unless you were supposed to put your hand in the dragon's mouth, which she would not.

She thought she'd run laps of Saint Peter's Square, but it was fenced off. So, she decided, fence to the Tiber and back, one lap. She tagged up and started back to the river, nodded warily to the dragon, who watched her closely. It was after midnight, but she'd not been able to sleep after the visit to Pigneto, the talk with Sister Georgia. And she had miles to go before she slept; Trastevere was too hilly and dark at this time of night to run there. The Vatican and its periphery, on the other hand, were flat. And oppressively quiet. She felt safe, but nervous, too.

Quiet nonetheless suited the run. Sister Felicity was right, running was praying, and both made her feel better. Whatever the outcome of this summer in Rome, she'd be ready for Milwaukee's marathon. The third time she tagged up outside Saint Peter's Square, a policeman stopped her. "Is not safe," he said, and waved his hand back and forth.

"Very safe," she said. Of course he'd presumed to speak to her in English. Who else would be out running this late?

"Not safe," he said. "Go home."

"It's safe because you are here," she said, trying flattery.

He said something; Claire wasn't sure what because it wasn't in English, but then he opened a partition in the gate and spread an arm: *This way*. Then he drew a finger in a horizontal circle. "This way, please to go." She could do her laps inside the cordon around the square, which of course wasn't a square but more of a keyhole shape, the vast space embraced by two broad colonnades. Each colonnade was topped by life-size statues of no fewer than one hundred-forty saints, seventy a side. She remembered the Clementine sisters of long ago bragging that Saint Clement had made the cut; had Saint Gertrude?

And who else looked down at Claire as she jogged around now—men behind security cameras, the two policemen sitting in the small police car parked in the square, Swiss Guards in harlequin pantaloons and maybe the pope himself, in whose general direction she waved each time she passed under the papal apartments? And then it was across the stairs in front of Saint Peter's and back down the other side of the square, the other set of saints, whom she nodded to as she passed beneath them. She thought about running up the stairs to the basilica itself, knocking on the door, but an unsettling green laser light swept the plaza before the church, heist-movie style. Hers would be called, *The Day I Was Anna*.

Two laps around. Four laps, twenty. Her watch said she'd gone ten miles. Plenty far. She needed to get back.

When she exited the fencing, the policeman waved to her, and she waved back and then he waved again more insistently: *Stop.* She stopped.

He held up a finger, talked into a radio hanging over his shoulder, and then nodded at the reply with a broad smile. He pointed back into the square. "Il papa, he is saying God bless you."

Claire looked back toward the papal balcony. More of a large window. The pope only made addresses from there; he slept elsewhere. He'd not be there now. There was a light on where none had been before, but she was too far away to see if anyone was out on the balcony. And when she moved to run back toward it, the policeman wordlessly stopped her. A little prank, maybe? She played along. She waved to the distant balcony, smiled, shouted, "Grazie, Papa!"

The policeman frowned and made the sign of the cross. She did, too, but still grinned like she was in on the joke and moved away from the square. She'd maybe seen the pope. He'd maybe seen her. She had definitely done midnight laps up and down Via della Conciliazione—her knees could attest to that.

But that wasn't the strangest part of the night. As she chugged back to the Convento di Santa Gertrudis, the first person she thought to tell the story to was not Sister Georgia, not Sister Thérèse, not Sister Felicity or Mother Saint Luke. It wasn't Monica or Dorothy. It wasn't Marcus.

No, the person she first thought about telling the story to was the drummer who'd started the trio off in Pigneto. Not that she'd ever see him again. But maybe she thought of him because he, like her tonight, had been unafraid. Maybe she thought of him because the memory of that early beat and swish he'd established had been tonight's mental metronome.

Maybe she thought of him because for a long stretch, he'd sat there alone.

Sister Georgia said she had to choose. But what if, for Claire, the choice wasn't yes or no or even maybe? What if the choice wasn't between convent life or marriage, two outdated, confining institutions?

What if the choice was to go it alone?

She ran on through the night, up and over the Gianicolo, the Vatican disappearing behind her, Rome rising on her left, Trastevere pooling in front of her, a dark expanse littered with lights. She reached the terminus of the Acqua Paola, its expanse of water looking as big as a bay. Finally, she was seeing it in person. It was softly lit and utterly empty. Claire felt like she'd arrived at a party after the last guest had left, the caterers invisibly packing up. Claire plunged her head into the water and drank.

Failure is part of the process: that was surely true, but also had to be something you learned from. If you *kept* failing, if you *couldn't* choose, then maybe you shouldn't. Sister Georgia was right to force her hand, just as right as the nuns who, years ago, had specified broken glass be spread atop the convent walls. It wasn't to keep men out or women in. It was to remind you that it wasn't a place to sit.

She began an easy trot home that accelerated with every step. She'd give herself a week to pray and think and make some more calls to buyers, brokers, boards. She'd buy the sisters some time after all, and some for herself, too.

And then she'd tell them.

Though she was exhausted, she smiled all the way home.

Back in Saint Peter's Square, a figure returned to the balcony, and, seeing no one in the square below, turned out the light.

IV. TESTACCIO

DOROTHY WAS NOT CONCERNED. HER mother was fine. Dorothy would know—just know—if she wasn't. It didn't matter that the locator app seemed to be breaking down—her mother's beacon had taken to disappearing for a day or a night, the app smugly reporting, "Location not found." Other times it would get stuck in a random spot. Most recently and bizarrely, her phone had circled Saint Peter's Square after midnight, round and round, as though carried on some mad clock's second hand.

Her mother would say it was a sign, and it was: Dorothy needed to get some sleep and stop tracking her mother so closely. Give her a day off, which would give them both a day off. And then?

The big Plan, the surprise.

Assuming it still was one by then.

Not to worry. Like all good mothers, like her own, Dorothy was good at secrets.

Such as: Did her mom know where Dorothy was headed now? Not likely. And if Claire gave the screen only a quick glance, she wouldn't have looked twice: Dorothy was in Madison.

What Dorothy loved most about her mom was that she never seemed at sea. Maybe all single mothers were like this, but her mom excelled. At ticket counters, on parent-teacher nights, looking for

Dorothy in a crowd, or even on lakeside beer terraces where her age was so discordant with the crowd's that she looked like an undercover cop, Claire was always steady, patient, smiling.

Her mother would make a very fine nun.

But what Dorothy wanted to know was why. Her mom had recently lost her dad, true. Grandpa's death had been hard on them both, but her mom kept saying after that she felt "lonely," which did and didn't make sense. They'd only ever seen him once or twice a year. Dorothy would probably see her mom even less if she disappeared into a life behind convent walls.

You can come see me anytime! her mom had said, and putting aside the fact that Rome was four thousand miles farther from Madison than New York, Dorothy could, sure. But what was so missing in her mom's life? After a long time away from the church—or as far as you could get while selling churches week in and week out—her mom had started going to Mass again, most every Sunday. Wasn't that enough? Honestly, it already felt pretty extra. Dorothy knew that fifty-year-olds did this, go crazy, but she thought they were mostly fifty-year-olds who were male or otherwise lost.

It might be—Dorothy didn't like to think this, but it might be because Claire hadn't had enough fun earlier in her adult life. Because how much fun was raising a toddler to teen on your own? Actually, a lot of fun, so far as Dorothy remembered, but maybe it had been different for her mom.

And if fun was what Claire had missed, why was she getting set to take vows?

Dorothy had asked everyone. Her ex-therapist, her neighbor, and even a religious studies professor. The professor mentioned that there was an ecumenical community of religious women across the lake. It wasn't exactly a convent, but the women were smart and wise, might be able to help.

The women lived in an old girls' boarding school at the edge of a prairie preserve. The day Dorothy visited, though, no one was at the front desk, and the quiet seemed so profound she didn't want to disturb it further by wandering deeper in. Maybe this was the kind of quiet her mother sought. (Then why not seek it here, Mom?)

Outside she followed a nature trail through some woods and along the way discovered three small cabins, each labeled HERMIT-AGE, each humbler than the one before. All were unlocked; the first two had a bed, desk, table, and kitchenette, all in one room. The smell, the spartan furnishings, active cobwebs, all reminded her of her YMCA summer camp, where, as a child, she had desperately wanted to go and, once there, just as desperately wanted to leave. The girls were mean. The boys were loud. The water had a metallic taste, like blood. Then they'd had a solo overnight. Each to their own patch of woods, supervised from afar, but still: alone. The next morning, when they all gathered, Dorothy was the only one to report solid sleep, not a moment's fear.

The third hermitage had a bed, desk, table, kitchenette—and a woman with close-cropped bright-white hair and a cross on a chain around her neck. She yelped when Dorothy entered without knocking.

"I'm so sorry," said Dorothy. "I was just..."

Part of Dorothy's plan—not the Plan, but today's plan—was to fake tears if she reached a roadblock with whatever nun she found.

But now actual tears welled up, not just because it was her mom she was worried about, but because in an instant she saw what her mom wanted, needed. Four walls. Quiet. A teakettle. A place to work and pray. A place to be present.

Dorothy tried to leave the little room, but she was fully crying now and so let herself be gathered up, served tea. The woman was a Catholic sister from California. She had been given the use of the hermitage to work on a book. She had postcards, portraits of saints, taped up above her desk. Dorothy asked about them to deflect attention. The sister—Laura—seemed to know perfectly well that Dorothy was stalling, but explained. The postcards featured tapestries from a cathedral in Los Angeles, a new one.

"Some people say the building's too modern, all these angles and planes crossing this way and that, but we live in a modern era; we're a modern church."

Right, thought Dorothy.

Sister Laura took down one of the cards and gave it to Dorothy. The art seemed both ancient and, sure, modern. The saint, a woman, appeared so lifelike that Dorothy felt guilty staring, but she couldn't look away. Above the tapestry woman's head was stitched the word LUCY. She looked young, entirely real.

"Saint Lucy is the patron saint of authors," said Sister Laura, "or maybe just people with glasses. Either way, she seemed like she'd be good company."

"Who's her friend?" Dorothy said, nodding to the wall.

"Saint Blaise, the patron saint of sore throat sufferers, and I had a touch of one. All better. We do a special blessing of throats, with crossed candles, around his feast day in February each year." She smiled. "I'm sure they're 'friends' in heaven, but centuries separated them on earth."

"I should go," Dorothy said.

The woman smiled pleasantly, not disagreeing, not rising to show Dorothy out.

After a moment, Dorothy said, "My mom was a nun once. Almost."

Sister Laura waited a long beat and then nodded thoughtfully. "When did she pass?"

Dorothy laughed, which she realized, too late, was not the right reaction. "She's alive and well. About to become a nun again." Sister Laura raised an eyebrow. "I know," Dorothy said. "I was surprised, too." Dorothy decided she could trust a woman in a Wisconsin prairie hermitage not to reveal any secrets and so briefly laid out Monica's Plan, which involved all of them—Monica, Dorothy, Marcus—going to Rome.

Sister Laura took it all in before she spoke. "Whatever you do, just be careful."

"'Careful' as in 'cautious'?"

"'Careful' as in 'careful,'" said Sister Laura. "As in slow. And a thirty-year walk back into vowed life may seem slow to her, but to you—to me—it does feel a bit fast. It's like falling in love. There's an infatuation phase where everything seems amazing, and then reality sets in. Not that reality's a bad thing."

"I don't think she knows what she really wants," Dorothy said.

"Neither do you, neither does Marco, and neither do I," Sister Laura said. "Again, I hope those sisters know what she wants, or are asking her that. They will. And it may be that they'll find out she really is called to be a sister. In which case your job, Dorothy, is to stand back and be a good daughter and let her get on with her life. It may also be that she'll find out she's not really suited to the life, and in that case, perhaps Marco should step forward and be a good friend."

"Marcus," corrected Dorothy quietly. "Don't you think he should talk with someone about all this, too?"

Sister Laura looked at the saints and then back down at Dorothy's phone. "He should talk with her," she said.

＊ ＊ ＊

Certain spaces in the convent functioned as whispering galleries—
the stone floors and walls transmitted the softest voices great
distances—and this was how Claire learned something was afoot.
Soon—tonight?—the sisters were going to host a kind of gathering
for her.

Unless the whispering was about Anna, the prospect who was
still putting them off.

Claire spent the day away from the convent, redoubling her efforts
to stall the convent's sale. Even if they *were* toasting Anna tonight, if
Claire came with good property news, they'd raise a glass to her, too.

And then Claire would tell them. She'd had a week since her midnight run around Saint Peter's Square, and that week had both agi-
tated and settled her. Yes: she would do it, she would tell the sisters
she wanted to begin the process of discernment, that she wanted to
become a sister of the Order of Saint Gertrude. Yes, she would tell
Dorothy and Monica and Marcus. Yes, she would tell herself, *Yes,
I've decided.*

And she had. She just hadn't decided when or how to tell the sisters. Maybe the sisters had figured that out—had figured Claire
out—maybe that was the occasion they were planning tonight.

Yes, that was it. "Yes": that's what she would say. And they would
ask, *Are you sure?* And she would—

What would she say?

Italian bureaucracy proving too congenial to the convent's sale,
Claire had begun courting other bureaucrats. An official at the
Vatican began outlining a process called "alienation"—this already
sounded good—wherein the property would be "alienated" from

church control, but—*clickety-clack* on a keyboard, and no, it turned out the Convento di Santa Gertrudis was not on their lists; the Vatican had no jurisdiction there. The Order of Saint Gertrude's casa generalizia must be consulted, however, the official insisted.

Given that the casa generalizia was the problem, this, too, was no help.

The Americans, though! If nothing else, visiting the American embassy would be distracting on a day she needed distraction. And so she spent hours being escorted from one embassy office to another, each handoff occurring with increased whispering between staffers. She talked about maps and dragons and roads, and hey, radon tests? Did they do those over here? A high reading might require lengthy remediation, even scuttle the sale.

The staffer sighed and said companies in Europe sold tour packages to *visit* high-radon spots; among some, it was believed to cure arthritis.

Now, *there* was an idea—but before Claire had fully fleshed it out, the staffer pointed out that radon was a carcinogen, and that it was five o'clock. Of course the staffer had been useless; he looked just like an old boyfriend of hers, Zack, who'd been sweet and thoughtful and kind and a little dumb; she'd had to break up with him three or four times before he understood.

Not long after, a marine—not a day older than Claire had been when she left Yale—was closing the outer gate behind her, while two others looked on from a booth nearby.

She remembered now: Zack had returned a box of her clothes by mail, and when she later turned it over to her local Saint Vincent de Paul store, she saw another woman's underwear in the box. Several pairs.

Who would she tell these stories to now?

Claire's phone rang. "Where are you?" It was Sister Thérèse.

"I'm at the American embassy. Just outside," Claire said. "No one seems to know how to navigate the red tape here, or even what color the tape is."

"Tape? I can't really hear you."

There was a pause; it sounded like Sister Thérèse was consulting someone nearby.

"We don't need any tape, and besides, our favorite market hall is experimenting with night hours!" Sister Thérèse said when she returned. "Come join us."

Was this the "party" Claire had overheard plans for? What if they *did* expect an announcement tonight? What if they sprung a pen and paper on her, what if there was something to sign and they had her sign it at the market? That made absolutely no sense, but what had made sense in Rome so far? Potatoes appeared on pizza. Pecorino in gelato. Marines secured buildings against her.

"I just sent you directions," Sister Thérèse said. "It's in Testaccio. Too far to walk. Take a cab. White cars. You can try to hail them, but it's easier to find them by an orange sign on a pole."

"Oh, Sister Thérèse, I don't know." Claire was ready, but not *ready* ready.

"Mercato di Testaccio, Claire," Sister Thérèse said. "We love it there! They love us! We think they won't love being open at night after being open all day, so we don't know if they'll ever do this again. There's supposed to be music! Wine! Or not! The market has lots of things. We can buy your tape!" More background din. "Sister Georgia said she's buying!" said Sister Thérèse, laughing, and then told Claire: "Don't walk."

Claire walked. Her legs needed the mileage and so did her mind. It took more than an hour, but the light held until almost the end and she saw everything. Up and over the hill of Santa Maria Maggiore, the basilica built on the spot where it miraculously snowed one August sixteen hundred years ago. Snow, in Rome, in August? Claire would have built a basilica, too. Then down past Nero's underground palace again. Past the Colosseum, where the arches made strange piecework of the sun. Tourists wandered, dazed; even the fake gladiators looked spent from a day hustling photos.

Past the Palatine Hill, legendary home of Rome's founders, green and quiet, now as then. And then the vast, grassy, empty Circus Maximus, no time for laps today. She was on an old road now, one Romans and visitors took when leaving by sea, just eleven leagues west.

But she wasn't walking nearly that far tonight. She left the crowds, wove into the neighborhoods, struggled up a walled-off street. Aventine Hill? The street's paving stones were much larger, rougher than the traditional cobblestones; tall stalks of grass grew in the crevices. Claire then found herself drawn through a gate into a serene courtyard. A grove of tall umbrella pines sheltered an ancient orchard of orange trees. Men and women sat on benches. Children played with a nasone. She followed a broad gravel path to an overlook that seemed to take in all of Rome. Her eye swept from the Vittoriano to the dome of Saint Peter's, the Gianicolo, Trastevere.

She was in Rome, she was part of it, better for it. Better, of course, because of the sisters, the Convento di Santa Gertrudis, Mother Saint Luke, her key, which unlocked nothing. But it didn't need to because Rome had unlocked something for Claire.

If only she could show Marcus this.

Time to exit.

She found herself on a narrow street that quickly gave up its sidewalk—and then most of its width, so that she was flattening herself as cars went by. Where was she? Her phone couldn't say exactly, but the surroundings were beautiful. It would be even more beautiful if the buildings she was passing—stucco apartment buildings, slender hotels, painted puréed-cherry red and blood orange and pale peach—had lower walls that she could see over, but for now, the sumptuous colors were enough. *Dorothy*, she thought, *look at this!*

Dorothy, she thought, *look at me.*

Claire knew her daughter worried about her, especially after Grandpa died. These last few years, Claire could see it in Dorothy's eyes, feel it in her every hug. And if those signs were too subtle, there were the links Dorothy texted, the books she suggested, like *Aging into Joy* or *Last Half, Best Half,* both of which advised giving up gluten, which apparently caused depression. Claire wasn't depressed. She loved carbs.

And she loved this life she'd found in Rome, in a convent in Rome. She loved the women, the work, the prayer, the rhythm of each day. She loved being part of something, a line of women that stretched unbroken back centuries, generations, far older and richer—spiritually—than, for example, that 318-year-old upstart, Yale. She loved the Claire that loved all this; she caught sight of her sometimes, in a shop window, a passing town car or limousine, the likes of which, if all went well, she'd never ride in again: that reflected, reflective woman, that Claire, looked great, no lie.

She would tell this, the truth, to Dorothy. She loved Dorothy. She loved that Dorothy loved her enough to worry about her, but she didn't want Dorothy to worry about her taking vows. This was bigger than Claire, than the two of them, certainly bigger than working with Monica selling old churches.

Come see me here, Dorothy! Come see me happy. I'm not disappearing. I'll live farther away, but that's what planes are for, phones are for; please, Dorothy, can I have just this?

And that was it, wasn't it? The selfish side to all this joy. After twenty-nine years of making every decision with Dorothy in mind—*What will she think or do or say if I take this job, date or marry this man, live this life?*—did Claire really want to do something without regard to what Dorothy needed or thought? Could Claire? She didn't know, only that she was in Rome, bearing down on joy.

Three steps into the market, she stopped.

This was like no other market she'd seen, even in Italy.

By now, she understood that American supermarkets had long lied to her. Stateside, those pale, flaccid green leaves hadn't been lettuce; the stubby orange sticks not carrots, and those reddish, sallow objects as round and hard as billiard balls? Not tomatoes. And nothing else in an American store would dare call itself a vegetable once it had visited Italy.

But here—she'd been to markets across Rome, but here—

She began to walk.

The colors were almost audible. And this was a sign. The colors in markets across town had been so bright when she'd first arrived in Rome; then she'd struggled to discern her calling and they'd dimmed; now they were vibrant again: The eggplants, iridescently purple-black. Tomatoes—shaped like teardrops or pearls or fists—

all so red she felt she had to squint. Peppers—red, green, yellow, orange—beamed from opposing stalls. Artichokes bloomed like flowering finials. And there were limes and oranges and sausages and a giant slab of cheese studded with spring-green pistachios. She bought it. She bought a carrot as large as a limb. She eyed a coffee cake the size of a car tire. She startled at the sight of a whole swordfish, massive, set atop its own bed of ice, sword tied to tail, so that it looked as if it was arcing out of the water, escaping the hook, ripplingly alive. Not the case next door. Here the swordfish heads had been chopped off and set on the counter, snout up, silver-blue obelisks three feet high. A man from a salumeria waved her over and she almost ran to him. He shook his head at the swordfish, handed her a thin sausage slice studded with all kinds of things, including orange rinds. She popped it in her mouth. A dozen flavors bloomed. Textures, too. His English was, unfortunately, quite good. Coppa di testa: sausage made from a pig's whole head, save the brain and the eyes. That crunchy bit? Likely the ear.

Claire took refuge at a pizza counter and almost bought an oblong pizza laden with caramelized onion and squash and olives and something that she and the baker, after two minutes of working through equivalences in English and Italian, gave up identifying.

A man at a wine stall waved her over and she went and then she was having a glass of wine. "Nebbiolo," he said with a shrug, as if to say, *I know you've had better, but this isn't bad.* In other words, he was flirting with her. To escape, she moved across to a stall that was selling purple paper cones full of—salt cod? No, calamari. She hated calamari. Rubbery and slick and, well: squid. She'd been through enough already. But these calamari—she looked back at the wine seller. He gravely nodded his endorsement. And the calamari's purple paper matched the plastic chairs and tables: she had a Realtor's love of a coherent setting. She wouldn't sell real estate anymore! She didn't go back to the tables. Shouting had arisen behind her, laughter, too, and she wasn't ready for that. She focused on the calamari. She just wanted her own private peace to last until the sisters showed. The man at the counter nodded to whatever was going on behind her. "Le sue amiche." She sighed. Something about friends. Of course he would assume that the drunk Americans (which was her own assumption) were her friends. She turned.

Chairs had been pushed aside, and in the middle, to Claire's shock, Sister Felicity was dancing and clapping, and now Sister Georgia went to join her. Sister Thérèse was on the sidelines, grinning, talking to a stout older woman in a beautiful forest-green drop-waist dress, encouraging her to join in. On a low riser nearby, a stage, two women, one playing piano, the other a clarinet. The wine seller appeared at Claire's elbow and asked to dance. Claire looked up at the sisters for help, approval, but none had seen her yet. Oh, what did one dance matter?

But he'd already interpreted her hesitation as a no and moved on to Sister Thérèse, who greeted his request with an exaggerated curtsy and then the two of them swung onto the floor, each lighter on their feet than the other; flight seemed imminent. Sister Felicity and Sister Georgia looked on with delight. So did Claire. Here was joy, there was joy. Here was community, there, too. And God, God was everywhere, but so very much here.

Sister Georgia said something to Claire, but she couldn't make out a word. The sister took her by the arm to a quieter stall—olive oil—and when that proved too loud, one quieter still. A locksmith.

"This place really does have everything," Claire said.

"Sera," said the locksmith. Sister Georgia waved a curt hand at him, and he frowned.

"I want to apologize for the other night," Sister Georgia said to Claire. "For telling you you had to hurry up and choose."

"*I* want to apologize," said Claire.

"Don't apologize," said Sister Georgia, and then stopped. "Apologies again. It seems I'm always telling you what to do."

"I need that," said Claire.

"No, you don't. You need to figure out for yourself what you're called to do. And you have all the time in the world to do that."

"I don't—we don't. The Convento di Santa Gertrudis closes September fourth. Less than thirty days."

"Pishposh," said Sister Georgia. "We'll buy another." The locksmith said something to her, and Sister Georgia shook her head.

"But the vote—the vote, the Order of Saint Gertrude," Claire said.

"God will provide," Sister Georgia said.

And God already had, so much, artichokes and swordfish and three sisters, countless runs, one spectacular convent, and one revivifying summer. So much.

But Dorothy, Monica, and even Marcus, even if they didn't quite understand this yet, had provided Claire. Claire began this summer thinking she'd spent her fifty-some years slowly grinding to a halt. Instead, she'd been built up, by her mom, her dad, those old Milwaukee nuns, and, she'd begrudgingly admit, even Yale.

But Monica and Marcus and Dorothy had made Claire who she was. And who she was now, or would be, was a vowed sister of the Order of Saint Gertrude.

"I have something to tell you," said Claire.

"Good. But we owe the man something for blocking his traffic. Do you have Mother Saint Luke's key? Of course you do."

The key, now? When she was on the verge of saying she'd stay? But Claire did have it; she dug it out and handed it to the man reluctantly. The man listened as Sister Georgia spoke to him in Italian. He turned it this way and that, rustled about in an old metal drawer full of hardware. Then he put the key back on the counter. His hands were small, which maybe served him well in his trade?

"He says it's an old key, which we know, and suggests we buy a new lock, which we won't."

"Can he at least tell us what kind of box it unlocks?"

"Door," said the man, who apparently knew English.

"He says it unlocks a door," Sister Georgia said, smiling, and then followed up with him in rapid Italian.

Grinning, he shook his head as he replied.

"I asked him what kind of door, and he said a door with a lock," said Sister Georgia. It was possible he was flirting with Sister Georgia. It was possible Sister Georgia was flirting back. He spoke. "He's asking you to dance," said Sister Georgia, still smiling, still shaking her head.

"Oh," said Claire, "I—"

Sister Georgia stuck a thumb in her chest. "Prima." Then she pointed to Claire: "Seconda."

"Sempre la prima!" the man said.

Claire watched them dance, watched them all, couples young and old. Monica occasionally accused Claire of being a flirt. Claire didn't understand how that was an accusation. She liked flirting. She liked kissing. She liked men. She liked imagining what was possible, and sometimes, even what wasn't.

* * *

The market's experimental night hours ended at nine.

Claire and the sisters left at midnight.

But not before the locksmith had taken a last spin with each of them, not before the last shopkeeper had stuffed a last free item in their last string bag, not before the last hug, the last *Pregherò per te!* Finally, the pianist and bassist could no longer be begged or bribed and the wine seller had retreated to his stand to rub his feet.

Trastevere was just across the river, but the women wandered in another direction, drawn by more talk and shouting and squeals a block or so away. Piazza Testaccio. Children up far too late played soccer on the paved piazza, where a few lonely plane trees grew. All around, parents, grandparents, aunts, uncles—locals—drank and smoked and talked and laughed. It was hard to tell where one restaurant's outdoor seating ended and the next began. One particularly popular spot was serving beer. Claire and the sisters took it all in. The kids playing soccer were very good. One boy, frustrated, took a sharp kick against the girl he'd been dueling with. He got the ball but at the cost of accidentally hitting a grandmother who'd been watching. She rubbed her shoulder where the ball had struck. He ran to her, eyes full of tears. The girl looked on, hands on hips. Time to go home.

In the taxi—Claire's treat—she asked if that much fun was regularly on tap in other seasons, not just summer. Sister Georgia said no. And then Sister Thérèse said, "You're going to laugh, but the truth is yes, it's like that every day, but here." And she put her hand over her heart.

Claire smiled. Sister Thérèse really meant what she said. Claire could see that and could see that what might look like sanctimony to Monica and Dorothy looked to Claire like Sister Thérèse was aging into carb-fueled joy well ahead of schedule.

The cab swayed through the city, the night swirled around them, the window glass reflected four private smiles, as twenty-five days left became twenty-four. At the Convento di Santa Gertrudis, the sisters, too tired for further conversation, bid one another good night. Sister Felicity and Sister Thérèse went up first, leaving Claire with Sister Georgia.

Claire opened her mouth to speak, and Sister Georgia put a gentle hand to Claire's cheek. "Tomorrow," Sister Georgia said, and then disappeared into the dark.

Keeping up with her mother could be exhausting, Dorothy found, but never more than now. Here Claire was, in Rome, living in a convent, and at roughly 1 a.m. Roman time, Claire had texted her daughter two words: *We danced.*

Dorothy began to tap out a reply. *What the—*

She deleted it and sat. *Do you remember, Mom…*

And then she quickly deleted that, too, because Dorothy wanted this dancing memory to herself for now: final year of high school, at an all-girls school that she loved but for one tradition, which took place in February. The father-daughter dance. Her dad never came to anything, wouldn't come to this. Claire and Dorothy usually went to a spa instead, but senior year, Dorothy asked Claire if she could ask Marcus. Claire said yes cautiously; Marcus said yes enthusiastically. But the night before the dance, Dorothy quailed. Marcus wasn't a star, but he was a someone, and the other girls would talk and look and not-look and point and giggle and be jealous but also judge, because did Dorothy really rate someone from Hollywood as her date? And where *was* her dad?

The dads would study them, too; Dorothy knew that they'd be the center of attention no matter how much they tried not to be (or, rather, especially if they tried not to be). Marcus would be cooler than anyone else's dad, and Dorothy would be mortified.

Marcus came anyway, to the house, a surprise, arriving at the door with a corsage for Dorothy and another for Claire and a boutonniere for himself and a hamper full of food that a clever assistant had ordered on his behalf. Mother and daughter were in sweats; he wore a tuxedo; no one changed. When dinner was done, he pulled a mix CD from a breast pocket that another clever assistant had compiled and Sharpie'd DANCE DANCE DANCE on. Tucked amid all the other tracks was exactly one slow song, and the first time through, he danced with Dorothy, and the second time, he danced with Claire.

But her mother and Marcus were just so *bad* at dancing, looked to be suffering, had even slowed to a stop while Dorothy had gone running for the camera, so that when Dorothy came back into the room, she crashed into the two of them, hugged them close, and the three of them slowly rocked with the song.

Don't let go.

Claire thought she heard Dorothy say it, Dorothy thought Claire thought it, and only Marcus knew the truth: for as long as they all held on, he might just be the happiest.

Years later, Dorothy had the app, but she didn't need a blue beacon to know her mother was nearby. She could just feel it. She'd tried explaining this to her once, and her mom probably didn't remember.

Dorothy hoped she didn't because Claire had said to Dorothy, *No, I don't know what you're talking about.*

What Dorothy was talking about was this: that when she was within a mile of her mom, a block, a dozen feet, or in the same living room, she could feel her, an electric charge, up and down, the two of them irrevocably together.

V. TERMINI

DOROTHY WOULD FEEL SUCH A charge twenty days later, September 1, ninety-seven days since her mother first went to Rome, fifty-nine days since Claire had returned, twenty-four hours since Dorothy herself had secretly arrived in Rome.

Against Dorothy's every expectation, The Plan was proceeding to plan.

Its core principle was that they would do whatever they had to do together. Dorothy, Monica, Marcus. So even though Dorothy had beaten them to Rome, she was to wait to see her mother until Monica and Marcus arrived. To have not seen her mom immediately felt bizarre, answering her mother's texts as though Dorothy was still in Madison even more so. *It's so*—quick app check—*sunny in Madison today, Mom!*

But it's 3 a.m.? her mom replied.

Ha! You know me, Mom, and Claire did, but, Dorothy hoped, not well enough to detect her daughter's presence nearby.

Dorothy had planned to meet Monica and Marcus at the airport. But they'd each waved her off, and that was okay, too. It would give her a few more hours to see Rome. It seemed doubtful that, after today, she—or her mother—would ever be back, so why not make the most of what time she had? A welcome distraction if nothing else. So she was off to see Saint Peter's this morning, then Castel Sant'Angelo, then a walk up the Gianicolo for the view of Rome, and finally, a stroll down past the Convento di Santa Gertrudis to scope things out one last time. If she happened to catch her mother out and about, so much the better. Monica said plans had to be flexible.

The first thing Dorothy wanted to do when she saw her mom was apologize. Or hug her, then apologize. For getting so upset in Madison, for going along with Monica's plan to disrupt whatever was happening now. Because while Dorothy didn't really get the whole convent thing, she did get that joining one meant joining a community—as countercultural a community as you'd find nowadays—and that there must be something powerful in that.

No wonder her mother sounded happier these days than she had in her entire life.

Dorothy refreshed the screen. Her mother hadn't moved. Satisfied, Dorothy headed off to join the line in Saint Peter's Square.

September, and the Plan, had finally begun.

Several North American congregations of nuns were pooling people and resources to have a small side-chapel Mass said at Saint Peter's for the intentions of their new postulants studying in Rome. A sidewalk café lunch in Prati would follow.

Sister Thérèse, Sister Felicity, and Sister Georgia knew some of the new women from teaching, and they invited Claire to join them—a Mass was a wonderful way to visit Saint Peter's, and it would be fun for Claire to meet their confreres in Rome. A happy occasion, but Claire felt more jittery than she had in years. For one, something was afoot among the sisters.

Claire had loved living in community this summer with the women, but she hadn't loved all of it. She hadn't had roommates for a long time. She hadn't wanted to be nudged about doing laundry. She was fairly sure Sister Georgia cheated at cards. And Sister Thérèse's effort to poison them all with her coffee making was relentless. She'd mismeasured how much to put into the Bialetti this very morning and given everyone the equivalent of a triple espresso. Which might have been fine, but Claire had also gotten up early, gone for a run, and stopped by Paolo's coffee bar on the way back.

Big day today, Paolo. I'm going to tell them.

Tell them what?

I don't know, she began. She meant to add, *How to say it in Italian,* but the words hung there unspoken, like she'd forgotten the English, too.

Paolo waited and then smiled. *Good*, he said. *In bocca al lupo.*

She chewed on that on the way home—it sounded like he'd said something about the mouth of a wolf, which made no sense, though maybe he understood what was coming better than she.

Tomorrow, Sister Georgia had told Claire at the end of the Testaccio market night, and she'd been right to hit pause; Claire had been so high on Rome, the sisters, dancing—and not a little wine—she would have signed up for anything. But when tomorrow had come, it had brought with it a thousand tasks and deadlines and locks to be tried. She'd been ready to commit but wanted to do so on a day when her mind was clear—clear enough, anyway, to know that it was time. Days passed; distractions mounted; the deadline loomed. The sisters' attention was scattered. And then this special trip to Saint Peter's had arisen. If this wasn't a day to tell them, what was?

Other than bouncing off the walls, Claire hadn't signaled to the sisters that any announcement was pending. Sister Felicity had raised an eyebrow when Claire had handed over her phone and asked her to safeguard it in the office, though she'd accepted Claire's explanation. A special trip to the Vatican: Claire wanted to be as present as possible.

But—*would* Dorothy call? Like all the mothers she knew, Claire had a gossamer tether to her child, one that could even stretch across oceans, and indeed, stretched that far, that tight, vibrated louder than when plucked closer to home.

Claire was also anxious that she'd been volunteered to do a reading (in English) at the Mass. The reading was from Psalm 19 and ended with this strange poetry: "The judgments of the Lord are true; they are righteous altogether. / They are more desirable than gold, yes, than much fine gold; / Sweeter also than honey and the drippings of the honeycomb." Much as Claire loved that unexpected word, *drippings*, she couldn't say it without stumbling over *honeycomb* when she practiced. She wasn't sure if it was because the words themselves seemed sticky or if it was the combination of consonants, but she knew that Marcus would absolutely be able to help her sort it out. She didn't have her phone, but she looked at her watch and did the math as if she could call him: 8 a.m. in Rome; 11 p.m. in Los Angeles. Where would he be?

Just out of sight. Marcus had given Dorothy the wrong flight number, a lie he hoped she'd later forgive—or at least forget, in the likely tumult that would ensue. He wanted to enter Rome alone. He liked Monica's plan fine. He didn't necessarily think it *was* a plan—show up at the front door of the convent and ring the bell was step one, and a big celebratory meal en route to the flight home was the last step. In between, much ad libbing, which he'd told Monica didn't happen as much as audiences thought it did.

He had his own plan, and it involved seeing Claire first, alone.

It was hardly the first trip to Saint Peter's for the sisters, but there was no such thing as an "ordinary" visit there, and so the plans had been worked out well in advance. Complicating matters was Sister Georgia's insistence that they stop by Borri Books in Termini on the way; she had to pick up a novel there that she'd ordered for a friend who'd be at the Vatican today. Then they'd transfer to the metro, and—

"It would be so much easier to *walk* straight to Saint Peter's," said Sister Thérèse for the fourth time that morning and perhaps the fortieth time this week. "You can pick up the book some other time."

Again, there was this side, too, to community life. Squabbling over books and buses, all while the largest edifice in Christendom awaited.

Claire began to feel ill.

Marcus's arms were laden with flowers. Roses had seemed cliché, but then not having them seemed a glaring omission, one he'd decided to make up for by overbuying. Asters and zinnias and coneflowers and dahlias. Black-eyed Susans. Lavender and lilies and lisianthus. He'd broken a sweat coming up the hill.

And then he'd seen them, the women, clustered on the street outside the convent. He slowed. He didn't want to explain, not with his face surrounded by flowers. He just wanted to see Claire for a minute, alone. Was that too much to ask, God? He'd tried talking to God in the last week or so, feeling like he'd won at least proxy access, having been Claire's friend for more than thirty years. *God? Do me a favor? Get these women inside and get Claire outside.* Where was Claire, for that matter? The women looked all dressed up.

Claire glowed like she had the first time he saw her.

She did not see him.

He felt unexpectedly small, seventeen again, scrawny and wet from the shower, when Claire hadn't initially seemed to see *him*—him, the Marcus Sardeson millions had seen, for better and worse, since then—rather, just a boy who didn't belong where he was.

The line was endless but moved steadily. Dorothy used her phone to read all about the square, the church, the pope, marble, Tuscany, wine, wild boar, one Wikipedia article leaping to countless others, while she waited. She and her mom had never tackled Europe; they'd been so busy with notching the fifty states, a quest that had ended in South Dakota.

She checked her watch: 9 a.m. Monica's flight would land at eleven, then customs, car or train from the airport to central Rome, check in at the hotel, where Dorothy had already stashed her luggage. She'd see Monica around two, earliest. Marcus's flight landed at one, so maybe Dorothy wouldn't see him until four, although he moved faster than Monica. In any case, they'd all meet at Monica's hotel at five, review the Plan one last time, and then march over to the Convento di Santa Gertrudis. In short, plenty of time. So why was her heart already racing?

The bus to Termini was late.

"Of *course* it's late," said Sister Thérèse.

"Enough," said Sister Felicity. "We'll take a taxi."

Claire ran inside to get the community purse. Anything to escape this awkwardness.

With Claire gone, the real source of the argument surfaced.

"Sister Georgia put Claire's name down on the list of women to be celebrated today," Sister Thérèse told Sister Felicity. "I said that would make it look like she was an actual postulant and Sister Georgia said—"

"Sister Georgia!" Sister Felicity said.

But Sister Georgia wasn't paying attention.

"Who do you think is getting all those flowers?" Sister Georgia said, squinting toward Marcus, who was too far away for her to recognize.

"Perhaps he's selling them," said Sister Thérèse, happy for the respite. "You should do that, Sister Georgia. You have such lovely roses. Though—"

"Flowers belong where they're planted. I've never seen the purpose of cutting them."

"Let's go inside," Sister Georgia said, and stepped back into the vestibule.

Just as Sister Thérèse and Sister Felicity made to follow her, the convent's shared cell phone rang. Sister Thérèse studied the caller ID.

"Delaware?" Sister Felicity asked. "Boston?"

"New York, looks like," Sister Thérèse said. "Anna?" Her eyes widened, but Sister Felicity waved the call off.

"I'll call her back," Sister Felicity said, staring toward Marcus. "I'll deal with this one first."

Marcus looked around wildly.

"Stammi lontano," said Sister Felicity as he approached.

"Such pretty flowers," Sister Thérèse said.

Sister Felicity noted that her poor Italian had registered no impact and so switched to English. "You'll find women dislike empty gestures," she said. "Good day."

He'd rehearsed many scenarios, even this one. Farfetched, he'd thought: Claire locked inside, two sisters outside, perhaps another of them just on the other side of the door, barring his entrance. But here he was. Action!

I need to marry her. We belong together and she is making a mistake.

But go ahead, try saying that to two angry nuns. Marcus put the flowers down and left. (Fled.)

Monica texted Claire again. Unforgivable. It was fine that Claire had needed space—she'd put an entire ocean between them—but not answering texts, or calls, or telepathic transmissions, for weeks was not acceptable. Never mind that Monica had endured vast empty mornings, evenings, weekends, when she normally would have been tending to Claire's life. Never mind that she'd had to spend part of that time cleaning up Claire's messes in the States, and in Rome, clients calling: *Why is Claire Murphy trying to sell me a pile of bricks in Italy that I can't even take possession of?*

Never mind. So long as Claire was okay, hadn't done anything rash yet, never mind.

Monica reread the last text she'd sent Claire. Hadn't she been clear? *Claire, I'm here. In Italy. My limo left because I was late through customs. Taking train. ETA 13:10 at something called "Termini." Meet me there? Much to discuss.*

Next, a text to Dorothy and another to Marcus. Except she couldn't bring herself to send them. Monica was no longer so certain of the Plan.

Sister Thérèse retrieved Sister Georgia from the vestibule.

"Claire's somewhere inside, taking forever," Sister Georgia said.

"She's obsessed with that key," Sister Felicity said. "She's probably trying to use it to unlock the office."

"It doesn't work in that lock," Sister Thérèse said.

"That's why it's taking her so long."

But when Sister Felicity went inside to rescue Claire from the office, she couldn't find her. Claire might have gone up to her room to retrieve her own money, but that was unacceptable, too, so Sister Felicity simply grabbed the community purse from the office and headed back to the front door.

When Sister Felicity got outside, the other sisters waved urgently. The bus was arriving.

"Go on ahead. Claire and I will follow you," Sister Felicity said. Sister Thérèse frowned but climbed aboard. Sister Georgia followed, looking pleased as the door closed behind her.

Claire's door was closed, too, when Sister Felicity went to check on her.

And why wouldn't it be? Claire was overcome, Sister Felicity thought; she was exhausted; she'd had her hand confusingly forced by Sister Georgia, who'd involved her in that Mass at Saint Peter's. That's why Claire was hiding; that's why she'd been a bundle of nerves.

Sister Felicity stood in the middle of the roseto and checked her watch. When Claire finally emerged, they would walk to Saint Peter's. They'd run if she wanted to! Whatever Claire wanted. How Sister Felicity had mishandled her. All those years in New York, she'd always known exactly what to do. She'd gotten rusty in Rome, particularly with respect to a flaw she'd always suffered, not knowing how best to get or give bad news. She cast one last glance up toward Claire's room. The door was still shut fast.

Sister Felicity turned and went into the office, shut the door, sat at her desk. She'd meant to cancel the landline to save money but hadn't. She now wished she had. She picked it up, dialed.

"Anna?"

When the call was done, she hung up the receiver and stared at it. It would not have been a silver bullet—or key—but it would have meant something. Money would mean more, ultimately. But Anna, whom they had waited for, prayed for, for so long, Anna would have meant a lot.

Sister Felicity could go on ahead, alone, to Saint Peter's. But she didn't want to. She wanted right now to be with her community, small as it was, and that community was headed to Termini. Knowing Rome's public transit, they'd likely as not be stranded there, well short of the goal. For once, that would work in Sister Felicity's favor.

She left the convent and began walking down the hill to the Tiber, talking to herself the whole way. Sister Felicity really had had hopes for Anna, but if she was being honest, even higher hopes for Claire. Something had happened to Claire over the summer, or was happening. Some sauces cooked slowly. Sister Georgia had ruined everything by turning it up to a boil.

Sister Felicity wondered if she was ruining things further by leaving Claire be, alone in the convent, but decided what Claire needed right now was time, quiet, solitude.

Claire most definitely did not need to hear from Sister Felicity that Anna had finally made her decision—*no, thank you*—and thus, barring miracles, the Convento di Santa Gertrudis would close, followed shortly thereafter by the Order of Saint Gertrude itself.

The entire convent had been quiet when Claire had come back inside; she'd thought it odd that the absence of three women could make the vast edifice feel any emptier, but it did. She climbed the steps to her room, to secretly borrow money from her own stash to spare the convent whatever expenses might arise today.

And then she entered her room and stopped and sat and stared.

Hanging on the back of her door was a hook and, on the hook, a long white gown and with the gown, a veil.

Not just white, supernova white. So bright it bleached everything else in the room of color, everything in the convent of sound.

It was a novice's habit, and it was beautiful.

She wouldn't remember moving across the room, but she did so, undressing, taking the habit from the hanger, and slipping it on. She'd expected it to be rough; it was smooth. Tucking her hair inside the veil and then arranging it around her forehead was simpler than she'd imagined, too.

The room, of course, had no mirror. None did, and she couldn't bring herself to dig in her purse. But she saw her reflection in the window and began to cry, both because she looked exactly the way she'd looked when she was twenty and because she didn't. She looked fifty-two in the mirror. She looked fifty-two and radiant.

She sat and prayed and wondered and prayed and sat and thought and didn't think for one moment about the sisters waiting for her outside—were they? was there still an outside?—and tried to make sense of it all. This was a novice habit; she was not a novice. She was, if anything, on the precipice of becoming a postulant. Postulants did not wear habits; they received them when entering their novitiate. A postulant might spend six months to a year in formation, studying, discerning, deciding. This was too soon.

Who had put the habit here?

Why had Claire put it on?

A thought occurred. Claire would do what whoever had left her this habit intended for her to do: experience vowed life as a novice, however briefly, take a kind of spacewalk through Rome. She'd go out front, find the sisters, explain that she wanted to make the trip to Saint Peter's on her own. Or she'd not find the sisters. In either case, she'd make her way across the city alone. She'd stop by Termini, where the sisters were headed. Along the way, she'd visit her favorite coffee bar, see Paolo, gauge his reaction, and then continue, seeing how the world saw her. If Rome saw her as a nun, as someone befitting vowed life, then Claire might finally, fully, see herself that way as well.

How very clever of these wise sisters of Saint Gertrude. It was odd they didn't tell her about this earlier. Maybe Sister Felicity had been about to, or the others had. Everyone had seemed distracted this morning.

Claire made her way to the front door. Then she turned back.

She'd forgotten Mother Saint Luke's key.

Once it was retrieved, she was on her way again and asked the air: *Where to, Mother Saint Luke?*

Then she paused, waited, as she'd been waiting for months, years, for some sort of reply.

As the silence stretched on, she realized that was the reply, and that now that she'd put on the habit, silence had enrobed her.

What's wrong??? texted Dorothy. When Marcus had earlier said he was in trouble, she'd thought he'd meant in trouble for lying to her, not telling her that he'd arrived in Rome hours before he'd told her he would. And he was in trouble for that. But that didn't matter now.

Meet me at the Termini station, Dorothy, Monica texted. *You, too, Marcus. Unless you want me to believe it was a stuntman who did the tough stuff in all those movies of yours.*

Yes, Marcus said. *I always had a stunt double when the script called for me to carry flowers to a convent.*

Texting with old people took too long, Dorothy thought. So much punctuation. She looked around Saint Peter's. She'd finally made it inside. What she'd not realized was that it wasn't just one church, but many; every alcove seemed to hold an altar or chapel. Some even had a priest saying a Mass; other pews were roped off, with signs noting who or what was due next. She watched a service for a few minutes. It wasn't in English, but like any cradle Catholic, she knew the rhythms of the Mass well enough to know exactly where in the service they were. It had been so long since she'd been in a pew. Maybe she'd catch a Mass before she left Rome. With Mom.

Termini, 3:45, texted Monica, which was thirty minutes after she was due to arrive.

Termini, 3:15, Monica texted separately to Claire, adding, *We'll have thirty minutes just to ourselves.* And then, because Claire hadn't been responding to any of her texts since she'd landed, Monica put the phone to her forehead and sent a backup message telepathically as well.

Then Monica googled, *how to pray beginner Rome urgent friend.*

Dorothy took a picture, as she thought she'd have been accused of hallucination otherwise. On her way out, she'd stopped by one of the side chapels. A sign hanging between two stanchions caught her eye: LA MESSA PER CELEBRARE L'INGRESSO DI QUESTE DONNE ALLA VITA RELIGIOSA GIURATA, a Mass, her phone told her, "to celebrate the entrance of these women to vowed religious life." A list of seven names followed. Two from the bottom: CLARE. Spelled differently, no last name, but given everything, wasn't it possible—likely—that this was her mom? And what was this ceremony? Dorothy had checked her watch. She'd just missed it. So after all this worrying, wondering, her mother, without telling her, had done this *today*?

One American couple saw her anxiously standing by the sign, computed their own translation, and then smiled and said congratulations.

Dorothy raced to Termini.

Monica saw Claire before Claire saw her. It was hard to miss Claire: she was in head-to-toe white; faces across the train station turned to her like leaves in a breeze. A couple of women walking by snapped photos and then studied the result, all without breaking stride.

So Monica was too late. Claire had gone and done it already? She was a nun. Monica hugged her, swore at her, asked her what the fuck was going on, and then hugged her again, this time not wanting to let go, crying into the fabric.

"You look beautiful," Monica said. "You look so fucking beautiful."

"What are you doing here?" asked Claire. "Why are you crying? What's the matter?"

Everyone spoke at once.

"Good Lord," said Sister Felicity.

"Romeo?" said Sister Georgia.

"*Claire*," said Marcus, falling to a knee.

"Mom!" Dorothy said.

"Claire," said Monica.

"Say yes, Mom," Dorothy said.

"She already has," said Sister Felicity quietly.

"Who *are* you?" Sister Thérèse asked Marcus.

An old friend, Claire thought. *A classmate. A floor mate. A library rooftop summiteer, a Saturday-night-party-avoiding study buddy, a father-daughter dancer.*

A tabletop singer.

An actor.

Claire shook her head. Because Marcus was no longer acting.

But Claire—Claire was.

PART III

....

I. IN CASO DI EMERGENZA

POSTULANT COMES FROM *POSTULATE*, FROM the Latin *postulare*, meaning "to ask," so here's a question. When your old love reappears in Rome and finally gets down on one knee, what do you do? Do you ask to be forgiven for sending mixed signals?

Or do you turn to the kind, tolerant, patient sisters who have been walking beside you throughout and ask for *their* forgiveness? Explain that you may have some unfinished business and need just a little more time before you even start to discern?

Or—

Or do you look at your daughter and your best friend and ask them to understand: you don't need rescuing; you are, finally, on the verge of rescuing yourself? You're not sure how, you're not sure how long it will last, but you know that this is the first step.

Which you take, releasing Marcus's hand, surveying all the faces arrayed. And then you take another step, backward, and another and another.

Are you acting now, and what's the role?

This last question may not be Claire's alone to answer, but it's too late regardless, as she's already begun to run.

Claire had never run in a habit, but she'd run in Rome, in New York, in Milwaukee, in a hundred other cities. She'd run with men and women, with people she didn't know and people she did, with a nun, by herself. She'd rarely run to get away from anyone and she wasn't sure she was doing so now. Shouldn't there be shouting? But for a single cry of Dorothy's—"Mom!," whose timbre called back to toddler days—there had only been the sounds of the train station. Track announcements, security warnings, a police dog's bark, the calls and laughter of friends. Claire thought she heard someone call her "Sorella," ask her why she was running. But it was a man's voice, and so on she ran.

One block, two blocks, five, and she was back in front of Santa Maria Maggiore, one of four major basilicas in Rome to have extraterritorial status—she'd be on foreign, Vatican, territory inside, and so no one could catch her.

But there was an entrance tent outside, soldiers with guns, magnetometers, who knows what they'd find if they could find her heart? Onward. Now another basilica, this one so small, Santa Prassede, and she slowed, *Go in, for God's sake*, and so she did. And then there she was, in the year 900 or thereabouts, a tiny jewel box of a church, the ceiling lapis lazuli blue, faded paintings on columns, the walls teeming with portraits. Forget what she said about special effects: *now*, now would be a good time to stop time, give her time to sit and think. Now, now, *now*, what now? Was *that* a prayer? She'd been asking for years.

The world spun on; she swept outside, to the curb. An elderly man, not much more than half her height, doffed his fedora when she waited with him to cross the street. "Buongiorno, Sorella," he said. What she needed to do was go back to Paolo's coffee bar, any coffee bar, and sit, or stand, and have a coffee, or not, and just catch her breath for a moment.

She heard a whistle—something like a referee or policeman might use—and stiffened. She reached into the folds of the fabric for her phone, to see who had called or texted and what they'd said—who would be first? (Monica?) Who would have sent the most texts? (Dorothy?) Who would have not called but whom did she most want to speak with right now? (The sisters.)

Then she remembered: she didn't have her phone.

Whom did she most want to be waiting for her on the next corner? Marcus.

She looked up. No phone, and she really wanted to know what was going on with the weather. Sunny a moment before, the sky had now darkened: Rain? Pedestrian-clogged streets told her she was nearing the Colosseum. No roof there, but there was a metro entrance. That could be her recovery time, place; she'd descend into the metro, take it a couple of stops south, get out and find a bus, or walk the rest of the way into Trastevere, to the Convento di Santa Gertrudis, where they'd all be waiting for her.

A year longer to discern, decide: that's what she would ask for.

No, that was nonsense. She'd decide today, by the time she'd reached the convent. She breathed deep as she felt it returning to her, the old wisdom, the old maturity, the old feeling of feeling old accompanied by a new one, pleasure at being this old. It was an accomplishment to have lived a life like hers. It was an accomplishment to be alive now. It was its own prize, being fifty-two. Fifty-two and able to draw three people across an ocean.

Though that made her feel guilty. And loved.

Dear alumni magazine, much has changed for me in the last year, and for the better.

No matter what she chose, she could start her note to the magazine that way.

She'd claim victory, whatever the competition. Her knees hurt but her head had never felt so clear. Running wasn't just a salve but salvation.

The first raindrop fell on her head, and she began to run again, chasing the decision that had always just outpaced her.

Back at Termini, passengers resumed ignoring them.

"I'm Marcus Sardeson," he said, and held out a hand to Sister Thérèse.

"Greetings, Romeo," said Sister Georgia.

"You must be Claire's daughter," said Sister Felicity to Dorothy. "Are you a runner, too?"

Yale at night, junior year, the last time Claire had been chased. A landscape of jagged slate paths and dirt-scarred lawns, castles with moats, one ancient lamppost after another losing a lopsided battle with the dark. Blue-lit emergency call boxes bloomed here and there, sentinels she found more ominous than reassuring.

A Saturday night, just the two of them, just like old times, except instead of sequestering themselves in a library, Claire and Marcus were out exploring.

High Street was a narrow avenue that crossed the main part of campus. At one end lay the library and law school; at the other end, sat a hodgepodge collection of buildings that housed the art gallery— and the building, or "tomb," of one of the school's secret societies, Skull and Bones.

Claire had heard about the societies her first year. She hadn't been impressed; they sounded like little more than fraternities. And only seniors belonged, which sounded stultifying. She'd resolved to pay no attention to them, but their windowless clubhouses were scattered across campus. You couldn't help but pass several daily. Skull and Bones was reportedly the most exclusive—and the most diabolical. Or so Claire assumed. She did know that they were one of the last to hold out against admitting women. That alone made them diabolical.

Which made her distressed that Marcus was now walking right up to the building itself.

"Claire," he hissed. He had detoured from the front door to head down a flagstone path that wound to the side, toward a narrow gap between the tomb and the art gallery.

She stood with hands on hips, deciding what to say, when he hissed again.

"Claire, we don't have much time!"

What was about to happen? Her imagination proposed a half dozen scenarios. She was surprised how many included Marcus kissing her. More reason not to listen.

"I'm tired, Marcus," she said in a normal voice.

She heard him muttering as he walked back to her. "I promise," he said, "this will be good."

"Why didn't you tell me you were in Bones? The *worst*—"

"For fuck's—for Pete's sake, Claire, I'm a junior, like you. And I'm just—not. That's why we're not going in the front door."

"Where *are* we going?" Claire said, but she was already gliding along, her hand in his, down the narrow path between the two buildings. It ended at a spiky wrought iron gate, about seven feet tall.

Marcus ran his hand along the wall, as though looking for a climbing hold.

"It's too tall," she whispered. "There's no way we can climb this. And—isn't someone going to notice?"

"That's why we have to hurry," Marcus whispered back. Then he turned and held out a palm to Claire. "Ta-da!" A key. "No climbing."

He put the key to the lock, and they stepped inside.

She would see Marcus in dozens of films in years to come. In good films and bad. In romantic comedies, explosive action movies, dark mysteries, and her favorites, quiet character studies where nothing much happened other than Marcus silently acting up a storm, often in tandem with a woman who, to Claire's eyes, never suited him. But even among her favorites, nothing compared with the imaginary movie that Claire took that night, stored carefully in her memory ever since, and played infrequently, for fear that repeated viewing might dull the colors, dim the voices, his and hers.

She had the first line.

It's so beautiful.

And the second.

Marcus, I—

And then the script (which only he knew in advance but whose broad outline she immediately understood) called for him to go to her, take her face in his hands, and kiss her.

But he didn't. He took her hand and pulled her deeper into the garden, to the fountain that sat at its center.

Skull and Bones had either not invested in security lighting or was brash enough to have forgone it in an area where no noninitiate dared tread. Above, half a moon peeked around one of the art gallery's turrets, turning the green lawn gray and the fountain a depthless black.

Marcus was spewing lines of dialogue that Claire would later

cut from the version she archived in memory, because they didn't
matter—Marcus had gone to his art history professor with a question about the Bethesda Fountain in Central Park, and the professor
had said if Marcus was interested in such things, he should check
out the fountain behind Skull and Bones, but hurry; Bones was having it crated up and sent away for restoration. The professor was consulting with them on the project—it was just a replica of a famous
fountain in Rome, but a quite fine copy, and if Marcus was discreet,
the professor would hide a key for him and—

"Please stop talking," Claire said. Water was barely flowing from
an upper basin into a lower one. *Tick, tick*, the drops wobbled and
fell, each one silvered in its fall by the moon. *Tick, tick*, a series of
bronze turtles struggled to make it into the upper basin of the fountain. There were four boys, also in bronze, to help the turtles in their
efforts. The central pediment looked to be marble. Around the lower
basin, four dragon-like fish spat water into four huge stone shells. It
looked like seven different people had designed it and each had gotten their way. She went to the fountain, put a hand out, caught some
of the drips. It was beautiful.

Thirty years later in Rome, she slowed to a walk. She was still being chased, but she needed to find Marcus, now, have him take her
to that fountain. She walked and watched as the film flickered on in
her head.

Out behind Skull and Bones, Marcus stood beside her, stared at the
fountain.

"The professor said this fountain sits in this tiny square in Rome,
and there's a story about a guy trying to win over his girlfriend's

wealthy dad by promising to build a fountain outside their house overnight. I mean, it's all made up, but he must have. The fountain's there, apparently. They got married. That's the story. I think."

"What did she think about all this?" she asked.

"Who?"

"The girl."

"The professor didn't say." Marcus looked at the fountain. "I hope she liked turtles," he mumbled.

Ask me, Claire thought. *Ask me what I think. About turtles. Fountains. Everything. Us.* He would, he did, he ruined every man after for Claire, men who rarely asked what she thought, or laughed when she asked them.

He was trembling. Claire will always remember that, him staring at the fountain, her staring at him, both of them trying to figure out how they'd gotten here, to this moment, this spot, and what should come next. Years later, in Rome, she looked behind her, as though he might be there, as though they might finish the conversation now. And where was he? Where was everyone? It was like the pieces of her life had been shaken out of a box and everything had been assembled in the wrong order. Now she was in Rome, discerning, fleeing— what? What would happen next?

"I guess it's not a very romantic story," he said to the fountain. He was trying very hard not to look at Claire.

I love—this, thought Claire. Fountains, darkness, silly Yale, spooky Yale. *This*, she'd thought, not *you*, though the unspoken words now hovered between them.

They'd talked about romantic attraction during her formation summers with the Clementines, that it was not only possible that a sister would fall in love someday but likely; they were human. So it wasn't something to fear, but one did have to be very, very mindful. Don't seek temptation. (She hadn't; tonight hadn't been her idea.) Be strong. (10–0 in intramural inner-tube water-polo, and she never wore a two-piece.) Know yourself.

And she did. But the sisters, wise as they were, had said nothing about fountains. About, specifically, Marcus. About what happened when the foundation you stood upon—which you'd painstakingly built, stone by stone, turned out to be water. She couldn't tell him she loved him because then everything would vanish, including these turtles, this night.

"Marcus?"

Light flooded the garden, and a jangly bell began to ring. Four students, boys, rep ties askew, had materialized at a corner of the garden opposite the gate that she and Marcus had come through. An older man, red-faced and heavyset, stood nearby, hands fisted at his sides. "What the *fuck* are you doing here?" the tallest boy said.

Claire recognized him from—Italian class, where his Italian name—they'd all selected one—was Giacomo.

"La pace sia con te, Giacomo. Mi piace la tua casa," Claire said, which, after four years, was still about all she knew how to say: Peace be with you. I like your house.

"Maria?" Giacomo said, which was not Claire's class name but did out Giacomo as one of the boys who'd taunted her in Commons freshman year.

"What the *fuck*?" one of the other boys said.

Arrivederci meant goodbye.

Claire and Marcus ran out the gate, down the street, and into Old Campus, their first-year redoubt. They ran for the statue with the lucky foot students rubbed and Marcus stopped there, panting. Claire ran on. She didn't know if they were still being chased, but if they were, she wanted to be somewhere they could call for help. She made for one of the blue emergency phones. When she got there, she stopped and leaned against it. The windows overlooking them were dark.

She felt overwhelmed, but happy. She didn't understand why and didn't want to. Couldn't you just let joy come? She wanted to press the button on the emergency phone box and shout into it or have it shout to her: *Yes, whatever the question is, yes!*

Marcus was running toward her.

She couldn't wait to tell him.

She was giddy. She might as well be drunk. She pressed the button. The speaker clicked into life, and she heard the line ring as though it was dialing someone. Oops. It *was* dialing someone. The police. What *was* she going to say? Marcus was almost upon her, his mouth open.

The line stopped ringing; a voice answered. "Yale Police. What's your emergency?"

"Keep running," Marcus said, looking back, chest heaving.

"We're fine," she whispered, even though one wrong step now meant everything would fall.

Marcus caught his breath, calmed, gently took her hand. What next? She'd rarely been around him when that had not been the consuming question.

"Yale Police," the phone repeated. "What's your emergency?"

"We're all right," she lied.

✣ ✣ ✣

"Claire!"

She should not have slowed to wander through memories. She should have kept running, and right past the front door of the Convento di Santa Gertrudis. But she didn't, and when she paused in front of the door, she heard her name and looked down the hill. Marcus was arriving at a slow trot. Monica and Dorothy were exiting a cab behind him.

"Claire!" Across the street now, exiting from another cab facing the opposite direction, the three sisters.

All Claire had wanted was a little time. True, by one measurement, she'd had thirty-four years, but that turned out not to be enough. She pushed on the door, left unlocked as always, and went inside.

She leaned her back against it briefly: *Think*.

The sisters thought their lock didn't work, but sometimes, beneath the housing, there was a little catch—there was.

Claire locked the door.

Apologies, Sister Felicity.

Time. It was all she wanted.

She hurried through the vestibule. They'd be in soon enough; one of them would have a key.

And then it occurred to her: Claire had Mother Saint Luke's.

She passed through the roseto, up and into the chapel, through the nave, into the sacristy, out the chapel's back door into the parco.

Voices.

That hadn't taken long.

It had always been so quiet in the parco; that had been its greatest treasure. It should have been the key to the parco that was marked *in case of emergency,* because this, here, this pocket wilderness, those serrated walls, this was refuge, was escape.

The voices grew closer.

Claire clutched Mother Saint Luke's key and started moving deeper into the garden, toward the back wall. If she burrowed deeply enough into the vegetation the others would give up, turn around, go back. No one ever went this far back anyway, not even animals. The path grew narrower and narrower until it disappeared altogether beneath a deep net of vines. What might lurk below? She turned.

She *wanted* to see the sisters and explain. She wanted to see Marcus and explain. She wanted to see her daughter, Monica, everyone, and have *them* explain to her what was going on. Where had the white postulant's habit come from? What would happen now?

She stopped. The voices had grown more distant, or quieted. Or given up.

She thought about them then. Sister Felicity, Sister Georgia, Sister Thérèse; Monica, Dorothy. Marcus. Six entirely different people who had nothing in common but this: not a one of them ever gave up.

And this: they were coming for her.

Why was she running? She loved these people. They all wanted the best for one another.

It was just that Claire wanted—*had* wanted—for it all to mean something. The tug in her heart, the pull on her soul, Rome, finding her way to the Convento di Santa Gertrudis, Mother Saint Luke. Her key.

Her key. Their key. What no one will ever, ever know is that Claire envisioned one day wearing the key after taking vows, wearing it on a chain, under her blouse, against her chest, always to remind her that she could always get out of what she'd gotten into. Somehow.

"Claire!"

Her heart throbbed—it sounded like Dorothy, but Dorothy would never call her *Claire*. Sister Thérèse, then. What had Claire ever done to merit this, a chase across Rome only to be cornered in a medieval walled garden?

With a door.

She'd reached the back wall, and though the vines knitted their own wall here, she saw between them that there was a gray patch amid the blush-pink stucco, and it was—she parted the vines now— it was a door. A metal door, not unlike the one at the front of the convent, except much older. That first day, the sisters had told her Mother Saint Luke had left a note with the key: *In case of emergency.* And now Claire saw: it was meant literally, not figuratively. There was simply a door, unlocked with a key, that led outside to safety. If the convent was on fire. If you were being pursued.

If you had had quite enough of community life and needed just a night, one night away, to converse and clink glasses at the American Academy or the Spanish Academy or the French Academy or the Testaccio market, and not have your sisters know, you'd slip in and out this door, your fellow sisters never the wiser. God would know, but you'd take that up with God.

Or you'd just walk out and close the door behind you one last time. Claire put the key to the lock. All this time, the lock had been right here.

It didn't fit.

She tried the knob. It wouldn't turn. She pulled. It wouldn't budge. She took two steps back and to the side to survey the situation, and then the earth swallowed her whole.

* * *

"What was that?"

"You all go back. I'll go on. She could be hurt."

"There's no way out?"

"You don't build a twenty-foot wall only to punch a hole in it."

It was dark and wet and things skittered. Her ankle was sore, but not broken as she'd initially feared. Her forearm, too: just bruised. She'd skinned her palms but was on her feet, standing in a small, brick-lined space at the bottom of an iron ladder, all of which had been invisible beneath the vines that Claire had unwittingly stepped into, thinking they covered solid ground. They had not; they covered the underground entrance to the GALLERIA ANTIAEREO: RIONE TRASTEVERE, or so a smudged sign said.

She'd dropped the key in the fall. She looked down. It was between her feet. She picked it up. She fitted it to the lock, but it wouldn't turn. She wiggled it. It finally scraped clockwise and then the door opened.

On the wall immediately inside was a large black-handled knife switch, the old-fashioned kind the mad scientist throws to bring the monster to life. But she feared nothing now. Not being found, not being lost. The key had worked. She threw the switch. *Pop, pop, pop.* A series of lightbulbs briefly illuminated what appeared to be a long, low tunnel, and then each winked out, all but for one about a dozen feet ahead and then a cluster far beyond. Everything was covered in dust layered so thickly it sloughed off her feet like snow.

A tunnel. An old wartime air-raid tunnel for the neighborhood. She walked forward.

To her right, a large medallion: VIGILI DEL FUOCO, the words surrounding the head of a fire-breathing dragon, the fire department's traditional coat of arms.

Sister Georgia's dragon map. It hadn't shown a road but this passage. Not proposed, real.

Rows of hooks ran along the wall, all labeled for things that were no longer there—tools, masks, gear. Beneath the one labeled TORCIA ELETTRICA, though, was not a flashlight but a bulky green canvas knapsack. She took it down, opened it up, and found bundles and bundles of cash. Not ones and fives or tens or twenties, but thousands. And bearing not Grover Cleveland's face but Giuseppe Verdi's, whose thousand-lire note—the bag, it would turn out, contained four thousand of them, four million lire—made the entire haul worth roughly two thousand dollars, had anyone known to exchange them for euros the last day they could have, which was eight years before. Sister Felicity had been right. There had been money hiding here, and, if they had shopped shrewdly with the proceeds, it might have just covered the sisters' airfare back to the United States. Now, though? Maybe a collector would be interested. Cents on the dollar. Maybe the sisters would get enough not for airfare, but to pay for an additional checked bag, one with all of Mother Saint Luke's memorabilia.

Voices again. Claire wished she had her phone. This truly would be something to photograph. The sign, the tunnel, the knapsack, the haul. The dark. She wished someone could leap forward in time, film it, and play it back for her. She was desperate to know what would happen next.

And it was a shame it didn't unfold that way, that she hadn't gotten a glimpse of the future but had strayed again into the past—Yale at night, water, turtles, running, secrets, what she once thought she was or would be—because she might have been able to position herself in such a way that she caught Marcus before he fell.

II. SALVATOR MUNDI

MONICA, YELLING, TRIED TO DIRECT rescue efforts, but once the rescue crew descended into the hole, Sister Georgia took over. The conversation went back and forth too quickly for her to understand, but Claire somehow knew exactly what the rescuers were saying.

What's he doing down here?

What's she *doing down here?*

What are we doing down here?

Sister Georgia answered that last question in such a way that the paramedics stiffened up and got to work: backboard, cervical collar, straps, discussion of ropes and pulleys or another way out, and then more rescuers arrived.

Marcus, like Claire before him, had fallen down an open manhole into the air-raid shelter's access tunnel. It wasn't a long drop, maybe twelve feet, but the tangle of vines that had slowed Claire had torn away beneath Marcus. He'd fallen hard.

The rescue did not look like a movie. It was dark and messy and slow. Eventually, Marcus, milk pale, was wrestled out of the hole. The door in the garden wall that Claire had unsuccessfully tried earlier was jimmied open, and the men carried him out of the convent, up the hill, and into an ambulance, which sped away.

Or so Claire assumed. She'd been quick to wave off help for herself—too quick, it turned out, and by the time she'd climbed out of the hole with Sister Thérèse's assistance, the ambulance was gone, Monica and Dorothy with it.

"Let's get you changed," Sister Felicity said, which was when Claire remembered she was wearing the habit. She began to ask where it had come from, to apologize for the state it was now in, but Sister Felicity only drew a breath and walked her to her room. Once there, Sister Felicity went into the bathroom and began running a shower, pulled clean clothes out of the closet, and set them on the room's sole chair.

"I can't—" Claire started to say.

"And when you're ready, I'll find a car to take us over. No bus," Sister Felicity said, and smiled. "We'll be there before you know it."

"I'm sorry, Sister," said Claire.

"What a needless thing to say," said Sister Felicity, and gently shut the door.

Later, outside, had Claire peered down from her upper floor into the roseto, she would have seen the three sisters in a circle, eyes shut, hands held, heads bowed. But Claire was busy in her room, getting dressed in her own clothes; trying, and failing, to find the words of her own prayer; trying, and failing, not to look at the habit where she'd hung it; trying, and failing, to avoid whispering one last deal into the empty air.

Monica was, finally, fully in charge. She met Claire's car as it arrived, left the sisters to deal with the driver, and swept Claire into the building as if it were Monica's own hospital, which, to judge from the deferential or terrified looks of staff they passed, it had become.

Marcus was fine, Monica began, though that statement became

more brittle as she continued. So far, what they knew was that he'd suffered no broken bones—or anything else that the doctors could detect, really, other than a blow to his head. Possibly a severe concussion, made worse by the fact that he had been injured before? Maybe the accident on that movie set during Claire's marathon had not just involved a stunt double, but Marcus, too. In any case, he was comfortable, he was being monitored, all was in order but for the fact that Monica had, earlier that day, discovered her best friend in the world at the bottom of a hole behind a convent, clutching a key. But Claire could explain that later. Earlier, there'd been a disagreement about which hospital to take Marcus to; the ambulanza crew had seemed to have different ideas. Frantic, Dorothy had researched options online and come up with this hospital, a private one, Salvator Mundi, just west of Trastevere.

"You'll like that it was founded by nuns," Monica said. "The Sisters of the Divine Savior."

"Where's Marcus?"

"*I* like that it turns out it's the celebrity hospital. Or was. The emergency entrance is quite discreet—and quite small. Liz Taylor came here during *Cleopatra*," said Monica. "Muriel Spark used to check herself in for a month at a time, take a 'rest cure.' Brigitte Bardot—"

Monica rattled along, but Claire was run-walking down the hallway, looking in rooms, most of which were empty. Historic photos, doctors and nuns in white posing stiffly beside ancient technologies, lined the walls. When she finally found Marcus, the room was bright and sunny, with fresh flowers. Other than a swollen nose, he looked fine. If he had bruises, they were invisible to her.

"Marcus?"

His eyes were closed. He didn't respond.

"If I've got it right, they don't understand why he keeps falling asleep," Monica said. "Marcus?" No response.

A nurse arrived and seemed startled to see them there. She clapped her hands and pointed to the door.

"It's fine we stay," Monica said. "The doctor said."

The nurse shook her head and kept pointing.

"You have to make an exception," Monica said, shoving Claire toward the bed. "This is his—his—"

The nurse waited.

"Friend," Claire said.

"You should have kept your nun outfit on," Monica told Claire.

The nurse said something in Italian.

"Marcus, we'll be right back," Monica said. "Stop pretending to sleep."

The nurse ushered them out the door and then yanked a shade across the door's window. But the shade swung clear, and Claire looked in at Marcus. She should have ignored the nurse. She should have at least touched him, a hand to his hand. She remembered him telling her about a role where he'd spent much of the movie in a hospital bed, the final scenes in something like this, a coma. *Not as easy as it looks*, he'd insisted, and Claire had laughed, because she'd once said the same thing about prayer. *But all you do is kneel and close your eyes*, Marcus said.

"Where's Dorothy?" said Claire.

"Just to be clear," Monica said, "I'm not worried because they're not worried. It's weird, I wish he was more… conscious, but everyone seems to think he will improve, and soon. So do I."

"He looks fine," Claire said. But he wasn't. She suddenly had to look away.

Monica sighed. "Dorothy didn't buy my optimism either. Said she had to go for a walk. I told her I would text her with any news."

"Go find her for me, would you?" Claire said.

Monica shook her head. "So they did mention this one possibility. He might have more than a concussion. A sub—subdural? Hema-something. A brain bleed. But the good kind, I guess, it's right there beneath the skull, and if that happens, you monitor it, and possibly drain it, drill the skull, little tube."

Claire put her hand over her mouth.

"Hang in there," Monica said. "I didn't mean *you* you; I meant *one*, I meant the doctor does it. Apparently, it works like a charm. But if they do it, I'm going to make sure they drill in the right place. Real estate, neurosurgery, where you stand on future red carpets so the paparazzi don't see the scar: it's all about location." She looked around. "So, I will stay here, stand watch."

"It's not funny," Claire said quietly, imagining Marcus not walking down a future red carpet but being wheeled down one.

"That's why I've thrown up twice so far," Monica said. "I'm pretty sure it's what got us kicked out of the room."

Claire looked in. The nurse was continuing to take his vitals. Numbers wavered across a screen atop an IV pole; Claire couldn't read them.

"The *second* he—"

"The doctor comes back top of the hour," Monica said. "Go find your daughter."

Claire had her choice of signs. PRIMO SOCCORSO, no; STUDI MEDICI, no; PISCINA PER FISIOTERAPIA, no. And then: PASSAGGIO DELLA CAP-PELLA. No, she would not find Dorothy in the chapel. She should have realized, years ago, that naming her for Dorothy Day meant you got the whole package: the height, the independence, the contrariness.

The fierce belief in the importance of a meal.

Claire stood just outside the café and stared. It was possible that the hospital had aerosolized some pleasant hallucinogenic for the benefit of patients and visitors. Something that would cause folks to see what they wanted to see but which could never be true in the real world. Like this: Dorothy, the girl who'd loudly argued with Claire in Madison, now sitting down, eating, laughing quietly with three sisters. Sister Felicity, Sister Georgia, Sister Thérèse. Claire stepped into the café. It looked more like a stage set of a café than an actual one. The drinks case was sparsely stocked. And as Monica had likely already noted, it lacked alcohol.

The woman behind the counter looked up, but the women seated did not. Dorothy dabbed her eyes with the back of her wrist, nodding as she did. "Seriously," Dorothy was saying, "she seriously did that." The sisters shook their heads and grinned.

Claire coughed. They turned. "I don't mean to interrupt..."

"You're not—" Sister Thérèse began.

Dorothy leapt up. "Is there news?"

Claire shook her head. Dorothy sat back down slowly. The sisters exchanged a look and rose.

"Don't get up on my account," said Claire.

"We've had such a lovely visit," said Sister Georgia, and then spoke to Dorothy. "It was a delight meeting you. You are your mother's daughter, every inch."

"She means that as a compliment," said Sister Felicity.

"I don't think they're anything alike," said Sister Thérèse.

"Her, I like," said Dorothy, pointing to Sister Thérèse.

They laughed. The sisters gave Claire hugs in turn, and Sister Felicity said to her, "Let us know. And let us know how we can help. If anyone needs a place to sleep, we have room. For a little while, anyway."

"Sister!" said Claire. "I'm so sorry—I can't believe I forgot—it's— the deadline is tomorrow."

"Not so fast," said Sister Felicity. "Thirty-six hours, give or take. Not that it—"

"I can still—we can still sort out something," Claire said. "With the Vatican. With Anna. I'll try the embassy again. We'll get the Boston sisters on a conference call. Tell them to postpone the vote."

"Anna and I spoke," Sister Felicity said, her face now tight, "and she said her discernment had led her to—"

"Anna said no," said Sister Georgia.

"Sister!" Claire said. She looked at each of them. Sister Thérèse turned away.

"We'll pray is what we'll do," said Sister Felicity. "For you and for your friend. And for your daughter. And we'll let God take care of the rest."

"Sister—"

"We'll talk," said Sister Felicity. "But first," she said, looking over her shoulder, "talk with your daughter."

"She's so worried about Marcus," Claire said, staring absently Dorothy's way.

Sister Felicity nodded slowly before she spoke. "She's worried about *you*."

"So," Claire began, but Dorothy just shook her head and leaned toward her. Claire gathered her up and held on tight. Claire had long worried—because every aspect of the culture, and some people directly, had told her—that she had been doing something wrong raising Dorothy alone, engaging her anti-engagement father as little as possible. But the truth was that Claire came to wonder how all those two-parent couples did it. How did you hug in a hospital with three? That was rugby; that wasn't parenting. No, there was always just room enough in Claire's arms for Dorothy, and Claire knew that no matter how angry Dorothy had ever been with or would ever get at Claire, there'd only be room in Dorothy's arms for her mom. At least until Dorothy's own daughter came along, and Claire suddenly hoped one would.

"I didn't see any food on the café table," Claire said. "When was the last time you ate?"

"The sisters said that the tomato plants got scared around you," Dorothy said.

"What?"

"That you ate everything they had," Dorothy said.

"That's not true," Claire said, wondering if it was.

"They offered to pray with me," Dorothy said, looking slightly confused, like the sisters had offered to take her to Mars. You could X-ray Dorothy all you wanted now and you'd not find much belief. Or maybe, thanks to the sisters, you would.

"They're good women," said Claire.

"Did any of this"—Dorothy said, looking around, and Claire felt a pang that a summer in Rome might be summarized this way, a fluorescent-lit, anemic café—"have to do with Marcus?"

Claire would have sat down with Dorothy eventually. She would have explained that "this," that Rome, that considering a future in the convent, had to do with her arriving at a crossroads that she recognized from long before. She'd gone one way then—out; she'd thought she might go the other way now, in. Because who got a chance to do that? Her wanting to join the Convento di Santa Gertrudis had everything to do with doing something intentional for a change, not riding the river but steering to a shore. It had to do with Dorothy, moreover, who deserved to have a mother who was, finally, fully alive. Dorothy wouldn't be losing a mother or whatever Dorothy's fear was. Granted, there was much that Claire herself hadn't fully understood: Why this call, why now?

Or so she had wondered until the question became, What now?

And it had nothing to do with Marcus: Did Claire have any lies left over from her reunion allotment?

Claire sat down gently at the table. "I didn't sleep the night before my college graduation," she said. "Sister Anastasia—she was the superior, or leader, of the Clementines, the religious community in Milwaukee I'd pledged myself to—she'd just arrived in New Haven and so had my father, your grandfather, and everything was so crazy. It felt like more than the end of college; it felt like the end of the world."

It was the end of the world, of course, her world. Claire had fallen in love with that world—with Yale, the people and the place and the damn library of teeth and Bibles—and she'd fallen in love with Marcus. Sister Anastasia must have known that, or sensed that, Claire explained, because she asked Claire to join her at the Saint Thomas More Chapel the afternoon before graduation to pray and reflect. Sister Anastasia led them in a rosary and then they both fell silent. Finally, Sister Anastasia rose, and when Claire began to as well, the sister put a gentle but firm hand on her shoulder: *Don't let me rush you*, Sister Anastasia said. Claire's cheeks glowed red with embarrassment, but who could see that in the empty chapel? God, probably.

What happened that night was family lore, but Claire told it once again to Dorothy now: the show, the stage, Marcus about to kiss his costar, Eva, until Claire climbed the stage and changed the script.

What did Eva do then? Dorothy wanted to know. Claire honestly couldn't remember. She remembered being barely able to see or hear, that after the kiss, Marcus said something—words—and she tried to say words in reply. She remembered the rest of the cast closing in on them, remembered thinking they were coming after her. But they were just gathering for the final bow. Marcus reached for Claire, but someone grabbed one of Marcus's hands, someone else the other, and they held on as Claire ran, ran.

After that, he was gone, gone, back to his movie shoot, his plane somewhere above while she zombie-walked through graduation, rode home to empty and lonely Milwaukee, the back of the car filled with her belongings, which she would have just as soon set fire to.

Then came New York, Dorothy's father, Len, the pairing, the parting. Claire always kept this brief and did so now, looking around the hospital café, which Len might just like, plain as it was. Though he'd never been, she knew he'd hate Rome, its layers of art, statues stuffed in every corner. "Your father and I see the world through different eyes," Claire said, "and so went our different ways."

"So you got what you wanted?" Dorothy asked, studying Claire carefully.

Claire had kissed Marcus onstage before the world. She'd put aside plans to become a sister. She'd had a successful career. She'd made good friends and one best friend. She'd helped some people who'd needed help. She'd saved an airport chaplain's chapel. She'd found her way to Rome and had spent four months being reborn, within and without, in a beautiful convent in a beautiful city. She'd had magical meals and drunk magical water. She'd met women she'd remember her whole life. She'd tried a single key in dozens of locks that had never worked until one did.

She'd had a daughter, a perfect, smiling, brilliant, and beautiful girl, and she'd named her Dorothy, and she was here with her now. Claire reached out for Dorothy's hand and took it. So much of Dorothy still felt small and childlike to her, or so Claire's mind insisted, but holding her hand, all grown-up, reminded Claire that her daughter was an adult now. Dorothy squeezed the hand. Claire squeezed back.

"I got exactly what I wanted," Claire said.

And what she wanted now? She wanted Marcus to be okay. After that, she could figure everything else out.

"Let's go back and see how Marcus is doing," said Dorothy.

Claire missed the stout walls of the convent, how they'd held the world at bay, until they hadn't.

Claire nodded, stood, and Dorothy did, too. Claire gave a last look around the café.

"The sisters do have room, you know," Claire said, "if you're interested."

"Don't push it," Dorothy said.

The doors to the café swung open, and Monica came through.

"Who's been praying here?" Monica boomed. She pointed at Dorothy, then Claire, and then at a cafeteria attendant who had rematerialized behind the counter. The attendant looked at Monica and shook her head.

"Is he okay?" said Dorothy.

"Okay?" Monica said. "He's dancing."

"He's *what*?"

"He's not. He's awake is what he is, and *as* it appears from your pained faces that you have *not* been praying, I will take full responsibility for his recovery, as I just did with his doctors, for which I received the honor of being once again ejected from the room."

"He's awake?" Dorothy said.

"He is, even though I'm sure he'd prefer to be asleep for whatever final barrage of tests they're putting him through. But: no drilling, no draining. We get to see him back in the room not too long from now."

Dorothy gave Monica a hug. "You're the best."

"I do what I can," Monica said. "Which is a *lot*."

Dorothy waved her phone. "I'm going to call Peter!"

Monica watched Dorothy leave. "That's good parenting," she said, something Monica used to shout on soccer sidelines when Dorothy scored a goal. "She was in a state before."

"Wasn't me," Claire said. "I found her here with the sisters."

"At some point, we need to talk about them. And their castle. And you in it," Monica said.

"Not now?"

"You choose. The other topic is cerebral hemorrhages. Did you know they could be aggravated by cell phone signals?"

"What?"

"Or so I gather from that nurse, who *took my phone from me while I was holding it* and put it in the staff fridge."

"She did not."

"It would be very helpful to me if you could pray loudly when we reach the nurses' station. She strikes me as the type who will go for that."

In the hallway outside the room, they got the briefing: concussion; no hematoma. The hospital wanted to keep him at least overnight, just in case, but all looked promising.

"No drilling?" Claire said, and the doctor frowned.

"A miracle," Monica said doubtfully.

The doctor—like a surprising number of the staff, from Pittsburgh—said no. But the body was mysterious and the brain the most mysterious of all. Then again, he'd not dealt with a lot of convent accidents before coming to Rome. No better place to fall, right? God's got your back in a town like this.

Monica and Claire remained silent.

The doctor coughed and started again. "So, which one of you is the wife?"

Marcus was given a pamphlet on concussion care: no sports, no reading, not much of anything for six weeks. But he can have a little wine if he wants, the doctor said. The nurse pantomimed leaving to get a bottle that very moment.

Marcus turned her down, confused.

"It's a real hospital?" he said after the nurse and doctor left.

"Yes," said Monica, "there's even a wing where they treat small animals, mostly cats."

Marcus tried to lift himself onto his elbows. "It's a veterinary hospital?"

"But the best," Monica said. "Liz Taylor's last Maltese was treated here."

"She's teasing you," said Claire.

"Claire," Marcus said with a weary smile. "I remember you."

"Really?" Claire said.

"We met—in college. You were planning to become—a nun." Marcus stopped smiling. "And years later, you started down that path again."

"I'll leave you alone," Monica said. "I'm going to liberate my phone, find the sommelier."

Claire and Marcus watched her go.

"She's in a good mood," Marcus said.

"You're alive," Claire said. "We're all in a good mood."

Marcus extended a hand and Claire took it. "I told the docs my memory was fuzzy, but that was only because they started in on what kind of insurance I had—"

"We'll sort that out."

"I remember everything," Marcus said. "I remember the accident, I remember everything before. I remember my first trip to Rome to see you and then this one. I remember our dinner—"

"I remember the dinner at Yale when you climbed on the table and sang."

"I remember," Marcus said, "when you climbed onstage at the senior show and—"

"And then ran from it crying," she said. "But no one saw that, other than my father, mother superior, and about two thousand parents and friends of the actors onstage whose finale I'd just ruined."

"Sense of humor: intact," he said. "All that nunning has been good for you."

"I've not run in days. Well, except—"

"*Nun*ning," Marcus clarified. "All your praying? Practicing to be a nun. I never thought you'd aim for convent life again, but then, here in Rome, I could finally see it. I can see it now. You're smiling."

"I'm smiling because you're okay."

She saw him try, very hard, to smile back.

"I'm not okay," he said quietly.

A nurse arrived, followed by a man wearing a rumpled guard's uniform, followed by Dorothy, who said, "Visiting hours are over, apparently. They've already kicked out Monica. She, um, kicked back. We should go."

"Go," said Marcus.

"Wait, but—"

The guard was at Claire's elbow.

"Go," Marcus said, and then they were gone.

Per the original plan, Monica had booked a luxe boutique hotel not far from the convent, three rooms.

"Could we walk?" Claire said as they left the hospital.

But Dorothy begged for a cab and so Monica found her one, and some quick hugs later, the two old friends were walking along alone, Monica's arm snaked through Claire's. No luggage; Monica had had the taxis deliver it. They walked along in silence until they reached the hotel's pea-gravel entrance court and then looked up: a brief vision of what the Convento di Santa Gertrudis would be like had anyone spent a dime on it in four hundred years.

Monica explained that she'd chosen the hotel based on its rooftop bar alone, but by the time they got to the roof, the bartender was packing up.

"Just as well," said Claire, who didn't want to talk, not yet. She wondered if the triple-layer feather beds advertised in the lobby would deliver anywhere near as good a sleep as her iron convent cot. She looked out over the rooftops and stopped short when she saw that just a block away rose the ramparts of the Convento di Santa Gertrudis.

Monica saw her startle and then went to the bartender, brokered some whispered transaction, and then reappeared with a bottle of wine and two glasses as he left.

"They had a good run," Monica said, nodding to the Convento di Santa Gertrudis. "I take it there's no surprise white knight arriving before noon New York time tomorrow?"

Claire shook her head.

"You tried," Monica said.

"You're a good friend," Claire said. She'd meant it, but the words sounded rote.

"I am," Monica said. "It's time you noticed who's really been at your side all this time. Me. *Claire's Darkest Hours*, seasons one through thirty, Monica Drumlin, showrunner."

"I'm sorry," Claire said. "I should have tried harder."

"You didn't do everything you did *and* run a bake sale, true," Monica said. "A few chocolate chip cookies might have put you over the top. I have a good recipe. The key is flake salt, lots."

"I failed the sisters. The firm. Marcus."

Monica waited until their eyes met before she spoke again.

"He's going to be all right," Monica said.

"He is, right?" Claire said. "But—that's not just wishful thinking? Why didn't they release him tonight?"

"You, of all people," Monica said. "It has nothing to do with wishes. It has to do with belief. This is what I believe."

Claire shook her head, her throat too clogged now from crying, from trying not to cry, from trying to sift the right words from the wrong ones.

"Listen to me, okay?" Monica said. "*You* know he's going to be fine. You believe. You don't want to, you haven't wanted to for years, you've treated faith like an affliction, but you believe in God, the whole thing, life hereafter. I don't. Or I don't know. It's a possibly beautiful thing that I don't understand, like quarks. But you, you've

occasionally tried to scrape that belief out of your heart and soul—
you have one—and you can't."

"I don't want to."

"Then stop trying to abandon him."

"God?"

"And Marcus. *And*, not *or*. You keep trying to choose, Claire. You
made your choice long ago. You asked the universe for everything,"
Monica said. "And unlike most of us, you got it."

Claire looked out at Rome.

"But the sisters," Claire said.

"The sisters, too. You got them, their key, their love, and what
sounds like most of their fresh vegetables."

"It's all gone tomorrow," Claire said. She looked at her watch.
"Today!"

Monica looked over toward the Convento di Santa Gertrudis. "It's
still there, Claire."

III. LA CAPPELLA DI BEATA VERGINE MARIA DI LORETO A FIUMICINO

MONICA WENT DOWNSTAIRS. Claire said she'd follow. Claire had everything, even a plush hotel room.

Marcus called from the hospital. He sounded better. They talked.

She'd tell Monica about it later.

She stayed on the roof.

She had nothing now.

The September deadline was hours away; they'd soon determine how many bids had arrived to beat Sister Rose's brother's: none. They'd vote on dissolving the order; opposing votes: only three. You couldn't count Mother Saint Luke's. And maybe you couldn't even count the three. Why should Sister Felicity, Sister Georgia, Sister Thérèse, vote against the inevitable now? Soon enough, they'd walk out the door for the last time.

Claire had never realized how well the massive convent hid itself in the dark. A single streetlight dimly illuminated the façade. But the interior, unlit, disappeared. Much of the city did. So many cities were scolded for spilling too much light into the night sky; Rome had an excess of dark. Scanning the city from a hilltop at night was like studying a dying fire. Some embers still burned bright—the Colosseum was lit, the Vittoriano blindingly so, and this or that palazzo glowed—but so much of the city lay dark and invisible.

What would happen now? To the sisters? They'd have to move.

They were not fragile; they'd find new homes and roles quickly enough. But they'd been so close to rescuing the convent, the order, and they hadn't. Claire hadn't. They'd put their trust in Claire and she hadn't come through.

She'd had deals fail before. Part of the business. Acrimony and lawyers and sometimes tears. This wasn't that. This wasn't even, as Monica pointed out, a deal. But it had been something, an agreement to be struck, if not with God, then with herself.

Sister Felicity said she wearied of women coming to their door to find themselves. That wasn't Claire. She knew who she was, where she was, always had, had always known she hadn't belonged. She hadn't come to Rome to find anything. But she had come to this decade of her life looking to be found and by something larger than her. Not the Yale Club.

What she'd learned at the Convento di Santa Gertrudis was that she did believe, but that she wasn't particularly good at it. Not as good as the sisters, anyway. She'd learned their life wasn't one that you could just try on, any more than she could just climb back onstage thirty years ago and stay this time at Marcus's side. That wasn't her role.

What was?

Moments before, when they'd spoken by phone, Claire had told Marcus she didn't know. She'd told him the sisters probably wouldn't ask her to join now; she'd made such a mess of things, and in a few hours, there'd be nothing to join. She'd told him he probably shouldn't ask her anything, either; she'd fled the stage for a different life long ago, and that was the one she was living. It came with a daughter, belief, friends, too, and Marcus was one of them. What else was there to say?

A lot, but in the end, they each just said goodbye.

She was tired. She checked her watch. Two a.m. On the street below, cats darted from one dark doorway to the next. Time for bed. Sleep for an hour or two, wake, figure out the rest of her life.

She was about to leave the roof when she saw something unusual. Better said, it was unusual that she'd never seen it before, especially in a city as covered in graffiti as Rome: someone in the act of painting graffiti. But there someone was.

On the front wall of the Convento di Santa Gertrudis.

Claire had a broker's knee-jerk dislike of graffiti. Its presence automatically discounted the sales price. On one of her walks around Rome with Marcus, Claire had muttered something about establishing a charitable foundation devoted to cover-up paint and pressure washing. Marcus had said not to; the graffiti added character. He'd doubled down, even: Romans *had* to cover their walls in graffiti, lest they risk being "smothered by the past." That's all graffiti was, and it was a lot: a way for the present to assert itself against what had come before. In so many places in the world, graffiti was taken as a sign that an area had been abandoned. In Rome, it seemed a way of declaring the opposite, of saying, *We're still here.* Given how much had come before in Rome—and how that history kept toppling down on Romans every day—graffiti, as Marcus said, was a matter of survival.

She cursed him now as she flew down the hotel stairs. Graffiti had nothing to do with survival, or if it did, only in a negative sense, as here: the convent's death sentence was hours old and the vultures were already out, shaking cans, *click-click.* If they needed to tag something, why not Monica's hotel? Or draw a big smiley face on the Spanish Steps. But leave the—*my*—Convento di Santa Gertrudis alone.

The convent had looked so close from the roof of the hotel, but

Trastevere put two litter-strewn staircases and one twisty, pitch-black alley between Claire and the convent's front door. She arrived just as the artist was finishing.

She looked at the street and knelt: the sanpietrini! Sister Georgia had taught her the etymology just last week. Rome's ubiquitous cobblestones, which herringboned one street after another, a bane to motorcyclists in rain and pedestrians in all weather, were quarried from volcanoes and known as *sanpietrini*, San Pietros, little Saint Peters; and Jesus said . . . *You are Peter, and upon this rock I will build My church.* And the little-known latter part of the verse: *And hey, Peter, if you ever see someone defacing a defunct convent in the middle of the night, dig up one of these little paving stones and chuck it at them; it won't be held against you. Verily.*

"Are you all right?"

Sister Thérèse's voice. Talking to the graffiti artist? Claire didn't turn. It would be just like Sister Thérèse to daffily ask after the welfare of the criminal instead of telling him to fuck off.

"Claire?"

Claire looked up. She'd identified a candidate sanpietrini. She no longer had the key and wished she did: this *was* an emergency, and the key would be just the tool to pry this block free. Give her fifteen minutes; she'd have it fully out. The artist would have run off by then, but let him run. Claire had been training for a marathon. She'd lap the city hunting him.

"Where'd he go?" Claire asked.

"Who?" said Sister Thérèse. "'He'? Was—was Marcus here? He should be resting."

"He is—who?—no, Marcus is at the hospital."

A light went on in an apartment above the café.

"We should talk more quietly," said Sister Thérèse.

"It would have been nice if the neighbors had woken earlier, scared off the guy."

"Who's this guy?"

"The graffiti artist. So-called artist," Claire went back to digging. It was possible, of course, that Claire had hit her own head while falling into the tunnel and was having a much-delayed coma dream. That made some sense, because nothing else right now did.

She'd discarded Marcus over the phone?

Sister Thérèse brightened. "That was me!"

Claire had caught Sister Thérèse tagging her own convent.

Claire continued kneeling in the street, and Sister Thérèse knelt beside her.

"Claire," she said, "why don't you come inside?"

In through the door, the vestibule, into the roseto, velvet gray at this hour. Up the stairs, down the corridor to Claire's old room, no need for a light, she knew where she was. Sheet, pillow, bed.

Sister Thérèse came for her at 8 a.m., though Claire was already stirring; she'd awoken, as she'd awoken every morning in Rome, to the tolling of bells: on the hour (*time for Mass!*), ten minutes before the hour (*start walking now!*), ten minutes after (*you're late*—or the carillonneur had overslept). She'd miss all that, too. The bells, this cot, this convent. And Sister Thérèse. Sister Georgia. Sister Felicity.

"Sister Felicity would like to see you in the parco, Mother Saint Luke's hermitage," Sister Thérèse said. "Come find me after," she added, her eyes almost twinkling.

So this was it. The convent's deadline had loomed so large for so long that Claire was surprised to see the building still stood this morning, Rome, too. Life, exasperatingly, went on. Which meant the sisters were still waiting for an answer from her, even though what was the point? It would be too late to count toward the twenty-one bodies; the convent's sale deadline had passed; the order's dissolution vote was about to happen or had already.

And still they wanted to know?

Worse—witness Sister Thérèse's twinkle—they might have convinced themselves that they already knew, and that they knew Claire still wanted to join.

And she did.

But she couldn't.

Claire still believed, and believed that she would have made a good nun once, in another time. But not this time. Too much had happened. She'd failed in every way you could fail, she told Sister Felicity, including the most important way, discerning what to do next.

"I disagree," said Sister Felicity. They were sitting in the garden, outside Mother Saint Luke's old hermitage.

The parco was not nearly so vast as Claire had once thought it. The greenery had been flattened by men and equipment and so it was possible to see clear to the rear wall. Bumblebees lumbered this way and that, tending to what flowers remained. When Claire had wandered the parco before, she'd have sworn she'd walked half a mile. But now it looked like the garden was no more than one hundred meters deep, maybe half that wide.

"I can't stay," said Claire.

"None of us can," said Sister Felicity, and waited. Claire found she could no longer meet her gaze, and turned away. Sister Felicity continued. "Discernment isn't a failure just because it doesn't lead to professing vows."

"It *is* a fucking failure," Claire said. Apparently she was going to burn all her bridges: send Marcus packing and have Sister Felicity's last memories of her be profanity laden. "When you run a race, they don't give you a medal for collapsing at mile eighteen."

"They do if that's the finish line," Sister Felicity said.

"I don't want to run that fucking race," Claire said. "I trained for a marathon, twenty-six point two."

"Does that work during negotiations," asked Sister Felicity, angry now, "swearing? Is that how you let people know you mean *business*?" Claire apologized and Sister Felicity waved it away. "Because it doesn't work with me. It's a shortcut, and not to sincerity."

"Business? I don't do deals anymore. Clearly."

"We've loved having you here, Claire. *I* loved running with you, talking with you, eating with you."

"Thank you."

"We loved having you here," Sister Felicity said. "We just wish you'd *been* here."

"I'm sorry?"

"Vowed life," Sister Felicity said. "It's not a convent in Rome, saying grace before meals—"

"I went to Mass, too."

"And you weren't there, either. Even when you were sitting with us, you were wandering around, running—"

"Praying!"

"And praying, and always coming back here, searching every cot, every corridor, searching for the *one* thing you know isn't in here."

The feeling was so strong, Claire turned to look beside her, but instead of Marcus, all she saw was air.

"*Claire,*" Sister Felicity said, "you've seen the inside of more churches and convents than I ever will. I hope you see many more, and not just to close them. I hope you finally find a spot from where you can really *see.*"

"Sister," Claire said quietly. "I *can* see. I—I believe. I really do."

Sister Felicity nodded and then took hold of Claire's hands as she had before their run. "I know," Sister Felicity said. "I just can't believe you choose to think there's only one way to show God that."

Claire stared at Sister Felicity, who held on, lowered her head, and closed her eyes. After a moment, Claire did the same. Silence, beautiful once more, no longer absence but presence, rose around them.

Claire found Sister Thérèse waiting for her near the vestibule.

"Everything go okay?" Sister Thérèse said.

"I used swear words in front of Sister Felicity," said Claire, still wobbly. What had just happened?

"She hates that," Sister Thérèse said, a look of concern flashing. "And I can see you set her off."

"You could say that," Claire said. It felt like her eyes were taking forever to feed information to her brain. She looked around uncertainly. Everything old, everything new.

"You need a walk."

"No, thank you. Maybe a bed."

"Bribe it is," Sister Thérèse said. "Signore Maritozzo is closing up for a month; they're renovating his building. This morning is our last chance."

✳ ✳ ✳

Another of Claire's failings: she could be bought.

But: maritozzi. The pope himself would be susceptible. Probably why he lived in Rome, Claire thought as she took another bite. Extra orange zest today; perfect. "Are you going to miss these?" Claire asked.

Sister Thérèse nodded, spoke with her mouth full. "They have these a lot of places around town. The best ones—the biggest ones, the free ones—are here, but they won't be hard to find elsewhere."

"You're not leaving Rome?"

"Eventually," said Sister Thérèse. "But I agreed to teach at the Collegium Sanctum Pontificum this fall; we'll see about spring. Depends on finding an apartment. We have a lot of discerning to do as a community."

"I'm sorry if I made it harder."

The truth was, they'd made it harder on Claire—too much laughter, too much stillness, too much running, too many tomatoes, too much prayer. They'd made it hard to leave. It was a shame the women hated money so much. She'd pay them Yale tuition for all that she'd learned.

"You *did* make it harder," Sister Thérèse said. "And more fun."

"I wish I'd found a better buyer for you," Claire said.

"We never wanted a buyer," Sister Thérèse said, "if we're being honest. We just wanted a forever."

"I'm sorry Anna said no," Claire said quietly.

"I'm sorry *for* her, but I don't fault her," Sister Thérèse said. "It's a choice and she made it. Better now than in a dozen years."

Claire waited for Sister Thérèse to ask about Claire's vocation, or rather, state the obvious, which was that Claire didn't have one.

But Sister Thérèse said nothing. Maybe the task would fall to Sister Felicity. Maybe they'd expect her to just figure it out.

"The last time we went out for maritozzi, you were going to tell me how you decided to become a nun," Claire said. "It's too late now, but—we got distracted."

Sister Thérèse laughed, dumped the remainder of her roll into a garbage can. "Claire, Claire, *Claire*," she said, and then led her to a nasone, washed her hands under the flowing tap, plugged it for a drink and sipped deep, and bade Claire do the same. She checked her watch. "I decided to be a nun about four hours ago."

Claire knew, from thirty years' experience, that religious life had an intimate grammar that might sound like everyday language but could be inflected to catalyze new meanings. Sometimes for the worse. Sometimes better. Sometimes, as here, just confusing.

"I was born a nun," Sister Thérèse said. "I dressed my Barbies in habits I made myself. I dressed *Ken* in habits. I led prayer services for the neighbor kids in my backyard. I asked my second-grade teacher when I could enter the convent. I ran away at age twelve, by city bus, to join a convent. I was sent home, but that changed nothing. I was voted 'most likely to become a nun' by my senior class, which was the first time they even had that category."

"Amazing," Claire said.

"No, the look on your face says, *crazy*, and of course: I scared almost everyone. But it wasn't a choice, never for me. From my first memory, I had perfect clarity of what God wanted for me."

And then something happened, explained Sister Thérèse, her first night in an actual convent, which she'd entered about five minutes after graduating college—not unlike what Claire's timeline would have been. There Thérèse was, finally, starting down the path she'd so long sought, and she felt horrible, alone, afraid. She barely made it through the night. She asked to leave before breakfast the next day. The sister in charge of the postulants told her to give it another day, decide the next morning.

"And you did?"

"I did. Prayer, some good sleep, much conversation, and I felt better."

"And here you are," said Claire.

Sister Thérèse shook her head. "The morning after *that*," she said, "the sister came back. 'What did you decide?' she asked. I said, 'I told you yesterday, I'm staying.' She said, 'What about today?' I said, 'Okay, then: yes, again.' And then—you can guess."

"I can't," said Claire.

"Every day," Sister Thérèse said. "The sister asked me every day, and finally—I was a bit thick—I learned to ask myself. We sisters take a series of vows. Simple vows, final vows. Those are choices. But we also make a choice every day. It can be hard to remember that in a city as busy and beautiful and whipped cream–filled as this—and sometimes visitors distract—"

"Sorry—"

"But I choose."

"You choose," Claire said.

"I choose," Sister Thérèse said, checking her watch, looking around. "And here we are."

Sister Thérèse had led them to the Fontana del Prigione.

The knowledge washed over Claire in waves. How had it taken her so long to figure this out? Mother Saint Luke had been obsessed with this fountain because the prisoner was missing from the pedestal rock; the prisoner had escaped, like *Mother Saint Luke* had wanted to escape, how she *did* choose to escape, night after night, toast of the town, Sister La Dolce Vita, only to find herself trapped in a convent that was crumbling, no way to get out except a key she wouldn't use.

Claire had been wrong about Sister Felicity's room of empty boxes, but she was right about this.

The words came tumbling out of Claire now; she all but grabbed Sister Thérèse by the shoulders and shook her: three months, thirty years it had taken Claire to figure this out. Marcus! She'd imprisoned him, never willing to let him go but never willing to let him in. And herself! Chaining herself to mutually exclusive lives, not thinking she would pull herself apart in the process. She'd been not only the prisoner, but the prison, the key, the lock.

Sister Thérèse looked shocked.

"Don't do like I did, Claire. It's a *fountain*," Sister Thérèse said. "The only thing that means is that there's water here."

"But Mother Saint Luke—"

The police had gone exploring in the tunnel after Marcus's fall, Sister Thérèse said. She pointed to a Vespa shop that burrowed into the hillside not far from the fountain. "The tunnel, which is probably also the 'road' Sister Georgia found on that map, exits there. The key works in a door at the rear of the shop. It was probably a way for Mother Saint Luke to get *into* the convent late at night. I think she was forever bringing me here to show me that. She must have thought, youngster that I was, I'd need a back door. But I didn't, and anyway, she chickened out: she never showed me."

"But it means..." Claire said, drifting off. It meant something. It had to. The fountain, this season in Rome, Claire's time in the convent, this walk with Sister Thérèse. That Claire still, after everything, still believed, was still waiting to have that acknowledged, that meant something—

"It means we're running out of time," Sister Thérèse said, and checked her watch once more.

"Again, I'm so sorry—"

"No, *you're* running out of time," Sister Thérèse said.

"Sister Felicity said I wasn't. She also said—although I probably misconstrued this, too—I think she was saying I should talk to Marcus."

"And say what?" Sister Thérèse asked.

Claire had loved Rome but hadn't loved how her insufficient Italian kept so much corked inside her each day. She could say *bel pomodoro* to the tomato seller but not say, *These tomatoes remind me of the ones that grew along our backyard fence when I was a girl; my father didn't care for them but my mother and I would pick them and slice them and salt them and eat them, sometimes right there in the yard.*

The bottled-up feeling had infected her English as well. She'd fallen silent before Sister Felicity many times, hadn't consistently returned Dorothy's or Monica's calls. When Marcus was with her, she'd been so lost in her thoughts, all those intersecting realities, that she hadn't even told him what she really needed to say. That he was the first person she thought of in the morning, that he'd been the one she'd imagined on the other side of every lock in Rome, that she'd wished she'd found him in Rome long, long ago.

"That," Claire told Sister Thérèse, "I love him."

Sister Thérèse stared at her a moment and then swept Claire into a hug and kissed her on the neck. "Sister Georgia was right," she said. They parted. "Don't ever tell her I said that."

"Right about what?" Claire asked. But Sister Thérèse seemed distracted. Somewhere nearby, an engine whined and coughed through a series of gears, faster and faster. *Claire* was distracted; she had only one thing to do now, and that was get to the hospital and talk to Marcus, assuming he'd still talk to her. "Sister Thérèse," Claire said, "if you'll excuse me, I'm going to go over to the hospital—"

The car she'd heard was grinding ever closer, and Sister Thérèse had turned away from her, in search of the noise. Wisely so, Claire thought, lest they wind up stretched out in the hospital alongside Marcus.

"He's not there!" Sister Thérèse said, stepping toward the onrushing car instead of away from it.

"Sister!" Claire shouted.

Sister Thérèse ignored her. "Here they are, finally!"

And here they were: Sister Georgia, Sister Felicity, fresh from the car share's parking space nearby, urging Claire and Sister Thérèse to get in, tearing away even before the doors closed.

"Is everything all right?" Claire asked.

"It is now," said Sister Felicity. "Sister Georgia used to drive a taxi in Boston."

"For women only," said Sister Thérèse.

"Gertrudans are problem solvers," said Sister Georgia. She kept one hand on the wheel and the other hovering above the horn as she accelerated.

"I didn't tell her," Sister Thérèse told the other sisters.

"For heaven's sake!" Sister Georgia said, checking the mirror.

"The next time you examine your conscience," Sister Felicity said, "I want you to look deep in your heart for the crush on Marcus Sardeson you tend there and scrub it out."

"It wasn't that!" said Sister Thérèse. "He swore us to secrecy!"

But out it came: Marcus had called the convent looking for Claire. Said he had checked himself out of the hospital, was on his way to the airport. Sister Thérèse had told him Claire was sleeping but that she would wake her. He then had a sudden change of mind.

"Loss of nerve," said Sister Georgia.

"And he said not to tell you that he'd called, that he was leaving the country."

"But he didn't know," Sister Felicity said.

"Know what?" asked Claire.

"That we sisters don't keep secrets from one another," said Sister Georgia.

"And that includes you," said Sister Felicity.

"And always will," said Sister Thérèse, "even if you marry him."

Gertrudans are problem solvers, and so when traffic delayed them and Sister Felicity and Sister Thérèse began arguing about whether they should have taken the train instead, Claire got to work from the back seat. GPS was estimating forty-five minutes before they arrived. Marcus's flight took off in forty minutes. But Claire had rarely faced a challenge that she couldn't solve with a call or two, and so began to dial.

At Leonardo da Vinci Fiumicino Airport, a small door in the international departures area of Terminal 3 leads to a Roman Catholic chapel. It is emphatically basic. Gray carpet, taupe walls, a drop ceiling done in white. The center aisle is extra-wide; luggage is welcome here. The chapel has a phone number, but it is mostly used internally, when airport staff need to find stranded souls blankets, food, clothing, a lawyer.

The chaplain has no power to get anyone on or off an airplane. He is a priest from the suburban, beachfront diocese in which the airport is located. He comes, says Mass, and leaves. There's good golf about twenty minutes south.

But there is also a woman on-site. She is a religious sister, and her name is Sylvia. Sister Sylvia is used to not only encountering unusual problems but solving them. Baby formula for the mother and baby separated from the rest of their family by immigration. A rosary for a grandmother from Peru who lost her beads on the plane. Tea and tissues for the young man who'd needed both.

And then there was the day when Sister Sylvia got the call from America. She recognized the woman calling right away—they'd met in Lagos ten years ago at an international conference of airport chaplains and have been money-saving roommates at the conference ever since—and so Sister Sylvia told the Rev. Susan Clark, *Of course, I will do this*. And because Sister Sylvia had done favors for so many at Rome's airport, she hardly even had to ask for any in return as she passed into the sterile zone, went to the gate Susan told her to, and asked the agents there to deplane a man who'd already boarded.

"You are needed in the chapel," Sister Sylvia said to the man once he appeared. Then, walking down the concourse, travelers parting before them, she called the priest, who had told her he was headed to the hospital for chaplaincy duties, but who she knew would play golf first. It was easy to get him to put his clubs back in his trunk and return to the airport.

It sounded like fun, for a change. He'd never said a wedding in the airport chapel before.

"Did you say 'wedding'?" Marcus asked Sister Sylvia in English, and then, Italian.

She replied the same way Marcus did as soon as he saw Claire, even before she spoke: "Yes!"

Just as the ceremony was about to begin, the chapel's phone rang. Sister Sylvia held up a finger. When she returned, she said they had to wait.

Claire almost lost it—no, no, they'd waited decades, they couldn't wait another second—but the sisters settled her, and they all waited together, forty-five more minutes, forty-four of which Monica spent narrating live via phone her and Dorothy's progress toward the airport.

"I may kiss the bride," said Monica when she arrived, breezing past the priest to do so.

"Sorry we're late!" Dorothy said, running in behind her.

"Took us thirty-four years to get here," said Marcus.

Claire backed up slightly, then stepped forward. Marcus looked ready to cry, but Claire's eyes were clear and bright. She put out her hands to take Marcus's, which were warm and trembled slightly. She tried to settle him, thumb massaging his palm. The priest whispered something—it sounded kind—and put his hand gently above theirs. Marcus looked at him.

"I think he means we can't hold hands yet," Marcus whispered to Claire.

Claire looked straight at Marcus, shook her head, did not let go.

The priest said something in Italian.

"He's asking if you're ready," said Sister Georgia.

Claire shook her head, exhaled long and low. "I'm not," she said finally. Marcus's eyes widened. She could feel Monica inch a half-step closer. "There's something I need to tell you. I made a deal once, a silly, stupid deal, that I can't really explain other than I was twenty and scared."

"Claire," Monica said.

Claire stared at Marcus. "You'd gotten that initial bad result from the movie physical, I prayed for you to be healed, and in exchange"—there was no way to say this without just saying it, she thought, consequences be damned—"I'd give you up."

"*Claire,*" Sister Thérèse said in a scolding hush.

"I gave you up," said Claire quietly.

Marcus looked at Claire, the sisters, the priest, took a long moment before speaking.

"I prayed, too," he said. "When you left me on that stage, I prayed that you'd run to New York City, have an extraordinarily wise and loving daughter, start a career helping religious communities figure out second, or third, or fifth acts. I didn't know how to pray but I'd watched you and knew the most important part was the believing part, and so I believed, I believed it would all work out. I prayed for you to come to Rome, meet three incredible women and one incredibly beautiful edifice in an impossibly beautiful city."

Claire opened her mouth to say something but couldn't.

"I prayed to live long enough to see all that," he said. "And—I did, thanks to you."

"To God," declared Sister Felicity.

Marcus nodded. "And all along, I figured if the cost of staying in your life was staying out of your love life, I'd pay it. You've no idea how many times I came close to proposing."

"Reunion," Monica said, almost to herself.

"Rome," Marcus said, round and clear.

"Marcus," Claire whispered.

He smiled a very, very quiet smile. "But mostly I prayed that just once more in my life, however long it lasted, in front of a large audience or a small one or none at all, that you would kiss me just once more the way you did that night onstage."

Claire stared at Marcus. The priest stared at them both. No one moved until Sister Georgia, softly but insistently, said, "Cue."

They froze. Then Claire inclined her head one way and Marcus the other, and they closed the distance between them slowly, cautiously, as if testing each inch to be sure it would bear the weight.

After roughly thirty years, they kissed.

They did not stop. The priest smiled and spoke to Sister Georgia, who smiled back.

"What did the priest say?" said Dorothy.

"That they're doing things out of order," Sister Georgia said.

"Tell him he doesn't know the half of it," said Monica.

Claire and Marcus broke apart and looked at each other.

Sister Georgia nodded to the priest. "Per favore, procedere."

And the priest was about to, but Claire and Marcus began kissing again.

The letter is difficult to read against the red brick, and maybe it's not a letter. It has the waiter at the café across the street from the convent confused. *Y*, it reads, the first letter of *yes, Yale, yet, youth, you* and *you* and *you*, words he doesn't think of because *Y* is the one letter in the Roman alphabet modern Romans don't use.

A week later, when three plainly dressed women—one old, one not so old, one young—sit down at his café, he learns they are from the ancient convent across the street. He thinks to ask them about the *Y* but forgets.

And then they are gone.

IV. THE ETERNAL CITY

After

THERE IS A CHURCH IN Rome with a line marked on the floor in bronze. Some forty-five meters long, the line stretches diagonally into the nave from the building's southernmost corner, precisely along Rome's meridian. It is an indoor sundial and marks the passing of time with the help of a tiny oculus near the top of the building's west wall. The hole is just inches wide, but from the nave, it is a pinprick, its light that of a stubborn sun.

Claire is forever falling in love with different churches around Rome but always returns to this one. Sometimes, depending on the hour, she attends a Mass. Her Italian still falters, but she can follow the service; the ritual is universal; in Los Angeles, in Milwaukee, in New Haven, in Rome, the Mass is the same, two parts, the Liturgy of the Word, the Liturgy of the Eucharist; it starts with a welcome, it ends with a farewell.

The pencil of light from the oculus traces a path along the floor; the hours and minutes are not marked—what means the passing of a day?—but the months are. Claire has watched it move from May to July, from July to October, from fall into winter. It has helped popes since 1702 predict the date of Easter; after all these years, it's perfectly accurate, though this doesn't matter to Claire, who knows the truth, which is that time moves too fast.

She likes the sundial's impossible geometry, how the straight line becomes, in effect, a circle; the sun starts close to the wall at the summer solstice and finishes deep and distant into the nave at the winter solstice, and it follows the same route every time. Time works exactly like this, the sun that crosses the stone floor here is the same one that crossed the stone floor on Beinecke Plaza at Yale so long ago.

There are loud voices in the rear of the church; she can't decipher them—the syllables race to the wall and then back, lapping one another like rings on a pond struck with a stone—but she knows what they mean, without looking at her watch, without looking at the floor. It's time.

"Closing, thank you, closing, thank you. Orario di chiusura, closing, thank you."

And then someone is at her right shoulder.

"It is closing time. Signora, è l'ora di chiusura."

Claire looks up. The man is wearing a black blazer that bears a busy red-and-orange patch, a coat of arms. Claire nods. *I understand.*

The man waits.

Claire sinks from her seat to her knees to pray.

The man waits, but then moves on.

Lord, Claire starts. *Give me just a little more time.*

More elevated voices.

And here let the camera fly up and away, not a drone, an old-fashioned crane. Let it take in Claire, rising, turning, let it take in the church, people filing out. Let it take in the altar beneath the painting of Jesus being baptized, let it take in the red marble, the turquoise, the maize, the magenta, the cobalt, the gold, the gold, the gold, let it take in the oculus, its leaked light, which burns a hole in the floor well ahead of where Claire embraces Marcus, who's finally arrived.

They watch the light, how it ushers time past them.

✳ ✳ ✳

Peter and Dorothy do not marry, but they promised themselves to each other at a dinner in Rome just a day after Marcus and Claire wed.

"'Promised,'" Claire said, "what does that mean?" Marcus quietly held her hand and smiled. It meant everything.

They had thought the young couple was going to follow in their footsteps and wed, right there, right now—why else would Peter have magically appeared from Madison?

"It means he loves me," Dorothy said.

"I do," Peter said, grinning.

"He sold his car to pay for the ticket here," Dorothy said.

"Alpheus," Peter said. "Named for my uncle."

"You sold your *car*?" Marcus said.

"Not everyone has bags of money like you and Mom," Dorothy said. They did then, but no longer do; with help from many friends, one in particular, Claire and Marcus will buy the Convento di Santa Gertrudis from Sister Rose's brother just weeks after this dinner. "Last-second transatlantic tickets? C'mon."

"But your *car*," said Claire. He'd have been better off selling Dorothy's artisanal bike.

"Technically," Peter said, "it was *his* car, Uncle Alfie's."

"It didn't run," said Dorothy.

"I was all set to donate it to Wisconsin Public Radio," Peter said, "but then Dorothy called from Italy. I mean, from here. So I went to the junkyard. They gave me three hundred and forty dollars."

"And then he found the rest of what he needed in a coat pocket," Dorothy said proudly.

Claire and Marcus looked at each other and did what Dorothy

and Peter had never done nor would ever do well, which was the math. Peter had found the necessary additional thousand dollars—at least—in a coat? Perhaps the uncle was missing that, too.

"Forty dollars!" Peter said, pleased.

"Three hundred forty, plus forty? That's an incredibly cheap ticket," Claire said, and it was, because, as Peter explained, he was due back at the airport in ninety minutes. The ticket only allowed him to spend six hours in Italy. Also, as he discovered on the way over: because he paid for the ticket in cash on the same day he traveled and was traveling with no luggage save a slim book of poetry, a neo-ancient/medieval bestiary by Marianne Boruch, he had to spend a longer time in security. He didn't mind, he said. It made him feel safe.

Claire and Marcus looked at Dorothy and then at Peter. "You are a beautiful man," Marcus said and took out his phone. He still had a friend who worked at a studio's travel office. The bill to change Peter's flight would come to Marcus personally, but it was worth it. Marcus would pay and pay for nights like this, stories like this, love like this, a city like this.

Dear classmates,

> *I miss the Class Book, but will settle for this venue, the alumni magazine's notes section. It's been a busy year for me; I went to Rome, fell in love with a convent there, and set about joining it. At the last moment, I decided I couldn't. My heart was called elsewhere. You may know him, a classmate, Marcus Sardeson. Fortunately I believe in a God who forgives and understands and understood that this was*

the path I was on all along. Marcus is forgiving, too, as are
my patient daughter, Dorothy, and wise friend, Monica.
I'm the only one who hasn't quite forgiven myself for
dragging everyone the long way round on this chase, but
I'm working on it.

We got married in an airport chapel. I know: What's the
rush? But I have found, like so many of you, that at fifty-
two, we don't have forever left—just a lifetime, which is both
shorter and longer than it seems.

Claire and Marcus ride out la pandemia in the Convento di Santa Gertrudis. That had not been the plan. The embassy had been sending one alert after another urging Americans to leave, and so they'd tried, and failed. And though their plan for the Convento di Santa Gertrudis was beginning to take shape, the building wasn't ready yet, and so they were alone there, with a decadent excess of space and garden in which to work, to exercise, to eat, to pray.

Even, finally, dance.

"Alone": Claire and Marcus often use the word in quotation marks, for they've learned the concept is all but meaningless in a Roman convent with four hundred years of history. Footfalls, bricks fall, a book placed here reappears there, tomatoes appear where they've not been planted, the bright white novice habit has disappeared, for good.

And then one day, the doorbell, which has never worked, begins to ring.

That was almost three years ago. Now it is 2022, and Claire, like many Romans, is rediscovering her city. The city moved outdoors with the pandemic and seems resolved to stay outdoors.

There is even a horrifying new trend, to-go coffee, branded "American Takeaway." One location evilly neighbors Sister Georgia's old foe, AD, American Donut. But Claire will not succumb. She is sitting at a café now, clear across town from Trastevere, not far from the Colosseum. She and Marcus are doing the sightseeing they never did. One stop a month; they're too busy to do more. The waiter brings the caffè and a laminated pictorial menu. She smiles and thanks him, and he goes back inside. She misses Paolo. *Gone to America,* the new barista had said. *I will be your new friend.*

She has a new friend: Marcus. He is not only a new friend but a new man since he quit Hollywood. And he did quit, has to keep quitting when calls come. It's not quite like Sister Thérèse's daily choice, but every so often he has to choose. He listens, declines. He's firm; she's learned that about him. Also: he snores like a building coming down. And: he can't abide anyone being late to anything, which makes him stand out more in Italy than his ash-blond hair. He's not above giving Claire a fake meeting time to compensate for her anticipated tardiness—what can she say? she's Roman now and she does as they do—and she wonders if he's done that today. They had separate errands this morning; hers finished early.

She could call Monica. Claire had worried that, her own life having settled down, Monica wouldn't know what to do with hers. But this is a needless concern; for Monica, the answer to *What next?* is everything: she will retire, buy a bookshop in Paris or Milwaukee or both. She bought an old seminary on Lake Winnebago to develop as a resort, then sold it.

Claire's offered to keep an eye on properties in Rome for her, but Monica says Kurt—their old waiter at the Yale Club, Monica's new love—doesn't like flying. Maybe Claire should start running Monica's life. Monica says Claire's inspired her (always has); Monica is going to change her life soon, start with an online intro to physics class or two. Claire's counting down the days until they meet again, which may be the next Yale reunion, already around the corner.

Claire takes a sip from her coffee, looks up and down the street. The Colosseum is just a half mile away, but she can't see it.

She puts her cup back down.

Across the street—

She rises.

The owner calls to her. She pulls a bill from her purse, leaves it on the table. She walks away, entranced.

She no longer believes in magic, in divine deals governed by spite, in loneliness as purifying pain. She renounced all that at the airport altar. What surprises her is that choosing Marcus has meant receiving so much of what she thought she'd receive if she chose the convent: companionship, contentment, grace, a faith no longer formed by fear. Peace. She knows peace, is peace, gives peace. She still prays, but she doesn't believe anymore that she can single-handedly save anyone's life except through CPR or the Heimlich maneuver, and she doesn't see coincidence as anything more than that: coincidence.

But she's here, right across the street from the Basilica of Saint Clement. Saint Clement, the patron saint of the Clementines from Milwaukee.

This church was the subject of much mythology in the order of nuns Claire had worked for as a teen. It was "their" church—of course it was; they were the Clementines!—but, vexingly, the church had been "given" by Pope Urban VIII to another order, the Irish Dominicans, in the 1600s. Still, Claire knew it to be a stop on any Clementine sister's pilgrimage to Rome. She also knew it to be a very unusual place, as would befit Saint Clement.

Saints are usually made saints once it's proven they've been the source of a miracle or two; in Saint Clement's case, a boy who'd drowned in the middle of the same ocean as Clement was miraculously returned to shore and life. How had Clement accomplished this? Because angels had built him a small underwater sanctuary on the seafloor. Of course. And the seas later parted once a year to permit his followers to visit and worship with him.

Or so Claire recalls the story. Which is why she's surprised and not to see a stairway leading down to—another basilica. Rome layering its history once again, the twelfth-century basilica built on top of a fourth-century basilica, plaques tell her.

She checks her watch. If Marcus is looking for her, he can call. She's at the basilica of Saint *Clement*! She pays an entrance fee and descends.

The basilica beneath the basilica has a lower ceiling and its walls are bare. But the faded murals she sees, the colorful, intricate mosaic floors she walks on—these are the same floors that worshippers walked on nine hundred years ago. Otherwise, the only color comes from mold of a brilliant green, which blooms on the wall in a broad corona above each of the stick lamps that light the space. It smells wet, but there's something to the wet, an extra ingredient she can't determine. Maybe it's not one ingredient but two thousand years of them. Tourists wander in little clumps from room to room. The space is simultaneously thrilling and ugly; part of it reminds her of every church basement she's ever been in. She half expects to find a mildewed bingo board.

Instead she turns a corner and finds a sign, in English, pointing down yet more stairs: TO THE MITHRAIC TEMPLE. So there's another layer still. Street level, twelfth century; basement, fourth century; subbasement, a second-century pagan church devoted to the Mithraic cult. The rooms are damp, some of the stone walls wet to the touch. There's a "classroom" and a "ritual room," grim spaces as would befit a religion that showered initiates in bulls' blood from a ceiling abattoir. But the ceiling, like the second century, is far away, and so it's quiet. She's surprised she can still hear traffic, though, a steady, rushing roar, and that's when she steps through another narrow arch and startles someone, she doesn't know who, but likely a woman, as all Claire sees is the briefest glimpse of a long white dress as it disappears around a corner. Claire will apologize when she catches up.

But first she stops and stares at what she's found, the source of the roar. Not traffic but water.

Claire later will tell Marcus, whom she's kept waiting, all about her visit to the basilica, the Mithraic ritual room; she'll even tell him about the rushing water, which was visible through a floor grate in one room, behind a glass panel in another, but running so cold, clean, and clear, it was as though she could taste it, and in that moment, she can.

She does not tell him about the subterranean street that runs between the Mithraic Temple and the second-century house that neighbors it. She does not tell him that it's tall and narrower than any other passage she's seen in Rome, that to walk it would mean shouldering through stone. She does not tell him that it's chained off, because then he wouldn't believe what she'd say next, that it's into this subterranean street the figure Claire startled fled, never to be seen again. She does not say what she knows, that it was one of the Clementine nuns she'd loved—Sister Ernest, the chef; Sister Mary Grace, the plumber; Sister Honora, the knitter; Sister Jane, who'd said, *Come back.* She will not tell him that Mother Saint Luke's *in case of emergency* key made no sound as she dropped it into the rushing water, it having unlocked its last mystery, the discovery that although she left the sisters in Milwaukee thirty-seven years ago, they had never left her. She will never fully know what they had, but she will know this, that those women had been the key.

The day the doorbell rang at the Convento di Santa Gertrudis for the first time after Claire and Marcus took ownership, it was a young woman and her elderly mother. An emergency shelter had turned them away. They'd heard that nuns would take them in.

They would and Claire and Marcus did.

After that, the doorbell rang and rang.

They had a roof, they had beds, they had an interrupted plan, which had been to convert the Convento di Santa Gertrudis into an interfaith retreat center, a place for women to rest, religiously affiliated or no, a kind of "spiritual spa," Monica, who'd fronted more than half the money the project required, called it.

But then came all these people—women with families—needing help. Which meant Claire and Marcus needed help. She took a deep breath and made a call.

Sister Felicity came first. Sister Thérèse next. They'd both been teaching just outside Rome. They begged Sister Georgia, who was back in the States, *not* to come—her age put her at risk—but Sister Georgia said Gertrudans were problem solvers and dissolution talks were dragging on so. More sisters came. Friends came. Sister Thérèse began shooting videos of the work and then Marcus started helping her and then more help showed up, more and more. And after Sister Thérèse and Marcus produced a short video called *How to Answer a Call*, which featured a phone falling to a picturesque Roman street from two stories up in excruciating slow motion while Sister Thérèse explained what you can hear when you can't hear your phone, so many women came trooping up the hill through Trastevere that they had to refer some to other, emptier convents.

Sister Georgia fell ill, recovered in the hospital, fell ill again, asked to recover in the parco, in the hermitage, where Mother Saint Luke could take care of her. And she did (along with a round-the-clock corps of sisters), and Sister Georgia survived, though Sister Georgia privately doubts this: all around her the convent appears full; one wing is an intergenerational shelter for single mothers who are taking care of their mothers along with their kids; the other wing is for the reinforcement sisters arrived from the States, with a whole hallway devoted to aspirants, women young and old from every continent save Australia (give it time) and Antarctica (more time) who have expressed a desire to discern with the Gertrudans. Not all will ultimately stay, of course, but in the meantime, they gather and pray and work and follow Sister Felicity's advice to, among other steps, visit Sister Georgia in the parco for Latin tutorials.

The straw poll in September 2019 had indeed called for closure: of the convent, the order. The pandemic delayed subsequent votes. And now all this activity has delayed a final vote indefinitely.

No, Sister Georgia is quite sure she didn't survive. Latin in the air, women in the convent, sun pouring over all of it? She has died and gone to heaven.

On the convent's façade, some clever Roman has added a solid circle between the two arms of Sister Thérèse's Y, making them into what they've already become, two arms outstretched in welcome.

Claire and Marcus want to get back for their thirty-fifth college reunion; they have a story to tell, and they want to hear others. They're eager to see this "film" Monica's been dropping hints about; Claire guesses it might be that new documentary about a beloved former Yale chaplain, Rev. Robert Beloin. But reunion fees are high and airfare expensive and though Monica will insist on paying for them, they don't want her to; she's already given them, and the convent, so much.

Monica decides it's only fair to let them have a preview of the film and sends Marcus the link.

While Monica's "spiritual spa" idea fell prey to the more pressing—and physical—needs that have arisen, the nonprofit foundation that Monica, Claire, and Marcus initially set up to run the spa survives, and they rent the Convento di Santa Gertrudis back to the Gertrudans for a dollar, "not a penny less!" as Monica says. She's told Dorothy that it's her best investment ever.

Claire and Marcus occasionally travel. Not far. When in Rome, they work at the convent; Claire in the kitchen and laundry, Marcus with Sister Thérèse or in whatever part of the building most urgently needs repair. He's learned a few things along the way. He should never tackle electrical problems without a pro. A hardware store in Rome is called an iron shop. Italian mice have sharp teeth. Some doors are best left locked. And don't let a day pass without kissing Claire.

He's in danger of missing that milestone today, though. She left for an early run and he's not seen her since. He checks his watch. He's not anxious, but he is eager to see the film Monica sent and won't watch it without Claire.

Weeks before, Claire swore Sister Felicity to secrecy. The two women lapped the Villa Pamphili gardens once, twice, and just like that, six miles were gone.

Which left twenty and two-tenths to go. Sister Felicity asked if Claire needed anything—water?—but Rome is a DIY marathoner's dream, fountains flowing everywhere. Claire was set. Sister Felicity ran out of the park with Claire to the top of the Gianicolo and then saw her off.

Cars, people, sanpietrini, made it less of a dream marathon, but Claire couldn't stop smiling. She ran around St. Peter's Square, waved to the pope's window. She ran across the Tiber to the Villa Borghese and then on to Termini. Then on to Pigneto, as far east as she'd go, tagged up at Frédéric's doorbell and began looping back to Testaccio. No time to stop at the market; she went on to the Circus Maximus, where she took a lap and then headed over to circle the Colosseum. She doubled back to the Tiber and started a long trek north along the river to the old 1960s Olympic district, then back south on the other side.

She ran, she walked, she climbed stairs, dodged scooters. She drank when she was thirsty. At mile eighteen, the mile where her father had found her after she fell, she raised her arms and face to the skies, shouted his name, and was drowned out by a scooter madly beeping behind her. The driver was smoking a cigarette; she plucked it from his lips and toed it out. He cursed; two women on the sidewalk applauded, as did, somewhere, Claire assumed, her mother.

A world-record marathon time hovers around two hours; Claire herself once had a goal of four. That day it would take six, and when she fell into Sister Felicity's embrace beside the Fontana dell'Acqua Paola she couldn't help thinking of all she'd won.

Dorothy has stopped checking the tracking app on her phone; she knows where her mom is now, which is where she was, which is, always, at her side. Dorothy visits Rome as often as she can, sometimes with Peter, sometimes without, sometimes she stays in the Convento di Santa Gertrudis, which she knows her mom prefers.

What Dorothy doesn't know is that Claire always knows where Dorothy is, even when Dorothy's not in Rome. Claire doesn't need a phone, just her heart, which flashes memories of Dorothy each night as she falls asleep, Dorothy in day care, Dorothy in Madison, Dorothy in Monica's arms, in Peter's, in Claire's. Pulse, pulse: Dorothy is close, ever closer, and Claire always sleeps with half an ear for Dorothy to crack the door and say, *Mom? Good night.*

Marcus is tired of waiting. He'd asked Sister Felicity earlier about Claire's whereabouts and had been told not to worry so he didn't. He knows well by now to trust whatever these women say. But no one told him not to watch the film Monica sent, so he clicks the link, waits for it to load, and presses play.

The opening seconds are murky, but once he realizes what he's watching, he enlarges the picture, stands, rewinds, presses play again.

Someone unearthed an old VHS tape of the pregraduation show, the night Claire climbed the stage, and Monica has had it digitally transferred.

There's no crispness to the images; the colors blare; the sound is loud then soft. The picture occasionally shakes; whosever parent shot this must have forgotten their tripod. Marcus wants to see every minute of the show but finds himself fast-forwarding to the end. He wishes he could see what would be impossible to see, the campus outside the theater, the fountain behind Bones, the Beinecke Library, fall leaves and spring daffodils, Sanford Hall and its lofty sextet.

But no, only the stage, himself, his costar, and dimly visible in the front row, Claire's dad, that sister from the Milwaukee convent.

And Claire, who eventually rises, moves to the wings, climbs the stairs, heads for center stage.

Marcus doesn't remember the noise, but it's unmistakable now, a rising roar. And he doesn't remember that it went on so long, so long that the roar became a hush, with Marcus and Claire, holding hands, about to kiss.

The video catches a stray voice, not from the stage, but from somewhere far back in the audience. "Claire!" it says, "Claire!" And again, "Claire!"

More than thirty years later, Marcus leans forward, squints as though that will help him hear, and when the voice calls her name again, Claire appears at the door.

"Here I am," she says, and comes inside.

RINGRAZIAMENTI

There are not words enough in English or Italian or any other language to adequately thank Maya Ziv for her unstinting work on this book. It exists because of her.

Thanks, too, to her colleague Lexy Cassola for her down-to-the-wire advice and to Elisabeth Weed, who's always believed, even when I didn't. Also from The Book Group, thanks to DJ Kim and, for just the right read just when I needed it, Louisa Skerry. From elsewhere in the book ecosystem, repeated thanks to Jamie Knapp, Wendy Pearl, Stefan Moorehead, Daniel Goldin, and everyone else who works so hard to get books into readers' hands.

Thank you to my family. To my daughters, Lucy, who launched me into writing, and Mary, Honor, and Jane, who sustain me. To my endlessly loving and patient wife, Susan, who puts up with so many travails of the writing life, including traipsing through moldy church basements in Rome.

And thanks to the many women religious whom I learned from during this project, including Sister Christine Bowman, OSF; Sister Charlotte Cummins, CJ; Sister Marie Isabel, SSEW; Sister Ginny Reichard, SSND; Sister Mary Swanson, SSND; Sister Emily TeKolste, SPSMW; the sisters and oblates of Holy Wisdom Monastery; the Agnesian sisters and staff of the Leo House in New York City; Rev. Judith Whelchel, MFA; and most especially, Sister Julia Walsh, FSPA.

To *none* of them, nor anyone cited below, should be ascribed any errors, omissions, or opinions in this book.

Thanks to Tiffany Parks for her smart and sensitive read of the manuscript with respect to matters Italian and otherwise; Bishop

Paul Tighe, Rev. James Martin, SJ, and Rev. Joe Simmons, SJ, for the books and conversations; Patrick Gallagher, CCIM, and Christopher Kelsey for real estate advice; Matt Linn and Lorni Fenton for estate and trust counsel; Michael Mazza for the canon law consult; Rev. Mark Bosco, SJ, for introducing me to the extraordinary mosaic of Jesus and Mary in the Basilica di Santa Maria in Trastevere—and to some fine restaurants nearby; Rev. John Quinn, SJ, whose account in *Loyola Magazine* of a minor seminary headmaster's demurral I drew upon to depict Claire's early inquiries; T. Geronimo Johnson, Prof. Giordana Poggioli-Kaftan, Elisabetta Luzzi, Teresa Fraioli, Katherine Rooks, Toni Brancatisano, and Sophie Minchilli for insights regarding Roman customs, cuisines, and more; Melissa Couch, Louise Henricot, and her colleagues at Italy Sotheby's International Realty Roma for their Italian property expertise; Rev. Otto Hentz, SJ, for his description of "mezzanine moments"; Prof. Richard Leson for fountain advice; Susie McGuinness for the quick Latin lesson; Peter Johnson, MD, and Jim Sanders, MD, for advice on medical miracles and mishaps; Rev. Jeremy Zipple, SJ, for his insights into documentary filmmaking, and Marisa Silver and Rae Canaan for how to shoot a tricky scene; Jeff Briggs, for the trip around the Warner Bros. lot; Kate Zbella for her care for Claire; Jane Delury, Merridith Frediani, Valerie Sayers, Lizzie Skurnick, Megan Staffel, and Emily Gray Tedrowe for suffering early drafts; and for ceaseless support, the world's best writing group, Christina Clancy, Lauren Fox, Aims McGuinness, Anuradha D. Rajurkar, and, gone from this world far too soon, Jon Olson.

Thanks to the University of Wisconsin–Milwaukee, the Council for Wisconsin Writers, and the Shake Rag Alley Center for the Arts for time and room to write.

Thanks, too, to the libraries: the Golda Meir Library of the University of Wisconsin–Milwaukee, the Mead Public Library of Sheboygan, Wisconsin, and the Beinecke Rare Book and Manuscript Library at Yale, whose holdings and scarily high interior rooftop are largely as described, though I decline to name the delightful administrator who permitted me and a classmate to take in that view once upon a time.

Thanks to Prof. Murray Biggs, who introduced me to acting in his Restoration Drama class, and to my college classmates, those named and not, for their support and community and for forgiving me for lies told at reunions and in this book. (Sanford Hall, for example, does not exist, though everyone should have a roommate such as I did, worth naming a building for.)

And grazie to the books, including, among others: Eleanor Clark's *Rome and a Villa*; H. V. Morton's *The Fountains of Rome*; Jan Herman's *A Talent for Trouble: The Life of Hollywood's Most Acclaimed Director, William Wyler*; Matt Murray's *The Father and the Son: My Father's Journey into the Monastic Life*; and Kathleen Norris's *The Cloister Walk*.

E. B. White's essay "Here Is New York," written in 1948, first appeared in *Horizon* magazine and is now published in a slender standalone volume by the Little Bookroom. Ladybird, Kettle of Fish, and Cassidy's are actual New York establishments; Goldie's and Flavio's are not, but should be.

The Marianne Boruch book Peter takes aboard his flight to Rome is the poet's wonderful *Bestiary Dark* (Copper Canyon, 2021).

Biblical quotations are from the New American Standard Bible (1971).

I tried to take as few liberties with Rome as possible. I did invent the restaurant at the top of the stairs, though if you want to try the pasta dish Claire and Marcus eat there, you'll find it in Trastevere at Trattoria da Enzo. Thanks to Natalie Kennedy's tip, Sister Thérèse favors the maritozzo at Il Maritozzaro, near the Roma Trastevere train station.

The Fontana delle Tartarughe can be found in Rome's Piazza Mattei; copies exist in San Francisco and several other locations in the United States, although the backyard of Skull and Bones is not one of them, so far as I know. The Fontana del Prigione is located in Trastevere where Via Luciano Manara meets Via Goffredo Mameli. The (or a) door to the air-raid tunnel is located to the left of the fountain beneath some vines; let me know if your key works.

My account of Mother Saint Luke and her interaction with William Wyler and *Roman Holiday* is fictional, although, as reported in Herman's biography, Wyler's daughter Judy, after ducking out of school early, did disappear for a few hours one afternoon, having been taken by a man with a bicycle. Wyler's wife said the episode made her "blood run cold."

The religious orders depicted herein are completely fictional or, if real, used fictitiously, but credit is due the novelist J. F. Powers (1917–1999), who in his work created a fictional order of priests, the Clementines, to which my own Clementines pay homage; and my great aunt, Gertrude Scanlan Cleary (1913–1999), for inspiring my creation of the Gertrudans. A woman of great faith, she was a writer and once wrote to bestselling author and priest Andrew Greeley for advice. He said to keep at it, which could be the Gertrudans' motto.

I've visited many airport chapels and interfaith spaces, including Rome's and Milwaukee's; the latter is in the parking garage but otherwise not burdened with any of the history I imagined for it here. Fiumicino's airport chapel is as described but the staff portrayed are invented. Readers wishing to impulsively marry at Fiumicino should know that's not possible in real life, not without the time-consuming pursuit of numerous forms prior (as for your VAT refund, that's available at a counter next door to the chapel). Italians already know this; others should check with their embassies.

That's not to say readers might not find their own religious sisters to work wonders; I hope they do.

ABOUT THE AUTHOR

Liam Callanan's novel *Paris by the Book*, a national bestseller, was translated into multiple languages and won the Edna Ferber Prize. He's also won the Hunt Prize, and his first novel, *The Cloud Atlas*, was a finalist for an Edgar Award. Liam's work has appeared in *The Wall Street Journal*, *Slate*, *The New York Times*, *The Washington Post*, and *The San Francisco Chronicle*, and he's recorded numerous essays for public radio. He has taught for the Warren Wilson MFA Program for Writers, the Bread Loaf Writers' Conference, and the University of Wisconsin–Milwaukee, and lives in Wisconsin with his wife and daughters.